The
Teacher
Evacuees

ROSE WARNER

CANELO

First published in the United Kingdom in 2025 by

Canelo, an imprint of
Canelo Digital Publishing Limited,
20 Vauxhall Bridge Road,
London SW1V 2SA
United Kingdom

A Penguin Random House Company
The authorised representative in the EEA is Dorling Kindersley Verlag GmbH. Arnulfstr. 124,
80636 Munich, Germany

A CIP catalogue record for this book is available from the British Library.

Print ISBN 978 1 83598 026 2
Ebook ISBN 978 1 83598 027 9

Cover design by The Brewster Project

Cover images © Arcangel, Shutterstock

Printed and bound in Great Britain by Clays Ltd, Elcograf S.p.A.

Look for more great books at
www.canelo.co | www.dk.com

1

For the many teachers in my life who have inspired, encouraged and believed in me. I am grateful to and appreciate all of you.

Chapter One

The post slid through the gleaming brass-plated letterbox at the tall, narrow North London house, landing on the black-and-white tiled floor with a soft thud.

'Drat.' Victoria McKaye stopped with one hand on the door, shoved a strand of thick, wavy, red-blonde hair beneath her straw summer hat and checked her diamond-studded wrist-watch, a twenty-first birthday present from her parents. She'd miss the bus but there was no help for it.

Holding her handbag over one arm, she bent to collect the scattered letters. House rules. Whoever happened to be near the door when the post arrived collected and sorted it.

At nearly thirty, she should have her own home rather than sharing digs. However, she had a bedroom to herself and from what she'd seen of them so far, the other girls seemed like good fun. Younger than her, of course, but by now she'd got used to that.

She picked up her own post and flipped through it. Two letters, one from her mother and the other from her youngest sister, both with the Canadian stamps which already looked foreign. Nestled in between them, a slim, tan-coloured envelope emblazoned with the crest of the school where she'd start work in a fortnight.

No more dreary girls' boarding school in the wilds of Yorkshire. She was finally in London – the heart of everything – and could build an independent life. As she put all the letters in her handbag, she paused. She already knew what her sister and mother would have said but perhaps the one from school was important.

She opened the front door and unsealed the letter, her shoe heels clicking down the front steps and along the walk bordered by pink and white roses, yellow dahlias and purple verbena in full August bloom.

Dear Miss McKaye.

She scanned the letter from the headmistress and then read it more closely, thoughts of the bus and her shopping trip forgotten.

'Excuse me, Miss?'

'Yes? Oh, sorry.' She stepped aside and made herself smile at next-door-but-one's maid, who today had a small, fair-haired girl with her, pushing a doll in a pram.

'You look like you've seen a ghost, Miss.'

'I'm fine. Ivy, isn't it?' Her landlady had mentioned the girl's name in passing. Victoria stuffed the letter back into its envelope and then into her handbag.

'Yes, Miss.' The girl, who didn't look more than fourteen or fifteen, nodded while the small girl at her side stared up at Victoria with solemn blue eyes.

'Are you going to the park? If so, I'll walk with you.'

'You?' Ivy put a hand to her mouth and then added 'Miss.'

'McKaye.' Until now, she'd only seen the girl at a distance beating rugs in the back garden or collecting milk bottles.

The maid gave her a hesitant half-smile. 'The milkman said you're from Canada. My, that's far away. My uncle went out there when I was little, and my mum never heard from him again except for one postcard when he reached Halifax. Mum says you can't be too careful in them foreign places. You never know what might happen with wild animals and such.'

Maybe Victoria wasn't the only one who'd wanted to disappear. In her case, though, she planned to go back to Canada one day, and she kept in regular touch with her family. Besides, England wasn't truly foreign. Her parents were English, born right here in London. And her father's parents, Granny and Grandad McKaye, were originally from Edinburgh in Scotland. Victoria had grown up with Canadian, English and Scottish traditions and took pride in her British ancestry. If things had been different… She shook her head and dismissed the unpleasant thought.

'Although I am from Canada, and it is indeed very far away, I live here now.' Victoria was a different person than she'd been back in Canada, in that sleepy rural town she wanted to forget. 'What's your name?' Victoria bent to the girl, a pang of loss tugging in a place she'd buried deep. Nowadays, she didn't let herself think about having children. The ones she taught at school had to be enough.

'Diana. And that's Lucinda.' She gestured to the flaxen-haired doll in the pram. 'Mummy's cross so she sent us out with Ivy.'

'All at sixes and sevens today, and no wonder.' Ivy clicked her tongue against her teeth.

'Daddy says we all have to do our duty, George and Harry shouted and Mummy cried.' When Diana took the hand Victoria held out, Victoria's heart squeezed at the trusting, chubby clasp. 'My brothers are big and going away to fight in the war soon.'

'Now, now. Don't worry your head about any talk of fighting and war. It'll all blow over. Won't it?' Ivy's voice quavered.

Until a few minutes ago, Victoria had thought talk of war was just that, merely talk. Now, she wasn't so certain. Over the past few months, her family's pleas for her to return to Canada had become increasingly insistent. Yet, although she loved them, she'd resisted, because of course Britain would be safe from any conflict. Wouldn't it? 'I'm sure the prime minister and his government have everything in hand.'

'See there, Miss Diana? I heard Miss McKaye's a teacher and teachers know what's right and proper. You trust your teachers, don't you?'

Diana nodded and squeezed Victoria's hand. 'I'm going to be seven soon. Will you be my teacher?'

At the corner of the road, they turned towards the park and entered it through a pair of ornate wrought-iron gates. The mid-afternoon heat hung heavy, the air had a dusty scent and even the few ducks drifted aimlessly on the water of the pond as if they too were waiting. But waiting for what?

'I don't know. Which school do you go to? I'm teaching at Park Road on the other side of the hill.'

That job, a permanent one after a temporary post at a gloomy, quasi-Edwardian-era boarding school on the Yorkshire moors, was the biggest reason Victoria didn't want to leave England. Here, nobody knew her and she didn't have to face the pity of her family and friends. Or her former fiancé, now married to the woman he'd betrayed her for, her own second cousin. Letitia with her honey-blonde hair, perfect oval face, indigo-blue eyes and helpless air that since their childhood had made boys and then men fall at her feet.

'Park Road is my school.' Diana's mouth curved into a cherubic smile.

'Well, maybe you'll be in my class.' Victoria's stomach lurched. The letter from the headmistress hadn't given any details but she wouldn't have called the entire staff together at nine o'clock on a Friday morning at the end of the school holidays if not for something important. 'Since it's so hot, why don't we get ice creams?' She pointed to an aproned seller with his cart near the pond. 'My treat.'

As Diana bounced with excitement, Ivy stepped back and retrieved the pram her charge had abandoned. 'I'll wait over by that tree while you—'

'I meant ice cream for you as well, Ivy. All of us.'

The girl's mouth dropped open and her freckled face flushed. 'It wouldn't be proper, Miss McKaye. If my mistress heard—'

'If your mistress says anything, tell her I insisted.' It was unusual, certainly, but why shouldn't Ivy have a treat? She worked hard enough. Besides, there was something about her that touched Victoria's heart and reminded her of the hired girl at home.

Skirting around several men digging a trench, she marched over to the ice cream seller and gestured to the others to follow.

Fumbling for money in her purse, and as Diana chattered about ice cream, Victoria glanced at the London skyline poking through the distant trees.

She wouldn't let herself think about that meeting with the headmistress. Yet an uneasy chill slithered through her, bringing goosebumps on her arms below the sleeves of the floral summer dress she'd bought in one of the big shops on Regent Street soon after she'd arrived here.

Despite her brave words to Ivy about the prime minister and his government, Victoria read the papers. Hitler had to be stopped and soon.

And if it was up to Britain to stop him, all those rumours about school evacuations she'd tried to dismiss might soon become a reality.

–

Two mornings later, Victoria went into Park Road School via the staff entrance near the tennis courts at the rear. This part of the school, a red-brick building with arched windows, had been built in Victorian times and then added on to. Today, the grounds covered almost half a block, although Victoria's infants' classroom would be here, in the oldest part.

She smoothed her full navy skirt and crisp white blouse with its stylish puffed sleeves, and hovered outside the staffroom door. A hubbub of raised female voices spilled into the corridor and somewhere a bell rang.

As if on cue, women of all ages, shapes and sizes came out of the staff room and streamed along the corridor. Swept up with them, Victoria clutched her handbag and did up the buttons on the smart peplum jacket of her skirt suit. While she'd hoped to meet her new colleagues individually, maybe this way would be easier. Whatever the news, they'd all hear it at once which would make Victoria less the 'new girl'.

'Come along. Don't dawdle.' At Victoria's side, a tall, thin woman with pale blonde hair pulled back in a tight bun gestured towards what Victoria remembered was the school's spacious main hall.

'Sorry.' She gave an apologetic smile which the woman didn't return. When she'd come here for her interview, Victoria had been impressed with how light the hall was, with high windows that overlooked the schoolyard and playing fields.

In the hall, she found a chair in the middle of an empty row near the back as the buzz of multiple conversations continued on around her.

'Is this seat free?'

At the soft, hesitant voice she looked up and then nodded. 'Yes, please, join me.'

'Thank you.' The young woman slid into the chair next to Victoria's. 'I'm new. When I got the letter from Miss Hopson, I didn't know what to think.'

'I'm new too.' Victoria introduced herself.

'I'm Nell… I mean Miss Potter.' Her face flushed and she fiddled with a loose strand of dark-brown hair curled into a chin-length bob.

'Victoria.' She spoke in a low voice. 'I'm in the infants department. You?'

'Juniors.' Nell's voice dropped further. 'It's my first post.'

'You'll soon understand how things work. We both will.' Victoria looked around the hall, now filled with women and a few men. The headmistress who'd interviewed her stood at the front and, at her side, was the severe-looking blonde from the corridor.

'Where did you teach before?' Beneath her too-big navy hat, Nell's brown eyes were frightened and she held her worn black handbag in a tight grip. Her navy-blue pleated skirt reminded Victoria of school uniform, while a washed-out pink blouse with a pointed collar did nothing for the girl's colouring.

'In Canada, at a school in my hometown and then at a girls' boarding school in Yorkshire.' Before coming to England, Victoria had always thought teaching was temporary and her real life would start when she married. How wrong she'd been.

'Lucky you.' Nell's lips turned up in a hesitant smile. 'You aren't going to go back to Canada then, what with all this war talk?'

'No.' Even if Victoria wanted to return home, it was likely too late. The thought, which before had flitted through her mind as light as the puff of dandelion seeds, now settled. Had she had her head in the sand these past months? 'If I want to go home, I'm sure I'd be able to by Christmas.' Yet even that thought wasn't as comforting as it had once been. 'Are you from London?' She couldn't place Nell's accent, which wasn't surprising since she'd only lived in England for eighteen months. However, there was something careful about her speech that made Victoria wonder if the other girl wanted to hide her background.

'Yes.' Nell dug in her handbag for a handkerchief.

'Which part? I'm still getting to know...' Victoria stopped as the headmistress rapped on a lectern for their attention.

'You have undoubtedly wondered why I called you all here today, cutting short a late-summer holiday for some.' Miss Hopson made an apologetic face as a murmur went around the seated rows of teachers. 'I wouldn't have done so unless it was urgent, of course.'

Victoria's stomach knotted. The sunlight coming through the windows tinted Miss Hopson's grey hair with silver and her face looked older and more strained than when Victoria had met her in April.

'It is my duty to tell you that our school life will soon change. Miss Wentworth, head of the junior school, and I were informed several days ago that...' She paused and looked at the woman by her side whose grim expression remained unchanged. 'In the care of teachers, pupils in London schools whose parents agree will be evacuated to the countryside beginning on the morning of the first of September. Given that the government's evacuation plan...' Miss Hopson raised a hand to quell the chatter. 'Please, ladies and gentlemen.'

As the room quietened again, the headmistress came out from behind her lectern. 'As many of you know, discussions about voluntary evacuation have been ongoing for several years now and formalised in the wake of last year's Anderson Committee Report. The evacuation of London schoolchildren is not unexpected, but I hoped... I know we all hoped that things would not reach this point. However, by working together we will endeavour to keep life as normal as possible for our pupils no matter where we may find ourselves.'

As the chatter broke out again, Victoria glanced at Nell.

'Do you think the school will be split up, then?' Nell twisted a starched white handkerchief with an embroidered daisy in each corner. It was beautifully worked and of much better quality than her clothes.

'Maybe; it would make sense, I suppose. How could a rural village school take in all of us?' At Victoria's interview, the headmistress had said that while some classes had as many as sixty children, Victoria would only have forty-five. 'From what I understand, many rural schools aren't separated into different levels either.'

'I've only ever lived in London.' A small smile crept across Nell's face and instead of fearful she now looked almost excited. 'The countryside sounds grand.'

To Nell, perhaps, but not Victoria. As Miss Hopson began speaking again, Victoria shuddered. She'd only escaped one pokey, dull place in the country and now, a scant month later, she was about to be shipped off to another. While she already knew life wasn't fair, having to leave London when she'd only got settled seemed particularly bad luck.

'Although some of our pupils' parents have registered them for evacuation previously, there are still many who have not.' Miss Hopson paused. 'I have also written to the parents to help prepare them for our departure, and while our school was used as a registration centre for private evacuations last month, there is still much work to do. I've asked Miss Wentworth to speak to you on that point.' She turned to her colleague.

'She's a dragon, that Miss Wentworth. She's one of the ones who interviewed me.' Nell made a disgusted face more like those Victoria had seen on girls she taught than fellow teachers.

As Miss Wentworth stepped over to the lectern, Victoria studied the woman more closely. Although she was likely only in her early forties, she appeared older and had a pinched look, not helped by her tight hairstyle, old-fashioned wire spectacles and severely cut grey jacket, white blouse and grey pleated skirt.

In another ten to fifteen years, would she be a Miss Wentworth? An old 'dragon', at least in the eyes of younger teachers. A woman who still lived in shared lodgings and marked the seasons of her life by the school calendar. Someone whose only treat was an annual trip to the seaside with other single teacher friends, and who stared down old age alone. Victoria's stomach rolled and she hugged herself. She wouldn't be a Miss Wentworth. She was still young enough and she'd make different choices. But what if she couldn't? If there *was* a war, what if it dragged on for years and she got stuck in a life and place that didn't fit?

'Oh no. Of all the ruddy bad luck.' For an instant, Nell's voice sounded more working-class East End than this part of leafy North London with its doctors, solicitors, civil servants and other middle-class professionals.

'What is it?' As Victoria jerked her head up, she caught her own name.

'You and me are stuck with Miss Wentworth visiting parents who haven't registered their kiddies for evacuation. Supposed to encourage them.' Nell's expression turned to horror. 'It'll be like being back at school ourselves with her bossing us about.'

At the lectern Miss Wentworth rapped for their attention. 'Please gather with your assigned group where you'll be given names, addresses and more information. Many hands make light work and at this time of national crisis, we must remember Lord Nelson's stirring words on the eve of the Battle of Trafalgar. "England expects that every man will do his duty." But now, over one hundred and thirty years later, and with our few male teachers planning to enlist, it's also we women, we teachers, who have a duty to our country and to our pupils, and we shall not fail.'

Stirring words indeed, but amidst the polite, muted applause, instead of feeling inspired, a cold chill slithered up from Victoria's stomach and through her windpipe.

Despite her age, she'd been a foolish girl, so sure war wouldn't touch her. And now instead of being inspired and suitably brave, all she felt was afraid.

Chapter Two

'Come along, Miss McKaye and Miss Potter. Only one more family. You're both doing splendidly.' Miss Wentworth stopped by a stone wall at the end of a road lined with tall, red-brick houses, much like the one Victoria lived in, and flipped through a list of pupil names and addresses.

Nell let out a heavy sigh as she sank onto the wall, and Victoria had half a mind to join her. At the end of their second day visiting parents who hadn't yet registered their children for evacuation, they'd walked miles criss-crossing what was ostensibly only a small area of North London.

Victoria's feet hurt and she felt that her lips must be permanently fixed into what was by now a pretence of a reassuring smile. She'd had so many cups of tea and different varieties of cake that she'd lost count. And underlying it all, whether in a painfully neat front room or determinedly middle-class drawing room, was an undercurrent of fear, thick, heavy and lodged in the pit of Victoria's stomach. For the first time since she'd left Canada, she longed for the cool shade under the big maple tree in the back garden at home with a chilled glass of Mother's lemonade.

'We took a wrong turn. The Foster-Daltons are the next road over.' Beneath an olive-green cloche hat with matching ribbon, Miss Wentworth took off her spectacles, replaced them in her capacious handbag and gestured back the way they'd walked a few minutes earlier. 'I'm surprised that such a family...' She stopped and glanced at Nell. 'Get up and don't loll about. Park Road staff must be role models for not only our pupils but the wider community. You aren't ill, are you?'

Nell shook her head and winced as she got to her feet.

'Come along, then.' Miss Wentworth went ahead at a brisk pace as Victoria and Nell followed her trim figure.

'Are you certain you're all right?' Victoria took Nell's arm, noting the curl of dark hair plastered to one cheek and greyish-purple circles beneath her eyes.

'Fine.' Nell shook Victoria's hand away and shoved her hair back beneath the same unattractive, too-big navy hat she'd worn three days running. 'I don't expect we've a choice but let's hope that wherever we end up we're not billeted with old sourpuss.' Nell's voice dropped and she spoke out of one side of her mouth.

'Don't be so hard on her.' Victoria made her expression non-committal. Nell was young, still almost a girl, and like Miss Wentworth, she was someone with whom, under ordinary circumstances, Victoria would have nothing in common. Still, after yesterday and today, she couldn't help but respect Miss Wentworth's efficiency and evident dedication to her pupils and the school.

'I board in this road.' Catching up with Miss Wentworth, Victoria once again tried not to see herself in fifteen to twenty years' time.

The older woman must have been pretty once. In fact, she was still pretty, when a child managed to coax a smile out of her. She had a delicate heart-shaped face, and if she wore less severe clothing and more flattering colours, pink perhaps or a soft blue, she'd make more of herself. 'If you dress your best, you feel your best.' That was Victoria's mother's motto and she'd instilled it in her four daughters.

'Diana Foster-Dalton.' Miss Wentworth stopped in front of a black, wrought-iron gate that mirrored the one in front of Victoria's lodgings. 'She'll be one of yours, Miss McKaye.'

'I met her several days ago walking to the park with the family's maid.' So much had happened, it already felt like another lifetime. Victoria paused with her hand on the sun-warmed gate. Everything and everyone looked the same, including her, but it all seemed so very different. 'I'm surprised Diana's parents haven't registered her.'

'Perhaps they've already made private plans to go to the country.' When they reached the front door, and for a moment before she lifted the shiny brass knocker, an expression flashed across Miss Wentworth's face which might have been sorrow.

Nell muttered something under her breath that Victoria didn't catch, and then the door swung open and Ivy appeared. 'Yes, Miss?' Beneath a white cap which she wore with an apron over a print dress, her freckles stood out on her pale face. 'Oh, Miss McKaye. It's you.'

'Yes.' Victoria gave the girl what was perhaps her first genuine smile of the day. 'And Miss Wentworth and Miss Potter from Park Road School. Is Mrs Foster-Dalton in?'

'She's...' Ivy glanced over her shoulder. 'I'll see. Please come in.'

'Miss McKaye.' Diana's curly-haired head poked around a half-open door at one side of the gracious entrance hall and then the rest of her appeared. Dressed in a short, pink floral dress with a white collar, white ankle socks and black shoes with straps and clutching her doll, Diana had a worried expression. 'Mummy's upstairs lying in her bed. Cook left and Mummy said—'

'I'm sure your mother will join us as soon as she can,' Miss Wentworth cut in. 'Perhaps you can show us into the drawing room?'

'Yes.' Diana's voice was a scared lisp as she led the three of them into a cluttered room with a jigsaw puzzle in progress on a table by the bay window and a bushy aspidistra in a shadowed corner.

Ivy reappeared as the teachers settled themselves where Diana gestured. 'Mrs Foster-Dalton will be with you shortly. I'll bring you some tea and—'

'That won't be necessary.' Miss Wentworth waved the maid away. 'I expect you have other work to do.'

'Yes, Miss. Thank you, Miss.' Ivy gave a brief bob and then disappeared again.

In the silence, broken only by the ponderous tick of a longcase clock, Victoria and Nell perched on the edge of a low-backed sofa with Diana between them while Miss Wentworth sat in a winged armchair beside the piano.

'Why don't you show Miss Potter the garden, Diana?' Miss Wentworth's gesture, as she indicated another window on the far side of the room, was almost regal.

Diana nodded and bounced to her feet, and Nell followed. As they left the room a woman with bobbed light-brown hair, who must be Mrs Foster-Dalton, entered.

'When Ivy said your name I...' She twisted a handkerchief between thin fingers. 'I didn't realise you taught at Park Road.'

'I only started there in the last summer term.' Miss Wentworth stood and took Diana's mother's hand.

'And we... Beatrice, I...' Mrs Foster-Dalton's voice trailed away again.

'It's no matter. When I saw the name I wondered if it could be you.' Miss Wentworth cleared her throat and glanced at Victoria. 'Unless you've made private arrangements, Miss McKaye and I are here to register Diana for the school's evacuation. You must see you have to send her away, Mary.'

'Yes.' Mrs Foster-Dalton still held Miss Wentworth's hand. 'Edward says I must as well but I've been such a coward and our families... well, there's nothing suitable. Edward's office, you remember he's with the civil service, will likely go to the country as well, but I didn't want to tell Diana. She's all I have left.'

'Nonsense.' Miss Wentworth patted Mrs Foster-Dalton's arm. 'Even if they're not at home, you still have your husband and the boys.'

'I'll take care of Diana.' Victoria had stood too and when Miss Wentworth beckoned to her, she joined the conversation. 'Diana's a lovely girl and will be in my class.'

'Thank you.' Mrs Foster-Dalton nodded. 'My husband says I shall have to find some war work but I don't know how to do anything.'

'Like us all, you'll have to learn, won't you? As we did before. You were a dab hand at rolling bandages and writing letters.' Miss Wentworth's voice was brisk.

'Yes, but that's all Mummy would let me do. It wasn't real work.' Mrs Foster-Dalton straightened, smoothed the wrinkled front of her lavender day-dress and in making herself taller she also seemed to gain confidence. 'Still, Alex wouldn't have wanted me to shirk my duty.'

'No, he wouldn't.' Miss Wentworth's voice caught and the two women exchanged a look that Victoria couldn't read.

'Mummy.' The sitting-room door was flung open and Diana rushed in followed, at a more sedate pace, by Nell. 'I showed Miss Potter our garden and we saw a butterfly and a bird and I petted the ginger cat from down the road.'

As Diana paused for breath, her mother ran a hand over her daughter's windblown hair. 'That's lovely, darling, but Mummy needs to tell you something very important.' She knelt to her daughter's level. 'You have to go away to the country for a while. It will be an adventure with other children from your school, and Miss Wentworth, Miss McKaye and Miss Potter will take good care of you.'

Although Mrs Foster-Dalton's voice was bright, Victoria caught the underlying quiver and crouched by Diana's side. 'We're going to have loads of fun in the country but you need to be a brave girl for Mummy and Daddy. Can you do that?'

'Like my brothers? George is going to learn how to fly an aeroplane, and Harry has joined the navy.' Diana's eyes filled with tears but she bit her lower lip and hugged her doll tight.

'In a way, yes.' Victoria glanced between Nell and Miss Wentworth. Would she ever be able to think of her as Beatrice?

'We all have to do our part.' She rose to stand next to Nell as Miss Wentworth joined them.

'We do.' Miss Wentworth nodded.

'For king and country. Countries. I expect Canada will also be part of whatever happens,' Nell added, beaming at Victoria.

Victoria tried to smile back and looked around the circle of faces: Nell's excited one, Mrs Foster-Dalton's grief-stricken one, and Miss Wentworth's, grim verging on wrathful.

Although Victoria had been too young to remember much about her father's absence, he'd been a surgeon with the medical corps in the last war. When he came back to his family as almost a stranger, neither he nor her mother ever talked about those years or what he'd experienced. Yet, as well as sending her husband, her mother had lost both her brothers, one at the Somme and the other at Vimy Ridge.

Although she understood why Mrs Foster-Dalton had called it that to Diana, war wasn't 'an adventure' and here in England, for better or worse, Victoria would be in the thick of it. While she still hoped for peace now, for the first time, all those preparations she'd almost dismissed because she'd been so caught up in her own life became truly, terrifyingly real.

She couldn't change what might happen but, like Miss Wentworth, Nell and even Mrs Foster-Dalton, she'd learn and do her best.

As Diana's hand crept into hers, Victoria squeezed it. 'I'll look after you, darling.'

'Lucinda too?' Diana held her doll aloft.

'Of course, Lucinda.' Victoria's voice hitched as Diana displayed the doll's pink gingham dress and lace-edged underclothes.

Victoria was a teacher and new pride in her work surged through her. Never more than now, she had a responsibility to the children these parents were entrusting to her care. And despite the fear, she wouldn't let any of them down.

Chapter Three

Under the vaulted roof in London's bustling Liverpool Street railway station, a labyrinth of dark tunnels and arches criss-crossed by footbridges, Victoria settled the new navy pillbox hat that matched her suit more firmly on her head and checked her list once again.

Evacuation day. 1st September 1939. A day she'd both dreaded and expected in equal measure, even before Germany had invaded Poland at dawn.

Her stomach rolled and a gust of wind blew cinders and a discarded newspaper near where she stood on the platform. At mid-morning, and after gathering at their individual schools and taking a coach here, the station was filled with parties like hers, pupils and teachers setting off into the unknown. Mothers and some fathers too who, despite well-intentioned advice against it, had come here desperate for a last glimpse of their children.

'Have you heard anything about the place we're going to?' At Victoria's elbow, Nell's voice was tinged with suppressed excitement. Like Victoria, she wore an armband and a cream cardboard London County Council badge edged in orange pinned to her coat, the latter with their names but both of which identified them as one of the adults accompanying evacuated children. 'I've never been further from London than Clacton-on-Sea. My auntie took me there for August Bank Holiday when I was twelve.' Her eyes shone, replacing what in only a few days Victoria had come to recognise was a sadness Nell sought to hide but often swirled about her like winter fog.

'No, although Miss Wentworth said it's likely to be some-where in East Anglia, Norfolk or Suffolk perhaps, since we're departing from this London station.' At a shout, Victoria looked up from her list which, as it had back at the school, still showed one child unaccounted for, Diana Foster-Dalton. 'Ralph, don't push Albert. Both of you boys get back into your groups.'

'Sorry, Miss. Yes, Miss.' Ralph stopped pretending to be an aeroplane, gave Victoria a cheeky smile and flapped the identity card on a cord around his neck.

Further along the platform, Miss Wentworth was huddled with one of the volunteer helpers, the two women surrounded by children clutching small cases or paper bags as well as card-board boxes with their gas masks hung by a string strap from one shoulder.

Victoria rubbed her temples. After a mostly sleepless night, the cries of children and an all-encompassing sense of worry mixed with trepidation pressed in on her. Where could Diana be?

'All set?' Miss Wentworth joined Victoria and Nell and gave them a brisk but what was undoubtedly meant to be an encouraging, bracing kind of smile. In a tweed coat that must once have been smart, and a tan-coloured hat with a jaunty feather, she carried a worn, brown-leather case with a monogram stamped in gold on the top.

'No, we're missing Diana Foster-Dalton. See?' Victoria passed Miss Wentworth her list.

'Evacuation *is* voluntary so I suppose...' Miss Wentworth squinted at the list, her neutral expression faltered and Victoria glimpsed what was perhaps the real woman, one who might be more vulnerable than her outward appearance would suggest.

'Here she is, Miss. I mean Miss Wentworth.' Nell's face went red as she pointed towards the ticket barrier and then dropped her hand as Miss Wentworth gave her a quelling look.

'In the nick of time too.' Miss Wentworth's tone was dry. Had Victoria imagined that brief hint of warmth and unfiltered, genuine emotion?

'I'm sorry.' Mrs Foster-Dalton sounded out of breath. She glanced at Miss Wentworth. 'I know I should have brought Diana to school to take the coach but I… we…'

'Mummy forgot my food parcel so we had to go back for it,' Diana said. 'Ivy gave me a packet of sweets as a goodbye present. Want to see?'

'You can show us later, dear, but now we need to be quick.' Victoria patted Diana's shoulder. Like all the mothers, Mrs Foster-Dalton was distraught. However, unlike most of the others she wasn't as successful at hiding it.

'I'll take you to join your group, Diana. You're with your friend Edith. Won't that be fun?' Nell held out her hand to the girl who took it.

'I'll see you soon, darling.' Mrs Foster-Dalton bent to embrace her daughter who whimpered. 'Be brave. It will be like a holiday.'

'But what if the bombs hit you and Daddy and Ivy?' Diana's blue eyes were wide and frightened.

'There's the shelter in the back garden for all of us, and if Daddy happens to be at work his office building has a basement so he'll be safe there.' Mrs Foster-Dalton's voice was too bright. 'We'll be fine.' With a final squeeze, she released Diana into Nell's care and stumbled backwards.

'You're doing the right thing, Mary.' Miss Wentworth patted the other woman's arm. 'Alex would be proud of you.'

'As he would of you.' Mrs Foster-Dalton's voice was choked and from behind Victoria a train whistle sounded and several children began to wail. 'Best be off.' She fumbled in her handbag for a handkerchief. 'Write as soon as you can.'

'I will.' Miss Wentworth hesitated as if she wanted to say something else but instead she stepped away and turned to Victoria and then Nell who re-joined them. 'For however long it may be, while our country is in peril these children are under our care. They – and their parents – are relying on us. Even though our school is being split up, our headmistress and I are relying on you.' She touched her evacuation identity card, gloved fingers lingering on the three numbers in stark black ink, the number of their school.

Victoria swallowed and nodded. 'Yes, Miss Wentworth.'

'Albert and Ralph.' Miss Wentworth raised her voice as the two boys whacked each other with their haversacks. 'I shall sit with those two on the train myself. In between them.' She gave Victoria and Nell a smile, as unexpected as it was surprising, before hurrying away.

Along with another volunteer helper, Victoria assembled her group with their luggage to board the train and then followed them into the already stuffy carriage. 'Keep your identity card around your neck, Thomas.' She gestured to a boy who was swinging it from his arm. 'Leave your chocolate in the food parcel for now, Edith.' She picked up a stray gas-mask box. 'Keep your gas mask with you at all times, remember?' She stowed her own case and coat in a rack, all the while resolving various disputes and trying to keep her voice calm and reassuring as whistles shrilled, more children cried and the train chuffed.

'Miss McKaye?' A hand tugged at her arm.

'Yes? Oh, Diana, what is it? Why aren't you sitting with Edith?'

'She wants to sit with Sheila instead.' Diana jerked her chin towards a seat several rows in front where two dark-haired girls had their heads together.

'You can sit with me, then. Here.' She gestured to an empty seat next to the window. 'Hurry, the train's already moving. Wave.' She peered out the window at the mothers lined up on the station platform, their faces almost as white as the handkerchiefs they flapped like small, steadfast flags.

'I want my mummy.' In the seat ahead of Victoria's, Peter, a boy who'd turned five three days before, wailed and several others joined in.

Of course the children wanted their mothers, the rest of their families too. It was likely the first time most of them had ever been parted from their parents and siblings.

'As soon as we reach where we're going, I'll help you send a postcard to your mothers. In the meantime why don't you draw special pictures for them?' She rummaged in her bag for the sheets of paper, each one divided into four, that she'd brought with her. 'I also have a surprise all the way from Canada.'

As Diana helped Peter find a clean handkerchief, they and several other children craned their heads over and between the seats to look.

'My mother sent you a present.' Victoria pulled out two boxes of new crayons. 'They're for you to share, but since Peter's the youngest he gets to choose the colour he'd like first.'

With the children distracted, Victoria glanced out the window where London's suburbs soon slipped by in a greyish-green blur. What would the city look like when she saw it again? With Nell and Miss Wentworth in other carriages with different groups of children, and except for the volunteer helpers they all shared, for now she was on her own. However, although she was new to Park Road School, she and the other teachers were the only link these boys and girls had with their lives before today. A lone connection with their parents, older siblings and extended families as well as their school and neighbourhood.

Evacuation meant the country was prepared for the worst, and for its children everything familiar had disappeared, as had the boundaries between home and school. Even if war didn't come and Victoria was back in London in a few days, she'd never be the woman she was before. For now, and no matter how long it took, she'd have to muddle through.

Chapter Four

'I'll visit you tomorrow, I promise.' As gently as she could, Victoria removed Peter's and Diana's clinging arms from around her waist. In the cavernous, echoing hall of the red-brick Victorian vicarage at the far end of Hazelbury, the North Norfolk village where they'd been billeted, the two children looked smaller and more frightened than ever.

'The pair of them will be fine, won't you?' Alice, the vicarage maid, patted Diana's head and took Peter's hand. 'Warm milk and an egg and toast then straight up to bed, I reckon. I have six younger brothers and sisters of my own so don't fret. The vicar and Mrs Russell will be home shortly. It's bad luck their car broke down the other side of Cromer after that funeral, that's all.' Alice, who Victoria guessed was around seventeen, gave her a dimpled smile.

'Thank you.' As Alice quickly closed the door with its blackout curtain, Victoria stepped onto the covered porch and then out into the drive. Was it only this morning she'd left London? Since arriving at the school at six before the children arrived at seven, she'd crammed what felt like several lifetimes and a gamut of emotions into the preceding fifteen or so hours.

At least Diana and Peter were the last two of her children to be settled with their foster family. Unlike those in some of the stories filtering in, Hazelbury's billeting officer had been organised. She and her team had allocated all the children to foster-parents in advance, sparing them from having to line up and be chosen like animals at a livestock auction. And when the coach from Norwich railway station pulled in, a committee of volunteers had greeted and welcomed the weary and dirty London evacuees to Hazelbury with iced buns and lemonade laid on in the village hall.

As Victoria made her way along the gravel drive between shadows cast by the moon and tall overarching trees, she glanced at the shapes made by shrubbery and garden statuary in what was now, after nine, a dark night. If only she had a torch – but since blackout regulations had been imposed from today, maybe even that small light wouldn't be allowed. After the Yorkshire girls' boarding school, she should be used to night-time in the countryside. However, before tonight, and whether in England or Canada, she'd never been out in it alone. She'd always been with other teachers in a school party – or at home, at the summer cabin, she'd been with her family.

Entering the lane that led to Hazelbury's high street, she stumbled into a hedgerow and caught her stockings in a branch. An owl hooted and when the moon slid behind a cloud, plunging the lane into almost pitch black, she hugged her handbag to her chest, gripped the string of her gas-mask box and broke into a run.

Was she right that there was pub on the corner that marked the outskirts of the village proper? Yes, there it was: The Crown, a squat, whitewashed building with a thatched roof. There were no lights there either, nor in the flint-fronted shops and houses that lined the high street, but there would be people behind those blacked-out windows and doors.

As she reached the corner of the pub, she pressed a hand to her chest and tried to get her bearings. The village hall couldn't be too far away and from there, after meeting up with Nell and Miss Wentworth, she could at last go to her own billet, wherever it might be.

The pub door opened and two men in dark jackets, trousers and cloth caps with scarves wrapped around their necks came out. 'Need help, Miss?'

'I… I don't know where the village hall is and I…' She squinted at them through the gloom and then held back a gasp as a dog barked and darted towards her.

'Now, now, Captain. Mind your manners with the lady.' The taller man grabbed the dog by its collar. 'You must be one of them who came with the school from London.' Behind a bushy, brown beard, he gave Victoria a kindly smile.

'Yes, I am.' She took a step back, giving the dog and men as wide a berth as she could.

'Don't mind us, nor Captain here neither.' The bearded man placed himself between Victoria and the dog. On closer inspection, the animal wasn't as big as she'd first thought. Some kind of medium-sized spaniel, perhaps? 'Between us, me and my brother have ten kiddies of our own up at the school. The name's Clarke. I'm Frank and he's Walter.' He jerked his chin towards his shorter, clean-shaven companion.

'Thank you.' Victoria's heartbeat slowed to its normal rate. 'I'm Miss McKaye. Actually, I like dogs. I shouldn't have been frightened.'

'Not to worry,' Frank said with another reassuring smile. 'Even without my brother's ugly mug, Captain jumping out in front of you there would have been right startling.'

Especially when she was tired and in a new place, and despite the taller Mr Clarke's, Frank's, gentle manner, the men and their dog had rattled her more than Victoria wanted to admit.

'The village hall's down past the chemist's and round the corner.' Walter gestured with a beefy hand. 'Frank and I'll show you. With this blackout none of us knows where we're going.' His deep-set eyes studied her. While some might have called him handsome, something about that intense, unblinking stare made Victoria uneasy.

'One of the teachers, are you?' Frank Clarke gave Victoria his arm to navigate an uneven piece of pavement. 'I have girls, but Walter's lads will keep you on your toes.'

'I am a teacher, yes, but I expect I'll only be teaching the London children.' She shivered as a wisp of fog spun along the high street and with it a cold breeze. She wouldn't have to cope with village children too, would she? She'd only managed to learn the names of her pupils from Park Road School.

'That billeting officer woman, Mrs Meldrum, didn't know what you'd be doing. "Be prepared for any eventuality" is what she said to us.' Walter shook his head. 'Me and my missus took a boy in, a lad of ten, to help on the farm. That's what we asked for, but not much good he'll be for chores, having never even seen a cow before. Spindly fellow, too.'

'All our pupils are Londoners with no experience of country life.' Victoria wasn't much better. Having grown up in a town, although in a rural area, she'd only seen cows grazing placidly in fields, almost part of the scenery. 'There's the hall.' It was the only building in the village apart from the pub and parish church she was certain to recognise. 'I can find my own way from here.' As they reached the corner, she nodded her thanks to the men and ventured to pat the top of Captain's head.

'Good luck, Miss.' Frank touched the brim of his cap and Walter followed suit before they continued along the high street and their footsteps faded into the distance.

Still gripping her handbag and gas-mask box, Victoria soon reached the hall with its peaked slate roof and double, white-painted wooden doors tucked beneath an open porch. 'Hello? I'm back.' Mindful of the blackout, she opened the door a crack and slipped through the opening as fast as she could. Inside, the hall was shadowed, the only light coming from an oil lamp and candles in tall holders.

'We were about to send out a search party for you.' Still wearing her tweed coat from the morning, but now with a considerably more harried expression, Miss Wentworth came towards her followed by Nell. The younger woman wore a peach-coloured dressing gown while the skirt, blouse and cardigan she'd had on earlier were draped over several wooden chairs.

'What's happened?' Victoria looked between them.

'We...' Miss Wentworth raised her hands and then dropped them again. 'Insofar as billets go, it seems we teachers have been forgotten.'

'And I slipped and fell into a pond chasing after two of your lot,' Nell said. 'Ralph and Albert are fine,' she added, forestalling one of Victoria's next questions.

'But what are we going to do?' Victoria sat on the only free chair and tugged burrs out of her ruined stockings.

Miss Wentworth's shoulders slumped. 'The billeting committee said they'd sort it out in the morning but at present there's not a spare bed to be found. We have to sleep here.'

–

In the weak light cast by the candles and oil lamp, Victoria wrestled with a folding camp bed. Next to her, struggling with her own bed, Nell muttered under her breath.

'You'd think they'd have expected us teachers too.' Nell rolled up a cardigan to make it into a pillow. 'It's not like the kiddies could have travelled by themselves, is it? Even the volunteer helpers are better off than us. Why did they get the rooms over the pub?'

'Likely because they're returning to London tomorrow.' Victoria made a cardigan-pillow roll as well. 'On the bright side, I suppose we could have been sent to sleep in a nearby barn.' She found one of the torches the billeting officer had left with the camp beds, clicked it on and rested it on the floor beside her bed. In a room the size of this hall, it didn't add much brightness but she'd be able to see enough to read.

'We'd have had hay for bedding, then.' Nell's laugh was hollow. 'I saw enough barns tramping round the countryside today.' She sat on the edge of her camp bed and it collapsed beneath her. 'Of all the ruddy—'

'More tea?' Miss Wentworth held up the flask several women from the local W.I. had provided, along with a plate of sandwiches, half a Bakewell tart, rock cakes and an assortment of crockery.

Victoria held out her cup and then cradled her hand around its warmth. During all those hours making sure children were safe in their billets, she'd thought longingly of a hearty meal, a hot bath, a clean bed and time to herself. Had it been too much to expect even one of those things?

'Be warned.' Nell crawled out from under the clothing she'd used for bedding. 'We might be better off sleeping on the floor. These camp beds smell so musty and horrible. Do you think someone might have died in them?' She pushed her bed back into position with a clatter.

'Don't be foolish.' Miss Wentworth gave her a quashing look. 'I expect they're used by the Scouts for camping trips and such. We've been fed, we're warm and dry, and we have shelter for the night. Although it's not what we expected, we have to put our best foot forwards.' Setting aside the tea flask, she sat on her own camp bed. 'Our pupils are counting on us. We must be… oh…' She yelped and pitched backwards.

'Miss Wentworth? Here, I'll…' Victoria set her cup on its saucer with a rattle, grabbed her torch and rushed through the semi-darkness to the other woman.

'I'm stuck.' Miss Wentworth's voice was muffled as her head now seemed to be caught beneath the bed frame and mattress.

'Hang on. Miss Potter, come and help me. Now, if you please?' Victoria gestured as Nell had a hand over her mouth, seemingly stifling laughter.

'Oh, no.' As she slipped on the polished floor, Nell bumped into Victoria and the two of them landed almost on top of their fellow teacher. 'I'm so sorry. It's my slippers on this floor.' She stared at Victoria wide-eyed, any hint of laughter gone.

Victoria gulped, pushed tweed fabric from her face and scrambled to her feet. 'Are you all right Miss Wentworth?' What if she was injured? Victoria fumbled for Miss Wentworth's hands and frantically tried to recall her first aid training. The village hall didn't have a telephone but if Nell ran to the pub—

'I'm fine.' Miss Wentworth stuck her head out from beneath the mattress. Strands of blonde hair tumbled around her face and several hair grips dropped to the floor with a faint ping. 'But I can't say the same for my hat.' Her voice shook as she tried to extricate herself but instead flopped backwards a second time, this time landing fully on the already crushed tan hat brim. 'Maybe if you both try to pull me out?'

Victoria kept hold of Miss Wentworth's right hand while Nell took her left and they tugged together.

'That's it.' Victoria braced herself. Although Miss Wentworth was slender, she was tall and wedged in an awkward position. 'There you go.'

'Thank you.' Miss Wentworth's voice shook harder and she took her hands away from Victoria and Nell to brush at her face. 'I… you…' Now sitting on the floor, her whole body vibrated.

'Do you think she's in shock?' Nell hovered at Victoria's side. 'Should we lie her down and put her legs up?'

'I'm not in shock. I'm…' Miss Wentworth looked between them. 'Who would think we… I…' Her words came out between gasps. 'It's dreadful but it's also amusing and…' She rummaged in her handbag for a handkerchief. 'I thought after the last one we were done with war. You're too young, you weren't even born.' She nodded at Nell. 'As for you, Miss McKaye…' She dabbed at her eyes with the delicate linen embroidered with pale-pink flowers. 'You were a child.'

'Yes, but my father served in the Canadian Army Medical Corps. He's a doctor.' As Victoria sat on the floor beside Miss Wentworth, her stomach knotted. For the most part, her mother had shielded Victoria and her younger sisters from that war. Even when the men came back, some lacking limbs and with still-livid scars, those were only the ones with visible injuries. She hugged herself at the memory of a man who used to sit outside the camp store near their summer cabin, rocking back and forth and talking to himself.

'Don't mind Mr Lewycky, children.' Victoria's mother's voice echoed across the years. 'He's to be pitied, not laughed at.'

Then she'd hurried them along, either into the store or towards the car, but always dropping several coins into the ragged cap at the man's side or making sure he had a cold drink and a sandwich.

Her mother had tried to shield her children from anything upsetting or unpleasant. She was still trying to shield them. That was the reason for all those letters asking, begging, Victoria to return to Canada. But now, thanks to her own pride and foolishness, Victoria was likely stuck here. Not only in England but in this Norfolk village where, except for these two other teachers she'd met less than a fortnight ago, she was on her own.

'Your father saw war then, all of it.' Miss Wentworth's voice caught. 'The horror. The dying and the dead. The men with missing arms and legs, shell shock. All the lives and families and hopes and dreams destroyed.'

Victoria exchanged a glance with Nell who retrieved a second flask of tea and the tin of rock cakes. 'Did you... Mrs Foster-Dalton mentioned someone and I wondered... Sorry.' She put a hand to her mouth. 'It's none of my business.'

'It's not, but I suppose I must explain. Diana's mother, Mary Foster-Dalton, and I were at school together. She was Mary Athill then.' Miss Wentworth sat up, her back ramrod straight and, in the flickering light, the others saw that her face held both pride and pain. 'Her brother, Alex, was my fiancé. He was twenty and I'd just turned nineteen – but then he was killed.'

'I'm... sorry.' Victoria reached for Miss Wentworth's hand and then stopped.

'Mary and I lost touch. She married and I... well, I didn't.' Miss Wentworth's usually brisk tone was softer, almost wistful. 'I made the best of things like so many other women and girls had to. No, no more tea or anything else, thank you, Miss Potter.' She waved Nell away. 'It's late. We need to settle our beds and put out the lights, such as they are.'

'Yes, Miss Wentworth.' Nell crept away and busied herself with her bedding.

Victoria retreated to her own bed and held her torch aloft as Miss Wentworth fixed her camp bed and made sure it was sturdy, then blew out the candles and the old-fashioned table lamp with the bulbous yellow floral shade one of the W.I. had also supplied. 'Good night.' Victoria turned off her torch and the darkness pressed in on her like a dark and malevolent being.

'Sleep as well as you can manage.' Miss Wentworth's bed creaked, and from Victoria's other side, Nell made a choked sound.

'It will be all right.' Victoria tried to make her voice bright.

'Of course it will,' Miss Wentworth said with a return of some of her normal bracing tone. 'Under ordinary circumstances, I wouldn't even think such a thing or suggest it, but we're not living in ordinary times. At school and whenever else we are with the children we will, of course, be Miss Wentworth, Miss McKaye and Miss Potter. But when we are together in private and must rely on each other as is the case at present, first names will be acceptable. If you wish, you may call me Beatrice.'

'Yes, Miss. I mean Beatrice.' To Victoria's right, Nell drew in a sharp breath. 'I expect when I can take a proper look at it in daylight I'll be able to fix your hat. I'm good with sewing and fixing bits of millinery, despite what you might think given my own hat's such a horror. I didn't have time to sort it or any of the rest of my clothes what with us being called to school early.'

'We all have more important things to concern ourselves with than hats or whatever else we may put on but thank you, that's most kind.' In the darkness, Miss Wentworth's voice was almost soothing.

Victoria shifted on the uncomfortable bed. While she couldn't yet think of Miss Wentworth – Beatrice – as a friend, maybe today the three of them had taken the first tentative step towards something else. A new kind of understanding that might make the situation they found themselves in bearable. At least for the duration, however long that might be.

Chapter Five

On Sunday morning, after her second restless night on a camp bed in the village hall, Victoria stole a glance at the congregation ranged in the pews around her. Under the wood-beamed roof of Hazelbury's parish church, and between shopkeepers, farmers and Mrs Russell, the vicar's wife and their four tall sons, she spotted some of her pupils. While she'd visited as many of them yesterday as she could, she'd see more after church. Already, though, she had a mountain of problems to sort, everything from a child who feared dogs billeted in a home with two large ones, to an elderly widow who'd requested a quiet, well-behaved girl being allocated two boisterous brothers.

For now, though, she'd make the most of the first uninterrupted hour she'd had to herself since leaving London. She gave Diana, who sat in the vicarage pew beside Peter, a small smile before turning back to her hymnal. She knew both the tune and words by heart, having sung 'Morning has Broken' often in both Canada and England and, especially in her early homesick days, it had seemed a comforting bridge between the two countries.

As she settled into her seat between Beatrice and Nell, and behind the pulpit the vicar gathered his notes to deliver the sermon, her gaze drifted to a nearby rose-stained glass window of elaborate design. It was a nineteenth century memorial to members of a local family, almost recent because according to an historical snippet on the porch notice board she'd read on her way in, Hazelbury's church dated from medieval times. With its great square tower, it stood in the centre of the village across from a small green and, as she'd also read, had been 'a stalwart beacon of hope and continuity through many centuries'.

Although it was only two days since she'd left London, Victoria had never needed such a reminder of hope and steadfast continuity more. Her thoughts wandered with the gentle cadence of the vicar's voice as he spoke about 'holding fast to God's promise' and faith, loyalty and duty.

'We must all remember that no matter how dark the shadows that threaten us—'

The rear door of the church banged open and a short, rotund and red-faced, hatless man appeared in the central aisle.

'Sorry, Vicar.' The man bobbed his shiny bald head as Mr Russell halted mid-sentence. 'I didn't even stop to put on me hat. I just heard Prime Minister Chamberlain on the wireless speaking from Downing Street. He said we're at war with Germany.'

As an anxious babble broke out, the vicar stepped down from the pulpit.

'Oh, dear God.' With a soft moan, Beatrice dropped her head into her hands.

'If Mr Chamberlain said so, it must be true.' Nell's voice held both excitement and fear.

Icy cold flooded Victoria's body and by reflex she grabbed her gas-mask box.

'So much for appeasing Hitler.' A man's voice rang out from the other side of the nave. 'We'll show him, won't we, lads? We can take whatever he plans on throwing at us.'

A cheer went up and Mr Russell raised a hand. 'Not in church.' Although the vicar's voice was calm, it carried an unmistakable note of authority.

'Tell us what you heard, Bob, all of it.' Mr Russell, now joined by his wife and sons, moved along the aisle, and men who'd gathered around the new arrival returned to their seats, falling silent.

'The prime minister didn't talk for long, only a few minutes. I were polishing glass behind the bar and listening to the Home

Service. Then Mr Chamberlain came on and I called the wife to come quick from the kitchen.' The man rubbed a hand across his forehead. 'After Chamberlain spoke, an announcer told about air raid warnings and said theatres, cinemas and other such "places of entertainment", as he called them, have to close straight away.'

'None of those 'round Hazelbury anyway,' another voice muttered.

'I want my mummy.' At a child's wail, Victoria turned to see Peter huddled alone with Diana in the vicarage pew.

The children. Even though she didn't know what to say, she had to somehow reassure her pupils. She touched Nell's arm and then Beatrice's. The three of them slipped out of their seats as Bob, evidently the publican at The Crown, continued to recount Mr Chamberlain's speech.

'Going to the aid of Poland… struggle to win peace has failed.'

The words washed over Victoria as she reached Peter's side, and he flung his arms around her neck as if she were his only defence against an invading German army. 'Hush, darling.' She patted his heaving back as Diana and then several other children clustered around her, their faces pale and etched with fear.

'Let us pray.' Once again, the vicar's voice rose above the hubbub.

As she held the children close, Victoria bowed her head. Now she knew for certain what she'd known in her heart for weeks, months even. She wouldn't be returning to London or even Canada any time soon. Her work, her *real* work, had only just begun.

Chapter Six

'If you and Miss Potter teach the juniors here in the hall, I can take the infants who turned up on a nature walk. Only around the village.' Victoria gestured to the crowded village hall which two days into what should be the regular school week, and in addition to the teachers' temporary sleeping accommodation, also now served as a makeshift classroom.

'I'd planned to keep to our London schedule, but without having use of a proper school building or schoolroom it's impossible. I can't fault the village teacher. She had no way of knowing how many of us there would be and in such a small school there's not enough space for—' Beatrice stopped and rapped on the table she'd commandeered as a desk with a ruler. 'Boys, stop pulling Sheila's plaits.'

'We have to adapt. I'm counting our lucky stars that Hazelbury still has a teacher and we aren't responsible for the village children as well.' Victoria marched over to Albert, took him back to his spot on the floor near the front of the hall, and gave him a picture book.

'Miss McKaye's right.' Nell put a hand to her mouth as if fearing she'd spoken out of turn. 'What I mean is—'

'I know what you mean, both of you.' Beatrice's eyes were smudged with purple and her already thin face seemed narrower. 'Thank you for wanting to help. A schedule would give the children continuity, but with us all here in one room we can't manage and—'

'Albert.' Nell darted across the room.

Victoria stifled a yawn and gave Beatrice a wry smile. 'I expect it will become easier once some more school supplies arrive from London.'

'And we have a proper place to live and manage a full night's sleep. The children whose first billets weren't suitable needed those rooms above the pub more than us. The publican and his wife will dote on them until permanent foster homes are available.' Beatrice returned Victoria's smile. 'I'll ring the billeting officer again later and we can only hope Mrs Meldrum finds places for us soon. Right.' She straightened. 'We'll do as you suggested. If you have the infants outdoors, Miss Potter and I should be able to manage here.'

'It's a plan.' Victoria glanced at Beatrice's white blouse. Immaculate when she'd started the school day, it now had a streak of dried blood across the front from a girl who'd had a nosebleed, and mud from cleaning up a boy who'd fallen into a farm ditch on his way to school.

'If a minor nosebleed and bit of country dirt are the worst of what happens whilst we're here, I'll consider myself a fortunate woman.' Beatrice glanced at her stained blouse too and then pulled on the cardigan she'd draped over the back of her chair. 'We also have to track down the children who didn't come to school at all today, and there are even more problems with billets.' She rubbed a hand across her face and tucked a loose strand of hair behind one ear.

Although her hair was still in a bun, Beatrice hadn't pulled it as tightly back as she had in London, and the looser style softened her fine features. She was less standoffish too, and although along with Nell the three of them were from different generations, that slight bond they'd forged over the collapsing camp beds had endured.

'I'll set out then.' Victoria clapped her hands. 'Infants' class. We're going on a special adventure. And Albert?' She waited until he turned to look at her with a sullen expression.

'What, Miss?'

'I have a very important job for you.' She beckoned to him. 'I want you and Ralph to walk at the back of our group to help me make sure nobody gets lost.' She nodded to the other boy. Maybe if she made the two of them feel responsible and important they'd have a reason to stop trying to cause trouble. 'Diana and Margaret will lead us at the front.' Diana needed a friend and with Edith and Sheila billeted together, Diana was now the odd one out. 'Follow me.'

Ten minutes later, and with her infants' class walking two-by-two around the back of the churchyard fence and into a country lane, Victoria let out a shaky breath. If not one of total relief, it was certainly a brief lessening of panic. And with Diana and Margaret at the head of the crocodile of children, and Ralph and Albert marching with soldier-like importance at the rear, some of Victoria's usual confidence returned.

'How many colours of flowers can you spot? Raise your hands and take turns.' It might be an outdoor classroom but that didn't mean standards had to slip. Victoria smothered a smile as hands shot up. She'd sounded like Beatrice, but the other teacher was an excellent classroom manager. Although they might never be close friends, Victoria could learn from her. 'Yes, Peter?'

'There's a red one, Miss.' Peter pointed to a clump of blooms on the verge.

'Do any of you know what that flower is called?' Victoria drew the group to a halt while Diana helped a younger girl pull up her socks.

'It's a poppy, Miss. My gran has some in her garden.' Ralph's voice was full of import.

'Flowers are for girls.' Albert kicked at the dirt track.

'Flowers are for everyone, poppies especially,' Victoria said, studying his bent head.

In wartime, poppies held even more meaning. These children were too young, but when Victoria was only a year or so older she and her classmates had recited Canadian physician

John McCrae's poem 'In Flanders Fields' at a special school assembly. Although, at the time, Victoria hadn't fully under-stood why some of the mothers, aunts, grandmothers and even a few of the younger teachers had cried.

'What's troubling you, Albert?' As the others exclaimed over the poppies, she moved closer and bent to speak softly to him.

'I hate it here, that's what.' Albert kicked up more dirt. 'My billet doesn't even have electric lights, and the lady said I'm dirty. I don't have no bugs. It weren't my fault Ralph was sick over me on the train.'

'No, it wasn't.' Many of the children had been sick on the journey and despite their mothers' efforts to send them away clean and tidy, most were bedraggled by the time they arrived here. Victoria made a mental note to pay Albert's billet another visit. While the majority of the village foster-parents were kind, she'd already discovered several cases where some, if not inten-tionally cruel, had no idea how to manage young children, especially those from a city like London. 'I know it's hard being away from your family and in such a different place but we all have to try and—'

A bellow interrupted her, and Victoria sprang backwards.

Several girls screamed and even Albert yelped.

'Stay calm, children, and move away slowly. It's only a cow.' However, it was big and bright red. As it stared at Victoria with its glittering, dark eyes, she wrapped one arm around Albert and gestured with the other. 'Shoo, go away, you.'

The cow continued to stare as the children huddled behind Victoria, and Peter howled.

'It must have come out of that field there. Fence has a gap.' Albert's freckles stood out on his face and his straw-blond hair stuck up on one side.

'I'm sure it will go back to where it came from.' Victoria gathered Peter into her arms and tried to sound more confident than she felt.

'Here comes another one, Miss McKaye. See?' Diana's voice quavered.

Now they were cornered. At a distance no further away than the width of an ordinary London road, two cows stood in the middle of the narrow lane which lay between them and the village. It was only mid-afternoon, but if they followed the lane too far the other way and got lost and it grew dark… No, she wouldn't let herself think about such things. *Stay calm*.

A cheerful whistle sounded and then a man in tailored light-grey trousers, a blue cotton shirt with the sleeves rolled to his elbows, stout walking boots and a battered hat came around the corner of the lane behind them. 'Hullo, there.' He carried a rucksack on his back, and a golden cocker spaniel walked at his side. He glanced between the children and Victoria. 'Are you lost?'

'No, but…' Victoria cleared her throat and jerked her chin towards the cows. The man looked to be around her age and beneath his hat, he had light-brown hair and eyes as blue as the prairie sky Victoria had grown up beneath. 'I… the children… we're from London and unused to the countryside.' Her face heated.

'You sound as if you've come from much further away than London.' His smile lit up his face and highlighted lines around his eyes and well-shaped mouth. 'Canada, perhaps?'

'Yes, although my family is British.' She put one hand to her warm cheek. 'I'm a teacher and these are my pupils. We were evacuated to Hazelbury several days ago. I was taking my infants' class on a nature walk but…' She again gestured to the cows still standing in the lane.

In the wake of her broken engagement, she'd considered herself immune to masculine charm, but when was the last time she'd met any man close to her age, let alone such an attractive one? On the ship coming to England she'd spent most of her time in her stateroom. And between the girls' boarding school and now this job, she was surrounded by other women.

'Don't be frightened. Walter Clarke's cows won't hurt you. They're used to people and dogs. However, if Walter spent more time tending his farm and less down the pub, his cattle wouldn't get out.' The man clipped a lead to the dog's collar, spread his arms wide and took several firm steps towards the animals. 'Stay calm and follow me. We'll walk around them. Don't make any sudden movements or shout out.'

Walter Clarke. One of the men Victoria had met coming out of the pub on her first night here. The shorter, clean-shaven one with the deep-set eyes and square face who, with his brother, had walked with her to the hall.

'Do what the man says,' Victoria instructed the children until all of them had scurried around the cattle in pairs with the man and his dog.

'Now you.' The man returned and gave her another smile. 'I'm Louis Grainger.' He held out his arm to Victoria.

'Victoria McKaye.' Although she'd felt nothing when taking Mr Frank Clarke's arm, her fingers tingled as her hand connected with this stranger's bare, sun-warmed forearm. As soon as they'd made it safely around the cows, she took her hand away. Given it was a warm day and a country walk with children, she hadn't worn gloves. That brief, unexpected skin-to-skin touch was the only reason she was unsettled.

'I'll walk with you and the children to the village crossroads.' His eyes twinkled, telling her he was teasing. 'In case you meet any other stray cows or sheep.'

'Thank you.' She stepped back. She was a teacher and a grown woman, not some foolish girl to be swayed by a smile, a handsome face and a bit of joking.

'I'm visiting my great-aunts in Hazelbury. They've been away but will return today. Before meeting them at the station, I decided to take Lady for a hike.' He gestured to the dog, which the children eyed almost as warily as they had the cows. 'Lady's a friendly girl. If Miss McKaye says it's all right, you can pet her and then take turns holding her lead if you'd like.'

As Victoria nodded and they turned another corner in the lane and left the cows behind, the children clamoured around Mr Grainger and Lady.

Victoria straightened her wide-brimmed straw hat and smoothed her floral day-dress. Mr Grainger was only visiting Hazelbury. Even if she wanted to – and she didn't – she wasn't likely to see him again.

Chapter Seven

'Beatrice, Nell, I have good news.' After seeing the children on their way to their billets safely, Victoria rushed back into the village hall. 'While I was with the last of the juniors, Bob from the pub came to tell me he'd a call from Mrs Meldrum. She's sorted out our billet and is bringing her car to take us there. She's on her way now.'

'Excellent. When I spoke to her, she said she was most hopeful.' Beatrice paused in tidying up scattered papers. 'It will be heavenly to sleep in a proper bed again.'

'And have a proper wash.' Along a wall near the hall's stage, Nell arranged six small chairs on loan from the Sunday school. 'I've only managed sponge baths since leaving London.'

'You and me both.' Victoria nodded agreement as she surveyed the makeshift schoolroom. 'An indoor lavatory would be welcome too, instead of having to tramp out into the dark near the garden allotments.'

'Indeed, but don't hold your breath.' Beatrice collected her handbag from the table beneath maps of Europe and the British Isles they'd pinned up earlier. 'The junior classes were full of complaints today. Many of their billets don't have indoor plumbing *or* electricity.'

'But surely for the teachers…' Victoria stopped as Beatrice shook her head.

'I had a letter from Miss Hopson.' Beatrice patted her handbag. 'I'll read parts of it to you later. Miss Hopson heard that accommodation is so scarce that teachers from another London school evacuated to the West Country with her group from Park Road are indeed sleeping in a barn. Presumably, they'll be moved elsewhere before winter, but for now they're making do with mattresses of hay and being woken each morning by early milking. We're fortunate by comparison.'

'I thought it was a joke our first night here, talking about barns and hay.' Nell exchanged a horrified glance with Victoria.

As Victoria's mother often reminded her, she should count her blessings, and that's what Victoria had to do in this situation. While she gathered her belongings, her thoughts once again drifted to Mr Grainger.

From his accent, clothing and demeanour, he wasn't a labouring man but he also didn't seem like a shopkeeper or entirely part of the professional class, either. He had to be from what her London landlady would call 'a good family' but so far, and apart from Mrs Meldrum, the vicar and his family and a widowed solicitor's wife, everyone Victoria had met here were farmers like the Clarke brothers or owned small shops and were of the same class as Bob the publican.

Who could a man like him be visiting? She smiled at the memory of his twinkly eyes and then sobered. Thanks to the new Act of Parliament passed the day war was declared, like all other British men between eighteen and forty-one, and unless he was in a reserved occupation or deemed medically unfit, he'd be conscripted to the war effort. Although here the war seemed far away, it could only be a matter of time until it reached even the most rural and remote parts of the country. Nowhere, not even Hazelbury, was safe.

She opened the door of the village hall and glanced up the road. 'I see Mrs Meldrum's car by the corner of the high street now.'

'We're all set.' Beatrice followed Victoria outside and Nell brought up the rear.

'I know we've only been here a few days but it feels like we're leaving home all over again.' Nell's gaze darted from one side of the road to the other in what Victoria had begun to privately think of as the younger girl's 'frightened rabbit' look. 'Oh, I do hope Mrs Meldrum's message means the three of us will be billeted together.'

'We'll soon know.' The car, a burgundy-coloured Austin Seven saloon, which Victoria only knew because Beatrice had previously mentioned the make and model, drew up in front of the hall and screeched to a stop.

Mrs Meldrum, a grey-haired woman aged somewhere between her late fifties and early sixties, waved from the driver's seat and tootled the horn. 'Don't worry about locking up.' She leaned from the half-open window to speak to them. 'I'm coming straight back for a W.I. meeting. The ladies and I expect you to join us once you're settled.'

Victoria's mother and aunts belonged to the Women's Institute in Canada. She'd resisted their encouragement to join, fearing she'd be out of place, too young to be one of the 'spinsters', but also not one of the young married women. However, here, and in such a small village, Mrs Meldrum hadn't left any room for her to decline.

As Victoria and Nell stored their cases and scrambled into the rear seats, leaving the front passenger seat for Beatrice, Victoria's heart sank. The W.I. would be one more obligation amongst what already seemed too many.

'Off we go, then.' Mrs Meldrum put the car in gear and drove off at speed.

'Gosh.' Nell leaned closer and spoke into Victoria's ear. 'She's like Mr Toad in *The Wind in the Willows* isn't she? Do you think we'll be safe?' Her face paled and her eyes widened in fright.

Victoria nodded as she slid sideways on the leather upholstery. 'I'm sure we'll be fine. We can't be going far and from what I've seen so far these roads don't have a lot of traffic. Here, hold on to me.' She held out her hand and Nell gripped it tight.

'All three of you will be staying at Hazelbury Manor,' Mrs Meldrum's voice boomed from in front of Victoria, 'with the Misses Grainger. They've been visiting friends near Lincoln but...'

Whatever else Mrs Meldrum said was drowned out as she hooted the horn again, scattering a flock of chickens onto a grassy verge.

Grainger. That was Louis's surname. If the Misses Grainger were his great-aunts, Victoria might indeed see him again and soon. She pressed her free hand to her queasy stomach as the vehicle swung around a corner and jolted into a tree-lined drive.

'Hazelbury Manor has medieval origins,' Mrs Meldrum continued. 'The Graingers were once one of Norfolk's finest families but since the last war they're sadly diminished. You may find the Misses Grainger a tad standoffish and set in their ways, but they are prepared to do their bit for king and country like the rest of us.'

The car clattered to a stop, and Nell's tight grip on Victoria's hand eased.

'Come along, then.' Mrs Meldrum glanced towards them. Her tightly crimped steel-grey hair never seemed to move as if it, like Victoria, was similarly intimidated by its imposing owner.

Victoria gave Nell an encouraging smile as they followed Beatrice and Mrs Meldrum across a well-kept lawn and up a set of stone steps to a massive wooden front door.

Mrs Meldrum pressed a bell and their small party waited in silence.

As the door swung open, Victoria took a step back. Instead of the maid she'd expected, Louis stood on the doorstep.

'Come in.' He greeted Mrs Meldrum and then his gaze darted to Victoria behind her. 'My great-aunts are waiting for you in the drawing room. Miss McKaye.' He nodded as she passed him and entered a dark and chilly hall. 'It's a pleasure to see you again.'

'Likewise, and thank you.' Victoria's face warmed as Beatrice, Nell and Mrs Meldrum all stared at her with raised eyebrows and barely disguised curiosity.

There was nothing for her to be embarrassed about. Her earlier meeting with Mr Grainger had been entirely innocent, so why did she feel such an inexplicable need to keep it to herself?

–

'Louis and my sister will show you to your rooms.' The elder Miss Grainger, a silver-haired woman wearing a dark-purple dress edged with black lace, waved a slender hand in dismissal. 'Although we are unfortunately lacking in staff, Marjorie, the daily, has already taken your cases up.'

As Beatrice and Nell had done, Victoria murmured her thanks. Declining an invitation to stay for a cup of tea, Mrs Meldrum had made a hasty departure and for the past half hour, Victoria and Nell had sat silent in a large, furniture-filled drawing room swathed in heavy green brocade draperies while Beatrice, the two Misses Grainger and Louis had discussed the war and several mutual acquaintances.

As the others left the drawing room, Miss Adelaide, the younger Miss Grainger, touched Victoria's sleeve to hold her back. 'You will find a lavatory outside the kitchen door and, should you need them, extra candles, lamp oil and matches are in the cupboard above the sink in the scullery.' Miss Adelaide was small of stature and feature, and her rather child-like face was surrounded by soft white hair with a slight curl. She gave Victoria an almost apologetic smile. 'We have an extra copper tub for you to use for bathing. Father wasn't one for change.'

'I'm sure it will be fine.' Victoria wasn't sure of anything at present except that, although basic, the village hall might still be preferable to Hazelbury Manor's faded grandeur.

'We only have Marjorie from the village.' Miss Adelaide led Victoria out of the drawing room with small, mouse-like steps. 'You shall have to make your own beds and so forth.'

Victoria swallowed an unexpected laugh. Although her family was what her father called 'comfortable', she'd never *not* made her own bed. And although they had a 'hired girl', her mother expected her daughters to do housework. 'I appreciate it's an inconvenience having us here. I know I speak for Miss Wentworth and Miss Potter as well when I say we'll try not to disrupt your lives too much.'

As they walked up a wide wooden staircase side by side before arriving in an upstairs hall with two corridors running off it in opposite directions, Miss Adelaide nodded. 'I, for one, am glad you're here.' Her bright blue eyes twinkled and reminded Victoria of Louis. 'My sister never shirks her duty, but Henrietta could do with shaking up a bit. We both could.'

Miss Adelaide whisked Victoria along the portrait-lined corridor to the left of the staircase and came to a stop outside two open doors where Beatrice's voice echoed from the nearer one.

'Ah, there you are.' Louis paused in showing Beatrice how to fix the blackout. 'I wondered where you and Aunt Addie had got to. Plotting a midnight feast, perhaps?'

'Don't tease, Louis.' Miss Adelaide gave him a fond smile before turning back to Victoria. 'You're next door with Miss Potter, and we've given you a smaller chamber across the corridor for a sitting room. Although the manor is large, it's not... well, we don't...' She stopped and twisted her hands together.

'Please don't trouble yourself,' Beatrice said. 'Between our bedrooms and that small parlour, we shall be perfectly comfortable.' She gave Miss Adelaide what Victoria now recognised as a polite but strained smile.

'We dine at seven. Nowadays, we don't dress for dinner but—'

'We will, of course, change. Smart frocks?' Beatrice moved away from the window to stand by Victoria.

'That will be fine.' Miss Adelaide exhaled.

'Ring if you need anything and I'll pop up.' Louis inclined his head towards a pull attached to a brass bell near the door.

'Louis!' Miss Adelaide chided him – but then chuckled. 'Don't let Hetty hear you. She still thinks we should have a houseful of staff.'

He laughed and patted her shoulder as they left the room together, the affection between great-aunt and nephew evident.

As Victoria made to follow them, Beatrice raised a hand to stop her. 'Get Nell and then come back here. I expect you have a smart frock but Nell won't. Between the two of us, we need to help her.'

'Of course.' Victoria spoke around an unexpected lump in her throat as a longing for home rose up in her so strongly she could almost taste it. Or even for her digs in London. She'd never had to share a bedroom or, except at the summer cabin, lived in a place without electricity and indoor plumbing. She gulped back tears.

'I suppose I should tell you to "buck up" or something similar but...' Beatrice's expression was more vulnerable than Victoria had ever seen it and then she shrugged. 'It's rotten luck, all of it. I'm still angry more than anything. After the last time, I—'

'Yoo-hoo.' Nell stuck her head around Beatrice's open bedroom door. 'I'm trying to fix the blackout and...' She stopped and came into the room. 'What's wrong?'

'Nothing.' Victoria bit her bottom lip. She hardly knew these women. She couldn't cry in front of them.

'Here.' Nell's voice was soft and she held out a clean handkerchief. 'I'd put the kettle on, but I'm too afraid of Miss Grainger to go back downstairs and find the kitchen.'

'I'm not frightened of Miss Grainger.' Beatrice gave a short laugh. 'But – here.' She dug in her school satchel. 'I still have a bar of chocolate and some boiled lemon sweets. We can share.' Her tone held a forced cheerfulness. 'While we do, we'll choose a dress for Nell to wear to dinner. I'm taller but one of mine should fit.'

'Mine too.' Victoria dried her eyes with the handkerchief. 'Sorry.'

'It's all right.' Beatrice sat on the edge of her bed and patted the eiderdown at her side. 'At least you *can* cry. I can't. I haven't, not really, since 1917.'

'Was that when your Alex…' Victoria sat and put a hand to her mouth.

'Yes, at the Battle of Arras in April.' Beatrice took foil from the chocolate and passed the bar to Victoria and Nell.

'One of my uncles was killed at Vimy Ridge that month too. He was with the Canadian Corps.' Victoria took a square of chocolate.

The bed creaked as Nell sat on Beatrice's other side. 'My dad lost friends. Dad didn't go with the rest of the lads because of his bad chest. Now, one of my brothers is a policeman and the other's with the fire brigade, so they're exempt.'

'War touches everyone no matter where you are. My two brothers were killed as well and I… my mother… our lives were never the same.' Beatrice's hand shook as she set the chocolate packet aside.

'How could they be?' Victoria covered Beatrice's thin hand with hers and then, after a momentary hesitation, Nell did the same.

'Right.' Beatrice avoided their gaze but for an instant let her hand lie beneath theirs. 'A smart frock.'

'Yes.' Nell pulled her hand back. 'I doubt I have anything the Misses Grainger would approve of.'

'Then that is their problem, not yours.' Victoria swallowed. 'I have a dark-blue dress with embroidered front panels that might suit you. It's a day-dress but also suitable for dinner. I'll get it.'

She went into the adjoining bedroom and rummaged in her case. Now that she had a fixed address, she could write and ask her London landlady to send her trunk on.

After finding the dress, she glanced around the room which, except for being larger and holding two beds, mirrored Beatrice's with its marble fireplace, leaf-patterned wallpaper, ornate furniture and dark-blue drapes over frilly white net.

'What do you think?' When Victoria returned, Nell stood by Beatrice's wardrobe and turned in a slow circle. The rich gold of the ankle-skimming dress set off Nell's dark hair and gave colour to her pale face. 'I pinned it in the shoulders and can take up the hem as well.'

'You look beautiful.' Behind Nell's back, Victoria smiled at Beatrice. 'Good choice.'

'I've never worn such a frock.' Nell stroked the fabric and her eyes shone. 'What if I spill my dinner on it?'

'Then we'll launder it.' Beatrice's voice was gruff. 'That dress suits you better than it ever did me. You can keep it if you wish.'

'Truly?' Nell's mouth dropped open. 'I…' She flushed.

'Try my dress too.' Victoria held out the navy embroidered frock as a diversion. 'If it suits and you like it, you can have it. If we have to change for dinner every night, you'll need more than one dress.'

'Oh, girls. I don't know what else to say but thank you.' Her lower lip trembled and she looked more schoolgirl than teacher.

Without thinking that these were her colleagues with whom she had to maintain a respectful distance, Victoria held out her arms and first Nell and then, more gingerly, Beatrice, joined the tentative hug.

'We hug in my family and although we're not family, we…' Victoria's tears returned and she sniffed.

'All we have right now is each other.' Nell's voice shook.

'And we'll make the best of things. That's all we can do.' Beatrice was the first to step away but as she studied Victoria a small smile played at the corners of her mouth. 'Now, tell us about the dashing Mr Grainger.'

'There's nothing much to tell.' Victoria made a show of fussing with Nell's dress.

Yet, as she recounted the story of the cows in the lane, and Beatrice and Nell listened avidly, it wasn't Louis Grainger who occupied the bulk of her thoughts.

Instead, it was the warmth of this unexpected bond she was forging with Beatrice and Nell. A friendship that might offer

49

the support and caring she needed to make the best of the myriad of unfamiliar and frightening things that were part of this new wartime life.

Chapter Eight

Two weeks later, standing at the front of her village hall classroom, Victoria clapped her hands. 'All right, children. You did good work today. Class dismissed.' She gathered up books and papers to store in a cupboard, because the local amateur dramatics society met here every Friday evening. 'Move your chairs against the far wall, please. Yes, Peter, you may take your drawing home to show the vicar and Mrs Russell.'

'Miss McKaye?' Diana hovered by the wall which held the maps of Europe and the British Isles.

'Yes, dear?' Victoria resisted the urge to ruffle the child's curly hair. Teachers couldn't have favourites, but she nevertheless had a special place in her heart for Diana.

'I told Albert he had to tell you but he won't.' The girl gestured over her shoulder to the boy who loitered near the fireplace.

'Tell me what?' Victoria beckoned to Albert as well. 'What's the trouble?'

'Nothing.' Albert studied his scuffed black shoes.

'Go on.' Peter, who'd joined them, bumped Albert's elbow. 'Miss McKaye will help, you'll see.'

'I want to help you if I can.' Victoria suppressed a tired sigh. Gone were the days when the problems she needed to solve were mostly in the classroom. 'But I can't do anything unless you tell me what's wrong.' She'd met with his foster-mum and supposedly the billeting issue had been resolved, but there was something more behind Albert's naughtiness than boyish high spirits.

'It's me brother, Wilf. Me mum said we ought to stick together, but he's up at Clarke's farm. Now the juniors are sharing big school round other side of village, I never see him.' Albert stuck his hands in the pockets of his frayed trousers and looked at his shoes again.

'I didn't know you had a brother.' Victoria would forgo correcting Albert's grammar for now. The school's London neighbourhood was mostly better off, like Diana's family, but thanks to a recent reorganisation, there was also a pocket of poorer households, and Albert came from one of the latter.

'He does and Wilf hasn't been at school this week.' Diana's tone was important. 'Mr Clarke said Wilf's poorly but he's not. Mr Clarke is making him work on the farm. Margaret's big sister told her and Margaret told me.'

'That's not right.' Victoria finished tidying school supplies away as she turned over ideas in her mind. Maybe she should speak to Beatrice, but, although reluctant, Albert had come to her first. She needed him to trust her. 'It's a lovely afternoon and there's no school tomorrow. Why don't I walk up with you to the Clarke's farm? You can see Wilf and I'll speak to Mr Clarke.' As she'd soon learned, the two Mr Clarkes had adjacent farms a quarter mile or so outside the village. 'Which Mr Clarke is it?'

'The one without the beard who has lots of big boys.' Albert's voice was a mumble. 'Wilf don't like his billet neither.'

'Are things no better with your foster family?' Victoria mentally berated herself. She should have visited Albert's billet again, but there were only so many hours in each day.

'The lady makes him eat outside in the garden instead of with the family,' Peter said. 'What will happen when it gets cold?'

'I'll sort it out, don't you worry.' Victoria patted Albert's shoulder. 'Come with me.'

'May we come too?' Diana tugged Peter along with her.

'I suppose so. We can leave a message at the vicarage on our way. I'll also send a message to the manor.' As she waved to one of the older pupils who passed the manor on his way home,

Victoria's thoughts whirled. The vicar's two youngest sons had returned to their boarding school and their elder brothers had joined the air force. Would there be a spare bedroom at the vicarage for Albert and Wilf to share? Mrs Russell was a kindly woman, and with boys of her own she'd be able to handle two lads. 'Come along then.' She put on her hat and gloves and picked up her handbag before sending the last of the other children on their way and locking the hall door behind them. 'Shall we play a game on our walk? What about counting how many animals we see?'

Half an hour and fifteen animals of various kinds later, Victoria picked her way along a rutted track and into a farmyard where a flock of chickens greeted her with a cacophony of squawks.

'It's all right, children.' Diana and Peter darted behind her, but Albert marched towards the chickens with his arms outstretched.

'Don't mind my hens.' A woman in a floral-print housedress covered with a voluminous white apron, came out of the red-brick and flint farmhouse. 'What have my boys done now?' She tucked loose strands of brown hair mixed with grey back into a net.

'Nothing as far as I know.' The Clarke brothers attended the village school and were taught by the local schoolmistress who kept to herself. Victoria held out her hand and introduced herself. 'I'm here about your evacuee, Wilf Glover. His brother, Albert, misses him. I also understand Wilf hasn't been at school this week.'

After returning Victoria's greeting, Mrs Clarke rubbed her reddened hands on her apron. 'I told my Walter he shouldn't have kept Wilf home. The boy's no good for farm work but it's not his fault neither. Come in, I'll put the kettle on and call Wilf. He's been missing his brother too.'

'Alma? What's with the racket – oh, Miss McKaye.' Walter Clarke came around the side of a well-kept outbuilding fronted in flint like the house and touched his cap.

'The teacher's here to see Wilf. I knew it were a bad idea keeping him home.' Mrs Clarke glanced in Victoria's direction.

'The boy's up in the loft reading.' Walter bellowed for him. 'You can take Wilf with you for all I care. I need a worker, not a lad who always has his nose stuck in a book.'

'That's our Wilf,' Albert murmured. After chasing the hens, he'd returned to Victoria's side. 'If he didn't look so much like our dad, me mum said Wilf could be one of those babies switched at birth like. There he is.' Albert let out an excited cry and dashed towards his brother who slunk out of the barn with his shoulders hunched and feet dragging.

'I'll contact the billeting officer, Mrs Meldrum, and make other arrangements.' Victoria made her voice polite. 'For tonight, though, I have a place in mind.' No child should look like Wilf did. While he might not have been beaten physically, from even the little she'd seen his spirit was well on the way to being broken.

'I think that would be for the best.' Mrs Clarke's expression was both troubled and relieved. 'Wilf don't fit in. Our boys are a bit rough, see? I… I thought of writing a letter to Mrs Meldrum myself but I didn't know…' She bobbed her head in Walter's direction.

'It's fine. Wilf?' Victoria raised her voice. 'Come here with Albert. I'm taking you with me.'

While Alma Clarke meant well, Walter was a different matter. She wouldn't want to leave a dog with him let alone a child, far from home and whose world had been turned upside down.

'You mean it, Miss?' Albert's eyes shone and he gave her a broad grin. 'Truly? This here's Miss McKaye, Wilf. I told you she's a good 'un.'

'Of course I mean it. Bring what you need with you for tonight and we'll come back for the rest of your things in the morning.' Victoria gave Wilf, a gangly tow-headed boy who looked older than ten, a reassuring smile.

'I don't have much. I can get everything now. Our Albert will help.' A flicker of what might have been hope flashed in Wilf's pale-blue eyes before the two boys disappeared into the house.

'Come make friends with my lovelies. The hens won't hurt you none.' Mrs Clarke gestured to Diana and Peter, and Victoria nodded. No matter how strange it might seem to them at first, she wanted the children to feel at home in the countryside.

As Victoria followed Mrs Clarke, Walter held out a hand to stop her. 'Settling in all right at the manor, then?'

'The Misses Grainger have been most welcoming.' Victoria kept her voice neutral. She'd never been a gossip and, in wartime especially, she wasn't about to engage in idle chatter.

'See much of their great-nephew? Them two old ladies raised him after his mum and dad died. An orphan, he was, losing his dad in the Great War and then his mum in the 'flu epidemic.' Walter pulled out a pocket knife and whittled a stick.

'I've met Mr Grainger, yes, but only briefly before he returned to London.' Victoria took several steps towards the children and hens.

'Posh bloke. Navy fellow, isn't he? One of them puffed-up officers with more gold braid than brains.'

'I wouldn't know.' Mr Grainger hadn't seemed arrogant, but since he'd been unexpectedly called back to London before dinner that first night, Victoria hadn't seen him since. Neither he nor the Misses Grainger had mentioned what he did in London, although since it sounded like an office job she'd assumed it was for some government department. And she'd made herself push away lingering disappointment that she hadn't had the chance to talk to him more.

'Well, don't be a stranger.' As Wilf and Albert returned to the farmyard, Walter straightened and gave her an almost too-familiar smile. 'Especially now your lot are at war too. Canada and the rest of us standing together against Germany.'

'Yes.' Victoria's stomach lurched. Her father was too old to go to war this time, but her sisters' husbands and her male cousins weren't. Schoolfriends and neighbours and other more distant family near and far. The war had hardly started but already its icy tentacles extended around the world, catching all of them in an iron-clad grip.

'You and your war talk, Walter.' Mrs Clarke re-joined them with all four children. 'We hear too much of it on the wireless and in the village. I can't even escape it at church. I don't want to hear about the Germans in my own farmyard.' She shook her head and rolled her eyes. 'Don't you agree, Miss McKaye?'

Victoria muttered something non-committal before she and the children said their goodbyes and went back down the lane.

Why would Mr Clarke be interested in Louis Grainger?

The sun had begun to slip low in the sky and streaks of red and gold patterned the fluffy clouds that drifted above the village. Somewhere, cattle lowed and, in the distance, the church spire reached up into the sky, solid, eternal and hopeful.

All the changes and upset of the past few weeks had made her unusually edgy. Mr Clarke hadn't meant anything by his questions. In such a small village, it was likely everyone took an interest in the family who lived at the manor.

Victoria already had enough to worry about. As her mother would have said, she had no need to borrow trouble.

Chapter Nine

'You two stay here. I'll only be a minute.' After leaving Peter and Diana at the vicarage, Victoria had gone to Albert's billet and then returned to Hazelbury Manor with both boys. She guided Wilf and Albert around the main part of the house to a wooden bench outside the scullery door. 'No running off – and be on your best behaviour, remember?'

'Yes, Miss.' Wilf nodded and nudged Albert in the ribs as the two of them set their paper carrier bags and haversacks on the grass before sitting side by side on the bench, their faces pale in the growing dusk.

'What on earth? I got your message but…' Nell came out of the scullery. She had a kerchief tied around her hair and wore a blue cardigan and white bib apron over her dress. 'I heard voices so I came out to see if those village boys were helping themselves to apples again. Miss Grainger already had me clear them off earlier.'

'I didn't see any boys from the village but…' Victoria drew in a shaky breath. 'I didn't know what else to do. The vicar and Mrs Russell are in Norwich overnight, and Albert and Wilf need a safe place to stay. Albert's billet won't take Wilf and the boys need to be together. I'll telephone Mrs Meldrum in the morning.' She rubbed a hand across her face.

'Miss Wentworth left for the amateur dramatics society meeting a quarter of an hour ago, and Miss Adelaide took flowers to the church to arrange for tomorrow's wedding. Miss Grainger's lying down with a headache and asked not to be disturbed.' Nell studied the boys. 'I'm doing the washing-up.

We ate early but there's plenty of food for you as well as these two, but where can we put them to sleep?'

'We won't take up much space, Miss Potter,' Wilf said.

'I thought you were poorly.' Nell came closer and her brow furrowed.

'It's not… I'll tell you later.' Victoria shook her head at Nell. 'There's our sitting room. We could make up beds for Albert and Wilf there. It would likely only be for tonight. I'll speak to Miss Adelaide when she returns and—' At an engine and crunch of tyres on gravel she turned around to peer into the growing darkness.

'That must be Mr Grainger,' Nell said. 'Miss Adelaide said they'd had a letter. He was to come up from London to Sheringham on the train and then borrow a friend's car to get here. She'll be sorry she's not back to welcome him.'

A car door slammed shut, and Victoria's insides quivered. Although Miss Adelaide would likely not mind having Wilf and Albert sleep in the sitting room, would Mr Grainger be as understanding?

'Let's take the boys into the kitchen and feed them and then I'll go upstairs and—'

'Hullo. What's all this about then? Has Mrs Meldrum given us two new evacuees?'

As Mr Grainger came around the side of the house, Victoria started and Nell made an instinctive bob. While it wasn't exactly a curtsy, more a jerk of her head and upper body, Victoria recognised the intent.

'No, Sir. Well, they are evacuees but Miss McKaye… we both want to help the boys.' Nell's voice came out in a high-pitched squeak.

'It's all my doing.' Victoria stood in front of the boys and Nell. 'Wilf was at Mr Clarke's farm, Walter Clarke, and Albert's billeted here in the village but they want to be together and… well… there were problems with both foster families so I had to bring them here. Only for tonight. I'm sorry. Miss Grainger is resting, but I'll speak with Miss Adelaide as soon as she's back from doing flowers at the church.'

'It's all right.' At Louis's half-smile, Victoria's tummy fluttered in a different, more pleasurable way. 'I'll fix things with my great-aunts. What do you say, boys? Do you want to bunk in with me in my room?'

'Oh, that's not necessary.' Victoria rushed to explain. 'I thought I could put them in the small room that's now our sitting room across the—'

'There's more space in mine. Two beds as well. That will suit you better, won't it, lads?' He gestured to Albert and Wilf who nodded with matching scared expressions.

'That's very kind of you.' Victoria followed Louis and the boys into the scullery as Nell scurried ahead.

'Will you eat in the dining room, Sir? I won't be a moment.' Nell stood in the kitchen doorway. 'I'll feed the boys in here.'

'I don't want to cause extra work. Besides, you're not a maid.' Louis gave Nell a warm smile. 'We'll all eat here.'

'In the kitchen?' Nell's eyes widened.

'Of course. I've eaten in this kitchen many a time. Cook had a soft spot for me.' Louis's smile slipped. 'Now let's see what we can rustle up from the pantry. Miss Potter, you lead the way while these lads lay the table.'

'After you wash your hands,' Victoria told the boys. 'Leave your bags in the scullery.'

A quarter of an hour later, the four of them sat around the long wooden kitchen table in front of plates piled high with what Nell called 'a simple cold supper'. Since Louis had put the blackout up, the lamplight shone on the circle of faces and Albert and Wilf ate as if they hadn't had a hearty meal in days.

'If you don't need anything else, I'll leave you and get on with my mending.' Nell hovered behind Victoria's chair.

'Surely the mending can wait? Do sit down and join us.' Louis waved to the empty chair next to Victoria.

As Victoria nodded, Nell took off her kerchief and sat.

'Now, tell me all the news. Any more cows in lanes?' At the end of the table beside Wilf, Louis's eyes danced with merriment as he picked up his teacup.

'No.' Victoria gave him a tentative smile in return.

'But we did meet hens at the Clarkes' farm,' Albert said. 'I scared them away.' His initial shyness forgotten, Albert proceeded to tell Louis all about their visit to the farm, his billet and how Victoria had helped him write a letter to his mum and dad several days before.

'Tell me more about Walter Clarke's farm.' Louis set his cutlery on his cleared plate and nodded when Nell offered him more tea and brought the remains of a blackberry tart from the pantry. 'What do you have to say for yourself, Wilf? You've been very quiet.'

'Our Wilf's always quiet,' Albert said. 'Never a word out of him, Mum says.'

'I didn't like being at the farm.' Wilf took a plate with a generous slice of tart from Nell. 'I never milked cows before or worked in fields.' His face went red. 'I shared a room with four of the boys and except for Jimmy they made fun of me. Said I was soft. Hid my pyjamas and put my boots in the cow byre and such like.'

'I'll find you a more suitable billet as soon as I can.' Victoria's heart hurt at the thought of what Wilf had gone through. 'Not everyone is cut out for farm chores and you shouldn't have been kept away from school to do them.'

'I'll work with you tomorrow and help you catch up on the lessons you missed.' Nell finished serving the tart and sat again. 'You're a clever boy and you'd have a good chance at a grammar school place.'

'Thanks, Miss, but my mum and dad wouldn't hear of more schooling.' Wilf's gaze dropped to his plate.

'You have a while yet. No need to decide right now.' Victoria made her tone encouraging. 'For a start, who knows what will happen with this war, but it will surely bring changes.'

Louis finished his slice of tart. 'It already has, even if we don't recognise all of them yet. Did Mr Clarke hire any other farm workers when you were with him?'

'No, not ones I saw, anyhow. Only his boys, he's got seven, and him and me.' Wilf screwed up his face as if thinking. 'Why?'

'I heard he was having building work done on his barn. Perhaps he changed his mind.' Louis pushed back his chair. 'What do you say to a game of snakes and ladders before bed? I haven't played it since I was a boy but my great-aunts never get rid of anything. Come and help me look for it? Aunt Addie used to be very good at board games. She'll be home soon so let's ask her to join us, shall we?'

As the boys darted after Louis, Victoria helped Nell clear up and take the crockery into the scullery to wash up.

First Walter Clarke had been interested in Louis, and now Louis was interested in Mr Clarke. Perhaps it *was* entirely innocent but even if it wasn't, all Victoria had to go on was a small but persistent prickle of unease. However, in wartime, they all had to do their bit. From now on, Victoria would keep her eyes and ears open and her mouth shut. In whatever way she could, she'd defend Britain with all her might.

Chapter Ten

A dog barked, water splashed and Victoria rolled over in bed, pulling the feather pillow, bolster and eiderdown with her. Surely on a Saturday morning she could have a bit of a lie-in?

'Victoria? It's a gorgeous day. Beatrice is practising on the piano in the drawing room, and I've already been out collecting eggs from next door's farm for our breakfast.' Nell's voice came from a corner of their shared bedroom and then more water splashed in the bowl on the washstand.

Victoria groaned and sat up. 'You're becoming a real country girl, aren't you?'

'I am. I like it here, don't you?' After brushing her hair, Nell returned to make her bed. 'If we had electric light and indoor plumbing it would be nigh on perfect but I'm getting used to making do. Marjorie said she'll show me how to light fires when the weather gets colder. The fireplaces here are bigger than at home.'

'She'll be glad of your help.' Once the Grainger family's scullery maid, the youthful Marjorie now did the work of several maids, a cook and a butler, trotting up and down stairs and along corridors wearing a uniform that must have once been smart but was now a shabby, worn relic of a bygone age. 'I can pitch in too. Our summer cabin has a fireplace.'

'You must miss it.' Nell's voice softened in sympathy.

'I do.' Victoria stifled a yawn and went to take down the blackout. She also missed having her own bedroom, something she'd always taken for granted but which now seemed a luxury. 'It's on a lake so in the summer, I used to almost live in my swimming costume. I'd go boating and catch fish and then cook my catch over a campfire.' Her mouth watered at the memory. 'We haven't had a day off since we got here. After you help Wilf with his lessons, and I telephone Mrs Meldrum, why don't we pack a picnic and go for a walk in the woods? We could bring the boys and Beatrice with us.' If only for a few hours, being away from the village, Hazelbury Manor and school life would do them all good.

'A picnic?' Nell bit her bottom lip, and her cheerful expression dimmed. 'I'd thought to write letters to parents of several evacuees and I still have my mending and…' She stopped. 'I suppose all those things can wait.'

'Good. When I go to the telephone box, I'll pop to the village shop and—'

Someone pounded on their bedroom door and then Albert's voice came from the other side. 'Miss McKaye, Miss Potter? You'll never guess. Mr Grainger has enough petrol and he said he'll take us in the car to the seaside. All of us and Miss Wentworth. We can watch the men putting up barbed wire and maybe even laying mines at the beach.'

Victoria scrambled back into bed and pulled the eiderdown to her chin as Mr Grainger's deeper voice said something to Albert.

'The seaside?' Nell, who was already dressed, opened the bedroom door a crack to keep Victoria hidden. 'Miss McKaye and I were talking about a picnic in the woods but seeing the sea, even though we can't get close to it, would be grand.' After some more murmured conversation, Nell turned back to Victoria. 'I'll leave you to get dressed. Mr Grainger says we'll set out at half twelve.'

'All right.' As the door closed behind Nell and the excited voices faded, Victoria returned to the bedroom window to look out across the manor's gardens, fields and woods beyond. Above, a cloudless sky of soft blue stretched into the distance towards the invisible sea.

The scene was peaceful, pastoral even, and for a moment it was almost possible for Victoria to forget the war, the battles ongoing in Poland, and Hitler's warning that Germany would never surrender. And closer to home, the barbed war, mines and concrete barriers being laid on Norfolk's beaches and in towns and villages bordering the North Sea.

Victoria shuddered, turned away from the window and opened the ornate, old-fashioned wardrobe she and Nell shared to find a summer dress and cardigan suitable for a day out. But not any day out: one with Louis Grainger. She hardly knew him and they'd never spent any time alone together but she liked him.

Her heart raced and this time her shiver was one of excitement. As she closed the wardrobe door, she caught sight of her flushed face and sparkling eyes in its glassed front.

Nobody here knew she'd been jilted almost at the altar. It was more than time to put all that business behind her and experience life like any other woman who wasn't yet thirty.

After getting dressed and making her bed, she dug in her vanity case for her favourite pink lipstick and applied it carefully. It was only breakfast and then going into the village but she wanted to look her best. For herself. A man like Louis Grainger wouldn't be interested in someone like her and even if he was, she couldn't reciprocate any feelings beyond friendship.

Still, she felt more alive than she had in months and as she almost skipped down the stairs to the dining room for breakfast, it was Louis she hoped to see sitting across the table from her. And when he appeared in the front hall, rosy-cheeked and windblown from a walk with Lady, his gaze connected with Victoria's and held.

It was also him she imagined dancing with to the piano music spilling from the drawing room where Beatrice practised 'My Reverie', a 1938 hit by Bea Wain and Larry Clinton and His Orchestra.

As she reached the bottom of the stairs, she felt her face get warm. It might not be so easy to stick to friendship with Louis, and now she wasn't certain she wanted to.

–

'My mother's parents lived in Norwich but had a summer home in Cromer.' Several hours later and having left Beatrice and Nell to look round the shops, Louis and Victoria stood side by side on the promenade behind the sea wall bordering the empty beach below. 'One of my earliest memories is visiting Cromer with my parents and walking on the pier. I insisted on carrying my bucket and spade rather than leaving it with my nanny.'

Victoria breathed in the crisp air and took in the vast panorama of sea and sky with the town perched on the cliffs above. White gulls soared overhead, and Albert and Wilf chased them, running along the promenade and waving their arms as they mimicked the birds' piercing cries.

'I suppose places like Cromer here on the coast might be on the frontlines of war. If things develop, I mean.' So far, almost a month in, not much had happened but that didn't mean it wouldn't. On the home front, the list of government restrictions seemed to grow daily as did fears of a German air attack.

Louis pointed to a stack of barbed wire and scaffolding. 'Up and down this coast, they're getting ready. If Britain were to be invaded, along with the south coast this eastern one is vulnerable. That's why beaches have been closed and defences are being built.'

'Do you think a German invasion is likely?' Victoria twisted her hands together. 'Park Road and other London schools were evacuated to East Anglia because it was supposed to be safer.'

Louis shrugged and turned to look at her. 'Hazelbury is safer than London, at least from aerial bombing, and it's not right on the coast either but…' He hesitated. His blue eyes had flecks of green and were surrounded by thick eyelashes. Beneath his hat, his cropped brown hair glinted gold in the sunshine. 'We need to be prepared, that's all.'

That's what everyone said, from the prime minister and his government down to village shopkeepers, but somehow Louis's quiet comment sent more of a cold chill of fear along Victoria's spine.

'What kind of work do you do in London? I don't think you ever said.' Was it too forward of her to ask? Over their picnic lunch, the four adults had talked of general things, and the boys were a distraction. Here looking out at the sea, and although Wilf and Albert played nearby, was the first time Victoria and Louis had been alone. 'I'm sorry, Mr Grainger. I shouldn't have—'

'It's fine and please, call me Louis.' His expression softened and the tight lines around his nose and mouth eased.

'I'm Victoria.' Her breath stuttered. Using first names brought new intimacy to whatever was between them.

'I'm a lieutenant commander with the Royal Navy, currently based in London, Whitehall. I could have had a naval commission when I finished school but to make my great-aunts happy I went to Cambridge and read history instead. Later, after a few years in Portsmouth, I was posted to Hong Kong, rose up the ranks and returned to England earlier this year.' He gave her a half-smile. 'It's a desk job. Nothing glamorous, I'm afraid.'

Victoria's mouth went dry. She'd never seen him in uniform but even in ordinary civilian clothes Louis had an undeniable air of glamour. As well as what many women would call 'film star looks', his good manners, polish and general amiability also made for what her young American cousins would label a 'dreamboat'. She bit back a smile at the memory of the girls oohing and aahing over 'movie magazines' on their family's last visit to Canada before Victoria had sailed for England.

'Teaching isn't glamorous, either.' She glanced at Wilf and Albert who, having abandoned chasing gulls, were now playing with two other boys and tossing a rubber ball between them.

'You're still doing your bit and it can't be easy.' He hesitated. 'You don't seem to get much time off.'

'No but that's because these children's entire lives have been turned upside down. I'm not only their teacher but in many ways I'm also a substitute parent.' A role for which Victoria felt woefully unprepared. 'I expect it will get easier in time. Besides, if it's safe to do so and there isn't any bombing we might even return to London soon.'

'Perhaps.' Louis let out a long breath and glanced at his wristwatch. A cloud slid across the sun and the sea turned choppy, its earlier serene blue now steel grey. 'Right. We need to meet Miss Wentworth and Miss Potter at that tea shop and make our way home. Boys?' He called to Wilf and Albert. 'Finish your game, please.'

As Albert ran up to Victoria, excited to tell her about the other boys and their ball, she tried to pay attention to his chatter but part of her still focused on what Louis had said. He hadn't exactly dismissed her but she couldn't shake the feeling there was something he wasn't telling her. Not only about his job but himself. However, why should he share something personal? They were acquaintances, not even friends, thrown together by chance and likely only for a few months.

As Albert and Wilf ran ahead of Louis and Victoria up the hill to Cromer proper, Louis touched Victoria's sleeve. 'In the parlance of her Victorian girlhood, Aunt Addie says you and the other teachers are 'bricks' to take on what you have. Even Aunt Hetty agreed, although that was only after breakfasting with Albert earlier.' His mouth quirked into a teasing smile.

Returning his smile, Victoria's heart pounded. 'Albert's high-spirited, but with proper guidance he'll make a good man.' She averted her gaze, fearing Louis might guess her thoughts. He was a good man too and she couldn't deny she was attracted to him in a way both unsettling and new.

'Between you at school and now the vicar and his wife ready to give Albert that guidance at home, he has a chance to make something of himself. It's decent of Mr and Mrs Russell to take the boys in. Wilf's an interesting character too. Did you hear him asking me all those questions about navigation at breakfast?'

Victoria nodded but she'd paid more attention to Louis and how he'd answered Wilf's questions with interest and respect than she had to the boy.

'If we win this war, and we must, because the alternative hardly bears thinking about, there will likely be more opportunities for young people like him, girls as well as boys. While my aunts wouldn't agree, I say it's more than time.' Louis's mouth was set in a determined line. 'Those children are the future and it will be up to the rest of us to adapt. I didn't want war but since we're in it, those children are also why we must hold off the Nazis. So that our young people and the rest of us have that future. One that's free and just and stands for everything good and right, no matter the personal cost.'

Victoria's heart seemed to expand in her chest. She felt pride, yes, but it was more than that. For perhaps the first time, she truly considered herself part of something bigger and more important than she could ever have imagined. Something that would not only change the world she'd grown up in but change her future too.

Chapter Eleven

'Two more of my infants are returning to London at the weekend.' As the weeks slipped by, the trees around Hazelbury were draped in the bright yellows, golds and reds of autumn, and flocks of migrating birds travelled high overhead. On a rainy mid-November morning, Victoria walked with Beatrice and Nell along the leaf-scattered lane that led from the manor to Hazelbury's high street. 'Edith Perkins and Thomas Lockery are being collected by Edith's father on Sunday.'

'I suppose it's understandable.' At Victoria's right and wearing the tan, feathered hat that Nell had made good as new, Beatrice set a rapid pace. 'The expected German aerial attacks haven't materialised and with Park Road and so many other schools reopening, parents want their children with them.'

'Will we...' Nell's breath caught. 'Will we go back to London soon, do you think?'

'That will be up to Miss Hopson and whatever other authorities are in charge of making such decisions,' Beatrice said. 'For the moment there are still enough evacuees here for us to teach, and with Miss Hopson and some of the staff who were in the West Country back in London, I expect we'll stay where we are at least until the new year.'

When they reached the corner by the post office where their paths diverged, Beatrice and Nell continued on to the overcrowded school where the junior classes met and Victoria went to the village hall. As she rounded the corner, she gripped her umbrella as a gust of wind threatened to send it and her into the path of the milkman's cart.

She'd settled into a routine, and while at first she'd have welcomed returning to London, both she and her life were different now. Several weekends a month and occasionally in between, Louis arrived in Hazelbury to visit his great-aunts. How did he get so much leave? Being in the navy, why was he based in London instead of nearer the sea? No matter how often Victoria pondered these questions, she never came any closer to answers.

'Miss McKaye.' Diana skidded to a halt outside the hall. Her face above a too-large mackintosh was rosy from running while Wilf followed behind her with an umbrella. 'You'll never guess what's happened.'

'I'm sure I wouldn't. No Peter or Albert this morning?' She glanced around the rain-soaked street lined with tidy, white-washed houses along with a butcher's shop, a greengrocer's, and a chemist's. Only a few months before, Hazelbury had seemed strange and foreign but now this otherwise unremarkable village had become home.

'No.' Diana's voice was important. 'They're what's happened. Albert woke up in the middle of the night, saw Peter's bed was empty and went looking for him. All by himself.' Diana's eyes went wide. 'But Peter was sleepwalking, and if Albert hadn't found him at the edge of the pond and brought him back to the vicarage, Peter could have fallen in and drowned. The doctor came and said Peter and Albert have to stay in bed today.'

'Oh my goodness.' Victoria glanced towards Wilf who in his usual quiet way had already continued on towards his own schoolroom.

'But that's not all.' Diana walked alongside Victoria and they took off their wet outdoor clothes in the hall's entryway. 'Daddy's office is going to be sent to work in Wales so Mummy is closing up our house and Ivy is coming here to help Mrs Russell. Alice, Mrs Russell's maid, had to go home because her mum fell off a ladder and broke her leg.'

As Diana paused for breath, Victoria tried to make sense of everything the girl had said. 'I'll call on Mrs Russell and

Peter and Albert after school.' She'd thought Peter was finally more settled, but sleepwalking suggested otherwise. Should she write to his parents and find out if it would be possible for him to either return to London to live with his father or join his mother who, as an expectant mother, had been evacuated to Yorkshire? There were different kinds of safety and if Peter was so desperately unhappy, Victoria had to do something. 'I'm sorry to hear about Alice's mother but how exciting for you seeing Ivy again.'

'It is. It's not the same as being with Mummy and Daddy and my brothers but Ivy is next best.'

As Diana darted into the main part of the hall, Victoria hung back to greet the last of her pupils and help the smallest ones with their coats and umbrellas.

'No, you can't go back for your reading book, Sheila. You may share with Diana today. Don't forget to bring in your gas mask, Ralph.' She ushered the children into the cold hall and rubbed her hands together. 'While I start a fire, take out your slates. Those in the first class, use your coloured chalk to practise the letters we learned yesterday. Diana, please hand out the exercise and sums books. The rest of you can check your work for mistakes.'

'Yes, Miss.' Voices rose in a chorus from around the two long tables several of the evacuees' foster-dads had built from scrap wood. Since the Sunday school needed the chairs that had been on loan, the children now used mismatched kitchen and parlour chairs collected from various village homes. The latter included a grand, green-velveteen set of four from the drawing room at Hazelbury Manor, and Victoria lived in constant fear of them being damaged.

She found kindling and then, when it caught, added a log from the wood box, all the time keeping one eye on the open fire and the other on the children. 'No, Ralph. Don't pull Margaret's plaits.'

'Sorry, Miss.'

'You also need to apologise to Margaret.' Victoria glanced around the hall. Beatrice, who was a talented artist, had drawn and painted a frieze of squirrels on the end of a roll of brown paper. Along with several framed prints of sailing ships Louis had given them, it brightened the pale-green walls.

'Miss?' Ralph raised his hand. 'There's rain coming through the roof. Hit me right on the head it did.'

Several other boys tittered and one of the girls started to cry.

When Victoria reached the middle of the room where Ralph sat, she saw the puddle forming on the floor herself. She gestured to Ralph and several other boys. 'Move the table and chairs out of the way of the leak and then fetch buckets from the cloakroom. The rest of you stand behind your chairs. Don't cry, Jean. It's only rain.'

She found a handkerchief for Jean and, after asking Diana and Margaret to take charge of her, tried to think. She couldn't dismiss the children when they'd only just arrived, but ordinary lessons were also out of the question.

The fire sputtered and hissed, its weak flame battling with damp wood, and the rain fell harder now and hammered against the windows. Except for the boys who clattered buckets in the entryway, the children stared at her with matching sad faces. Victoria had to do something – but what?

'Why don't we play a game? A counting one.' She improvised. 'With singing and marching.' That would cover arithmetic, music and physical exercise all in one. It was unusual, but thanks to the war, which so far wasn't anything like the kind of war any of them expected, these weren't usual times. She'd leave the daily air raid safety practice, where they all donned their gas masks and sheltered beneath the tables, for later. Right now, they were too gloomy and it was up to her to bring a note of cheer. 'Follow me and let's sing "This Old Man" and count from one to twenty.'

As she led the children in a snake-like line, the stamping of twenty-two pairs of feet echoed against the wooden floorboards and voices rose in the familiar rhyme.

'Swing your arms like me, see?' Diana instructed the younger children as they completed one circuit of the hall.

Soon, laughter rang out and when Jean asked if they could sing the folk song they'd been practising, Victoria was quick to agree. It often took so little for children to forget their troubles, and she could learn from her pupils in that way and many others.

As they rounded the corner near the main hall door again, it opened and Louis appeared, shaking raindrops from his naval greatcoat.

Victoria stopped and grabbed the door which caused several children marching behind to bump into her. Her face warmed and she put her free hand to her cheek. 'Children.' She raised her voice to get their attention. 'Go back to your seats, please. Mr Grainger is here.'

'He's not a mister, he's an officer. Look at him buttons and gold on them shoulder boards.' In the sudden silence, Ralph's voice rang out.

'I'm sorry, I…' Victoria closed the door against the gusty wind and tried to regain her composure. 'It's *his* buttons and the gold on *his* or *those* shoulder boards, Ralph.' Grammatically correct or not, both were impressive and her face burned hotter.

'It's no matter.' Louis grinned. 'Mister Grainger is fine. I was passing and since it sounded like a herd of elephants had taken over the village hall, I thought I'd investigate.'

'It's cold and the roof's leaking so Miss McKaye were helping us get warmed up.'

'Ralph, please raise your hand when you wish to speak. All right, what is it?'

'I were only trying to help tell the man what we was doing. Your face is all red. Maybe you're sickening for something like Albert and Peter.' Ralph and the rest of the children stared at Victoria and then Louis.

'Miss McKaye had a good idea.' Louis sounded as if he was holding back laughter. 'If you're "warmed up" now, I have some chocolate you might like to share at your break, but only if you can sit quietly and listen to Miss McKaye.' He made a show of digging in his coat pockets as the children settled. 'I'll take a look at the ceiling,' he said to Victoria. 'May need to get Bob from the pub in. He's handy and can fix almost anything.'

'Thank you.' Victoria hugged herself and took a step back. No wonder so many women were attracted to men in uniform. 'Even though we don't have a proper classroom here, the children usually work well but today… they're still very young and far from their families. Sometimes I have to make allowances.'

'I said as much to Mrs Meldrum.' Louis shook his head and glanced at the pupils now sitting back at their tables.

'Mrs Meldrum?' The billeting officer was involved in everything of any consequence in Hazelbury and while, unlike Nell, Victoria didn't fear her, the woman still perpetually made her feel wrong-footed.

'When I came out of the post office, she was telling all and sundry passing about the noise from the hall.' Louis spoke softly so the children wouldn't hear. 'I jolly well told her to mind her own business.' His eyes twinkled, and Victoria's breath caught in her throat. 'Don't mind her. Beneath the bluster Mrs Meldrum's kind-hearted and she also has four sons in the Forces.'

As Victoria made her way to the front of the hall, leaving Louis to examine the ceiling, she swallowed a lump in her throat. In Louis's case, it was more than the uniform which made him attractive. She'd been drawn to him from that first meeting in the lane and she couldn't dismiss it or what seemed like an intangible connection between them any longer. However, now she'd admitted it, what on earth was she going to do about it?

Chapter Twelve

An hour later and in the vicarage front hall, a house Victoria now knew as 'The Three Chimneys', she put on her coat and thanked Mrs Russell. 'I'll speak to Miss Wentworth and we'll write Miss Hopson to ask her advice as well. Until we hear back, I'll keep an extra close eye on Peter at school.'

'I'll do the same at home.' Mrs Russell's usually placid face wore an anxious expression. 'If only Richard and I had heard the boy. And why didn't Albert call us or wake Wilf when he saw Peter was missing?' She shook her head and smoothed the cardigan she wore over a white blouse and tweed skirt. 'If we'd lost either of those boys, I'd never have forgiven myself. I don't know how I'd ever have faced their parents, either.'

'You can't blame yourself.' Victoria had more than enough of her own guilt. Had she not watched over Peter as much as he needed her to? 'I'll have a quiet word with Albert at school tomorrow. Hopefully, the hall roof will be repaired by then so the children can return.' After Louis and then Bob from the pub had assessed the situation, the hall had been deemed unsafe, so Victoria had sent her pupils home early and walked with Diana to the vicarage. 'Between us, we'll sort something out. Perhaps Peter's mother could even come here to Hazelbury. I didn't realise Peter's father had joined the navy. With no fixed home in London or anywhere else, it's no wonder the boy's unsettled.'

Mrs Russell nodded as she showed Victoria to the door. 'The weather's cleared up nicely, hasn't it? If the boys and Diana help me, I might get my broad beans sowed. Given we may soon have food rationing, I'm planning an early vegetable crop next year.'

'We're doing the same at the manor.' Along with Beatrice and Nell, and despite none of them having gardened much before, Victoria had spent several recent evenings poring over seed catalogues and considering how best to use the gardens surrounding the manor to grow food. Since all the local able-bodied young men had been called up, Miss Grainger and Miss Adelaide had also applied for a land girl.

Leaving the vicarage, Victoria tilted her face towards the afternoon sunshine which gilded the remaining leaves and burnished the nearby woodland with warmth and splotches of red, yellow and orange. At the gate, she glanced towards the bustling village high street and then back at the woods. Following a public footpath to the manor by way of fields and woods wouldn't take much longer, and while she could fill these unexpected free hours with lesson planning or housework, time to herself to walk and think was rare.

Decision made, she turned right instead of left and, walking away from the village, made her way into a country lane, then through a stile and onto the footpath leading to the woods.

Keeping a watchful eye for stray cows, she walked along the edge of the golden harvested field, swung her arms wide and drew in a lungful of crisp country air. The clear blue sky encircled her and although it wasn't as big and endless as on the Canadian prairies, it was still larger than most English skies. And similar to the prairie, sometimes the sky seemed to move almost like a living thing. She stopped at the entrance to the woodland and stood still, filling her soul with the expanse of azure overhead.

Behind her in the woods, a twig snapped and she whirled around. Nothing and nobody greeted her except the leaf-covered path edged by its canopy of ancient trees. The noise was likely an animal. A hare or badger or even a fox or small deer. She'd borrowed a book about the Norfolk countryside from the manor's library to learn about local wildlife.

Victoria shook herself and continued on the path. She was being foolish. An animal would be as keen to avoid her as she it. A breeze tugged at her hair and on impulse she took off her felt slouch hat, folded it in her satchel along with her gloves and then undid her low roll to feel the wind in her hair and against her hands as she had as a child. Above her head, branches creaked and deeper in the woods a bird called.

She stopped and cupped an ear to listen. Were those voices? She eased behind a thick tree trunk and peered around. Men from the village or a nearby farm cutting timber for fuel perhaps? As the voices drew closer, she moved further behind the tree and into underbrush. Although she didn't know if she needed to be fearful, some instinct told her to stay hidden.

'You're certain?'

A tall, blond man with a beard whom Victoria didn't recognise came around the curve of the path, and she pressed a hand to her mouth to hold back an exclamation. Louis was walking at the stranger's side – but not Louis as she'd seen him that morning in her schoolroom. Now, instead of his naval officer's uniform he wore dark trousers and a rough jacket, and a cap like those favoured by local farmers covered his head.

Hardly daring to breathe, Victoria leaned as close as she could without being seen to try to hear their conversation.

'Yes, he'll be on the train from London tonight.' Louis's voice was clipped, familiar but not. 'You'll find everything in order.'

'Good.' The stranger glanced around with a furtive air. 'What about the others?'

'All arranged.' Louis handed the man a tan-coloured envelope of the kind sold at Hazelbury's post office and which Victoria had in her own writing case. 'You have the money, a map and telephone number. Don't ring from the village. There's a phone box a mile or so out on the road towards Cromer. Use it instead.'

'Right.' Although the other man spoke English, he didn't sound like any other British person Victoria knew and with his pale straw-blond beard and hair, he didn't look like them either. If Victoria were to guess, she'd suspect he was German or Dutch. In fact, between his hair colour, ruddy complexion and stature, he resembled one of the Verstappen boys from home, a family who'd come to Canada from Amsterdam after the last war. 'I'll be in touch, then.'

Victoria blinked. Almost as if she'd imagined him, the bearded man seemed to melt away into the trees.

Louis stood in the middle of the path for a few seconds and only then did she see his shoulders relax. He pulled a small notebook and pencil from his jacket pocket and jotted something down.

Another twig cracked, and a squirrel chattered from a branch above Victoria's head.

'Who's there?' Louis turned and called out before moving towards her hiding place.

'Only me. I decided to walk back to the manor this way and...'

She stopped at the expression on Louis's face. Not anger, but one that reminded her of a fox she'd seen long ago lurking behind a cousin's henhouse. Cunning and a trickster, according to a story in the book of wilderness tales that sat on a shelf in the cabin.

'It's a fine afternoon, unlike the rain earlier. That's living on an island for you.' He gave Victoria a tight smile followed by a hollow laugh. 'I'll be on my way. Enjoy your walk.'

'Wait.' She raised a hand to stop him as a government poster she'd seen somewhere popped into her mind. *Warning! Beware of Spies* its large red letters had proclaimed. *Don't Talk. The Enemy Has Ears Everywhere.*

Could there be spies on their doorstep? If so, was Louis somehow involved? 'I saw you with a strange man. What was that all about?'

'Nothing.' He gave her another smile but wouldn't meet her gaze. 'At least, nothing for you to concern yourself with.'

'I thought better of you.' Filled with a mix of anger and fright, Victoria faced him. 'You're an officer in His Majesty's Navy and that man—'

'Hush.' Louis grabbed her arm and clapped a hand over her mouth. 'Come with me and don't say another word.'

Victoria tried to pull away but although Louis uncovered her mouth, he kept her forearm in a firm grip.

'It's not what you may think.' He hissed the words into her ear and pulled her even closer to wrap one arm tight around her shoulders. 'For now, do exactly as I say because both our lives could depend on it.'

Chapter Thirteen

To any distant observer, Victoria supposed she and Louis must look like a farmhand and his girl who'd snuck away for an afternoon tryst. With her handbag, gas-mask box and satchel bumping against her hip, she tried to match Louis's long strides as he bundled her out of the woods, back along the footpath by the field and then onto an overgrown track that eventually brought them out behind Hazelbury Manor by a tall and bushy cedar hedge.

'Are you all right?' Louis glanced around before he opened the door of a small brick building with a thatched roof and tugged her inside.

'Yes.' Although Louis had released her, Victoria's heart still pounded and her legs trembled.

'Here.' He pulled out a wicker chair and helped her sit. 'We're safe now.' He slid over another chair and sat across from her. 'When my great-aunts were young, this place was a summerhouse. It hasn't been used in years so has fallen into disrepair. I'm sorry I can't offer you a cup of tea.'

'But you *can* offer me the truth.' Victoria set aside her gas-mask box and folded her damp hands on top of her handbag and satchel so he wouldn't see them shake. 'If you don't, I'll go straight to the local police constable.' Nevertheless, given the Grainger family's standing in the village, would Constable Smith believe her? 'Or someone else in authority like the military police.' She made herself sound braver than she felt.

'I don't doubt it.' Louis gave her a wry smile. 'It's people like you who will end up winning this war for us. You were magnificent, Victoria. You *are* magnificent.' A faint flush crept across his cheeks and he cleared his throat. 'Many women would have caused a ruckus or worse but you didn't and I'm grateful.'

Despite what had appeared to be damning circumstances, there was still a part of her that trusted Louis. Or, trusted him more than the other man. Victoria clasped her hands tighter. 'Was that meeting in the woods something to do with your work?'

'Yes.' For an endless moment, Louis stared at the cracked flagstone floor and then raised his head to pin her gaze with his. 'I can't tell you the whole truth but since you saw what you did I'll tell you what little I can. But before I do, you must give me your word that it goes no further. I'm not exaggerating when I say that national security and thousands of innocent lives could depend on us keeping mum.'

She nodded and shivered. As a teacher Victoria had to be discreet, but until now any secrets she'd needed to keep had been related to school or her family. Never anything so immense that it would impact more than a few people. 'I promise – but does anyone else here know?'

'Aunt Hetty, but that's it.' He gave a light, almost boyish chuckle. 'She quite fancies being part of clandestine operations. I had to tell her since I'm likely to be here more often than usual. However, I'm going to suggest that you don't speak to her about any of this – best if you both appear to be completely oblivious, and that might be hard if you each know the other knows, as it were.'

'Of course.' Victoria tried to mask her surprise. Grim, straightlaced Miss Henrietta Grainger, who gave the impression of having never left the previous century, was the last person she'd have suspected to be enthusiastic about any kind of secret work.

'Aunt Hetty has hidden depths.' Louis edged his chair closer until his knees almost touched Victoria's. 'Like you, I imagine.'

Her face heated. 'I don't have any idea what you mean.' Louis couldn't be flirting with her, could he? Still, she didn't move her knees away, although wearing her coat, serviceable navy skirt, ribbed-wool grey winter stockings and walking shoes, she must be a world away from the women he knew in London.

'One day I'll tell you what I imagine.' He sat back in the chair and steepled his hands on his lap. 'But right now…' He let out a breath. 'You know I'm with the Royal Navy. A lieutenant commander, hence the gold braid that so impressed Ralph.' A brief smile broke his otherwise serious expression. 'After I returned from Hong Kong, and given the way things were then going with Germany, I was assigned to a unit doing special government work. Intelligence, national security and the like. It helps that I have a gift for languages and speak several. My mother was half-French.'

Victoria nodded as if she understood but in truth she didn't, not fully. However, now that Louis had started to confide in her, she didn't want to divert him by asking questions.

'Your being in those woods this afternoon may have been a blessing in disguise. That man – well I can't tell you the details but there are several like him all along the Norfolk and Suffolk coasts. They slip in and out under cover of darkness and meet up with men like me. Slowly, I'm convincing him to trust me.'

'You're like a… spy?' Victoria stumbled over what had always seemed to her a traitorous word. 'But you're an officer in the Royal Navy.' If one were to believe the papers, there were spies in all walks of life. However, Victoria had never considered that might also include those serving in the armed forces. Yet why couldn't they be as duplicitous as anyone else? Her stomach curled into a tight knot.

'As I said, I'm in intelligence work. Despite what you saw in the woods, most of what I do is collect and analyse information that might be useful to my superiors. In the process, I help to identify and neutralise threats to this country and its allies. Do you believe me?'

'I suppose so but… I…' She stopped, unsure. Louis was convincing and he'd almost, but not quite, convinced Victoria too. She still had questions, though. Ones he likely couldn't answer. Doubts as well. She only had his word that he was working in intelligence, and thanks to Roy, her former fiancé, she'd already learned that both words and appearances could be deceiving. 'I promise I won't tell anyone what I saw this afternoon or about your work either.' Unless Louis or someone else gave her a good reason not to keep her word. Although Victoria considered herself a person of integrity, in certain circumstances concealing a secret could be more harmful than telling the truth.

'I appreciate your discretion but that's not all.' Louis hesitated. 'I know I'm asking a great deal and I'll have to clear it with my commanding officer, of course, but if he agrees I'd like you to help us.'

'Me? Help you how?' Victoria clutched the strap of her satchel. 'I'm a teacher. I don't know anything about how the government or armed forces intelligence work.'

'That's precisely why and how you can be of use. Nobody would suspect you because you're ordinary.'

She flinched as if he'd struck her. 'Ordinary.' That was how Roy had described her when he'd broken their engagement. He had wanted someone more exciting, more glamorous and prettier who stood out in a crowd. Someone like Letitia who had beauty and grace, and who would be the perfect wife for a man who not only had his sights set on rising to the top of the legal profession, but also had political ambitions far beyond their small-town world.

'What? Being "ordinary" is a good thing. I didn't mean to offend you.' Louis took off his cap and raked a hand through his hair.

Victoria put her own hand to her head, all of a sudden remembering that she'd taken off her hat in the woods and hadn't put it back on again. Her windblown hair tumbled around her shoulders and she couldn't tidy it because in their dash across fields and footpaths, she'd lost the hair grips tucked into her palm. 'It's fine. I…' She swallowed a sob.

'You're lovely, Victoria, exactly as you are and don't let anyone make you think otherwise.' He dug in his pocket and passed her a clean handkerchief.

'Thank you.' She sniffed and patted her eyes. 'If I were to help you, what would I do?' She had to deflect this conversation. It was bad enough that she'd broken down in front of Louis, but if he ever learned the truth she'd never be able to face him again. She had let everyone, including her parents, believe ending her engagement had been her decision as much as Roy's. It had been the only way to hold on to some semblance of dignity and pride. Victoria wasn't about to share that secret now, especially with Louis whom she hardly knew.

'You'd observe what's going on in Hazelbury and the surrounding area and report back to me. If you think of it, working as a teacher makes the perfect cover. You have both a respected position in the community and reason to be involved in village life. You also have a reason to be part of the lives of those fostering your evacuated pupils.'

'I do, but I'm not involved in much here yet because I haven't had time. I go to church, and Mrs Russell invited me to join the choir, but I'm only attending my first W.I. meeting next month.' To get to know the women serving as her pupils' foster-mothers rather than at Mrs Meldrum's pointed insistence. 'If we're still here then, Beatrice, Nell and I have also talked about putting on a small play in the summer term to bring the Londoners and villagers together. Beatrice is keen on amateur dramatics, and Nell's a wonderful seamstress.'

'That's exactly what we need.' Louis's eyes shone. 'You'd simply go about your everyday life but keeping your eyes and ears open for anything that seemed the least bit unusual or out of order. Even a hunch that something wasn't quite right. I'd want to hear everything as you saw it.'

'A hunch?' She paused and then leaned towards Louis. 'You remember you once asked me about Walter Clarke? The one at Upper Yarrow Farm. His brother Frank is at Lower Yarrow.'

Louis nodded and leaned even closer to Victoria until their foreheads almost touched.

'Well, the day I went up there to get Wilf, Walter Clarke asked me about you and it struck me as odd, is all. I can't put my finger on why, but since then I've seen him in the village a few times and there's something about him I don't trust.' Victoria exhaled. 'It likely sounds ridiculous but—'

'No, it doesn't.' Louis grinned and then sobered. 'I can't tell you more but when it comes to Walter you're not wrong. Keep him in your sights but don't let him suspect you have more than a passing interest in what he might be up to. Make a mental note of what might be any unusual comings and goings at his farm or in the village. Nothing is too small or insignificant.'

The village was easy but how was she supposed to monitor Upper Yarrow Farm? With Wilf no longer living there, it wasn't as if she could drop by, but perhaps through the W.I.... 'Mrs Clarke, Walter's wife, seems friendly enough. If she's a member of the W.I., I could maybe find a reason to visit.'

'Exactly.' Louis's smile warmed Victoria. It held approval, excitement and something else that made her heart skip a beat and her palms tingle. 'I knew I could count on you. We'll work well together, you'll see.'

'But you said your commanding officer had to give his approval.' What had she got herself into?

Louis hadn't actually said he wasn't a spy, but since Victoria's only knowledge of spies came from books and Hollywood films, was working in intelligence much different? And why did Louis want her to watch Walter Clarke? Was Walter involved in some kind of espionage too? Victoria already had her own doubts about the man, but only because from her few interactions with him he seemed unpleasant and not be trusted. But – she was trying to be fair – being unpleasant and untrustworthy was a far cry from being a spy. It was all too confusing. And if she hadn't decided to walk home through the woods, she'd never have been caught up in any of it.

'My CO's approval is a formality.' Louis shrugged and his smile broadened. 'You want to do your bit, don't you?'

'Of course.' However, apart from teaching, Victoria had expected that 'bit' to be knitting socks, learning how to grow vegetables and keeping up morale — not dangerous work tracking down possible Nazi sympathisers and German informers.

Or, as part of that work, spending more time with Louis who might be dangerous in a quite different way.

Chapter Fourteen

Tonight was Victoria's first W.I. meeting and now she had a hidden agenda. On Wednesday evening in the second week of December she glanced around Hazelbury's village hall, decorated with the red and green paper chains the children had made out of newspaper and painted. In a nod to the season, Beatrice had taken down her autumn squirrel frieze and, using the other side of the brown paper roll, drawn one featuring robins, holly and more squirrels. The latter were dressed in cloaks and bonnets much like those worn by animals in Beatrix Potter's stories.

In the middle of a row, Victoria shifted her chair in a futile attempt to get closer to the fire while Mrs Meldrum, Miss Grainger, Beatrice and several other women chatted behind the table ordinarily used as the teacher's desk. Cocooned by the blackout and thanks to the decorations, the room looked cosy even if it didn't feel so warm. It was also filled almost to capacity with women of all ages, shapes and sizes from what must be both the village proper and surrounding area.

'It's good we came early.' At Victoria's left, Nell spoke into her ear. 'Otherwise, we'd have been at the back near the door.' She shivered and rubbed her gloved hands together. 'Nippy, isn't it?'

Victoria nodded. Nowadays, she was always cold, despite wearing a knitted vest during the day and bed socks at night, both of which her mother had sent in her most recent parcel. But was it only the weather or her nerves as well that made her perpetually chilled? So far, she hadn't spotted anything out of the ordinary but she hadn't yet found a reason to visit Walter Clarke's farm, either. Still, Mrs Clarke was at tonight's meeting and Victoria had made it her mission to speak with her.

'Those ships colliding in Scotland yesterday were a bad business. I read in the paper there were more than a hundred men lost.' To Victoria's right, a middle-aged woman she recognised from church, who also hosted a pupil in the junior part of the school, chatted with her neighbour on the other side. 'Terrible for their mums. I have to say I'd feel the same if it had been a German ship involved instead of two British ones. We're all mothers no matter where we live or what language we speak.' The woman clicked her tongue. 'Alma Clarke said her Walter were up near Glasgow last weekend for a family funeral. A cousin who came over from Ireland about twenty years back. Walter's home now but terrible journey he had what with train delays. As I said to Alma, at least he's not one of them poor fellows at the bottom of the sea.'

'Ladies.' Mrs Meldrum rapped on the table to bring the meeting to order, and Victoria almost groaned in frustration. As soon as she'd heard something interesting the conversation ceased. Still, when Victoria had heard the report of the accident on the wireless, along with sorrow for the men lost, she'd also had a pang of guilty relief because Louis was safe at his desk in London.

At Mrs Meldrum's other side, Miss Grainger bowed her head as Mrs Russell opened the meeting with a prayer.

Victoria bowed her own head, her thoughts racing. The collision of those two ships in thick fog in the sea off the Mull of Kintyre was certainly an accident – but had Walter Clarke been in Scotland for anything other than a funeral?

'Thank you, Mrs Russell.' In her navy-blue tweed skirt and jacket, Mrs Meldrum resembled an upholstered sofa Victoria's parents once had in their living room. She held back a smile and tried to listen as Mrs Meldrum acknowledged the vicar's wife and then spoke about the knitting the W.I. was doing for the Forces. 'Our vice-president, Miss Grainger, will now speak to us on that matter.'

Miss Grainger stood. 'Since our November meeting, many of you have made excellent progress with socks, scarves and other items for our enlisted men.'

Did her gaze linger on Victoria and Nell who, owing to their work at school, hadn't yet completed one scarf or pair of socks between them? *Must try harder.* The comment Victoria had written earlier today in Ralph's exercise book popped into her mind. When it came to war work the same could be said of her, but like Beatrice's and Nell's, her day extended long beyond the classroom, and she was busy from the time she woke up in the morning until she went to bed at night.

'It has been suggested we hold a whist drive to raise funds to buy more knitting wool.' Miss Grainger pushed her spectacles farther up her nose and checked her notes. 'Mrs Walter Clarke, and her sister-in-law Mrs Frank Clarke, have volunteered to organise and host such an event on the Thursday evening before Christmas.' She gestured to the two women who sat side by side several rows across from Victoria and Nell nearer Miss Adelaide and now Beatrice. 'Please let them know if you'd like to take part. At this point, it is my pleasure to introduce tonight's guest speaker, Retired Major Bertram from Whittleton Hall, who was one of Norfolk's most distinguished army officers during the First World War. He will tell us about the important role of Britain's allies in this war; after which Mrs Meldrum will announce the winner of our Christmas stocking competition and we will enjoy refreshments.'

Clapping broke out as Major Bertram, a tall, grey-haired man with a handlebar moustache, took the platform. 'Thank you, Miss Grainger, and good evening, ladies.' He gave them a courtly nod before, in plummy vowels, launching into a speech which while although undoubtedly worthy and important, failed to hold Victoria's interest. Instead, her thoughts wandered.

Although she'd never played whist, she could learn. If Beatrice and Nell played, perhaps they could teach her and she could convince them to join the party. Since four players were needed for a table, maybe Miss Adelaide would make up their number. Victoria's pulse sped up and her breath quickened. It would be a chance to do something practical that might make a real difference to the war effort beyond knitting and having a vegetable garden. For now, she'd managed to set aside her questions and vague doubts and accept that Louis was telling her the truth.

And if she were honest with herself, she wanted to help Louis too. He wasn't only handsome and charming but honourable, kind and patriotic. She liked him, he wasn't Roy, and he wasn't dodgy like Walter Clarke either. Maybe if there was a dance in the village one Saturday night, they'd both be there and—

She started as amidst more applause Nell prodded her in the ribs. 'Sorry?' She glanced around.

'Major Bertram wants to meet you.' Nell gave Victoria another nudge. 'Miss Grainger or Mrs Meldrum must have told him you're from Canada so you're one of those allies he talked about.'

'Oh, of course.' Victoria stood and smiled to greet the major when Miss Grainger, accompanied by Miss Adelaide and Beatrice, drew her forwards to introduce them, nodding and answering his questions patiently and politely. 'My father was a surgeon in the last war. Yes, my parents were born in London and came to Canada as small children so I have British ancestry. Canadians are happy to pitch in with the war effort and help Britain in her hour of need.'

Goodness, she sounded like a recruiting poster – but the major was the kind of person who naturally inspired such talk. While her family and many other Canadians hadn't wanted another war, now that they were in it, they didn't have much choice in supporting Britain.

'Yes, I'm a teacher.' She smiled harder. 'Our evacuees have settled in well here, thank you.'

'Good, good.' The major clapped his hands, as big as small hams. 'That's the spirit. Come next summer you must bring your pupils to Whittleton Hall. Won't likely be able to spare the petrol but I'll send several wagons. By that time I should have some land girls about the place. I expect the children would enjoy seeing the animals and going up our tower. Make a day of it. Mrs Bertram would be delighted to have young people running about again. My wife was born in Canada so I'm certain she would enjoy meeting you. We'll lay on refreshments, assuming there's still any to be had.'

'Thank you, that's most kind.' There was nothing else for Victoria to say because it had all been decided without any input from her. Still, if they were here then, it would be lovely for the children, and her as well. Except for that day in Cromer with Louis, she'd hardly seen anything of Norfolk, and Whittleton Hall wasn't far.

'Most kind indeed.' The Misses Grainger, Nell and Beatrice all murmured while nodding agreement like the animated bobbing wooden monkey toys a distant cousin had once given Victoria and her sisters.

As the major was drawn aside by Mrs Meldrum, Victoria made her way through the small groups of women clustered around the tea urn and plotted her next move. Where could Alma Clarke have got to? The meeting hadn't ended yet so unless she'd left early... no, there she was, near one of the blacked-out windows.

'Mrs Clarke.' Victoria reached her after evading several foster-mums who undoubtedly wanted her help in resolving yet more problems related to their evacuees. 'I'll be with you in a moment.' She waved away an especially persistent mother. 'I need to have a word with Mrs Clarke first. Sorry about that.' She turned back to Alma. 'For the whist drive—'

'Oh, would you be willing to help? I'd be ever so grateful. Walter says he won't have no truck with whist drives and the like at Upper Yarrow so Olive, Frank's wife, is hosting it at their farm.' Her shoulders slumped. 'I only want to do my part.'

'We all do and I'm happy to help.' As she told her pupils, Victoria needed to keep an open mind and not jump to conclusions.

'Olive and me could use help making sandwiches and such but...' Her head darted from side to side like a sparrow pecking for crumbs. 'That's not what's truly worrying me. It's my youngest lad, our Jimmy. He needs help with his reading, on the quiet like.'

'But Jimmy's not one of my pupils. Surely the local schoolmistress, Mrs Mann, can work with him and—'

'She could, but Walter won't hear of it. You now, Walter seems to have taken a real shine to you. He says you remind him of his young sister. We lost our Florrie to the 'flu in 1918. Only a little lass she were then.'

'I'm sorry about Florrie, but...' Victoria hesitated. Mrs Mann, Hazelbury's schoolmistress, was a middle-aged widow who'd made it clear that she had her own what she called 'educational methods'. Apart from having to share the schoolhouse with Beatrice and Nell, what the London pupils and teachers did was none of her concern. Yet, despite likely being seen as interfering and ruffling feathers, Victoria had to take that risk for the greater good.

'I can try to help Jimmy, I suppose. Shall I come up to the farm for eleven on Saturday morning?'

'Thank you, that would be fine.' Mrs Clarke straightened, less sparrow-like and more a fierce mother bear protecting her cub. 'I'll see you on Saturday, Miss McKaye.'

Victoria turned back to the foster-mum and tried to pay attention to her complaint about the noise her evacuee made going up and down stairs.

Yet, in another part of her mind, she focused on Saturday. She had to find a way to tell Louis what she'd arranged, but when she did would he have more instructions for her?

Chapter Fifteen

In the country lane behind the vicarage, Victoria waved at Ivy, Diana and Peter over the garden fence. Ivy, who'd arrived from London the week before, was hanging up washing on a line strung between two now leafless trees. While Saturday morning had dawned bright and sunny, the fields surrounding Hazelbury were tipped silver with frost and the sky was an icy blue.

'Miss McKaye.' Peter ran to the fence. 'Miss Wentworth. I got a letter from my mum this morning. She's coming here after Christmas and we'll live together. She also said she'll have a special surprise for me.'

'How wonderful, Peter.' Victoria exchanged a glance with Beatrice as they both greeted the boy. So many letters had gone back and forth but, in the end, the authorities had agreed that after the baby arrived, Peter would be reunited with his mum and new sibling here in Hazelbury.

'It is.' The boy grinned. 'I like Mrs Russell and all but she's not my mum. My dad says I have to be the man of the family while he's away.' He puffed out his small chest and stood, soldier-like, by a patch of winter cabbage. 'It won't be long now until we can go back to London, though. Ivy says nothing's happening there so the war will be over soon.'

As Beatrice talked to Peter, Victoria's heart squeezed. While each week one or two more children returned home to their parents, Park Road's headmistress, Miss Hopson, continued to say that Beatrice, Nell and Victoria should stay in the country with their remaining pupils.

Apart from insisting that Victoria take Beatrice with her to Upper Yarrow Farm today, Louis hadn't had any further instructions for her but his expression had been grave when he'd arrived from London last night. Although he hadn't said so, Louis didn't expect the war to be over soon so Victoria didn't, either.

'Right, we need to be on our way.' After they'd said goodbye to the children and Ivy, Beatrice turned to Victoria. 'I'm still not happy about you agreeing to help Jimmy Clarke, and, when she finds out, Mrs Mann won't be either. You have more than enough to do without taking on extra tutoring, especially for a child who isn't even our pupil.'

Victoria did indeed, but tutoring Jimmy was the only way she could have a look round Upper Yarrow Farm. 'Mrs Clarke asked me because she's worried over Jimmy so how could I refuse? As for Mrs Mann, we'll have to see she doesn't find out.' As they continued along the lane and onto the track leading to Walter Clarke's farm, Victoria's stomach lurched. It was all very well to sound brave, but now she had to make herself believe it.

'It's dishonest. If Mrs Mann asks me outright, I'll have to tell her the truth.' Beatrice stopped at the entrance to the farmyard. 'I also don't see why you wanted me to come with you. You're perfectly capable of working with Jimmy on his reading by yourself.'

'You're head of the junior school.' It was a feeble excuse but the best Victoria could come up with. 'If he was one of ours, Jimmy would be in one of the junior classes.'

'There isn't truly a junior school at the moment, as you're well aware.' Beatrice gave an exasperated shrug. 'I shall make the best of things, but don't say I didn't warn you.' Then, she gave an unexpected chuckle. 'I grew up in the country near a small Berkshire village. I miss country life and when I retire I always fancied having a small farm with a cottage near the sea. I suppose I should have been careful what I wished for.' She shooed several inquisitive chickens away from her black lace-up boots and shook her head at two cows who, to Victoria's relief, were safely behind a pasture fence near where a small car was parked.

Victoria rapped on the front door of the farmhouse using a brass knocker shaped like a horseshoe. Beatrice didn't often share anything personal and while Victoria wanted to continue that conversational path, the door opened and Alma Clarke appeared with Jimmy held tight by one shoulder.

'Good morning.' She made her voice bright as Mrs Clarke greeted them.

Jimmy, a gawky, red-haired boy of ten, grunted.

'Speak properly to the teachers.' Mrs Clarke cuffed him around the ear and then after taking their coats, led them through a dim hall into a small parlour. A Victorian sofa covered in dark-red fabric sat along one wall and several chairs were arranged at precise right-angles around a centre table which held a stack of schoolbooks.

'I keep this room for best.' Mrs Clarke smoothed her hair, the movement once again reminding Victoria of a sparrow.

'Thank you.' Beatrice gave Jimmy a quelling look as he started over to the window hung with frilly lace curtains.

'Shall we make a start, then?' Victoria took off her gloves and pulled out one of the straight-backed chairs and sat as Beatrice did the same.

'I'll bring you some tea.' Mrs Clarke left the room but, since she didn't close the door behind her, they soon heard the clatter of crockery from elsewhere in the house.

'What seems to be the trouble with your reading?' Beatrice drew one of the books towards her while Jimmy took the chair across from them.

'Don't like it.' Jimmy rested his elbows on the table but, with another severe look from Beatrice, took them away and folded his hands in his lap instead. 'Don't like school.'

'That may be so, but the government says you must stay at school until you're fourteen,' Victoria said.

'Which is as it should be,' Beatrice added. 'Now, take this book and read this passage to us so we know where you're at.'

As Jimmy's halting voice began to read a story which Diana, several years younger, managed with ease, Victoria looked around the room, which was decorated with floral wallpaper and filled up with framed family photos interspersed with several landscapes, and another small table topped with a family Bible. It was entirely ordinary and much like many of the other homes Victoria had visited here.

Voices echoed from the farmyard, and Victoria slid back in her chair to peer through a gap in the curtain. Walter Clarke stood talking with his brother and another man outside the fence with the cattle. So far, there was nothing unusual there either.

'Them letters make no sense to me.' Jimmy gestured to the page. 'I try but...' He worried his lower lip. 'I expect I'm stupid, that's all.'

'You're not stupid,' Victoria said. 'Perhaps it's that you learn differently from other children. One of my sisters struggles with reading like you do.' With the means to afford it, Victoria's parents had taken Stella to Toronto for special help. Children like Jimmy weren't as lucky, but maybe from what she'd learned with Stella, Victoria could help him.

'I've read about the Montessori method and several other approaches,' Beatrice said. 'I wonder if any of those might work.'

'All we can do is try.' Victoria studied the boy now slouched in his chair. 'Will you work with us, Jimmy?' She took an exercise book from her satchel.

'I suppose it couldn't hurt. I'm not lazy despite what Dad and me brothers says.' He gestured towards the window where Walter now gesticulated at the other men.

'I'm sure you're not.' Beatrice's voice was firm. 'Let's use this exercise book so you can write some letters for us.'

'I'll be back in a moment.' Something was happening in the farmyard, and Victoria needed to find out what. Mrs Clarke had indicated that the brick lavatory was around the side of the house in the back garden. To reach it, Victoria could go out through the front door and pass the men.

Beatrice nodded as she handed Jimmy a pencil, speaking to him in a gentle and encouraging voice.

Victoria darted out of the room and into the hall, looking both ways to make sure that Mrs Clarke was still busy in the kitchen.

Then, she took a deep breath and opened the door. The other Mr Clarke, Frank, had disappeared but Walter and the stranger still stood in the yard beside the small motor parked beside the pasture fence.

'Hello.' She gave the men, who'd stopped talking as soon as she appeared, a careless wave.

'Trying to teach my Jimmy, are you?' Walter shook his head. 'I shouldn't bother. The lad's a dullard. Still, it don't take brains to weed and dig potatoes, only muscle.' He guffawed.

'Jimmy may surprise you.' Victoria tried to keep her expression neutral. Unlike Walter, who was dressed for farm work, the stranger wore a belted tan trench coat and hat as well as a smart suit, gloves and glossy brown shoes.

'I doubt it.' Walter shook his head. 'Mr Knight here is a government chap. Wants to see what kind of land we have and where we can plough up to grow more crops.' He turned to the other man. 'Miss McKaye's one of them teachers from London. Came up here with evacuees and their school.'

Mr Knight, in his late forties or early fifties and of medium height with dark-brown hair threaded with silver, nodded as Walter introduced them. 'A pleasure to meet you, Miss McKaye. You teachers are doing important work and at considerable personal inconvenience. As a father myself, I am most grateful.' His clothing and sophisticated, dapper air were in marked contrast to Walter's appearance and manner. 'I must be off. Other farms to visit.' He touched his camel-coloured fedora with its darker-brown hatband to Victoria and gave her an almost courtly bow. Then he turned back to Walter as they walked towards the car.

Unlike the man she'd seen in the woods with Louis, there was nothing unusual about Mr Knight's appearance or accent. She could have passed him on any British high street without giving him a second look. Still, although she was likely being too suspicious, she hovered by the side of the farmhouse, shielded by a holly tree with its shiny green foliage and red berries.

As the two men continued their conversation, too far away for Victoria to hear what was being said, she rubbed her hands together in the chill wind. There was nothing to be gained from standing here so she'd visit the lavatory and then return to the house.

Taking one last look at the farmyard, she stilled. About to get into his car, Mr Knight had at first gone to the *wrong* side. The side of the vehicle that in North America and Europe would be for the driver, but in England was where the front passenger sat.

It was the same mistake she'd made her first few months in Yorkshire when she'd ridden in the boarding school's car to accompany girls to or from the railway station or to hospital in a nearby town. She pressed a hand to her mouth as Walter laughed and said something more while Mr Knight moved around the bonnet.

Victoria scuttled along the side of the house towards the lavatory and closed the stout wooden door behind her. Her heart pounded and her throat was so tight she could hardly breathe.

Mr Knight wasn't a government chap at all, at least not a British one. Her thoughts whirled.

She'd left the supposed dangers of German bombs landing in London for quiet rural Norfolk. But maybe the real danger lurked here amidst that which, on the surface was ordinary, everyday life.

Chapter Sixteen

'Well done.' Sitting in an armchair across from Victoria by the fireplace in the manor house's library, Louis moved a chess piece on the board which sat on the table between them. The firelight flickered and shadowed the planes of his face. By his feet, Lady snored and her paws twitched in her sleep. 'Don't do anything more for now until I'm able to report back.'

Victoria pretended to study the chess board. Since she hadn't been able to catch Louis alone, after dinner she'd suggested this game. Then, while at the opposite side of the large room his great-aunts and Beatrice and Nell knitted and listened to a concert on the wireless, she'd told him what she'd seen at Walter Clarke's farm. 'Should I still go to the whist drive?'

'With the others, yes.' Louis reached down to pat Lady. 'You don't want to draw attention to yourself or attract questions.'

'Of course.' Victoria tried to work moisture into her dry mouth. Louis's fingers were long and lean. What would it be like to wrap her own fingers around his and hold them tight? She couldn't let her thoughts veer down that path, no matter how tempting. 'There's a Christmas party and dance in the village as well. I'll go to it with Beatrice and Nell.' Not to imply she was fishing for an invitation. She turned her face towards the fire so Louis wouldn't see her blush.

'It sounds as if you're becoming a real part of life here.' A small smile played around Louis's mouth as he rubbed Lady's ears.

'I'm trying to, because if I don't think of Hazelbury as home, I'll never settle.' If she didn't put down roots, one day neither

Canada nor England would be home and then where would she be?

'About that party.' Louis leaned closer. Like her, he seemed to have forgotten the chess game. 'I expect we'll go as a group but I hope you'll save a few dances for me.'

'I'd be pleased to.' Victoria's gaze locked with his.

'Good.' He cleared his throat. 'What would you think of—'

'Louis?' Miss Grainger's voice reached them from the other side of the library. 'Would you be a dear boy and fetch my white shawl, please? I left it in the dining room and I'm feeling a chill.'

'Of course, Aunt Hetty.' Louis stood. 'We'll have to finish our game another time. I need to write some letters before turning in.'

'Certainly. I planned to write my parents tonight.' Victoria got to her feet as well, the top of her head hovering near his shoulder.

As Louis made his apologies and Victoria re-joined the others, Miss Adelaide tucked the navy-blue sock she was knitting into a basket and took off her spectacles. 'I like to imagine the soldier, sailor or airman who will wear these socks. I hope they bring him a bit of comfort and warmth.'

'You've always been too fanciful, Addie.' Miss Grainger continued knitting, her metal needles making a steady clicking sound in a counterpoint rhythm to the rain that pattered against the blacked-out windows. 'It doesn't do to let one's imagination run wild.'

Beatrice made a small sound which turned into a cough before she drank the last of what by now must be the cold dregs of her tea.

'That's it for me tonight.' Nell stretched, reminding Victoria of a sleek, sinuous cat. She was a pretty girl – which many of the local unattached farmers had noticed. She seemed unaware, though, never prolonging their attempts at conversation in the village shop or church, and unless Beatrice or Victoria were with her, she stayed at the manor when she wasn't at school. 'Beatrice? Victoria? Are you ready to come with me?'

'Yes.' Beatrice gathered up her knitting and the torches they used to find their way around the manor at night – safer, Victoria thought, than carrying a candle or lamp along what felt like endless draughty corridors stuffed with furniture and ornaments.

As they said their goodnights and then made their way from the library to the wing containing their bedrooms, Victoria stole covert glances at Beatrice who marched ahead, her shoulders stiff.

'Last cup of tea, anyone? I can put the kettle on.' Oblivious to any undercurrents, Nell paused at the doorway of their shared sitting room.

As the wind shrieked around the eaves and rain hit the windowpanes with even greater force, Victoria shook her head. More tea would mean having to use the chamber pot or making a middle-of-the-night trip to the outdoor lavatory, both of which she tried to avoid at all costs.

'No but…' Beatrice hugged herself, looking almost uncertain. 'We won't be able to sleep with that wind, but I can't knit another stitch or mark more incomprehensible maths papers. We could play cards, I suppose, or listen to my wireless. I had the batteries recharged yesterday.'

'We could.' Nell glanced between them. 'Or play one of those old board games Miss Adelaide found when she was doing a clear-out.'

Victoria's shoulders dropped as if she was a marionette and someone had snipped the strings keeping her upright. All of a sudden, she was tired. Of teaching, problems with billets and writing to the parents of her evacuees. Of the war that didn't feel like a war. Scrabbling around in the dark without electricity and indoor plumbing and making do in every part of her life. Even if she did have a few dances with Louis at the Christmas party, she was a teacher and couldn't ever escape the watchful eyes of the Misses Grainger, Mrs Meldrum and everyone else in the village.

She brushed a hand against her face, tried not to sniff and rummaged in her cardigan pocket for a handkerchief.

'I suspect we're all feeling a bit low. I know I am.' Beatrice found the matches, lit several lamps and gestured to Victoria and Nell to join her in their sitting room.

'You?' Victoria's mouth dropped open. 'I thought... well, you always seem as if everything is fine.'

'Years of pretending, I expect.' Beatrice's tone was wry and her smile revealed a dimple in her left cheek. 'Either that, or it's because of how I was brought up. Neither my parents nor my nanny would tolerate any sign of weakness. Mother still doesn't. I also had two elder brothers to toughen me up.' She sat on one end of a high-backed sofa and fiddled with the wireless dial.

Had. As Victoria sat at the other end of the sofa and Nell took an armchair, she noted the past tense. Although Beatrice rarely shared anything personal, she'd mentioned that her brothers had been killed in the last war.

'I only have sisters,' Victoria said. 'Three of them, all younger. They're married with children of their own.' In addition to her broken engagement, the fear of becoming the spinster aunt was another reason Victoria had wanted a fresh start.

'I have two brothers and three sisters.' Nell took out some mending. 'I'm right in the middle. We're all working now but so far I'm the only one who's left home. Reg is the policeman and Fred got promoted in the fire service. He's walking out with a nice girl and my mum's expecting an engagement one of these days.'

Victoria shrugged into the extra cardigan she'd left on an arm of the sofa. Her sisters and friends had moved on without her, and she hadn't got to know and make friends with anyone in London before Park Road School had been evacuated. So, like Beatrice and Nell, she was stuck here, almost in limbo.

'Come along. Nothing like a bit of dancing to make one feel better.' As lively music spilled from the wireless, Beatrice gestured to Victoria and Nell. 'Forget about that tiresome sewing, Nell. You're putting Victoria and me to shame.'

'Dancing?' Victoria glanced at Nell.

'Why not?' Beatrice's laugh was warm and rich. 'Except for a duty dance with the vicar and any retired military boys who pitch up, I'm too old, but you two will be the centre of attention at Hazelbury's Christmas party and dance. It's bound to be the social event of the year. I expect Mr Grainger will monopolise Victoria.' She winked. 'And don't think I haven't noticed those farmers making eyes at Nell. I can't have either of you letting the side down.'

'You're not too old and I... Mr Grainger... we're friends, nothing more.' Victoria was certain her face had gone red.

'I'm not interested in those farmers or anyone else.' Nell's voice was unexpectedly sharp. 'Besides, we need men to dance.'

'Not when it's only us here at home. What about starting with a Palais Glide or Lambeth Walk? We can do those in a line. It will warm us up *and* boost our spirits. Nell has a face like a wet weekend, and Victoria's lips are blue.'

Although she shook her head, Nell set aside her mending. 'My mum doesn't hold with dancing but she's not here to see me, is she?'

'No, and besides, what are friends for?' Beatrice started them off and Victoria and Nell followed, trying to match the walking dance to the music.

Victoria laughed until her tummy hurt and she collapsed into the armchair. She'd never suspected that the reserved Beatrice could be such a comic, strutting around the room and slapping her thighs. Or that timid Nell would follow, swinging her hips like a chorus girl treading the boards in London's West End.

'Come on.' Beatrice tugged her back to her feet. 'You can't stop until the music ends.'

As Victoria joined back in, copying Nell's exaggerated movements and Beatrice's hops, she forgot her tiredness or that she'd been gloomy.

Friends, fun and frolic. Somehow Beatrice had guessed she'd needed all three. And in a moment of certainty, Victoria knew she'd be likely to need them even more in the weeks and months to come.

Chapter Seventeen

'I'm sorry I missed the dance, and Christmas.' Louis held a low tree branch aside for Victoria and then joined her to continue what Miss Grainger called their traditional 'New Year's Day walk'. No matter that, owing to Louis's absence, the ladies had postponed it until after lunch on the first Sunday in January.

'You didn't miss much.' Victoria matched her steps to his as they moved ahead of Beatrice, Nell and the Misses Grainger. 'The vicar cancelled the midnight church service because the stained-glass windows couldn't be blacked out satisfactorily. There was also the worry of people having accidents in the dark. As for the dance, the hall roof leaked again so Mrs Meldrum ended what she called "the festivities" before nine.' Victoria chuckled at the memory. 'Not that there were many "festivities" to begin with. The few young men stood on one side of the hall staring at the young women on the other, and the two groups were too shy to approach each other. I danced with the vicar and that was it.'

'While I'm sorry you didn't have a good time, I'm glad nobody swept you off your feet.' Louis tucked his arm through Victoria's and squeezed it. 'It's a shame I was called back to London, but duty must.'

There wasn't a chance of any other man sweeping Victoria off her feet. There was only Louis, and before she'd understood what was happening, she was well on her way to falling for him. His arm felt right tucked in hers and so she left it there for now, when they were around a curve in the path and out of view of the others.

'Christmas and New Year were quiet. We tried to be jolly but I can't say it was a great success. And while the whist drive raised a good sum to buy knitting wool, I didn't see or hear anything remotely interesting while I made sandwiches or kept teacups filled.' She'd also missed Louis more than she'd expected. His presence added colour and interest to the grey dullness of everyday life, and he made Victoria feel like herself again, a woman whom, without her noticing, she'd let Roy diminish.

'Still, you went to the dance and whist drive and were seen there.' Louis gave her forearm another squeeze. 'Building trust takes time.'

'Yes.' And only an instant to break it. Victoria pushed away the reminder of Roy's betrayal. He was in the past and letting herself think of him gave him more attention than he deserved. 'Both Mr Clarkes were at the dance and whist drive. Mr Frank Clarke appears to be a fine man.'

'We're watching both of them but yes, Frank's a different "kettle of fish" as the saying goes.'

'I feel sorry for Walter's wife. Mrs Clarke seems lovely.'

Whenever one of them spoke, their breath came out in a frosty cloud. The sky was an icy blue, and a thin dusting of snow covered the path and nearby fields. The winter sun shone bright, making what Victoria's father called 'diamond snow', a carpet of silvery sparkles against the white. Yet, it wasn't the sunshine, her thick coat or the cosy blue scarf, mittens and hat her mother had knitted and sent in the family Christmas box that filled Victoria with warmth. It was being with Louis.

'Alma *is* lovely. As a girl she worked at the manor for several years in the kitchen and then as a housemaid before she married Walter. She's a hard worker and well liked in the village. It's a shame she ended up with a man like him. He was handsome back then, still is, I suppose, and she was taken in.'

Like Victoria had been 'taken in' by Roy? If she was honest with herself, there had always been something about him she hadn't fully trusted, but at first she'd been dazzled by his good looks, smart motor, fine clothes and ambition. Since their families were friends and everyone approved and said how lucky she was, she'd silenced those niggles of unease. She might not be much older now but she was certainly wiser.

'Oh look, those are Canada geese.' She took her arm away from Louis under the guise of gesturing to a flock flying high overhead.

'Norfolk's good for birdwatching, especially in winter.' Louis wasn't anything like Roy – but could she truly trust him? 'I have a bird book at the house. You're welcome to borrow it. You ought to keep an eye out for snow buntings. They're arctic birds but winter along the Norfolk coast. Some people call them snowflakes. Bit special, they are.'

'Thank you.' As they came out of the woods into an open area that bordered a field, Victoria hugged herself against a sudden chill breeze. 'I expect the children would enjoy learning about birds as well.'

'I'll look the book up for you.' With his gloved hands now clasped behind his back, Louis studied the sky. 'I hope I didn't speak out of turn or do anything to make you uncomfortable. I expect you have a fellow in London or Canada.'

'No, you didn't, and I don't have a fellow anywhere.' Victoria's words came out in a rush, and she tugged at her scarf to shield her face. 'I mean, I did have a fellow once, in Canada. But it ended before I came to England. We were engaged and he... well... it turned out he wanted to marry someone else instead.'

'I'm sorry.' His voice was soft. 'I had a girl, too. Like you, we were engaged, briefly, but a fortnight later she... well, it doesn't matter. It's long over.'

'I'm sorry for you as well.' Victoria's face must be bright red. Hopefully Louis would think it was because of the cold.

'Don't be.' His laugh was bitter. 'I won't be ungentlemanly but it was for the best.'

She wouldn't be unladylike and press him further, but part of her yearned to know what had happened. Although she hadn't thought so then, with time and distance, she realised that Roy breaking their engagement had saved her from what might have been a greater hurt later on.

'The next time there's a dance and I'm able to get leave, would you like to go with me?' Louis's cheeks were flushed too and for such a seemingly confident man, he appeared almost bashful.

'Yes, I would, thank you.' Victoria met his gaze and for several seconds something flickered between them. That intimacy she'd felt before but stronger this time, perhaps because they knew more of where they stood with each other. Friends, yes, but a friendship holding the possibility of more.

'We're making predictions for what nineteen forty will bring.' Nell came up behind them where they'd stopped under a tall, leafless oak. 'Despite shortages and food rationing, it has to be better than nineteen thirty-nine, don't you think?'

'Don't tempt fate.' Beatrice joined them with Miss Adelaide and Miss Grainger. 'Let's leave it at happy new year wishes and make the next months the best we can.'

'Indeed.' Miss Grainger looked over her spectacles at Victoria and Louis before taking his arm. 'I am too old to offer much in the way of a new year greeting or prediction. Time passes and, as I always have, I shall cope with whatever it may bring.'

'Surely we must have hope for the future?' In a dark-red coat trimmed with white and a cheery red hat, Miss Adelaide looked more bird-like than ever. 'I, for one, look forward to each new year for a fresh start.' She took Louis's other arm as they started down a low hill slick with ice.

'I'm with you, Miss Adelaide.' Victoria linked arms with Beatrice and Nell. 'Let's not invite misfortune. Maybe the war will be over soon and we'll wonder what we were so worried about.'

Louis glanced over his shoulder and as his gaze lingered on Victoria, her stomach lurched with a mixture of excitement and fear.

As before, he didn't believe the war would be over soon. She read that and more in his sombre expression. But whatever happened, his expression also told her they'd face it together.

Chapter Eighteen

'Well done, children.' On a Friday afternoon in mid-April when rain rattled against the windows in the village hall, Victoria clapped her hands. 'We'll practise the folk song again on Monday, but all your pageant parts are coming along nicely.'

Albert and Ralph poked their heads out from under the blankets that had transformed them into medieval war horses and grinned.

'That Albert is quite droll, isn't he?' From her seat at Victoria's side, Mrs Meldrum clapped too. Beatrice's initial idea of having the evacuees and local children put on a play had evolved into a much more ambitious affair, an historical pageant in support of the Red Cross which had become a joint initiative between the schools and the Women's Institute. As W.I. president, Mrs Meldrum had dropped by the various classes to lend support. Or, as Nell had said to Victoria on their walk to school earlier, 'More like sticking her nose in where she's not wanted.'

'Albert's certainly showing unexpected talents.' Not only in his pageant role. Without Victoria having to remind him, he was now cleaning the tables while Ralph swept the hall floor.

'He may have a future on the stage.' Mrs Meldrum nodded her approval.

'Or in the pulpit.' Victoria smiled her thanks at the boys as she tied Margaret's hair ribbon before retrieving another girl's missing pencil tin. Her classes had grown again in late February when many of the children who'd initially returned to London came back to the country. They'd been joined by others whose parents had kept them at home during the first evacuation in September 1939. 'Albert's a bright lad and Mrs Russell says he's taken a real shine to the vicar.' She took the stack of exercise books Sheila had collected.

'Being evacuated could be the making of him and of many of these children. Goodness knows how long they'll be with us. It might be years.' Beneath her hat brim, Mrs Meldrum's forehead wrinkled into a worried crease. 'Hitler won't stop at invading Denmark and Norway.'

Victoria shook her head and put a finger to her lips. Inasmuch as she could manage, she tried to keep talk of war out of the classroom. The children were already unsettled enough and with many having fathers, brothers and uncles in the Forces, she wanted school to be a safe and happy place where they could momentarily forget their troubles.

On that new year's walk only three months earlier, Victoria had sought to be optimistic. But now, with Denmark having surrendered to Germany, and Norway, with Britain's help, fighting for her independence, what many had called the 'Phoney War' was well and truly over. Along with Beatrice, Nell and the Misses Grainger, Victoria was glued to the wireless every evening for each increasingly grim news bulletin.

Mrs Meldrum tucked her bulky brown handbag over one arm. 'While watching the infants' performance, I made a few notes which I'll go over at our meeting tomorrow. I'd like to hear a bit more volume and energy from the children in that folk song. In the banquet scene, Peter tends to mumble, doesn't he? As the local lord, he needs to have more presence.' Mrs Meldrum put a hand to her bosom as if to demonstrate.

'He's not yet six.' Victoria suppressed a smile. 'He'll become more comfortable with the part in time.'

'I do hope so.' Mrs Meldrum adjusted her suit jacket and walked with Victoria towards the door, her gait reminiscent of a ship in full sail. 'It's kind of the Misses Grainger to let the W.I. gather at the manor for our extra meeting.'

'They're happy to support the W.I. and now the Red Cross as well.' In the entryway, Victoria sent her pupils on their way home, making sure they all had their satchels and mackintoshes. 'Diana, there's Ivy coming out of the post office. You can walk with her.'

'Yes, but Miss McKaye, I need to speak with you first. It's important.' Diana waved at Ivy to wait.

'All right.' As the months had gone on, Diana had become ever dearer to her, almost like the daughter she'd once hoped to have. 'Shall we go back into the hall?' After saying goodbye to Mrs Meldrum, Victoria gestured to her makeshift desk.

'I need to speak with you *in private*.' Diana jerked her chin towards Albert and Ralph who were still cleaning. 'Peter does too.' She tugged him forwards from where he hovered at her side.

'You've done enough cleaning, boys. I'll finish the rest later, thank you.' Mrs Meldrum was right. Peter did need more of a presence in his pageant role and Victoria had given him the part to help build his confidence. Despite his mother and baby sister having come to Hazelbury after Christmas, and the three of them being billeted with an elderly couple who lived near the vicarage, he was still bashful, and Victoria was running out of ideas to help bring him out of himself.

She took the broom from Ralph and dustpan from Albert. 'Please ask Ivy to wait for Diana and Peter. They'll only be a minute and I'd rather Peter had someone to walk home with.'

'What is it?' Victoria sat on the edge of her table and studied the two small and serious faces in front of her.

'It's…' Diana glanced at Peter. 'You know how everyone says we all, young and old, have to do our bit?'

'Yes, like you're both helping Mrs Russell with her garden.' Victoria made her tone encouraging. Something was worrying the children but she needed to wait so they could tell her in their own way.

'Well, what if we heard something that might be important? We weren't snooping, honestly. We were working in the garden and…' Diana twisted her hands together. 'Mummy always says if I see someone doing wrong, I should tell her and Daddy but they're not here and we didn't *see* anything.'

'What did you hear?' Victoria's hands tingled. All winter she'd watched and waited, making sure to attend every village dance and party, W.I. meeting, choir practice, whist drive and jumble sale. Yet, she'd had nothing to report to Louis and lately there had been bigger gaps between his visits.

They hadn't even managed to go to a dance together. He couldn't tell her where he'd been, and Victoria hadn't asked, but now they wrote to each other and his most recent letter had been postmarked Inverness. A cold chill snaked up her spine. The north of Scotland wasn't so far away from Norway. 'If you heard something that's making you upset or worried, you need to tell me or Mrs Russell or the vicar.'

Diana straightened her shoulders. 'It was when Peter and I were digging by the hedge in the vicarage garden yesterday after school. The one nearest the lane.'

'And I was hot from all the digging so Mrs Russell went inside to get me a glass of water,' Peter said. 'Wilf and Albert were doing their homework in the dining room, and Ivy was dusting the vicar's study while he was out.'

'So, what did you hear?' Victoria tried to keep the anxiety from her voice. There was likely only several minutes before Ivy and Albert would come in to see what was keeping Diana and Peter.

'It was Mr Clarke. The one from Upper Yarrow Farm. I saw him through the hedge,' Diana said.

'And he were with another man,' Peter added.

Was with. Victoria let the correction pass.

'A stranger,' Diana explained. 'They talked about a parcel arriving on Saturday night, but the postman doesn't deliver at night, especially not Saturdays. They also said something about going to the beach, but nobody's allowed to go to any beach.'

Victoria drew closer to the children. 'What did the man look like?'

'A bit taller than Mr Clarke but not tall like Mr Grainger,' Diana said. 'I couldn't see his hair beneath his hat. He wore a suit like Daddy does when he goes to his office and shiny brown shoes. He sounded English, though, not like the foreign spy in the comic Albert's mum sent him.'

Victoria's heart banged against her ribs. Mr Knight, the government chap she'd met that day at Upper Yarrow Farm, was only an inch or so taller than Walter Clarke and had worn a smart suit and glossy brown shoes too. 'I expect Mr Clarke was talking about a food parcel. He likely has family coming to visit,' she improvised. 'With the rationing, visitors often bring extra food, don't they? Perhaps one of the visitors arrived early and the others are following tomorrow night. As for the beach, I expect they meant walking along a promenade, perhaps the one in Cromer. I appreciate you telling me but there's nothing for you to fret about.'

'All right.' Diana nodded.

'I miss Mrs Russell's cakes,' Peter said. 'She said she'd make one special for my birthday but without enough butter and sugar how can she?'

'I'm sure she'll find a way round and you'll have your cake, but your birthday isn't for months yet.' Victoria shepherded Peter and Diana to the hall door. 'Run along with Ivy and Albert. I'll likely see you later when Miss Potter and I come to practise our choir solo with Mrs Russell.'

As she shut the door behind them, Victoria leaned against it and pressed a hand to her throat.

Finally, something had happened – and if what the children overheard was correct, something else would happen tomorrow night. Somehow, she had to get word to Louis.

Chapter Nineteen

Outside the pub, Victoria glanced around and tried to look nonchalant. The rain had stopped, a watery sun had come out and the telephone box across the road on a patch of green grass by a hedge was as reassuringly red as always. It was empty, so there was no reason for her not to use it. In fact, she'd look more suspicious if she lingered.

She crossed the road, found several coins in her purse and entered the phone box closing the door behind her. Since the manor didn't have a telephone, it wasn't unusual for her to make a call here but this time she felt exposed and obvious. She'd memorised the number Louis had written on a card for her so she picked up the handset, put a coin into one of the slots and spoke to the operator.

When the call connected, a woman answered. 'I'm sorry, Lieutenant Commander Grainger is out. How may I help you?'

How could this woman with her crisp, clipped vowels in distant London help Victoria here in a small Norfolk village? 'Do you know when he'll be back? I'm telephoning from Hazelbury. I live with his great-aunts.'

'Is it Miss McKaye?' The woman's voice sharpened.

'Yes.' Victoria glanced towards the village green where several white ducks glided on the pond.

'I'm Miss Skene, Lieutenant Commander Grainger's secretary. Please hold for a moment.'

At the pips, Victoria added another coin. Hopefully, Miss Skene wouldn't keep her waiting too long since she didn't have much change. A tractor came around the corner and rumbled onto the high street. As it passed the telephone box, she glimpsed Frank Clarke in the driver's seat with the dog, Captain. Her stomach knotted. At least it wasn't Walter – but would Frank tell his brother he'd seen her here? It had only taken Victoria a few weeks to realise nothing in this village remained private for long.

'Miss McKaye?' Miss Skene was back. 'I can get a message to Lieutenant Commander Grainger for you.' Her voice was cool, the accent an older version of the one favoured by the aristocratic girls Victoria had taught at the Yorkshire boarding school.

'Thank you. Please tell him…' She turned as someone rapped on the door. Mrs Yallop, one of the foster-mums who was always complaining about her evacuees. Victoria smiled and waved to indicate she'd be done shortly. 'He asked me to ring about the garden. The cabbage, I mean, and expecting a delivery tomorrow evening.' She fed her last coins into the phone. Cabbage was one of the code words Louis had given her months ago but until today she'd never had an occasion to use it.

'I see.' Miss Skene paused.

Victoria gripped the receiver in her clammy hand.

'Please hold.' There was a rustling sound and then within seconds Miss Skene returned. 'You can expect Lieutenant Commander Grainger on the noon train tomorrow. Do you drive and, if so, could you meet him in Cromer?'

'Yes.' Although she hadn't yet driven in England, her father had taught Victoria to drive the family car at home. 'We have petrol coupons as well.' Miss Grainger had applied for them so Louis could drive their late father's car which sat in the carriage house.

'Jolly good.' Miss Skene's voice turned brisk. 'I'm glad to hear the gardening is going well. Perhaps you'll send some vegetables down to London for us at harvest time.'

'Yes, and thank you.' Victoria rang off and opened the door of the telephone box, making her expression neutral.

'Calling London were you?' Mrs Yallop paused, her brown eyes wide with curiosity.

How had the woman known or had she made a lucky guess? 'Evacuee business, you know how it is.' Victoria forced a smile. 'Like you foster-parents, we teachers rarely have a moment to ourselves.'

Mrs Yallop nodded and under her blue snood several loose curls of brown hair bobbed. 'I hear that pageant is keeping you busy. I said I'd sew some of the costumes, but where I'll find the time I don't know. I've just put the garden in.'

'We've done the same at the manor.' Had she overheard what Victoria had said?

'We haven't seen young Mr Grainger in a while. About a month, isn't it? His great-aunts must miss him.'

'They do.' Victoria clenched her hand around her purse. 'I thought you needed to use the telephone?' She gestured towards the box.

'Oh, yes. I'm ringing our Dot in Fakenham. She said she'd be beside her phone waiting but knowing her she's likely late. My sister would forget her head if it weren't screwed on. Give my best to the Misses Grainger won't you? I expect I'll see you at the extra W.I. meeting tomorrow afternoon?'

Drat. In Victoria's nervousness, she'd forgotten about that meeting. However, if the train was on time and Louis arrived at noon, she'd be back for the W.I. by two. She'd also have to arrange to borrow the car which would mean confiding in Miss Grainger. And she'd need to find an excuse and ask Beatrice to tutor Jimmy Clarke on her own. Sir Walter Scott's quote about weaving a tangled web when starting to deceive ran through her mind.

Victoria muttered something non-committal and made her escape. One step at a time. She'd done the hardest part in tracking down Louis and getting him to come here. Now she could only hope she wasn't wasting his time.

The next day at noon, Victoria paced the sunny platform at the railway station in Cromer. She held Lady's lead in one hand; walking the dog gave her an excuse to burn off some nervous energy. The Norwich train was late, but even when Louis arrived she doubted she'd truly relax.

When she reached the far end of the platform for a second time, a grey-haired woman wearing a fashionable knee-length white coat nodded and smiled. 'Beautiful day, isn't it? Feels so spring-like.'

'Yes, it does.' Victoria tugged Lady's paws away from the woman's coat.

'Oh, what a lovely dog. Don't give my coat a second thought. I have dogs of my own.' She crouched to Lady's level and rubbed the dog's silky ears. 'Have we met before?' The woman glanced at Victoria.

'I don't think so. I live in Hazelbury.' The woman had what Victoria considered a mid-Atlantic accent, neither British nor North American either. An accent Victoria would have remembered if she'd met its owner here.

'Oh, I know.' The woman straightened. 'I'm Mrs Bertram from Whittleton Hall. My husband spoke to Hazelbury's W.I. late last year. I was supposed to be there but had a cold so stayed at home. I saw your photograph in the local newspaper. You must be the Canadian teacher that Sidney, Major Bertram, told me about.' She extended a hand and Victoria took it.

'Yes, I am.' Victoria introduced herself. 'Major Bertram mentioned you were born in Canada.'

At that W.I. meeting, Mrs Meldrum had gathered everyone together for a photo and when it had appeared in the paper in the 'Hazelbury Notes' section, Victoria had cut it out and sent it to her parents. Nowadays, her family often seemed like people she'd known in another life, forever as they'd been when she'd last seen them. Did she seem the same to them? It was something she could ask in person, she supposed, but couldn't find the right words to express in a letter.

Mrs Bertram gave Victoria an even warmer smile. 'Yes, I was born in Vancouver and grew up in Montréal when my father was transferred there for work. I met my husband in London when I was touring Europe and the British Isles with my mother and sister. We were introduced by mutual family friends.'

'I see.' Victoria had got used to British reserve and Mrs Bertram's easy informality, although welcome, was unexpected and somewhat puzzling.

'You're billeted at Hazelbury Manor, aren't you?' Mrs Bertram went on. 'From what Sidney's told me they used to have wonderful parties there. Is it Louis you're meeting?'

'Yes.' Victoria glanced around but apart from Mrs Bertram and a man who looked rather like the Hollywood actor Clark Gable and who'd got out of a baker's van parked nearby, the platform was empty.

'Louis was such a lovely boy. Good friends with our three sons and our daughter as well. And now...' Her bright expression slipped. 'Well, they're all doing their duty, aren't they? Oh, here's the train. I'm meeting Sidney's mother. With things looking dicier in London, she finally agreed to close up her house and come to us.' She gestured to the track and a puff of smoke in the distance. 'Sidney said he'd invited you and your pupils to visit the hall. Please do come soon. I'd love to hear children's voices around the old place again.'

'Thank you but we wouldn't want to disturb you. The children are *very* lively, some of the boys especially.' Although Mrs Bertram had boys of her own, the London evacuees and some of the recent arrivals in particular would not be the sort of children she was accustomed to.

'The livelier the better.' Was that a hint of yearning in Mrs Bertram's expression? 'I'll write and suggest a date.'

As clanking and a hiss of steam from the arriving train made further conversation impossible, Victoria nodded and smiled.

What would she tell Beatrice? Soon after Major Bertram had voiced the invitation, Beatrice had advised Victoria that if pressed she should decline with thanks. Released from the confines of a schoolroom, the prospect of a horde of unruly children rampaging across the manicured lawns of Whittleton Hall – with Victoria, Beatrice and Nell in pursuit – didn't bear thinking about.

As a motley collection of passengers streamed from the train's carriages, Victoria watched for Louis. What would she do if he'd missed the train? Call his office, she guessed, but it was unlikely there would be anyone there on Saturday afternoon.

Mrs Bertram greeted a white-haired, well-dressed woman who gave the lone elderly porter instructions about her luggage.

Several young men in RAF uniform with kit bags slung over their shoulders followed an officer directing them to a military vehicle parked near the seafront.

A clergyman in a clerical collar and several women with small valises or string bags walked in the direction of the town centre, while the man from the baker's van still stood on the platform seemingly waiting for a passenger rather than unloading or making a delivery.

But still no Louis.

Victoria gripped Lady's lead. 'What do you think, girl? Where could he be?'

The dog whined and tugged on the lead as Mrs Bertram and her mother-in-law followed the porter who pushed a trolley piled high with cases.

'What? No, wait… Lady.' Victoria lurched forwards as the dog yanked her towards a man in a cloth cap and workman's clothes who'd alighted from a carriage at the far end of the train.

'I'm dreadfully sorry, stop it, Lady.' She spoke above the dog's excited barking.

'It's all right.' The man bent to pat Lady and, from under the cap covering most of his face, gave Victoria a sideways grin.

'You... what... I...' She stopped as he shook his head. It was Louis, but why was he wearing those odd clothes and speaking in such a peculiar way? She'd been looking for a man in naval uniform or at least a smart suit.

'Shall we be off, then? Miss McKaye from Hazelbury Manor isn't it?' He tipped his grease-stained cap with the hand not holding a battered canvas bag.

'Yes.' Victoria gestured to the Grainger's motor as Louis, with Lady still bouncing around his legs, walked at what she supposed was meant to be a respectful distance slightly behind her.

'You drive. I'll sit in the back.' As they reached the car, he spoke in his usual voice but still softly, even though apart from that fellow from the baker's van, now speaking to a man in a suit, they were alone.

Victoria nodded, opened a rear door to let Lady in and then, as Louis followed, went around to the driver's seat and started the car's engine. Her hands trembled as she eased out of the parking spot and navigated through the narrow streets out of the town. Even though she wanted to, she sensed she couldn't ask Louis any questions, not yet. And even when they reached the coast road, she still didn't dare chat about anything more than the weather.

'Thank you.' Louis leaned over the rear seat.

She nodded and kept her eyes on the road. Although she'd never been a nervous driver, the combination of managing a British car and Louis seemingly watching her every move, rattled her.

'I expect you're wondering what's going on?'

'Yes.'

'I'm sorry I couldn't warn you. I didn't expect you'd have Lady with you or that Mrs Bertram would also be on the platform, but things could have been worse.' He let out a long breath. 'That fellow with the baker's delivery van is a cousin of the Clarke brothers and well... let's say he's currently a person of interest. The man he met off the train is someone else we have in our sights. When you rang my office and mentioned "the cabbage" Miss Skene knew to reach me, but I couldn't risk being recognised on my journey.'

'Oh.' Victoria's scalp prickled. 'I felt silly ringing you, actually, with nothing more to go on than two of my pupils having overheard Walter Clarke talking to a stranger about a delivery tonight, but you said nothing was too insignificant so I took a chance.'

'I'm glad you did.' Louis's voice was warm with approval, and Victoria's tight breathing eased.

'Diana and Peter were in the vicarage garden. They were on the other side of a hedge so Walter didn't know they were there.' She explained what the children had said and how she'd reassured them. 'People underestimate children but they're observant, often more so than adults. Now with the war, boys and girls pass around not only British but those American spy, detective and superhero adventure comics. As a result, many of them are inclined to see evil round every corner and be the hero who defeats it. However, from Diana's description, I did wonder if the strange man could have been that Mr Knight I told you I saw at Walter Clarke's farm before.'

Had the number of comics she'd confiscated during lesson time influenced Victoria as well? Or was it government messaging about staying alert and prepared for the possibility of a German invasion, combined with the work Louis had asked her to do, that made her more suspicious than she'd ever been before?

'Good job, all of you.' Louis knocked his knuckles against the back of the seat in a staccato rhythm. 'I was right, then.'

'Right about what?' Victoria turned into a side road, a shortcut to the manor which avoided the route through the centre of the village.

'Sorry, thinking aloud.' His laugh was low. 'There's a dance in Whittleton tonight. I don't suppose you'd fancy going with me? Lots from the nearby RAF base and local villages will be there.'

'A dance?' Victoria stopped for a cattle crossing and waved at the farmer, one of Nell's many admirers and to whom, like the others, she remained oblivious.

'Yes, a dance. You know when a man and woman move together to music?' Louis chuckled and then paused until the cattle crossed and the farmer moved on. 'But I'd also need your help. You wouldn't be in any danger, you'd only watch, listen and report back as you're doing now.'

Which already felt like too much. She was inexorably being pulled into both the war and Louis's life, and while part of her wanted to exercise her usual caution, another wanted to leap forwards without considering the consequences. She changed gear and watched a flock of birds soar above a newly ploughed field.

'Or we'd just dance and drink lemonade and talk. More than anything else, I'd like your company. It's up to you.'

As the silence between them lengthened, Victoria mentally shook herself. Except for Nell, Beatrice and the Misses Grainger, women went to dances all the time. If Louis hadn't been called away because of work, she'd have gone to a dance with him long before now.

'Yes, I'd be pleased to go with you.' She turned the motor into the entrance to the manor, a long, gravel drive lined with tall oak trees. 'I'll help as well.' Because it was another way of doing her duty.

'Good.' Louis leaned over the seat and squeezed Victoria's shoulder.

She wanted to go to the dance for more than wartime duty. And despite the barrier of her dress and coat, even as they left the car she could still sense the warm imprint of Louis's hand lingering on her skin.

Chapter Twenty

After Louis excused himself to speak with several men in RAF officer uniforms, Victoria sat alone at a small round table near the door in Whittleton's village hall, sipped from her glass of lemonade and watched the dancers. Although Whittleton was less than five miles from Hazelbury, with petrol rationing and only one bicycle for all three teachers to use, it was her first visit here.

From what she'd seen in the purple April twilight, sweet with the fragrance of new blossom, Whittleton had a similar high street to Hazelbury's, and was also lined with flint and pebble or whitewashed buildings. However, unlike Hazelbury, Whittleton hadn't been chosen to host evacuees but instead served an air base which had recently opened nearby. Since she hadn't yet spotted any Hazelbury foster-parents, for one of the few times since arriving in Norfolk all those months ago, Victoria felt less like Miss McKaye the teacher and more the person she used to be before she had to live and breathe school most of her waking hours.

Yet, she still wasn't truly off duty. She had to keep her eyes and ears open for anything that might be of interest to Louis and whomever he worked for in London.

She scanned the couples circling the floor as a three-piece band played Glenn Miller's 'In the Mood', competing with the chatter of voices drifting through a thick cloud of cigarette smoke. Men in Forces uniforms of all ranks mingled with local girls in light dresses, and Victoria's heart squeezed. Once, she'd been as carefree as those girls, but with her thirtieth birthday only weeks away, she'd long ago left girlhood behind. Apart from her career, she'd nothing to show for her twenties except for that broken engagement and the years she'd wasted on a man unworthy of not only her love but also her respect.

'Sorry to leave you on your own so long.' Louis returned and gave Victoria an apologetic smile.

'It's fine.' Yet Victoria was happier with him by her side. She guessed why he'd chosen this table for two – so they didn't have to make small talk with others – but it made them look like a couple. Although she wanted that closeness with him, she also wasn't sure if she was quite ready to take the next step.

'Having fun?' Louis leaned closer and his warm breath brushed Victoria's cheek.

'Yes, although I didn't expect it to be so crowded.' She gave a carefree laugh as if unaffected by his nearness. 'These days, when I'm not with the children, I'm more used to W.I. meetings, pageant rehearsals and choir practice.'

'That's a pity.' Louis's blue gaze lingered on her, and Victoria felt herself flush.

She was also more used to wearing sensible skirts, blouses, jackets and cardigans than this figure-hugging pale-pink cock-tail dress with its flared skirt, which she hadn't put on since leaving Canada. Even then, she'd only tucked it into her trunk because her mother insisted. And she'd only donned it tonight because Beatrice said no matter what the other women wore, a man like Louis would expect her to be properly, as she put it, 'kitted out'.

'Shall we dance?' He continued to study her and, feeling bolder than usual, Victoria looked at him in return. Albeit in a civilian suit rather than naval uniform, he was still more impressive than any of the other men here. And from his discreet gold-initialled cufflinks to crisp white shirt and striped tie, he was a world away from the labourer who'd stepped from the train a few hours before.

She finished her lemonade, nodded and then took his hand as he led them onto the dance floor and drew her close in a waltz.

'I feel rather out of place, but I had to leave my uniform in London. Still, being a naval man perhaps it's better I don't try to compete with the air force.' He gave her a teasing smile. 'What is it you women say about pilots?'

'I wouldn't know.' Victoria's breath caught at both that smile and the softness in Louis's eyes. 'I live with your great-aunts and two other teachers. None of them talk about pilots or any servicemen except you. I mean...' Her tongue tripped over the words. 'We don't talk about you in that way, either. We're interested in your work and want you to be safe.' She ducked her head which resulted in her almost resting the side of her face against his broad chest. 'Sorry, I—'

'No need to apologise.' As the music changed, Louis guided her into a smooth foxtrot. 'I'm glad you're concerned for my welfare.'

Had he put a particular emphasis on 'you'? Victoria made herself concentrate on the steps. 'You dance well.'

'So do you.' His voice was low, almost intimate.

His hand in hers made her entire body tingle. She was venturing into dangerous water. *Change the subject.* 'You can thank my mother. She insisted my sisters and I take dancing lessons. We went to a studio downtown on Friday after school. It was behind the drugstore with a soda fountain so afterwards we went there for milkshakes. Back then, I couldn't have imagined going to a dance in England.' Or with someone like Louis.

'Tell me more about your family and life in Canada.' He shielded Victoria as several boisterous couples would have bumped into them.

'There's not much to tell. I grew up in a town, not a village. Neepawa, Manitoba. You've likely never heard of it but it was home. Still is in a way.' Her throat tightened as she pictured the big brick house with the wraparound porch set on a leafy corner lot. 'I went ice skating in the winter and swimming at a nearby lake in summer. My family has a summer home, a cabin there so I canoed and hiked, and as a child, one of my favourite things was to stay up late and look at the night sky. All the stars and constellations were magical and with water lapping against the dock and the crackle of a campfire...' Her voice hitched and she swallowed hard. When, if ever, would she do such things again?

'It sounds idyllic.'

'It was.' As she talked on, telling him about her parents and sisters, her teacher training course and coming to England, the gap between her two worlds – two lives – closed, if not fully, then somewhat. She also felt whole in a way she hadn't since Canada had disappeared into the mist when she'd set sail for England and left everything familiar behind.

'I'd like to visit Canada one day.'

'You should.' Even as she mentioned places Louis might enjoy, Victoria knew it was a dream, much like the fairytales she'd once read to her younger sisters. They were pretending, a way of marking time until their real lives resumed, whether with an Allied victory or the unthinkable, under Nazi rule. 'The Rocky Mountains are awe-inspiring. One summer, Mother and I took the train to Vancouver to visit my aunt and uncle and when we stopped in Banff, we...' She paused and looked over Louis's shoulder towards the door.

'What is it?' Louis tightened his hold on her hand.

'No, don't look.' She leaned closer and spoke into his ear. 'One of Walter Clarke's sons, Gerald, is here with several other Hazelbury boys. The Clarke lad looks to be leaving but... could he be meeting someone else?' Victoria tugged Louis towards the door, behind a group of girls flirting with RAF fellows.

When they reached the door and stepped out into the inky night, Louis wrapped one arm around Victoria's shoulders. It didn't mean anything important. He was playing a role, nothing more, but nevertheless she let herself nestle close, like he was truly her sweetheart.

'Which one is the Clarke boy?' Louis twirled a loose strand of Victoria's hair as he spoke into her ear, and awareness flared along her nerve endings.

'The tallest, fair-haired one by the churchyard wall.' She tilted her head towards the darker outline of the parish church next to the hall. Whittleton's church and hall had been built away from the village which huddled over a low rise nearer the sea beyond.

The moon had slipped behind a cloud and with the blackout, the world was filled with shadowy, indistinct wraiths. In the distance, a dog barked, and a girl's high-pitched laugh echoed from a copse of trees.

Louis hugged Victoria tighter as they ambled along a path strewn with dainty, white and pink blossoms from fruit trees in full bloom, which filled Victoria's senses with sweet fragrance. When they reached a low stone wall separating the churchyard from the hall, he guided them behind a bushy hawthorn tree.

An engine sound drew nearer before stopping in front of the church gate.

Victoria held her breath as she and Louis stood, statue-like, hidden by low-hanging branches.

'Hang on, lads. It's me dad.'

Gerald Clarke's voice. He'd been taunting his younger brothers last Saturday when Victoria and Beatrice had arrived to tutor Jimmy. At seventeen, he was already the size of a full-grown man and, from what she'd seen, he didn't hesitate to use his brawn to intimidate anyone smaller or weaker.

'Put that light out.' Gerald's voice was a low growl, and the aroma of a cigarette drifted through the trees. 'I'll go see what Dad wants. Probably thinks I've got a girl.'

Ribald male laughter and jibes rang out as Gerald made his way to the vehicle, swearing when he tripped over a root.

'Over here.' Louis led Victoria deeper into the shadows and then they crouched close together in the damp grass.

'I can't see what they're doing.' She hitched her dress up.

'Nothing – except Walter's giving his son a telling off from the sounds of it.' Louis's voice was threaded with amusement. 'Wait, there's someone else there as well. Keep your head down.'

Victoria did as he said and listened to the murmured voices, too far away to hear what they said.

A door slammed and then the voices stopped as an engine started up again and footsteps crunched on a gravel path.

'Don't know what me dad and Joe are doing here at this time of night.' Gerald's aggrieved voice came from the other side of the trees. 'Where am I going to meet a girl with him keeping me on that farm from dawn to dusk? I goes out for a few hours on a Saturday and it's like I done disgraced him. What'll he say when I turns eighteen and joins the army?'

His mates laughed.

'Here, see what else I got for us. Nicked it from back of pub.' A different voice spoke and appreciative murmurs broke out as what sounded like a bottle was passed around.

Victoria shifted and a stick cracked.

'Hey, who's there?' Gerald shouted.

As he crashed through the trees towards them, Louis pulled Victoria to her feet and covered her mouth with his.

'Oh, sorry. Didn't mean to bother you. Thought it was lads from Whittleton spoiling our fun.' Gerald's voice slurred.

As Louis ended the kiss, Victoria's legs trembled and she buried her face in the front of his jacket.

'Miss McKaye?' Gerald sounded nearer now. 'And Mr Grainger?'

'It's fine. Go about your business.' Louis's voice was firm, like an officer giving an order to a young recruit.

'Yes, Sir, sorry, Sir.' Gerald backed away followed by more laughter from his friends.

'Don't worry.' Louis smoothed Victoria's tumbled hair. 'Gerald and the others will be too embarrassed to say anything – and that's if they even remember what they saw. My guess is they've been at the beer before coming here. If I hear any gossip, I'll deal with it.'

'I doubt anyone will talk around you.' If word got out she'd been kissing Louis by a churchyard like some village girl and her flyboy, how would she ever live down the humiliation? 'What if someone tells your great-aunts or Beatrice? As a teacher, I have to be respectable. I *am* respectable.' Thanks to her broken engagement she'd already become the subject of gossip once before, and knew how hurtful it could be. However, although the kiss was an act, she'd liked it more than she should have. Her face burned as she stepped away.

'Nobody's doubting your respectability, least of all me. If Beatrice or my aunts say anything, tell me and I'll deal with it.' Louis's voice was strained. 'But you're a fine and beautiful woman. I can't be sorry for kissing you.'

She flushed even further at the compliment. He was a hand-some man, one she was attracted to in ways she'd never been to anyone before. If she was honest with herself, she didn't regret kissing him either, only that they'd been interrupted.

'What do we do now?' Victoria shivered in her thin dress, and Louis took off his jacket and wrapped her in its warmth.

'What I'd like to do isn't what we need to, since duty calls.' He gave her a teasing smile and then sobered. 'What do you say about following Walter and Joe to Whittleton?'

Chapter Twenty-One

From her place in the choir stalls, Victoria glanced around Hazelbury's parish church. On this third Sunday morning in May, the ancient building was full. Since Germany had invaded Belgium, Luxembourg, the Netherlands and France over a week earlier, the anxiety in the pews was palpable.

'Let us pray,' Mr Russell intoned.

She bent her head and closed her eyes, but still her thoughts whirled. Logically, she'd understood that German troops reaching Britain was a possibility but now, with the enemy only the width of the English Channel away, the reality of a summer invasion had become terrifyingly real. While skulking around Whittleton with Louis in pursuit of Walter Clarke and Joe, who'd turned out to be the man with the baker's van at Cromer railway station, had been fruitless, that didn't mean the two men hadn't collected their delivery somewhere else.

From the small part of it Victoria had seen, the Norfolk coast was isolated, wild and dotted with hiding places for those who needed them. Her stomach rolled, and she gripped the edges of her hymn book harder.

'Victoria.' Beatrice's voice hissed by her ear.

'Right, sorry.' As the organ wheezed into life, she stood with the rest of the choir for the final hymn, and then the now familiar words of 'Jerusalem' washed over her.

To Victoria's right, Nell's beautiful high soprano rose above the others and echoed off the stone walls. This church and village had withstood previous wars and Victoria had to keep the faith and remain hopeful like everyone else.

Her gaze rested on Louis in the manor pew between Miss Grainger and Miss Adelaide. The two women stood ramrod straight as if single-handedly prepared to defy even a lone German from reaching England's shores.

After the hymn came to its rousing conclusion and the vicar dismissed the congregation, Mrs Meldrum helped Victoria gather up the anthem music and hymnbooks.

'I do think "Abide with Me" would have been more appropriate than "Jerusalem" but, of course, we must defer to what our dear vicar thinks best.'

'Of course.' Victoria kept her expression solemn. Trust Mrs Meldrum to never be short of an opinion. However, as she'd got to know her, Victoria had also come to recognise that she was always the first to offer a helping hand and, despite her propensity to gossip, beneath her often gruff exterior and critical manner lay a kind and generous heart.

'We're almost finished making the pageant costumes, so they'll be ready for the dress rehearsal. Many hands made light work, as the saying goes.' Mrs Meldrum finished stacking music and hymnals into tidy piles as Beatrice and Nell hung up the dark-red choir gowns.

'We appreciate all you and everyone else are doing to support the pageant. The whole village is involved in one way or another. From sewing to making scenery and selling tickets, it's truly a community effort.' Victoria left the choir stalls and followed Mrs Meldrum into the main body of the church.

'It's our duty, isn't it? The usual social distinctions don't apply in wartime.' Mrs Meldrum chivvied Wilf along from where he'd paused to study one of the stained-glass windows. 'We're all in it together is what I say, even though some might not agree with me.' She jerked her chin towards Major Bertram's mother, who was visiting Hazelbury at the invitation of a former school friend. 'The Misses Grainger understand the old ways are changing. Look at how they've accepted Miss Potter.'

'What about her?' Victoria lowered her voice as they came out of the church and into the fresh May day.

'Well, you know – a girl like her. Working class, although to her credit she must have got a scholarship place at a grammar school and is certainly trying to better herself.' Mrs Meldrum spoke out of one side of her mouth. 'I knew what and where she came from as soon as she got off the coach that day. She's a Cockney make no mistake, right from London's East End.'

'I hope you aren't suggesting Nell should be ashamed of her family or where she grew up?' Victoria bristled on behalf of her friend.

'No, indeed.' Mrs Meldrum shook her head so vigorously the brooch pinned to her hat vibrated. 'I expect they're good, honest, hardworking people even though they're not *our* sort. Certainly not Miss Wentworth's either. Such a shame about her family. Their circumstances were so greatly reduced after the last war.'

'If you'll excuse me, Miss Grainger is summoning me.' Victoria made her escape and let out a sigh of relief as she joined the group from the manor at the church gate. Whatever had happened to Beatrice's family was Beatrice's business. Like that kiss Victoria couldn't stop thinking about was only between herself and Louis. No gossip had reached Victoria's ears and now, several weeks later, it was likely Gerald Clarke had either decided discretion was the better part of valour or had indeed been too drunk to remember what he'd seen.

'What did Mrs Meldrum want?' Nell fell into step in between Beatrice and Victoria as they followed Louis and the Misses Grainger back to the manor.

'Nothing, really. It was about the pageant costumes mostly. Just think, in under a month it will be over.'

Beatrice groaned. 'Please don't remind me. I found more grey hairs this morning. I'm certain those recitations our juniors are doing are responsible. One of the boys still hasn't learned his poem, despite me working with him for weeks now.'

'Your hair is so fair any grey doesn't show.' Nell patted her own dark tresses. 'When I get my first grey hair, it will stand out for sure.'

Although Victoria hadn't found any grey hairs yet, they couldn't be far off. Hopefully, her thirtieth birthday this coming Wednesday would go unremarked. She hadn't mentioned it, so there was no way for anyone here to know.

As Beatrice and Nell talked about the pageant, she blinked away unexpected moisture behind her eyes. She wasn't a child and her birthday wasn't important. She was missing her family and worried about the war, was all. Slowing her steps, she pulled out a handkerchief and patted her eyes.

'All right?' As they left the village, Louis hung back and waited for Victoria while the others went ahead.

'Fine.' She blinked. 'Lots of blossom out. It's making me sneezy.' She gestured to the fragrant hedgerow that lined both sides of the narrow country lane.

'I see.' Louis dug in his jacket pocket and passed her a pristine white handkerchief to replace her ink-stained one.

'Sorry.' She swallowed hard and gave him a bright smile. 'My sisters used to tease me about never having a clean handkerchief.'

He nodded as if it were of no consequence. 'Everyone at church was talking about the pageant. What you, Beatrice and Nell are doing is fantastic for morale.' Louis kept his gaze averted as Victoria blew her nose and got her emotions under control.

'It's become much bigger than we expected, but it's helping the evacuees become a true part of the village.' Thank goodness Louis had changed the subject. Victoria didn't want to think or talk about her family right now. Or how, even once her children reached adulthood, her mother still celebrated their birthdays as the special days she insisted they were. 'I've heard that elsewhere the London children haven't been made to feel so welcome as they are here. It's lovely to see the local boys and girls bringing the Londoners into their games. We want our children to learn from the villagers and vice versa.'

A group of boys tore past them in the lane, and Ralph waved as he and Jimmy Clarke whooped.

'We're hunting big game in Africa, Miss,' Ralph shouted. 'I'm a hunter and Jimmy's a lion.' He brandished a stick like it was a gun.

Louis laughed. 'Is that the kind of mutual learning you had in mind?'

'Not on a Sunday, no, but they're having fun.' As they turned in at the manor's gate, Victoria had to laugh too, especially because Beatrice glanced over her shoulder at the boys and shook her head with a disapproving expression. 'Children don't have enough chances to be carefree these days. When I think about the ones in other countries, the Jewish children especially, I appreciate every moment of light-hearted fun and any semblance of ordinary life my pupils can find.'

'That's what we're fighting for, isn't it? The future of all our children. Like our parents did for us,' Louis said.

'Yes, although mine never expected the world to be engulfed in another war so soon.' As they walked up the drive to the front steps, the ache in Victoria's chest throbbed. She couldn't let herself think of anything but the here and now on this bright May day with Louis. 'I wonder what we're having for lunch. Beatrice and Nell wouldn't let me help earlier and—'

'Surprise.' The front door of the manor house flew open and Nell's face popped out followed by Beatrice and then the Misses Grainger. 'Happy Birthday,' they sang as Lady, wearing an enormous pink ribbon bow around her neck, barked.

'Happy Birthday,' Louis joined in.

'How... you knew? All of you?' She glanced around the circle. 'But my birthday's not until Wednesday.'

'I won't be here then.' Louis took her arm as they went up the steps and into the hall where a homemade birthday banner hung above the dining-room door. 'It's not much but your mother wrote to Aunt Addie about your birthday and said your family always made birthdays special for you. From there, we all plotted.'

'I made you a chocolate cake because your mum wrote that it's your favourite.' Nell's face shone with excitement. 'It was tricky with no eggs, milk or butter but I managed. I got the recipe out of one of the magazines Mrs Meldrum shared with me.'

'I made the banner from the end of a worn sheet left over from a pageant costume.' Beatrice gestured to the profusion of spring flowers painted around the colourful 'Happy Birthday' script.

'Come into the dining room.' Miss Adelaide took Victoria's other arm and gave it a gentle squeeze. 'We're having a cold luncheon. I hope that's all right? More a tea party, really, but your mother was certain that's what you'd prefer.'

'It's perfect.' Victoria put a hand to her face as she took in the table set with starched linen and the finest dishes and crystal and, at her place, Nell's cake and a small stack of parcels wrapped in brown paper. 'Thank you, Miss Grainger. Miss Adelaide. All of you.' She found Louis's handkerchief and patted her eyes again.

'We haven't had a party here for goodness knows how long.' Miss Grainger's voice was almost jovial. 'Not since Louis was a little lad, I suppose.' As Louis and Miss Adelaide guided Victoria to her chair, Miss Grainger followed. 'Whether we like it or not, the world is different now and it will undoubtedly change even more before this war business is over. As such, and after thinking things over, my sister and I have decided that for the duration, the three of you may call us Miss Hetty and Miss Addie.'

'So we must be Beatrice, Nell and Victoria,' Beatrice said.

'Yes,' Victoria agreed and gave Nell an encouraging nod as she went to the kitchen to boil water for tea.

As Miss Hetty chided Louis to 'remove that dog' from the dining room, and Beatrice and Miss Addie followed Nell to the kitchen, Victoria looked from the presents to the cake and then to the gilt-framed portraits of Grainger ancestors that hung on the dark-green papered walls.

Home was a place, but it was also where there were people who cared about you and who you cared about in return.

While she'd always carry her home and family in her heart, now Hazelbury Manor, Nell, Beatrice and the Misses Grainger had a place there too.

Her gaze lingered on Louis as he shut the dining-room door on a disgruntled Lady. While Victoria wasn't ready to put a name to her feelings, Louis had an extra special place in both her life *and* heart.

Chapter Twenty-Two

'That superstition about a frightful dress rehearsal meaning a good show on the day comes to mind, does it not?' On a Thursday afternoon in June, two days before the pageant opened to what Nell grandly called 'their public', Victoria rolled her eyes at Beatrice who stood beside her in front of the village hall's stage.

'Don't wriggle about so.' Crouched on her knees at Albert's side, Ivy, who was helping the children with their costumes, smoothed what was supposed to be Henry the Eighth's cloak. 'There.' She slipped it off Albert's shoulders. 'It will only take me a minute to sew that hem and then you won't trip over it.'

'Maybe we've been too ambitious.' Victoria inclined her head to where Nell tried to remove colourful butterfly wings from ten over-excited small girls. 'That's what Mrs Mann thinks, anyway. I heard her say so when I was in the post office yesterday.' Amidst the bustle of pupils, teachers and mums, the local schoolteacher sat behind Victoria's desk marking exercise books, ignoring the commotion.

'I had a word with her last week.' Beatrice's brow puckered. 'The most recent of many, to be frank. I don't know why Mrs Mann won't pitch in with us. Surely some feud with Mrs Meldrum going back decades can't be the only reason.' In a floral-patterned summer dress and her hair in soft curls pulled back from her face, Beatrice looked younger and more approachable than the severe woman Victoria had met last September. 'Still, it's important that all the children in the village take part, and since we're leading the pageant with the W.I., I suppose Mrs Mann's classes are our responsibility.'

'Except she'll likely take some of the credit if it's a success.' Victoria moved what would be several rows back on the day of the performance. 'Remember to project your voice, Margaret. We want to hear you. You're meant to be a queen. The rest of you, sit quietly and listen.'

As the different scenes, a story of England from the Middle Ages to the modern day, followed one another, Victoria was inclined to agree with Mrs Mann that they'd tackled too big a project. Rather than sweeping open on a medieval village, the red velvet curtain instead fell on top of the actors. Many of the children forgot their lines, and the mums and W.I. members behind the scenes were kept busy altering ill-fitting costumes.

By the time they reached what was supposed to be the grand finale, Victoria had stopped letting herself imagine what else might go wrong. She only wanted the dress rehearsal to be over so she could go home and put her feet up, preferably in a dark, quiet room. However, given the dire news coming from the German assault on France, none of them could relax at home either. If France fell, Great Britain would stand alone – the thought of which made Victoria's stomach churn and wish she could hide under the bed like she'd done as a child during thunderstorms.

'Peter, turn to face the audience, like Diana does.' Victoria gestured to the children on stage. 'That's right. Now for Diana's song.' At the piano, Beatrice played the opening chords, and Victoria exhaled. Diana was a natural performer and the one child they could count on. No matter what else was an abysmal failure, they'd end on a high note.

A crash sounded, children screamed and Victoria stumbled and fell as Jimmy Clarke dragged her from her spot.

'What on earth?' In the sudden silence and covered in plaster dust, Victoria stared at what should have been the ceiling almost above her head where a triangular piece of blue sky was now visible.

'Were it a bomb, miss? Is Hitler come here to get us?' A child's voice quavered and muffled sobs broke out.

'It wasn't a bomb and of course Hitler's not here.' From behind the piano, Beatrice's calm voice rose above the hubbub. 'Don't worry, children. Stay where you are for a moment, please. We'll come to you. Are any of you hurt? If you can, raise one hand.'

'All right, Miss?' Jimmy still held Victoria's arm as she half-lay near an overturned chair.

'I think so.' She put her other hand to her head, blinked and brushed away dust. 'But the ceiling and roof...' Her voice trailed away as she looked at the gaping hole.

'I reckon it weren't fixed properly after that there leak neither at Christmas nor before,' Jimmy said.

'But both those leaks happened months ago.' Victoria coughed and shook herself like Lady did after rolling in garden clippings. *The children.* She had to see to her pupils. If only she weren't so dizzy.

'Here.' Nell eased Victoria into a sitting position. 'If not for Jimmy's quick thinking, parts of the ceiling and roof would have landed right on top of you. Good work, lad.'

Jimmy mumbled and flushed red.

'But our pupils... the pageant.' Jumbled thoughts buzzed in Victoria's head.

'Nobody's injured, only a bit of shock. As for the pageant... I doubt the ceiling and roof can be fixed in time for Saturday.' Nell frowned.

Victoria dropped her head into her hands. All the work they'd done for naught – to say nothing of the children's disappointment.

'What's this about the pageant?' Mrs Meldrum's voice rang out. 'You won't let a partially collapsed roof and ceiling stop it, will you? We're made of sterner stuff in Hazelbury. All of us, even you London lot.'

'Of course we are,' Mrs Mann added with a nod to Mrs Meldrum, whatever old grievance that had kept them at loggerheads for years temporarily forgotten in the moment of crisis.

Murmured agreement echoed around the room.

'But I… I didn't think you were keen on the pageant.' Victoria raised her head, and Mrs Mann patted her shoulder.

'I wasn't at first. But now? Well, especially because you aren't being moved on, we all have to work together, don't we? Muck in, as the young people say even though I don't hold with slang.' Mrs Mann shook her head. 'I said from the beginning of the evacuation scheme that the coast was no place to bring children or their teachers. Finally, the government has seen sense.'

Victoria gave a non-committal nod. In late May, the government had extended the evacuation zone so children from Great Yarmouth to Cromer, locals as well as evacuees, were moved farther inland. Here in Hazelbury, they were a half-mile far enough from the coast for the children and teachers from Park Road School to stay where they were. However, while the teachers tried to keep life as normal and ordinary as possible for their pupils, true safety from German bombers anywhere was an illusion, even more so close to an RAF base as they were to Whittleton.

'Besides…' Mrs Mann lowered her voice and knelt at Victoria's side. 'I'm grateful for what you and Miss Wentworth are doing for young Jimmy. I tried but…' She shrugged.

'I didn't know you knew. We didn't mean to overstep.' Victoria's gaze darted to Jimmy who, along with several mums, was directing children out of the hall.

Mrs Mann harrumphed. 'How could I not? Jimmy's finally reading with greater fluency, isn't he? He must have had help from someone. I asked a few questions and then put two and two together. I may be set in my ways but I suppose I need to heed my own advice. As I tell my pupils, it's never too late to learn.'

'Thank you.' Victoria stood. As she and Mrs Mann had been speaking, the hall had emptied and children and adults now congregated on the small patch of lawn fronting onto the road.

'Pop along and tidy yourself while I help Miss Wentworth and Miss Potter get the children out of their costumes and dismiss them. Then we can clear up here, put our heads together and find somewhere else to hold the pageant.' Mrs Mann pushed her shoulders back. 'Whittleton Hall might be a possibility. The terrace overlooking the gardens could be just the thing. Or, I should say – what *were* the gardens before they were ploughed up to grow vegetables.'

Even as a glimmer of hope flickered in Victoria's heart, she had to be practical. 'What if it rains on Saturday?'

'Folk can bring umbrellas, can't they? We'll also set up tents. Major Bertram will have what's needed or if he doesn't, he'll know how and where to find them. The Scouts used to camp at Whittleton. My son had wonderful times there.' Mrs Mann's expression softened before she turned away.

Before today, Victoria had never exchanged more than a few words with Mrs Mann, and only about school matters. She'd never heard mention of her having a son, either, but perhaps she'd been too quick to judge based solely on the teacher's brusque manner. From now on, she'd try harder to get to know her.

Skirting scattered debris, Victoria made her way to the small kitchen tucked on one side of the hall, but prior to using the pitcher of water and basin to wash her face, she'd shake the dust from her clothes. Opening the kitchen door, she went into the narrow paved area abutted by the brick-and-stone lavatory, its door propped open and fields and woods beyond.

Hidden from any passersby, she raised her skirt and shook it and then took off her cardigan and shook it too.

At a sneeze, she clutched her cardigan close to her blouse. There wasn't anyone in the lavatory. The door was still propped open as it had been moments ago, and she'd have seen or heard someone coming around the side of the hall.

Victoria backed towards the open kitchen door and scanned the fields. Empty. Then her gaze slid to the woods in time to see a figure dart into them and disappear. With the angle of the afternoon sun, she couldn't tell whether it was a man or woman, young or old, in uniform or not.

She drew in a shaky breath, went into the kitchen and locked the door behind her. Had the person been watching her from behind the lavatory? A fast runner could cover the distance between the hall and woods in less than a minute. If they'd run in a straight line behind the lavatory, they wouldn't have been visible until having to cut across to the trees.

She hadn't taken off her clothes but whoever it was would have seen her legs and the tops of her stockings. Although it wasn't much more than she'd have displayed in her swimming costume, her heart still pounded and heat flashed through her body at the subterfuge and being spied on.

The local police constable hosted one of her evacuees. She'd call in there on her way back to the manor and make a report. If there was a Peeping Tom in the village, Constable Smith needed to be informed. Then, as she smoothed her clothing and splashed water on her face, fear replaced her initial anger and made her insides freeze.

She and everyone else had assumed the hall's ceiling falling in was an accident because of where the roof had leaked before. But what if it wasn't? And what if that shadowy figure wasn't interested in Victoria at all but had instead been watching and waiting for something or someone else?

Chapter Twenty-Three

Despite Victoria's worries about the weather, the day of the pageant dawned sunny and warm. And while Whittleton Hall's wide stone terrace overlooked a potato patch instead of what less than a year ago had been a rose garden, it was still a more than adequate substitute for the village hall's stage.

In the nearby drawing room, which Major and Mrs Bertram had mostly cleared of furniture so it could serve as a backstage area and dressing space, Nell and Victoria peeked through a gap in the damask curtains at the gathered crowd.

'I heard people have come from all over,' Nell said. 'Cromer, Sheringham and even beyond. Took buses, they did and are making a day of it.'

'It makes sense, what with the petrol shortage and most people not having a car anyway.' Victoria twitched the curtains closed and turned back to the drawing room. She'd decided not to involve Constable Smith and set aside her undoubtedly overactive imaginings when it came to the hall roof and that figure running into the woods, until she spoke to Louis. He'd been away since Dunkirk, that nail-biting time when British and Allied forces were evacuated from northern France, and Victoria and the others had sat by the wireless, their only consolation knowing Louis was safe in London. However, he was supposed to arrive in Hazelbury by midday. Now, he was presumably in the audience with Miss Hetty and Miss Addie, but today was only about the children and the pageant they'd spent months working on.

Here, backstage, a sense of calm purpose had replaced the chaos of the dress rehearsal. From the quiet hum of children having a last run-through of lines with their teachers, now including Mrs Mann, to a group of older boys making some last-minute adjustments to props and scenery, an excited buzz filled the air.

As Major Bertram and Mr Russell entered the drawing room to wish everyone good luck and then continued out to the terrace to welcome the audience, Beatrice and Nell hovered with Victoria by the piano that had been placed by a door leading to the terrace.

'In a way, not being able to use the village hall may have been a blessing in disguise.' Beatrice sat on the piano bench and opened her sheet music for the opening song. 'I don't mean it hasn't been difficult to move the performance here, but everyone has pitched in and petty differences seem to have been forgotten.' She nodded towards Mrs Mann who, since their arrival, had told anybody within earshot that the pageant was precisely what Hazelbury needed.

'Mrs Mann also told the vicar's wife that our pageant was "a bit of cheer" in these dark times,' Nell said from where she now stood holding the prompt book. 'You could have knocked me over with a feather when I heard her.'

Victoria smiled to herself. Mrs Mann had certainly come up trumps and nothing had been too much trouble for her, or indeed Major and Mrs Bertram. Even Major Bertram's mother, still as imposing as that day she'd swept off the train in Cromer, had said it was 'all quite exciting' and reminded her of 'theatricals' in her youth.

'Is everyone ready?' Victoria turned back to the children who nodded gravely. 'We know you'll do your best but if something does go wrong, keep going.' An adage that was apt for life as well. 'All right.' She nodded to Beatrice at the piano to begin the overture and guided the first performers onto the terrace, staying out of sight behind a curtain strung between two sides of a garden trellis.

When the music ended, Pauline, one of the village girls and Mrs Mann's pupil, moved forwards to the centre of the stage. As Clio, the muse of history, she held a scroll and told the audience about the programme to come.

'Our Wilf's sweet on that Pauline,' Albert said in a loud whisper from where he waited with the other infants ready to portray birds and animals of the Norfolk countryside. 'Whenever he sees her in her dad's shop or says her name, his ears go all red.'

'No talking backstage, remember?' Victoria hid a smile. Over the past months, she'd grown to love these children and seeing them grow and flourish filled her with pride. 'There, hear Miss Wentworth's music? That's your cue.'

One by one, a brown hare, badger, barn owl, hedgehog, red fox, golden oriole and others, all in ingenious homemade costumes, hopped, skipped and wriggled across the terrace in a simple dance as Beatrice accompanied them on the piano. When Peter, a grey seal, waved a small flipper at his mum and baby sister, the audience broke into applause, and Victoria's heart swelled with even more pride.

Almost an hour later, Ivy murmured into Victoria's ear as they stood together in the makeshift wings, 'The children are doing ever so well, aren't they?'

Victoria nodded and kept her gaze fixed on the stage where Diana and two other girls marched as suffragettes carrying purple, white and green banners inscribed with 'Votes for Women'. From medieval times through the English Civil War to a lively tableau focused on the coastal fishing industry and more, they'd almost reached Norfolk in the present day.

'Hold on, Albert. All you boys, be quiet.' Ivy grabbed Albert's arm as he mimicked the suffragettes, including the smallest one who dropped her banner and narrowly escaped getting her feet caught up in it.

'Sorry, Miss.'

Victoria gave them her sternest look, but Albert's cheeky grin was enough to soften the hardest heart – which hers wasn't.

'When's it time for the fruit cordial and buns Mrs Bertram said her cook made for us?' Ralph tugged Ivy's arm.

'You'll be having your drinks and such soon, but first you're all on stage for the finale,' Ivy said as the suffragettes came into the wings. 'Get into your places and no pushing.'

Until the dress rehearsal and now again today, Victoria hadn't recognised Ivy's leadership potential. The girl was intelligent as well. It was a shame she hadn't been able to continue her education, but it wasn't too late for her to make more of herself. If Victoria spoke to Beatrice and Mrs Russell, perhaps Ivy could help with the infants' class next year. Almost without noticing, Victoria had finally resigned herself to the war not being over soon.

She rolled her tight shoulders. If only she could have a proper bath in a tub with hot water from the tap instead of heating water which, once it reached that wretched copper tub, was only lukewarm. Although she'd adjusted to many things here, the lack of indoor plumbing was still a daily annoyance. At least she could enjoy the gorgeous cake of rose-scented soap Louis had given her for her birthday. He'd also given her a book about British birds, perfectly acceptable presents for her to open in front of his great-aunts and the others. Nevertheless, there had been a look in his eyes as she opened them that—

'Miss?' A childish voice pulled her out of her preoccupation.

'What is it, Sheila?'

'You said I could be the oriole for the finale and Betty's to be the mole but Betty won't give me the bird costume.' An aggrieved face framed by curly dark hair looked up at Victoria.

'So I did. Come quickly and I'll help you both change.' As Victoria passed Beatrice at the piano she gestured to her to play the between scenes music longer. 'In here.' She ushered Sheila and Betty behind a large wardrobe and curtained area in front of a fireplace. A telephone rang in the front hall outside the drawing room, and then Major Bertram's voice rumbled. 'All set.' She adjusted the oriole's wings, now worn by Sheila. 'Don't argue, Betty. If I hear any more grumbling you won't take part in the finale at all. There you go, right behind Peter.'

As the entire cast filed out onto the terrace, Diana took her place front and centre between Pauline, still the muse of history, and Wilf as the new prime minister, Winston Churchill, in a borrowed brown Homburg hat, jutted jaw and unlit cigar stuck out one corner of his mouth.

'Almost there.' Nell patted Victoria's shoulder.

'Thank goodness. After these last few weeks I…' Victoria paused as Beatrice stopped playing mid-chord, and Major Bertram brushed past them. 'What now?' she mouthed.

Beatrice shrugged and shook her head.

'I'm sorry to interrupt what has I'm sure we all agree been a wonderful performance from these talented children.' Major Bertram spoke into the sudden silence. 'However, I have only moments ago received a telephone call from London.' He hesitated. 'France has today conceded defeat to Germany. Great Britain is left to stand alone, undefeated and defiant against the enemy in its relentless surge across European soil.'

Amidst gasps and exclamations, Victoria glanced between Nell and Beatrice. What were they to do now?

As the younger children milled about and the older ones stood motionless, Victoria met Beatrice's gaze. Together they moved onto the stage followed by Nell and Mrs Mann. It was up to them to set an example and reassure the children.

Reaching Major Bertram's side, Beatrice asked him to call for quiet as all the teachers got their pupils back into place.

'There is no better time for our final number,' Beatrice said, her clear voice carrying above the last bit of murmuring. 'The children have worked hard and we will finish the pageant as planned.'

As Beatrice returned to the piano, and Pauline and Wilf delivered their closing lines, Victoria got a lump in her throat.

'In this time of peril, we stand together as one.' Wilf's voice rang out like an ancient battle cry.

'And we are still writing our history.' Pauline stood tall and graceful with her scroll. 'Do not lose faith or hope.'

Then, after Beatrice's piano introduction, Diana sang the first words of 'There'll Always Be an England'.

The backs of Victoria's eyes stung and she blinked away tears when everyone, children and audience, joined in to drown out the piano and carry the song on their own.

She linked arms with Nell and Beatrice who came back onto the terrace as the crowd started the song again, this time unaccompanied. They were in this war together, a real war, London teachers, pupils and villagers. Her gaze scanned the audience. Although she couldn't see him, Louis was here. She knew and felt it with the same certainty as her own name.

Together. The word slid through her mind and settled. Solid, right and enduring.

Chapter Twenty-Four

'What do you think?' On the Saturday a fortnight after the pageant, Louis glanced at Victoria from the seat of one of the two bicycles Major and Mrs Bertram had found stored in a shed at Whittleton Hall.

'It's a miracle. Having a bicycle for each of us will save so much time on walking, especially when visiting evacuees in their host family homes.' Victoria pedalled along the lane beside him, the warm breeze blowing loose strands of hair around her face. 'With the summer holidays coming up we'll also be able to go farther afield for picnics and such.'

'Even if we're not truly on holiday, and the only time off we'll have from teaching is just over a fortnight because of the war.' On Victoria's other side, Beatrice sat astride another cycle and Nell brought up the rear on Louis's old one which Beatrice and Victoria had taught her how to ride. 'Last summer, my mother and I went to Paris with friends and I also had a week by the sea in Torquay. Still, we have to make the best of things. There's lots much worse off.'

'Even when they're not in the classroom for formal lessons, the children will still need us. We give them continuity. It's nice to be needed, don't you think?' Nell said as they all braked to a stop at the village crossroads.

'It is, but apart from actual classroom teaching, I expect our so-called holiday will be more of the same work we're already doing.' Beatrice straightened her straw hat as they waited for a tractor driven by a land girl to pass. 'Even in the past forty-eight hours, I've had to sort two problems with foster-parents and take Wilf to hospital in Norwich.'

'At least he didn't have appendicitis the day of the pageant,' Victoria said.

'There is that, but I'm not Wilf's mother, I'm his teacher. I shouldn't have to deal with something like that.' Beatrice shook her head.

'With the vicar and Mrs Russell away, you did the best you could and Wilf's recovering well.' Victoria watched as Louis helped the land girl fix a problem with the farm wagon hitched to the tractor.

'Thank goodness.' Beatrice remounted her bicycle. 'See you later. Good luck with Jimmy, and enjoy your picnic.'

Nell and Beatrice waved as they continued on into the village, Beatrice to the chemist's and draper's shops for Miss Addie, and Nell to help Mrs Russell and Ivy with baking for the church fete.

'The Clarke farm next?' Louis cleaned his grease-stained hands on a rag and returned it to the land girl, who drove the tractor and wagon into the lane. 'We can cut along the edge of the fields and then through the path in the woods.'

'Yes.' Victoria's stomach knotted. On the outside, she was an ordinary schoolmistress dropping off books and work for a pupil who'd missed several days of school. Underneath, she was increasingly being drawn into a clandestine world she didn't understand but, according to Louis, one in which she had an important role to play. 'Any more news?' She spoke softly and out of the side of her mouth.

He nodded. 'The net is closing in on the drake.'

On the bike's handlebars, Victoria's palms grew clammy. The drake was the name Louis had given Mr Knight, Walter Clarke's visitor who'd gone to the wrong side of the car the first day Victoria and Beatrice were at Upper Yarrow Farm to tutor Jimmy. He had also likely been the stranger in the lane with Walter whom Diana and Peter had seen from the vicarage garden.

'What about the ducklings?' She glanced around as they rode onto a bumpy track alongside a golden wheat crop that waved gently in the breeze.

'All growing nicely.' Louis glanced over his shoulder. 'Watch for ruts.'

Victoria swerved. The 'ducklings' were Walter Clarke and several others, including Joe who'd alighted from the baker's van at Cromer station. While the identity of whoever had been behind the lavatory after the pageant dress rehearsal was still a mystery, the cause of the hall's roof collapse was 'almost certainly an accident'. That's what the builder who'd come from Norwich to repair it said, but Victoria couldn't shake a persistent niggle of doubt.

She wiped a hand across her hot face. Only a few more minutes and they'd enter the cooler shade of the woods. The path would be wider there and they could cycle side by side.

'If we – get down.' Aircraft engines roared, Louis grabbed Victoria's bicycle and she slid off it.

Heart pounding, she covered her head with her book bag and lay flat amidst the wheat. 'Us or them?'

'Them.' The bicycles rattled as Louis shoved them aside and then he rolled half on top of her.

The noise increased until the ground shuddered beneath them.

So far, the Luftwaffe had mostly bombed English Channel convoys and ports. *RAF airfields*. Were they targeting Whittleton or maybe the defences being built along England's East Coast? Those pillboxes and other fortified structures meant to protect the country from invasion.

After what felt like hours but was likely only minutes, the aeroplane noise faded, Louis slid off her and Victoria raised her head. The big blue Norfolk sky dotted with puffy white clouds soared above them as tranquil as usual.

Louis scanned the sky. 'They're gone.'

'What… how did you… was it the aircraft markings? That's how you knew they weren't ours?' Despite the sunshine, she trembled.

He nodded and held out a hand to help Victoria to her feet. 'I've also seen them before on the south coast.'

'Oh.' A part of Louis's life she couldn't ask him about.

He brushed dirt and grass off his shirt and trousers and gestured to the flattened stalks of wheat. 'I'll explain what happened to the farmer. He's a good sort and will understand.'

'Thank you.' Victoria spoke through numb lips. 'I… I…' She stuttered to a stop and hugged herself.

The German pilots would have seen them from their cockpits. Like a cat pouncing on a mouse, they could have ended Victoria's life in an instant. She would never have seen her family and friends in Canada again. Nor Beatrice, Nell nor her pupils. Thirty, which on her birthday had seemed old, was no age at all to die. She had so many things she wanted to do and experience – and to think that, but by chance, it could have ended here in a sunny forenoon in an ordinary English field. Although the pilots likely wouldn't have wasted a bomb or other ammunition on two people out for a bicycle ride, she couldn't think rationally right now. Her whole body shook, and she clutched Louis's hand.

'It's all right.' All of a sudden Louis's arms were around her and his hands threaded through her loosened hair. Her hat must have fallen off as she'd scrambled to the ground. Or maybe it had been because of her book bag. Then, not knowing whether she moved first or he did, their mouths met, for real this time, not like that evening of the dance.

As he kissed her, she kissed him back and wrapped her arms around him, the muscles in his back tight beneath his shirt.

In the distance, an air raid siren wailed and explosions rang out. Louis stopped, took his mouth away from where it hovered close to Victoria's but he still clasped her tight.

Emotions rushed through her: fear, desire and, despite everything, maybe even that love she'd tried to suppress. She touched a hand to her lips which held the imprint of Louis's kiss.

'That's Hazelbury's siren at the police station – and see?' He pointed to a flotilla of black dots soaring up into the sky towards the coast. 'Those are our fighter planes. They'll be from Whittleton. And the Luftwaffe.' He pointed at the aircraft the RAF planes pursued. 'The Germans must have circled around and attacked from the northeast. They can't have been spotted on radar until the last minute.'

Victoria shook even more as clouds of smoke rose in the distant haze. 'Did they bomb Whittleton airfield?'

'Must have.' Louis drew her back into his chest so her face rested on his shoulder, the beat of his heart through his shirt steadying her. 'It wasn't a civilian target.'

'Civilian or military, there are people on airfields. Like the vicar and Mrs Russell's sons, Diana's brother. Mrs Meldrum's niece who works in a canteen on an RAF base. The boys at that dance.' All young and with their whole lives ahead of them.

'It's war, Victoria.' Louis's voice was gruff.

She buried her face in his shoulder and hot tears leaked out of the corners of her eyes. She knew it was war and understood what it meant, but for the first time, the destruction wasn't something she'd heard about on the wireless or saw in news-paper photographs but immediate, visceral and close to home.

Chapter Twenty-Five

Victoria shook her head at Louis when he drew his bicycle to a halt by a bubbling woodland stream. 'I can't eat anything, but you go ahead.' Although she'd stopped shaking, almost half an hour later she kept replaying the German bombing over and over again in her mind. The roar of the planes. The smoke drifting across the horizon. And the black dots in the air where young men were intent on killing each other.

'I'm not hungry either. Doesn't feel quite right to picnic, does it?' Louis gave her a half-smile as he replaced the top on his water flask.

'No.' Victoria pressed a hand to her rolling stomach. Happiness and horror. Horror and happiness. Kissing Louis and then the bombing.

'The only way to cope with it all is to not let yourself think about it.'

'War, you mean?' The air was heavy with heat, and small insects skittered across the narrow stream. 'How can I not when the Luftwaffe are on our doorstep? Next thing you know, Nazis will be goose-stepping along Hazelbury's high street.' As they set off again, Victoria rode alongside Louis on a path near the lane to the Clarke's farm.

'Never! None of us will let the Germans take over our country.' Louis's voice was grim. 'Up and down the coast and whether by land, air or sea, we're ready for them. If they do somehow make it past the coastal fortifications, every man, woman and even child will defend England to their last breath. I know I will.'

Victoria hesitated. With his valiant words, Louis meant to reassure her, but all across Europe countries had already fallen to Germany. The Belgians, Dutch and French were no less brave or determined to resist than the British but now they and others were all under Nazi rule.

'I know what you're thinking.' Louis's expression was bleak. 'But I can't let myself doubt. If I do, then it would be as if the Germans have already won.' He stopped and stared into the distance.

Victoria nodded. As at the dance when they'd talked about Louis visiting Canada, they were pretending because the alternative was too awful to contemplate. So, like him, she tried to play the game. 'If any Nazi so much as sets one foot inside my schoolroom they'll wish they hadn't. I'll go after them with… with the fireplace poker.'

'Never underestimate a woman with a fireplace poker.' Louis laughed, lightening the mood. 'Hopefully it won't come to that but we must all be prepared come what may.'

'At the last W.I. meeting, I overheard the postmistress imply that Miss Hetty didn't need to have the cellar in the manor cleared out and made into an air raid shelter. I expect she'll think differently after today. There's a shelter beneath the vicarage too and a tunnel under the pub. That's where I'm to take the children in case of a raid.'

They left the woods and cycled down a low rise into the hedgerow-lined lane, picking up speed as they went.

'When I said all of us will defend England, I didn't mean to take unnecessary risks. Promise me you'll keep yourself safe?' While Louis kept his gaze on the lane the soft care in his tone made Victoria's heartbeat speed up.

'I promise.' Her throat clogged with emotion. 'If you'll do the same. Today, with the aircraft, you protected me in the only way you could and I… I don't think I even thanked you.'

Without thinking of himself, and even though in retrospect they might not have been in any real danger, Louis had instinctively covered Victoria's body with his to try to keep her safe.

Unlike Roy. At a Sunday-school picnic, when they'd been caught in a severe thunderstorm on the open prairie, Roy had found shelter for himself, only belatedly remembering Victoria and the children in her care.

'No thanks needed. If there had been a cave nearby, I'd have hauled you into it but in a field I did the best I could.' Louis glanced over his shoulder as they approached the entrance to Upper Yarrow Farm. 'All set?'

'Yes.' She got off her bicycle and wheeled it up the rutted land as Louis did the same. There was no need to be frightened. She only had to be herself, Jimmy's tutor, and she and Louis had been out for a Saturday cycle and picnic while he had a weekend's leave. Taking a deep breath, she scanned the farm-yard, empty except for several of Mrs Clarke's chickens pecking in the dirt.

'Everyone must be out in the fields.' The curtains on the house were drawn, windows closed, and the place appeared deserted. Leaving her bicycle with Louis, she went to the front door and rapped with the shiny brass horseshoe knocker.

Louis propped both bicycles against the farmyard fence and greeted a bay horse that came over to investigate.

After receiving no answer to her knock, Victoria walked around the side of the house towards the lavatory. A flour-ishing vegetable crop grew in the back garden and the kitchen window was open. She peeked inside, but the wooden table was scrubbed clean and the counter empty except for a wicker basket. At this time of day, she'd have expected to see signs of a midday dinner. Unless, of course, they'd taken their lunch to the fields. Still, why wouldn't Mrs Clarke be here?

She craned her neck to see further and put a hand to her mouth as she glimpsed the basket's contents. Where had all that butter come from? And bacon, ham and sugar? Even for a farming family who were eligible for more rations because of doing manual labour, she hadn't seen such a quantity of foodstuffs in any home since before the war.

Hearing men's voices, Victoria darted away from the window and back around the house.

'Miss McKaye? I didn't expect to see you here today.' Mrs Clarke came out of the lavatory as Victoria sauntered by, pretending to admire the tall pink, white and purple hollyhocks growing beside the house.

'I hoped Jimmy would be at home. I knocked on the front door but there was no answer so I thought to try around back.' She patted her book bag. 'I have some reading and exercises for Jimmy to work on since Miss Potter said he missed lessons this week. He's making wonderful progress.' She forced an innocent smile.

'I see.' Mrs Clarke smoothed her striped housedress. 'That's good, for Jimmy, I mean.' Her hands were red and chapped raw. 'Walter's in the barn but the others are out in the fields. Jimmy too.'

'Have you got any land girls yet?' They came into the farmyard and Victoria spotted Louis speaking with Jimmy and Walter. 'I should think with the size of your farm you'd have been one of the first to be approved.'

'Not yet.' Mrs Clarke stuck her hands in her dress pockets and glanced towards the barn. 'We don't need them really what with all our boys.'

'Miss McKaye.' Jimmy came across the yard to greet her with a broad and honest smile. 'I were telling Mr Grainger about them books you promised me.' His smile turned bashful. 'I mean – *was* telling and *those* books – like you and Miss Wentworth taught me.'

Victoria smiled back, a genuine one this time.

'The boy don't need to spend the weekend doing lessons. He has enough to do on the farm. That's why I kept him home from school.' In contrast to his son, Walter's expression was thunderous. 'Get along to the beet field, lad. You'd no need to come up to the barn in the first place.'

'But that plough blade broke and our Gerald sent me for a—'

158

'The blade's in the shed, not the barn. I'll tan Gerald's hide and yours too. Now git. Begging your pardon Miss McKaye, Sir.' Walter made a shooing motion at his son.

'Please let Jimmy stay for a few minutes,' Victoria said and took an exercise book from her bag. 'I need to explain about the work we've set for him. I understand the farm is important, but if Jimmy doesn't keep up with his lessons, he'll lose some of the good progress he's made.'

'What does a lump like Jimmy need book learning for?' Walter leered at his son. 'He were doin' all right with Mrs Mann, but no, Alma had to stick her oar in and give the boy notions above his station.' He turned to his wife. 'What are you doing out here? It's not time to feed the chickens.'

'I met Miss McKaye outside. I were in the garden when she came looking for Jimmy.' Mrs Clarke's face went pink and she patted her hair. 'I say Jimmy needs book learning. All the boys do. Times are changing.'

Walter's mouth dropped open and he stared at his wife before turning to Victoria. 'Jimmy better be quick about it then. Five minutes and right here in the yard where his mum can keep an eye on him so he don't wander off. He has his head in the clouds most of the time. I'll find the plough blade myself.'

'I'm interested in what you're doing with your sugar beets. My great-aunts will soon have a land girl and…' Louis's voice faded as he walked towards the shed with Walter.

'I'm sorry for Walter's manner. He don't mean nothing by it.' Mrs Clarke's words spilled out. 'It's the war causing him upset. Those German aeroplanes that went over earlier gave me a right turn, circled round our place three times, they did. The house and the barn both. I didn't know what to do, but when they came close and I saw they didn't look like the machines our boys at Whittleton fly, I dashed into the house and hid under the kitchen table since we don't have no cellar. Walter said to pay them no mind. He were in the barn, but I was dreadful shook up.'

'No wonder. It was terrifying. The planes flew over Mr Grainger and me when we were cycling.' Remembering her own fear, Victoria didn't have to feign sympathy. 'Let's sit on the doorstep in the shade. I'll explain the exercises Miss Potter has given Jimmy and you can have a few minutes' rest.' With Walter and the boys, Mrs Clarke must be on her feet from dawn to dusk.

As Victoria sat on the stone stoop between Jimmy and his mum, her thoughts spun. Why would those Luftwaffe planes have circled round Upper Yarrow Farm? Louis had asked her to keep watch here, but were the Germans doing the same? And if so, why?

While the butter, sugar and bacon in that basket in Mrs Clarke's kitchen might have come from the black market or profiteering, whatever was going on went beyond avoiding government rationing and price controls. It was more sinister – and frightening.

Chapter Twenty-Six

After leaving Upper Yarrow Farm and going back by the woodland stream, Victoria spread out a picnic rug and arranged the food she'd packed earlier. 'Now I'm hungry, famished actually.' She sat on the rug and opened the packet of grated carrot, cabbage and chutney sandwiches.

'Thanks.' Louis grinned and took a sandwich from her. 'Do you know, I never thought I'd miss thick-cut ham sandwiches so much? With lashings of good country butter. Not that Nell's chutney isn't good and we're all making do on the ration, but it's the simple, ordinary things I yearn for.'

'You'd have enough butter and ham if you lived with Walter Clarke and his family.' Victoria took a bite of her own sandwich and chewed. She missed having as much ham as she wanted, and butter too, now even more after seeing the lavish provisions in the Clarke's kitchen.

Louis paused mid-bite. 'What do you mean?'

'They're not having to live on the ration.' While leaving the farm and cycling into the woods, mindful of possible eavesdroppers, she and Louis had spoken about everyday things but now, certain they were alone, Victoria couldn't hold back. 'I looked through the kitchen window and almost couldn't believe my eyes. Ham, butter, sugar, bacon and likely more, all in enough quantities to feed the Clarke family and half of Hazelbury.' Anger burned in her chest at the unfairness of it. 'We're all supposed to be sacrificing together – and most of us are.' She gestured to their sandwiches as well as the syrup loaf and carrot biscuits she'd made from government wartime recipes published in one of the newspapers. 'Meanwhile, they're living high with no consideration for anyone else. I've heard of people getting extra food on the black market but I never expected one of our neighbours to be doing it.'

Louis clenched his jaw and his eyes narrowed. 'It goes on more than we'd like to think, even here, and farmers are some of the worst offenders.'

'Oh yes.' Louis nodded at Victoria's wide-eyed stare. 'Farmers make more money selling food on the black market than they do selling it to the government. If you asked Walter Clarke where those extra provisions came from he'd have an excuse like "they fell off the back of a lorry" or some such tale.'

'I suppose the government inspectors can't keep up.'

'No, they can't, so despite the threat of a fine and a prison sentence, people like Walter get away with selling and receiving black market goods.'

'It's treason, that's what it is.' Victoria finished her sandwich. 'I'd report him but I suspect that's not the worst of what Walter's involved in.' She leaned closer to Louis and recounted what Mrs Clarke had said about the German aeroplanes circling the house and barn.

'You're right to suspect his conduct.' Louis glanced around as if to check they were still alone. 'I asked Walter about his sugar beets because one of those fields is near the main barn, and I wanted to have a look round. Although I couldn't get into the barn, luckily a side door hadn't been fully closed. Possibly Gerald looking for that plough blade.'

'And?' Victoria's hand trembled as she packed away the greaseproof paper so it could be reused.

'I only took a quick look, anything more would have been too obvious, but from what I saw the barn was mostly empty. No animal feed or machinery and on the other side of the barn from the sugar beets, there wasn't a crop growing at all. It looked like hedges had been cut down and a ditch filled to try to flatten the land.'

'If it's arable why wouldn't a farmer grow crops there? The country needs any available growing space for food.' Victoria's voice was a mere whisper, and she jumped when a squirrel chattered from a branch overhead.

'Exactly.' Louis's mouth set into a grim line.

'Do you think… could it be that Walter's making an airstrip? For a German plane to land?' Even as she said it, Victoria shook her head. The idea was preposterous, like a story from one of the sensational American dime novels her young cousins devoured. 'Talk in the village is about the Nazis approaching from the sea and then landing and breaching the coastal defences, but what if instead they invaded by air, relying on Nazi sympathisers here to help them?'

'Yes.' Louis beamed and his blue eyes glowed. 'Someone who is to all intents and purposes an ordinary and patriotic British citizen.' He rocked back and forth. 'Of course, we don't have any other evidence and it's certainly not a crime to fill in a ditch or cut down bushes.'

'Walter might have a perfectly good reason for doing those things, and that land might not even be suitable for growing crops. Maybe he's already cleared it with the War Ags.' But Victoria shuddered remembering how Walter had spoken to his wife and Jimmy. Along with all the extra food, such a man didn't seem like someone who'd be concerned with basic human decency, let alone rules and regulations.

'Or maybe not.' Louis paused. 'I say, isn't Mrs Meldrum on the local War Agricultural Executive Committee? When I spoke with her after the pageant, I'm sure she mentioned something. It's not only farmers in the War Ags.'

'I expect she is.' Victoria smiled. Mrs Meldrum never missed an opportunity to be involved in any village or county affair. Local gossip was that she even had her sights set on being elected to the W.I.'s national committee one day.

Louis gave her a boyish grin. 'It should be easy enough to find out. A few minutes in the post office or village shop and some carefully worded questions and—'

'You'll learn more than you ever wanted or needed about all the ways Mrs Meldrum is doing her bit.' They shared a laugh. 'Come to think of it, I've never heard any mention of a Mr Meldrum but not that she's a widow, either. What about him?'

'Before he retired early to spend more time golfing, Mr Meldrum owned several drapers' and haberdashery shops. He started with one and built up a successful business with operations in village high streets across the county. Then he sold the lot and made what's by all accounts a handsome profit.' Louis took one of the carrot biscuits and a slice of syrup cake. 'He's a pleasant fellow but doesn't get out much apart from the golf club. He leaves what he calls the "gadding about" to his wife.'

'Smart man.' Victoria laughed again.

'A self-made one, and in trade, although Mrs Meldrum would never admit it.' Louis shrugged. 'Not that anyone should mind but it still matters to some. Major Bertram's mother, for instance.'

Maybe it mattered to the Misses Grainger as well. Would they disapprove of Louis becoming involved with a woman like Victoria? While she came from a respectable middle-class family, it wasn't one like Louis's with its links to the peerage and centuries of formal ancestral portraits that lined the picture gallery at Hazelbury Manor. On her mother's side Victoria was descended from Lancashire textile merchants while, like him, her father's Edinburgh ancestors were medical and army men.

'We should go back. I have a Red Cross meeting tonight.' Even to her own ears, Victoria's voice sounded brittle.

'It's only gone half-two. Unless the time has all of a sudden changed, your meeting isn't until seven.' Louis rubbed his chin. 'Aunt Hetty and Aunt Addie mentioned going.'

'It's still at seven but I have letters to write and lesson preparation to do beforehand. I also promised Nell and Beatrice I'd help them weed the smaller vegetable garden.' She scattered remaining crumbs for the birds and repacked the picnic, doing her best to avoid his scrutiny. 'You must have things to do as well and since we've done what we came for, we should—'

'We've only done part of what *I* came for.' Louis took Victoria's hands. 'Before, when we kissed but then the bombs dropped, I wanted to tell you… I've wanted to tell you for weeks now, but there's always been someone else around.'

She caught her breath and tried to pull away but he held her hands tight. Was she ready for what he might be about to say? 'I… you mustn't.'

'I mustn't what?' His blue eyes surrounded by thick lashes held her gaze.

'Your great-aunts… they… we can't.' She looked away towards the small stream where water splashed and tumbled against rocks. Insects hummed and a light wind rustled the green leaves, the only sounds to break the stillness.

'I'm my own man, Victoria. I'm also old enough to know my own mind.' He cupped her chin and gently turned her face back towards his. 'As are you.'

'Yes.' With that recent thirtieth birthday, she'd left any last vestiges of girlhood behind. Or maybe she'd become a woman when Roy broke their engagement – but that betrayal had made her wary of trusting another man again.

'I care about you a great deal.' In Louis's clear eyes and face, she saw honesty, yearning and maybe even love.

'I care about you too.' Despite trying to keep her heart safe, she might even love him, but her feelings were too new and fragile to fully understand or trust, let alone express.

'Good.' His eyes twinkled and his smile turned teasing. 'You had me worried there for a moment. As for my great-aunts, have they ever given you a reason to think they might disapprove of us having any kind of understanding with each other?'

'No, not specifically, although Miss Hetty looks at me with what seems like disapproval and as if she suspects there might be something between us. I can't help thinking that she must expect so much more for you than someone like me. You're her only close family.'

'Someone like you?' Louis clasped her hands tighter. 'Don't underestimate yourself. You're intelligent, brave, independent and strong of character. You're also beautiful, the loveliest woman I've ever known.'

'Thank you.' Her breath hitched. When Roy had left her for Letitia, Victoria's confidence and self-belief had been knocked, and it was only now she'd got back the person she'd once been. A woman who didn't need a man to complete her, but one determined to choose the right one for who she was now. 'Apart from the beautiful and lovely part, some men don't see those other things as good qualities.'

'Then they're foolish.' Louis leaned closer until his warm breath feathered Victoria's loose hair. 'As for Aunt Hetty, she's more pragmatic than you might think. The woman I was once engaged to should have been ideal and exactly who she and Aunt Addie would have chosen for me. Until, well, she wasn't. It turns out Evelyn had higher aspirations. She ran off with the youngest son of an earl at a country house party. Left me to "face the music" so to speak.'

'That must have hurt.' Victoria squeezed his hands.

'It did, but I found out who my true friends were.' He gave a half-hearted shrug. 'I kept the details from my great-aunts, let them think it was a mutual decision. No man wants to admit he's been dropped the way I was.'

No woman, either. 'I thought my fiancé dropping me for my second cousin was bad enough, but at least Roy did it privately. My parents and sisters supported me, although it was still awkward. Like you, I didn't share the details with them, but that's why I came to England, to leave all that mess behind.' Roy, whose parents were British like Victoria's, had once said it would be good fun to live in England for several years after they married. Although he'd lied about that too, Victoria had still made it here, albeit not how she'd first planned.

'While I regret you had to experience that kind of heart-break, you've put it behind you and now we both have a fresh start.' Louis paused and, still clasping Victoria's hands, he pressed her fingers to his lips. 'It's not my place to share their stories, but both Hetty and Addie had their own romantic disappointments and, in Aunt Hetty's case, a disapproving parent. Above all, they want me to be happy. I understand you're not ready for me to say anything more but we've skirted around the issue long enough. For now, and if it doesn't sound foolish at the grand old ages of thirty and thirty-one, I want you to be my girl. What do you say?'

'I say yes.' She leaned forwards to meet his kiss. In wartime, none of them knew how much time they'd have together or even have left. Those German planes earlier had shown her how short and unpredictable life could be. If she didn't take a risk now, when would she? She tugged Louis even closer as he deepened the kiss. She had one life and it was time she lived it – and she wouldn't let herself think about either the past or unknown future.

Chapter Twenty-Seven

'How did the weekend pass by so quickly? None of us did anything special, did we?' Nell swung her satchel from side to side as the three of them walked along the lane on their way to school Monday morning.

'I suspect Victoria did something special.' Beatrice gave her a knowing glance. 'She hasn't stopped smiling since returning from that picnic and cycle ride to Upper Yarrow Farm with Louis.'

'But Louis was only here less than twenty-four hours in the end.' Victoria pretended to frown but couldn't manage it. 'It's such a shame he was called back from leave because of the Plymouth bombing.'

'A much greater shame for the people of Plymouth.' Beatrice's voice was tart.

'You know what I mean. Of course the Germans dropping bombs on those poor people in Plymouth was dreadful, as it was on Whittleton. Thankfully, unlike in Plymouth, nobody in Whittleton was killed, but on our picnic Louis asked me to be his girl. Now I'm even more afraid for him. Who knows when he'll next get leave?'

If Victoria couldn't share her happiness and worry with Beatrice and Nell, who could she share it with? Victoria was so happy she feared doing or saying something to jinx it – which was why she hadn't said anything to them before. Instead, all of what had remained of Saturday and then Sunday she'd hugged the precious secret and memory of Louis's kisses to her heart, oblivious to ordinary life going on around her.

'You must learn to be happy with what you have, and when you and Louis can't be together, I expect the two of you will help keep the postal service in business.' Beatrice's gentle smile tempered her previous prickliness. 'The village postman is elderly. I foresee him being bent almost double coming up the drive under the weight of cards, letters and parcels.'

'Stop it.' Victoria laughed with the others. 'You're both happy for me, truly? In spite of everything?' An army vehicle rumbled past, leaving a cloud of dust in its wake. 'Louis had to leave so quickly he didn't have time to tell Miss Hetty and Miss Addie about us, but he said he'd write them a letter on the train.'

Would he? Victoria mentally shook herself. She had no reason to distrust him. The telegram from London had been waiting when they'd returned to the manor, and Louis had caught a bus to go straight to the railway station. His great-aunts hadn't even been at home so Victoria had had to give them his apologies.

'Of course, we're happy for you,' Nell assured her. 'Louis is a lovely chap.'

'He'll do.' A small smile played around Beatrice's mouth. 'Mind, in a uniform even the most ordinary man has a certain air, don't you agree, Nell?'

'Oh, go on with you. Wait until you two meet someone special,' Victoria teased back.

'I'm too old,' Beatrice said.

'And I'm not looking,' Nell completed what had become their familiar refrain with a decided shake of her head.

'You're…' Victoria stopped. At the end of the lane leading into Hazelbury's high street, a lorry towing a large Queen Mary trailer holding a badly damaged Spitfire passed.

The driver, a young man in an RAF uniform, waved.

'The poor fellow flying that machine.' Nell stared after the trailer as it disappeared in the direction of Whittleton. 'If he even survived, his injures must be horrific.'

'He'd have been better off dying outright, then.' Beatrice had continued ahead of them along the high street, and Victoria and Nell walked faster to catch her up. 'What?' She looked between them. 'I'm pragmatic. You both should learn to be the same.'

The only way to cope with it all is to not let yourself think about it.

Louis's words to her on Saturday, when the Luftwaffe had bombed Whittleton, echoed in Victoria's head. But what if something happened to Louis? No matter how badly hurt, she'd want him to live.

'Don't mind me. You're young.' Beatrice's tone was bitter. 'I only meant that life is harder for those who feel things deeply and in wartime, well… each of us learns how best to cope. Who am I to tell you what to do? I still have nightmares from some of the things I saw and experienced in the First World War. The injured, dying and dead and still the ambulances didn't stop coming.'

Behind Beatrice's back, Victoria and Nell exchanged agonised glances. There was nothing they could do or say to make Beatrice feel better, and despite their friendship and moments of connection, once again the gap between their ages – and life experience – was wide.

'Here we are.' Beatrice turned to them, her face wiped clean of emotion. 'Off to the village hall for Victoria and the infants this morning, and then we'll swap round this afternoon for the health inspector's visit. Don't forget we're meeting with Mrs Mann after school to finalise the room-use schedule for the last few weeks before the holidays.'

Victoria nodded, still thinking about what Beatrice had said. Was her fiancé killed outright or had he lingered in agony? Of course, it wasn't something she could ask, even of a less buttoned-up type of person than Beatrice. Still, in the past months, she'd learned there was much more to Beatrice – and Nell too – than she'd first thought.

She started as Nell nudged her. 'Sorry, what did you say?'

'I said…' Beatrice exhaled. 'Mrs Mann is squeezing all her lot into the smaller classroom this afternoon so you'll have the bigger one for the infants. Now some of the oldest boys have left to work on the farms, she told me she won't need as much space. One of the Clarke boys took up the space of several grown men all by himself.'

'Right, I hope Jimmy's back at school today.' Victoria clutched her satchel and handbag. 'His father doesn't appreciate the importance of education, that's for certain.'

'Poor Jimmy. He's not been any trouble since both of you have taken him in hand.' Nell beamed.

There was a sweet gentleness to the younger woman, but although she didn't know how, Victoria sensed that life hadn't always been easy for Nell. A sensitive soul, something had bruised her, something other than life in a cramped London terraced house where there were too many children and not enough money. Something else beyond being a scholarship girl trying to fit in at a grammar school and then 'better herself' as a teacher.

'See you later,' Victoria said as she made her way to the village hall. 'And welcome to you, Ivy.' She gestured to the girl who hovered at a suitable distance, waiting for her.

'Thanks, Miss.' Ivy's face went red beneath her freckles. 'I can't hardly believe it. Me here helping and you asking Miss Wentworth and Mrs Russell about me and all.'

'I appreciate it, especially owing to the shorter summer holiday.' The day after the pageant, Victoria had spoken to Beatrice and then, with her approval, Mrs Russell and asked if she'd consider letting Ivy join the infants' class for several hours each day in the autumn. However, the kindly vicar's wife had seen Victoria's need, and Ivy's potential, for herself so the girl was starting now instead of in September.

'From now on, the children are to call you Miss Byrne, don't forget. Even you two.' Victoria spoke to Diana and Albert who'd come to school with Ivy.

'Yes, Miss McKaye,' Diana said. 'See my new hair bow? Mummy brought it for me when she came to visit. One for Lucinda as well.'

'It's beautiful.' As Victoria unlocked the hall door, she admired the pink be-ribboned confections that adorned Diana and her doll. While some of the children hadn't seen their parents since last autumn others, like Diana, had had several visits from family. Dealing with the tearful aftermath the following day at school, Victoria was torn as to whether it helped or hindered. These days, Diana usually left Lucinda at home, but bringing the doll with her meant she felt more lost and uncertain so needed comfort.

'I'm glad I'm still here with you for the summer.' Diana's hand crept into Victoria's, the confiding gesture filling Victoria's heart with warmth. 'Even though you said I could have gone up to the junior's, I'd have been the youngest.'

'I'm glad you're staying here with me too.' Victoria looked around the group of children arriving singly and in groups of twos, threes and more, most chattering about the air raid siren and Whittleton bombing. 'I have loads of fun planned for all of us. Until autumn, it won't be a usual school term as we'll be outdoors playing games and having different sorts of lessons.'

'Will there be art? I like art,' Albert said.

'Yes, indeed.' Victoria smiled. 'I've even managed to get some poster paint.' In addition, her mother and sisters had gone in together to send a parcel with new books or a game for the children to enjoy as a surprise for each week school would be in session when ordinarily they'd have had a longer summer holiday.

'Yes, what is it, Peter?' Victoria looked down as the boy came to her desk. Despite fresh air and country life, he was still small for his age and pale with blue veins showing through his skin. 'Everything all right at home?'

'Yes, Miss McKaye. Baby Beryl's crawling now.'

'How lovely. I'll be out to see you and your mum and sister later this week.' She made regular visits to the families of her children, even Peter, whose real family was now with him.

'You know you said I could tell you anything, Miss?' Peter leaned closer.

'Yes, of course.' Victoria gave him her full attention. There were still a few minutes until she had to ring the bell, and everything else could wait.

Peter tilted his head to one side. 'Why would Jimmy Clarke's dad paint his barn roof red?'

'I don't know.' Victoria pulled out her desk chair and sat. 'How do you know he did that?'

'I went with Mrs Russell when she dropped off some of her ladies' magazines for Mrs Clarke on Friday after school. Mrs Russell were looking after me when Mum took Beryl to the doctor and Diana were with Margaret for tea.'

'And?'

'Mr Clarke came around outside of barn, covered in red paint, he was.' Peter gave a solemn nod. 'Mrs Clarke took Mrs Russell to look at her vegetables but I stayed in the yard to play with one of the cats. Before he saw me, Mr Clarke said some bad words.'

'Adults do, sometimes, when they don't think children are around.' Victoria's mouth went dry.

'Then he said sorry but he said it were because he were cross because he knocked over a tin of paint.'

'But how did you know he was painting the barn roof red?' The classroom chatter was a low hum as Victoria focused solely on Peter.

'I looked up and saw it.' He studied her with childhood innocence. 'There was a big stripe of red paint from one side of the roof to the other right at the front. When I asked him why, he said young lads like me should mind their own business and not ask questions.'

Victoria made herself laugh. 'I don't know why Mr Clarke would do such a thing but he must have had a good reason. Also, although I encourage you to ask questions here at school, not all adults are like me.'

'My mum says, "curiosity killed the cat" but she'll never tell me which cat.' Peter huffed. 'Or, she says I'll understand when I'm older. When will I be older?'

'All too soon.' Victoria's breath caught. 'One day you'll be a fine man and I'm sure you'll answer all the questions children ask you. Now go find your seat at the table. See? Diana has saved it for you, and I'll ring the bell.'

Like the cut hedges and filled-in ditch, a red marking on a barn roof might also mean nothing, but what if it didn't?

And what if Peter had provided another piece of the puzzle Louis and Victoria were working on, one that might mean national security was at stake?

Chapter Twenty-Eight

Early the next morning, Victoria sat bolt upright in bed as aircraft thundered overhead. 'No air raid siren?'

'Cover your head and get away from the window.' In the bed across from Victoria's, Nell ducked under the eiderdown.

Victoria fumbled for her eiderdown and when she couldn't find it, rolled out of bed and underneath it.

'They're gone.' Nell clicked on her torch and poked her head under Victoria's bed. 'The planes must have been our lot heading back to Whittleton. There's your eiderdown, clear across the room.' She folded it and then found her slippers and dressing gown. 'Since I'm up, I'll put the kettle on for a cuppa, shall I?'

'Good idea, thanks. There are some biscuits left from the batch I made to send to Louis. In the tin in our sitting room.' Rolling back out from under her bed, Victoria shrugged into her own wrap and slippers and yawned. 'What time is it anyway?' She fumbled for her torch and wristwatch. 'Almost five. How are we going to get back to sleep now?'

'We won't – so we'll have to make the best of it.' Nell's voice was cheery as she peeked behind the blackout.

'Girls?' After a rap on their bedroom door, Beatrice stuck her head in. 'Shall we have breakfast now? I expect Miss Hetty and Miss Addie can't have slept through that racket either.'

'If I eat breakfast so early, I'll be ravenous by mid-morning.' Victoria rubbed her stomach.

'That's why we have elevenses – but pack extra in your lunch.' Nell grinned. 'Let's start with tea and biscuits in our dressing gowns first.'

'I am not and will never be a morning person.' Victoria remade her bed as Nell and Beatrice laughed.

'Which you remind us of almost daily,' Beatrice said, taking her arm as they followed Nell down the stairs. 'Chin up. If there *had* been an air raid warning, we'd now be huddled in the dank cellar worried we're about to meet our maker.'

'True – but given we're living with the constant threat of invasion, when I'm sound asleep is the only time I'm *not* worried.' Wide awake, the seriousness of the war situation coiled around Victoria like the coloured picture of a snake she'd been terrified by in a book an older cousin had been reading one summer at the cabin.

'Good morning, girls.' Miss Addie met them at the top of the stairs, dressed and carrying a rose-patterned ewer from her washstand. Tail wagging, Lady followed at her heels. 'An early one, isn't it?'

'You could say that,' Victoria muttered beneath her breath as Miss Hetty joined her sister. Unlike the teachers, the two ladies could have a nap later if they wished.

'We were told life would be quieter in the country. Who knew we'd be on the flight path to an air base? Still, I wouldn't exchange Hazelbury for London any day.' Nell's laugh trilled. The fearful, mouse-like girl Victoria had met that day last September had blossomed as both teacher and woman.

'I suppose so. Not London or any other big city at present anyway.' Following Nell to the kitchen, Victoria once more reminded herself to count her blessings. Like Nell, she wasn't the same person she'd been last autumn either, even though the face reflected back at her in the looking glass over the washstand each morning and evening was unchanged. It was inside, where it counted most, that the changes had been greatest. Changes that had made her more confident in herself and maybe even willing to take a chance on love again.

She'd had a letter from Louis yesterday. A nice, big fat one she'd already read three times. Mindful of the censor, he'd only written about his everyday doings but he'd included a salutation and sign-off that brought a blush to her cheeks and flutter to her heart.

'If you have a moment for a word?' Miss Hetty stopped Victoria with a brief touch to her arm.

'Of course.' It was easy to think of and address Miss Adelaide as Miss Addie. However, in Victoria's mind, tall, white-haired Henrietta Grainger remained Miss Grainger. As such, any request she made was the Hazelbury equivalent of a royal command.

'In the drawing room, if you please.' Like her sister, Miss Hetty wore a dark-patterned day-dress with an elaborate lace collar, making Victoria even more conscious of her quilted blue dressing gown and matching slippers. 'No, Lady.' Miss Hetty shut the drawing room door on the dog and gestured to Victoria to sit on one of the sofas.

'The blackout? I could take it down now, at least one of the windows.' Victoria squinted through the gloom. Miss Hetty's manner often made Victoria feel like a schoolgirl summoned into the presence of a stern headmistress.

Miss Hetty gave a gracious nod as she sat in an armchair upholstered in the same green fabric as the sofa.

'There, that's better, isn't it? Such a beautiful sunrise.' With the tall, narrow window freed from its black covering, rosy rays of dawn spilled through the glass panes. Silver dew coated the garden in front of the manor, now also dug up for growing vegetables, and tendrils of mist draped the hedgerow by the gate.

'I've seen many sunrises. I doubt this one is any more memorable than the others. Nevertheless, we're here to see it and these days more than ever that is by no means guaranteed.' Miss Hetty's voice was curt.

Victoria's mouth went dry and she folded her hands in her lap to stop herself fiddling with a loose thread on her dressing gown.

'Addie and I had a letter from Louis in yesterday's post. I gather you had one as well.' Although the same blue as her nephew's, Miss Hetty's eyes currently held none of Louis's warmth.

'I did.' Which Miss Hetty already knew since the letter had been at Victoria's place in the dining room when she'd come down for dinner.

'I understand my great-nephew has…' She paused and only then did Victoria spot a faint tremble in the other woman's hands. 'Certain feelings for you. Feelings which you seemingly return.'

'Yes, I do.' Louis had written to his great-aunts as he'd promised. She'd had no reason to doubt him.

'Although the world is sadly much changed since I was a girl, certain conventions, at least in our family, have not.' Miss Hetty's eyes drilled into Victoria and she forced herself not to flinch. 'Louis is a fine man and I… we… thought he'd be settled long before now. My sister and I worry over him. We'd hoped… well, a young man in London has certain temptations, doesn't he? Sowing wild oats, as the expression goes.'

'I wouldn't know.' Victoria clenched her hands tighter. What *was* Miss Hetty getting at?

'Although we can't fault Louis for bestowing his affections, such as they may be, on you… I hope you recognise that he also has certain responsibilities not only to his family and country but Hazelbury. This house will be his one day, you know.' Miss Hetty sat ramrod straight and, in the shadows, the strong lines of her face reminded Victoria of one of the stone effigies she'd seen of a seventeenth-century Grainger in the village church.

'I didn't know, not about the house I mean.' She should have suspected, though. The Misses Grainger didn't have other close family.

Miss Hetty gave another regal nod. 'While I have no particular fault to find with *you*, you must also realise that affections given in wartime are, by their very nature, often transitory. Furthermore, you are from Canada and will presumably return there when the conflict is over, regardless of whether we or the Nazis prevail.'

'I… I hadn't thought that far ahead.' Victoria's voice cracked. Where was one of Nell's endless cups of tea when she needed it? 'But there is no formal understanding between Louis and me.' Now she sounded like one of Jane Austen's heroines.

'Of course there isn't. In the regrettable absence of his mother and father, Louis would, of course, make any such intentions known to my sister and myself first.' Miss Hetty sat even straighter. 'You may be a colonial but at least you come from a respectable family. Not one like Beatrice's but still…' Her voice trailed off. 'Addie is a romantic but, like me, Louis is more sensible. He would not be swayed by just any pretty face and despite her many virtues, Nell is… well…'

'A modest, kind, intelligent and hardworking young woman,' Victoria couldn't stop herself from adding.

'Indeed, for her class.' Miss Hetty exhaled. 'Louis knows his responsibilities and will make up his own mind but I would not want either of you to be hurt.' Now her tone was magnanimous. 'I presume he told you about his erstwhile fiancée?'

'He mentioned her name but that was all.' Victoria's fingernails dug into her palms. 'He would never be indiscreet.'

'Evelyn is recently widowed. She and Louis move in the same London circles so you never know, do you?'

'No.' Anger sparked hot and sharp and Victoria bit her lip. She couldn't let her temper get the better of her, not if she didn't want to have to find a new billet.

'Good. We understand each other, then?' Miss Hetty rose.

Victoria stumbled to her feet. 'Perfectly.'

'Oh, and one more thing.' Aunt Hetty stopped partway to the door. 'I suspect that you may be involved in this cloak-and-dagger business with Louis. I don't know the details, of course, but do be careful, won't you? I expect he's warned you to trust no one? One can't be too careful.'

Then, without waiting for Victoria to respond, Miss Hetty swept out of the drawing room, as much as anyone in an old-fashioned day-dress could be said to sweep.

Victoria stood in the middle of the room twisting her dressing gown cord as Nell burst in, followed by Lady.

'What on earth was she talking to you about? Your tea is likely cold now. I'll make you another cup straight away. Breakfast is almost ready as well. Beatrice and I made it because Miss Addie... Victoria?' Nell came closer. 'What's wrong? You're pale. Are you coming down with something?'

'No and nothing's wrong.' Or perhaps everything. She manufactured a smile and bent to pat the dog.

She'd be polite to Miss Grainger, of course. Victoria could no longer even try to think of her as Miss Hetty. And she wouldn't tell Louis about this conversation. He loved and respected his great-aunts and Victoria wouldn't come between him and them.

But what Henrietta Grainger had said was yet another reminder that Victoria had to be mindful in giving her trust. Perhaps even to Louis most of all.

Chapter Twenty-Nine

Sitting on picnic rugs and shaded by one of the ancient oaks that dotted the grounds of Whittleton Hall, Victoria, Beatrice and Nell watched all but their youngest pupils play a rounders match. It was Wednesday in the first week of July and the day of the school visit Major Bertram had first proposed to Victoria last autumn. From riding in the horse-drawn carts which Major Bertram had sent to collect the children and teachers to bring them the short distance from Hazelbury to their arrival, picnic lunch and time for games – it had all gone more smoothly than Victoria had dared hope.

Albert swung his bat, hit the ball with a resounding crack and took off at a run around the pitch Major Bertram had set out earlier.

'Yes, keep going.' Victoria sprang to her feet and cheered him on. 'That's it. Good lad. What?' She glanced at Beatrice and Nell's amused expressions.

'We didn't know you were such a keen sporting fan, that's all.' Nell took several plums grown in the hall's kitchen garden from the hamper Mrs Bertram's cook had packed for them.

'I used to play baseball with my sisters and cousins at home. It's similar to rounders.' Her mind drifted back to those lazy summer days of her childhood and youth. 'Each year, we'd have a family competition. I was the pitcher, somewhat like you'd call the bowler, for one of the teams. We usually won. It was good fun.'

'Sounds it.' Beatrice passed around a plate of arrowroot biscuits. 'I used to watch my brothers play cricket. Except for tennis and horse riding, my mother didn't approve of girls taking part in sport.' She shook her head. 'I always fancied playing hockey.'

'I never played sport at all,' Nell said and stared at her hands. 'Unless you count running round after my younger sisters.'

'Miss Hetty told me that when she was a girl they often had tennis parties at Hazelbury Manor. She showed me photographs,' Beatrice said. 'It seems that in her day she was an exceptional player. There was even talk of Wimbledon, but her father wouldn't hear of it.'

Victoria busied herself with packing up the hamper. Her talk with Miss Grainger still stung. She'd tried to hide her distress from Beatrice and Nell and avoid Miss Grainger as much she could, so on the surface life went on as usual at home.

'Miss Addie's such a pet, but Miss Hetty still scares me. It's as if she always expects me to do something wrong,' Nell said.

'Her manner can be off-putting, but she's not as bad as you may think, truly. Her bark's worse than her bite.' Beatrice stood and went to referee a dispute between two of her juniors.

Beatrice was entitled to her opinion, but it was no surprise that she was chummier with Miss Grainger than Victoria and Nell. Although from different generations, the two of them came from the same world, one which had its own rules and expectations learned in childhood. And one which, despite the so-called equalisation of social classes with the war, people like Victoria and Nell would forever be excluded from.

'It's been lovely to have a break, but duty calls.' Victoria stood as well. 'I must go and see how Mrs Bertram and Ivy are getting on with my smallest infants. When I left them on the terrace, Mrs Bertram had brought out the toy cars her boys used to play with and, for the girls, a dolls house. She also had some of them playing hopscotch. It was sweet.'

'There are times when I envy you your infants.' Nell laugh was rueful. 'I had to dissuade some of my boys from playing hide-and-seek earlier. That lot are likely to hide with the intention of not being found. We'd have to call out a search party.'

'The infants have their moments, but I wouldn't trade them. Even the new arrivals are settling.' Those new London children who either hadn't been evacuated last September or who'd returned home within a few weeks reminded Victoria how far she and the longstanding evacuees had come in ten months. 'Yesterday, I overheard Albert telling two of the new boys not to trample a patch of wildflowers behind the village hall. Quite outraged he was. He gave them a brief lesson about the importance of wildflower seeds.'

'Children listen more than we may think. Little sponges, they are.' Nell turned at a piercing wail from the rounders game. 'Arthur, mind how you swing that bat. Watch for anyone behind you. Did you fall and scrape your knee, Lizzie?'

As Nell and Beatrice restored order and, in Nell's case, administered minor first aid, Victoria walked along the hall's drive to the house. Much grander than Hazelbury Manor, Whittleton Hall was an elegant red-brick house that dated from Tudor times. With turrets on each side at the front, its mullioned windows sparkled in the afternoon sun, and the only reminder of the modern era was the roomy black saloon car parked by the stable block.

As Victoria neared the massive front entrance and adjacent fish pond, Major Bertram came out through the open doorway, followed by a white-haired butler carrying a valise.

'I won't be a moment, Sir.' The butler, whom Victoria had spotted when they'd arrived, buttoned his uniform coat.

Children's laughter rang out and then Ivy, followed by Victoria's infants, burst through a green door in a brick wall surrounding the kitchen garden, apparently playing a 'follow the leader' game.

'Whatever is the matter, Sidney?' Bringing up the rear of the children and holding Diana's hand, Mrs Bertram called to her husband. 'I'd hoped you could join us for tea. At luncheon, the boys so enjoyed your stories of India.'

'It can't be helped, Julia. Miss McKaye.' Major Bertram touched his hat to her before going to speak to his wife. 'That call was from London. No, don't fuss. I'll stay at the house in town.'

Surrounded by her excited pupils all talking at once, Victoria couldn't hear what else Major and Mrs Bertram were saying but from her gestures and facial expressions, it was clear Mrs Bertram was in some distress.

'The major was in the kitchen garden with us and then he was called indoors to the telephone.' At Victoria's side, Ivy handed out chalks from her apron pocket. 'It had got too hot and sunny on the terrace so Mrs Bertram brought us to look at the vegetables and play games. There's a flagstone path and it's ever so nice in the shade. I didn't do something wrong coming out here, did I? Only the children wanted to see what was on the other side of the door.' She lowered her voice and gave Victoria a frightened look.

'Of course not. Major and Mrs Bertram have given us the run of their estate.' Victoria glanced towards the house where a blonde woman in a smart summer dress and hat, and carrying a leather case, came out through the still open front door to join the Bertrams.

'That there is Mrs Wallace, Miss Bertram she once were,' Ivy said. 'Lives in London but she's home for a few days. Said she needed a rest from her war work. She's a widow, but a right young and glamorous one, don't you think?'

'Indeed.' Victoria covertly studied the woman. Mrs Wallace was around her age but that was where any similarity ended. Instinctively, Victoria smoothed her own summer dress, an old blue cotton one from before the war she'd pulled from the back of the wardrobe for its serviceability rather than style. 'Let's go back into the garden, children, shall we? And let's see how softly we can speak while we do.' She put a finger to her lips.

From where she stood with her parents, Mrs Wallace darted annoyed glances towards the infants as Victoria marshalled them back into line.

'Oh, Miss McKaye.' Mrs Bertram came towards them and put a hand to her windblown hair. 'The major had a call from the War Office and he has to go to London unexpectedly. Our daughter only arrived at the weekend but she's going with him. I'd hoped we could all have tea together but I must give you their apologies.'

'Of course – and thank you.' As Victoria murmured a polite response, Diana tugged on her hand. 'What is it, dear?'

'Mrs Wallace knows Mummy in London.' Diana gave Victoria a sunny smile. 'She took me upstairs and showed me her dressing table and let me try on her hat and scent. I smell like roses.' She leaned closer so Victoria could sniff the fragrance.

'You do.' The car pulled up and stopped on the gravel drive and the butler-turned-chauffeur got out to open the rear doors.

Major Bertram got in followed by his daughter who gave a languid wave in her mother's and Victoria's general direction.

'Oh, Evelyn, dear.' Mrs Bertram called to her daughter. 'When you're back in town, don't forget to…'

Victoria stopped in the drive, the children, Ivy and Major Bertram and whatever else Mrs Bertram said forgotten.

Evelyn. A widow. The words ricocheted in Victoria's head like a rounders ball.

Miss Grainger had mentioned Louis's former fiancée who was widowed and called Evelyn.

So that must mean… that Louis had once been engaged to the Bertrams' daughter. There couldn't be two such people in this small area, could there?

As the car whisked by, Victoria glimpsed blonde hair beneath that smart hat. And, so fleeting she almost missed it, a sharp assessing gaze through narrowed, distinctly unfriendly eyes.

–

'Another letter for you from Louis.' Two days later, on their return from school, Nell passed Victoria an envelope from a table inside the front door at Hazelbury Manor, where Marjorie sometimes left any post for them to collect. 'Three letters and a postcard so far. Keen, isn't he?'

'Don't tease.' Victoria made a face at Nell as she took the precious letter with its 'Opened by Censor' stamp.

'He's a gentleman of the best sort, and you're fortunate. Enjoy your happiness.' Nell flicked through the rest of the post, setting aside several letters and a magazine for Beatrice who'd stopped at the village library on her way home.

'He is, and I am.' Victoria sat on one of the hall chairs to remove a pebble from her shoe. Yet, despite that happiness, the thought of Evelyn Bertram, now Wallace, nagged at her like a sore tooth. Even if she and Louis had been engaged, it was years ago and Louis would have had no reason to tell Victoria. So why had Miss Grainger implied that Louis and his former fiancée might reunite? And why was Victoria obsessing over it?

Having dealt with the pebble, she took the rest of her post from Nell and, unable to wait any longer, opened Louis's letter and extracted the thin sheet of pale-blue paper from its envelope.

My darling Victoria.

Her cheeks warmed at the endearment.

I have good news. Whilst it's not Hazelbury, I'll be nearby on Thursday, 11th July. Would you be able to meet me in Cromer that evening? I'd like to take you for supper and to the cinema or dancing.

I'll arrange for a WAAF from Whittleton to collect you at the manor after school. I'll meet you at the railway station at half five. That should give you time to do some shopping or whatever else you fancy. Perhaps that order you mentioned from the stationer's will have come in?

Please ring my secretary Thursday morning, sweetheart, and let me know if you can make it. Miss Skene will be able to reach me with a message.

I hope that the W.I., church choir or some other worthy activity doesn't stand in our way as I'm longing

to see you again. Of course, I'll also arrange for a driver
to bring you back to Hazelbury. There's always someone
going from the coast to Whittleton so there won't be any
difficulty stopping by the manor.

Affectionately yours,
Louis X

A date with Louis – and not in Hazelbury where everyone would gawk and talk about them. With paper rationing, school supplies were limited but she'd managed to order some drawing pads from a shop in Cromer, and had had a letter yesterday to say that they'd indeed come in. Perhaps, if Beatrice gave permission, Victoria could put Ivy in charge of the infants and leave school early so she'd have time to fix her hair and change clothes. Not that she had anything new to wear, but maybe her pink dress with the—

'Girls, you'll never guess what's happening.' Absorbed in her happy daydream, Victoria raised her head at an exclamation from Beatrice who'd come in from the library and held a letter aloft.

'What?' Nell paused in fixing Lady's lead to her collar.

'I've had word from Miss Hopson.' Beatrice waved a sheet of paper on the school's letterhead. 'She's coming here, arriving the evening a week from Sunday. To visit us and, of course, our pupils.'

'Miss Hopson here?' Nell's face paled.

Victoria's heartbeat sped up. With their headmistress dividing her time between their London school and its teachers and evacuees in the West Country, she'd almost forgotten about her, and addressed any concerns to Beatrice. It was also Beatrice who occasionally sat in on Victoria's classes and checked the children's work to ensure it was to standard. 'Where will she stay?'

'If, as she writes, the Misses Grainger agree, she'll stay here at the manor.' Beatrice briefly covered her mouth. 'It's sensible, of course, what with the rooms over the pub booked with the overflow of RAF officers from Whittleton, the army camp up the coast at Weybourne and troops in Cromer. All the hotels and guest houses are undoubtedly full.'

'Perhaps Miss Hopson could stay at the vicarage instead?' Nell's voice had the mouse-like tone Victoria hadn't heard in months. 'She'd be more comfortable there than here.'

'I could go round to the vicarage and ask but…' Beatrice paused and returned to Miss Hopson's letter. 'She says she doesn't want to put anyone out and it will be "splendid" to live as we do.'

'During afternoon break, Diana told me that the vicar and Mrs Russell's eldest son is coming home on leave that week,' Victoria said. 'We can't ask them to have Miss Hopson at the same time. The Russells already do so much.'

'Quite right: and of course not.' Beatrice worried her lower lip. 'There's nothing for it but having Miss Hopson to stay here. If I come in with both of you, she can have my room.'

'There's Louis's room, I suppose, but that would inconvenience Miss Hetty and Miss Addie, and Marjorie most of all.' Nell sat on the chair beside Victoria and rubbed Lady's ears. 'They like to keep his room ready for him and the other rooms aren't…' Her voice trailed off and her face went red.

'I don't expect there's anything else suitable at such short notice.' Victoria finished Nell's sentence. She'd only ever peeped into the bedrooms in the other wing, but disused for years, perhaps decades, they weren't fit for any overnight guest, let alone their headmistress. 'It will be a squash with the three of us in our room but we'll manage.'

'Of course we will.' Beatrice put the letter back in the envelope. 'Besides, it will only be for a few days. I'll speak with Miss Hetty now and then write to Miss Hopson. With luck, I'll catch the evening post.' She turned away and marched up the curving staircase, the thud of her shoes on the worn carpet and her stiff bearing letting it be known that Beatrice Wentworth would never be one to shirk her duty.

Nell's appalled gaze locked with Victoria's. 'Us all in the same bedroom? She's a… I'm a girl from…' She stopped and stared at her shoes.

'We're three teachers doing what needs must in wartime.' Victoria took a deep breath. 'No matter how you might feel or how things would have been done before the war, in this instance Beatrice is only our superior because she is a more experienced teacher and heads the junior school. Like Mr Russell said in his last sermon, paraphrasing Galatians, "We are all equal in the eyes of God". Understood?'

Nell gave a frightened nod.

'Good.' She gave the younger woman an encouraging smile. 'The three of us are now much more than colleagues. We're friends, and there's nothing Miss Hopson's visit will do to change that.' Victoria sounded more confident than she felt. Unlike Beatrice, she and Nell hadn't got to know or worked with Miss Hopson before they were evacuated.

War or not, they couldn't let standards slip. Only a few moments before, all Victoria could think of was her date with Louis, but now her apprehension about Miss Hopson's visit superseded it. What if the headmistress found the children weren't up to standard in their learning, and that Victoria was lacking as a teacher?

Chapter Thirty

'Well done, Albert.' On the morning of her date with Louis, Victoria clapped and the rest of the children joined in after the boy had finished his short talk about North Norfolk wild-flowers. 'Your drawings are also very fine.'

'Thank you, Miss.' Albert's face reddened as he returned to his seat and Ralph and several others guffawed.

'Only girls draw flowers.' One of the new London arrivals sneered, reminding Victoria of when Albert had once said almost the same thing.

'Quiet, boys.' Victoria rapped a ruler on the desk for their attention. 'There is nothing amusing or unusual about a boy being interested in flowers. Botany is the study of plant life. Some of the world's greatest botanists have been men.'

'What about girls?' Diana raised her hand as she spoke. 'I like flowers but I also want to learn more about how they grow.'

'There are many women botanists too. I'll look for a book in the library, and next week we can learn about the women and men who have studied and advanced this branch of science. I'll also bring in another book I have with coloured pictures of flower paintings by famous artists, both men and women.'

As the children settled, Victoria's chest grew cold. Would Miss Hopson disapprove of her classroom management and how she often diverged from the standard curriculum to follow a pupil's interest? Lacking both school supplies and classroom space, she'd got used to making do. From outdoor geography and natural history lessons to applying simple mathematical principles to rationing, she'd done her best to help these evacuated children learn and be curious about the world around them.

'Right, who is next? Sheila isn't it? And you chose to show us—?'

'Excuse me, Miss McKaye. Mr Russell would like a word, if you please.' At the back of the hall, Ivy hovered by the half-open inner door, presumably having answered a knock while Victoria was dealing with Ralph and the others.

'Thank you, Miss Byrne.' She glanced at her wristwatch. 'We'll have Sheila's talk after morning break. While I speak with the vicar, Miss Byrne will continue reading this week's story to you.'

'Yes, Miss.' The children nodded and there was a rustle as they settled back in their chairs.

Victoria nodded to Ivy as she reached the door and then went into the entryway and closed the inner door behind her.

'Yes, Mr Russell?' Under his black Homburg hat, the vicar's thin face had a greyish tinge. 'What's wrong?'

He put his gold pocket watch away and smoothed his white clerical collar before glancing around. 'I had a telephone call from Major Bertram in London an hour ago. Early this morning, the Luftwaffe dropped bombs on Cromer.'

Victoria put a hand to her mouth to suppress a gasp. 'Was anyone hurt?' The major's call would have come through as the children were arriving at school.

Louis. She'd planned to ring Miss Skene from the telephone box near the pub at morning break. She was supposed to meet Louis in Cromer later. They were going to have supper and go dancing or to the cinema. His letter… Her legs trembled and she grabbed for the door handle to steady herself.

'There have unfortunately been casualties but I don't yet know how many. Several houses and shops took a direct hit.' He hesitated and briefly bowed his head. 'Some of your pupils' foster families have aunts, uncles, cousins and, in one case, grandparents in Cromer which naturally gives this attack, while dreadful in and of itself, a particularly worrisome dimension.'

'Yes, of course.' Victoria spoke around the lump in her throat. 'How can I help?' *If* Louis was already in Cromer, if he'd arrived there last night... the WAAF whom he'd arranged to collect her, Miss Skene... she had to telephone. Victoria's thoughts whirled while she tried to pay attention to the vicar.

'Miss McKaye? Do you need to sit down? I realise this news must come as a shock and I'm sorry to have caused you such distress.' The vicar took Victoria's arm and his cultured voice reached her as if through the crackle and hiss of a long-distance telephone line.

'I'm fine.' Victoria straightened. 'It's only... you see, Mr Grainger invited me to meet him in Cromer for supper later today. I was about to call his secretary and...' She put a hand to her head. 'He may already be in Cromer and his great-aunts, the Misses Grainger, if Louis is injured or lost... they will... I need to find out where he is or...' She couldn't make herself say the words.

'I understand.' Mr Russell patted Victoria's arm. 'I suggest you ring Mr Grainger's secretary now. I will stay with the children and Ivy. Use the vicarage telephone in the front hall. The door is unlocked.'

'Thank you.' Victoria fumbled for her handkerchief. 'I expect news of the Cromer bombing is spreading rapidly.' Hazelbury had close connections with the coastal towns and although the war limited travel, there was still regular traffic between them with farmers shipping goods to market, shopkeepers collecting deliveries and now a flow of soldiers, sailors and airmen between Norfolk's many military bases.

Mr Russell nodded. 'The village – and its rumour mill – are already abuzz. That's why I came here, and Mrs Russell has gone to the schoolhouse to tell the other teachers. We must prepare the children carefully and gently for what they will hear when they're out and about and in their foster homes.'

'I'll be as quick as I can.'

As Victoria made her way along Hazelbury's high street to the vicarage, and villagers came out of shops and homes asking questions she couldn't answer, she prayed as she'd never prayed before that Louis, and everyone else, would be all right.

–

Three-quarters of an hour later, Victoria sat in one of the rear seats of Mr Russell's car while he drove her, Mrs Meldrum and Mrs Bertram to Cromer. As they rattled along the narrow road, Victoria was hardly aware of the passing scenery or even the steady click of Mrs Meldrum's knitting needles at her side. Instead, she replayed her conversation with Miss Skene in her mind.

I'm afraid I haven't been able to reach Lieutenant Commander Grainger but he arrived in Cromer last night. Staying at the Red Lion. Yes, the hotel on the seafront. The secretary's usually crisp and dispassionate voice was tinged with concern, even as she promised to ring RAF Whittleton and cancel Victoria's transport arrangements.

'If you leave Mrs Meldrum, Miss McKaye and me right in the town, we shall see what's what and help as we can while you continue on to the vicarage.' Mrs Bertram looked over her shoulder and gave Victoria an encouraging smile. In her grey-green long-sleeved Women's Voluntary Service summer dress and hat, both with the red-embroidered WVS badge, she exuded calm capability.

'You must not worry about leaving the children, either,' Mrs Meldrum, in a matching WVS uniform, said. 'With Miss Potter and Ivy, they're in eminently capable hands.'

Realising that Victoria would be no use in the classroom, Beatrice had insisted she go to Cromer to search for Louis and had dispatched Nell to help with the infants for the rest of the day. Beatrice and Mrs Mann would manage what for today would be combined junior classes of village pupils and evacuees.

Victoria held one end of Mrs Meldrum's navy-blue sock as the other lady counted stitches. She'd never before left her classroom in the middle of a school day. What would Miss Hopson say if she found out?

As they entered Cromer, the car slowed, and Mrs Meldrum gasped and dropped her knitting. 'Oh my word.' She pointed out a window to where smoke rose from a partially collapsed building.

'I'm afraid we shall have to stop here,' the vicar said as he braked and parked across the road. 'We can't go any further, see?'

Victoria's stomach knotted as she took in the destruction. Members of the fire brigade and air raid precautions teams were hard at work and a first aid station had been set up at the next corner.

'Come along.' Mrs Bertram was already out of the car and waving down an ARP warden.

Victoria clambered out of the car and joined by Mrs Meldrum, they stepped around fallen masonry and shattered glass.

'Ruddy Jerries. Sorry, Sir, ladies.' Beneath his tin hat, the ARP warden's round face fringed with grey hair was grim. 'One of their planes dropped bombs all across town, but the café got the worst of it along with the road where the cinema is. Lucky it was so early. Otherwise, both places would have been packed with folk.'

Victoria pressed a hand to her throat. The same cinema where tonight she could have been with Louis and so many others.

'Munday's Newsagents in Church Street were hit too, and Mr Munday and his sister killed.' The warden dipped his head. 'Then the Germans machined-gunned the streets and sea aiming for soldiers having an early swim.' He rubbed a hand across his face. 'There's a rest centre in the Methodist Hall. The WVS are serving tea and buns and finding shelter and clothes and such for those who've been bombed out.'

'I'll continue on foot and see what help and comfort I can give.' Mr Russell patted the warden's arm.

'We'll leave you both to your work, then. The Methodist Hall is where we women can best do our bit.' Just as her husband the major must once have marshalled his troops, Mrs Bertram gestured to Victoria and Mrs Meldrum.

'Coming, but…' Victoria moved closer to the warden. 'Do you know anything about the Red Lion Hotel? A friend stayed there last night and his family in Hazelbury is most anxious.' While Victoria hadn't returned to the manor before leaving Hazelbury, after visiting the school Mrs Russell had been on her way to see the Misses Grainger and she'd also insisted Victoria go to Cromer and try to find out news of Louis.

'The hotel's still standing, but that's all I can tell you, Miss. That whole area's blocked off so you best go to the Methodist Hall and wait for news.' He turned away to wield a shovel, leaving Victoria to follow the others along a road where, in less time than it would have taken her to make a cup of tea, lives and families had been ripped apart.

'Dreadful, isn't it?' Mrs Meldrum tutted, tucking her handbag more firmly under her arm as they passed the corner of Church Street where, farther along, the newsagent had been bombed. 'Poor souls.'

Victoria nodded, unable to find the words. She'd bought a copy of *The Lady* there only six weeks ago. The café that had been flattened was where she and Louis had met Beatrice and Nell that day last autumn when they'd taken Wilf and Albert to the seaside.

'Sorry.' She stepped back so a man pushing a wheelbarrow piled high with building debris could manoeuvre by, followed by a wan-faced young woman with a crying baby in a pram.

The man touched his cap and Victoria hurried to catch up with Mrs Meldrum and Mrs Bertram. In the distance, the sea, calm and a tranquil grey-blue, stretched into a misty haze. She pulled her cardigan tight, all of a sudden chilled to her bones.

How could the sea look the same when so much else here had changed?

'Miss McKaye?'

Her head jerked up as a man's voice said her name. 'Yes? I... oh, Mr Clarke.' Her heart pounded.

'I weren't expecting to see you here today.' Walter Clarke edged nearer to her as two men carrying a ladder squeezed around them on the broken pavement. 'Shouldn't you be at school?'

'Under ordinary circumstances I would be, yes, but I came to help.' She kept her voice prim. Some instinct told her not to mention Louis. 'I'm with Mrs Bertram and Mrs Meldrum. They're in the WVS.' She gestured to the two women now half a block ahead. 'Mr Russell, the vicar, brought us in his car.'

'I hadn't pictured a young lady such as yourself taking up with that lot. Don't you have enough to keep you busy with the children?' His dark eyes narrowed.

'In wartime, we all have to do our bit. It's our duty, isn't it?' Sweat trickled down the back of Victoria's neck. 'You must excuse me, I...' She stopped as out of the corner of one eye she glimpsed Louis and another man she didn't recognise smoking in a doorway.

Louis gave an almost imperceptible shake of his head and put a finger to his lips.

'I didn't expect to see you here today either, what with your farm work and petrol being in such short supply.' She studied Walter Clarke in return.

A dark-red flush crept up his cheeks. 'Me and the wife have got family here.' He jerked a thumb along the road before sticking both hands in his trouser pockets.

'I do hope they're safe.' She managed a concerned expression even though part of her wondered if he was telling her the truth. Louis had said that Joe with the baker's van lived near Cromer rather than in the town itself.

'All right far as I know.' His voice was gruff. 'Our Jimmy likes you, and you always did put me in mind of my young sister,

Flora, but…' He paused and Victoria's breath quickened. 'You don't want to be making friends with my wife, nosing round my farm nor getting mixed up with Louis Grainger neither.'

'I'm sure I don't know what you mean. My visits to your farm have only been to help Jimmy with his schoolwork, and Mrs Clarke and I are in the W.I. together. It would be odd if we weren't friendly.' Victoria gave him a neutral smile. 'As for Mr Grainger, you know I'm billeted with his great-aunts. As with your wife, I'm friendly with him, that's all.'

'So you say.' Walter's voice was both measured and menacing. 'I'm telling you for your own good. A nice girl like you, I wouldn't want you getting hurt or into trouble, like.'

'Thank you for your concern, I do appreciate it.' Victoria spoke through numb lips. 'Now I must be going.' She returned Mrs Meldrum's energetic wave.

Victoria manufactured another smile as Walter tipped his cap and continued up the road. As she sped by the doorway where Louis and the other man were half-hidden, she was careful to keep her face averted. She didn't have any illusions. Walter meant a different kind of trouble than what was usually meant by a girl in 'trouble'. A trouble she couldn't so easily protect herself from, but in which she was also now involved too deeply to back out.

'Mrs Bertram went on ahead but I said I'd wait for you.' Mrs Meldrum took Victoria's arm and hustled her in the direction of the Methodist Hall. 'What on earth is Walter Clarke doing here?'

'He said he came to check on family.' Victoria kept her explanation vague.

'If he did, that will be a first.' Mrs Meldrum grimaced. 'Out for himself is Walter and always has been right from when he was a lad. He was never much for book learning, but he's got an eye for the main chance, that's for certain.'

Which was another reason Victoria needed to be on her guard around him. He suspected her of something, but while that brief glimpse of Louis had reassured Victoria of his safety, maybe she needed to be wary of him as much, if not even more, than Walter. She only had Louis's word that he was working in naval intelligence. What if he wasn't?

Chapter Thirty-One

'Tea?' Carrying a tray, Victoria came out the scullery door at the side of Hazelbury Manor and walked towards Louis in the vegetable garden. 'There's a few carrot biscuits left as well from the batch Nell made.' Two days after the Cromer bombing, Louis had stopped in Hazelbury for the Saturday afternoon, and now was the first time Victoria had managed to see him on her own.

'Thanks.' He straightened in the middle of a row of potato plants and wiped his forehead with a handkerchief. 'What do you think?' He gestured to the newly weeded crop planted in what had, before the war, been the manor's herbaceous border.

'Impressive.' As she set the tray on a wrought-iron table shaded by a wooden arbour, Victoria gave him a stiff smile. After two largely sleepless nights going round in circles about whether or not Louis was telling her the truth about his work, part of her wished she'd never got drawn into it in the first place. Initially, it had been almost a game, but one that now was deadly serious. In addition to everything else was how much she liked Louis, maybe even loved him. 'Mind you don't put our new land girl out of a job.' Miss Pilch, a jolly young woman from Leeds, had arrived the previous week and lived in a house on the edge of Hazelbury that had been turned into a hostel for half a dozen land girls.

'Hardly. Miss Pilch's job is safe.' Louis sat on the bench under the arbour and patted the empty space beside him. 'There would be enough work for several land girls *and* me if all the manor's outlying fields were brought into full production.

With the way the war's going, I suppose that may happen soon enough.' He stared at the tranquil garden drowsing in the heat. Bumblebees hovered over Miss Addie's lavender, and in the hay meadow beyond, Norfolk poppies waved their rosy heads in the sweet-scented July breeze.

'Britain can't fall.' Victoria poured tea for them both as the ever-present icy fear knotted her tummy. 'We won't let it whether by air, land or sea.' Her thoughts drifted to what she'd seen and experienced after the Cromer bombing. Along with the shock of destruction and loss, there had also been inspiring resilience. As she'd served cups of hot, strong tea, distributed buns and comforted frightened children, she'd been even more determined to do her bit in whatever ways she could.

'If only everyone had your faith and resolve.' Louis cradled his teacup.

'Most have much more than me.' Victoria considered how to ask the questions that had troubled her ever since she'd seen Louis in Cromer. 'The men are the ones fighting but we women are right alongside them. If Mrs Bertram and Mrs Meldrum had been born male, I could picture both of them commanding entire fleets.'

Louis chuckled. 'It's their sort who will continue to keep the railways, factories, post office and every other essential service going. They're doing their bit in the Forces as well. If women are conscripted, those contributions will only increase.' He ate a carrot biscuit in one mouthful. 'I expect you want to know what I was doing in Cromer.'

Had he read her mind? Victoria suppressed a sigh. How could she and Louis have any kind of real relationship if they couldn't be honest? It was wartime, though, and many couples had to keep secrets from each other. Since Major Bertram now worked for the War Office, he undoubtedly couldn't tell Mrs Bertram much about his job, either. Was she imagining problems where there weren't any and blowing whatever Louis was involved in entirely out of proportion?

'I expect you can't tell me why you were in Cromer.'

'I can't, but that doesn't mean I don't want to.' His lips pressed together in a slight grimace. 'What did Walter Clarke have to say to you?'

'Amongst other things, he warned me not to get involved with you.' Victoria hugged herself against more prickles of unease.

'A bit late for that, isn't it?' Louis wrapped one arm around Victoria's tight shoulders, his skin beneath the rolled-up sleeve of his blue shirt warm through the thin cotton of her dress.

'Yes.' She couldn't tell him that Miss Grainger had given her a similar warning. 'I also think Walter suspects me of keeping an eye on him. He didn't say so in as many words, but that was his intent.'

'If everything goes as planned, you should only have to keep watch for another few weeks.' Louis squeezed her shoulder and brushed a loose strand of Victoria's hair away from her cheek. 'You trust me, don't you?'

'Of course.' But did she, truly? Even though she didn't want to take what Walter had said seriously, he'd nevertheless planted more seeds of doubt in Victoria's mind. Louis was certainly a British naval officer. Why would she think otherwise? And that telephone number for his office and Miss Skene had to be on the up and up. Miss Skene had sounded almost as worried about Louis as Victoria was. Or was it all an act?

She couldn't ask Miss Hetty. Louis was her great-nephew and she'd obviously be biased in his favour. He'd also told Victoria not to say much, if anything, to Miss Hetty about them working together. At the time, his reasoning – that it was best for both of them to be oblivious – had made sense. She'd been so guarded the day she'd had to ask to borrow the car to meet Louis in Cromer, and Miss Hetty had seemed to accept the request and been guarded too. However, was Louis deceiving both of them?

'I should soon be able to tell you everything.' Louis curled the strand of hair around one finger, and Victoria quivered.

'Don't. Your great-aunts are in the house. If they look out a window and see you, us…' She felt herself flush. 'They could also say something to Miss Hopson. Our London headmistress arrives tomorrow and…' Louis dropped a kiss on Victoria's cheek.

'Aren't teachers allowed to have a life outside the schoolroom?' With another quick kiss, he drew back.

'Don't tease. You know my job extends far beyond the schoolroom.' She tapped one foot on the gravel path and tried not to groan in frustration. 'Only yesterday, I had to cycle to an ARP post halfway to Whittleton to get replacement gas masks for two of the new boys who lost theirs in a pond. Then, I had to visit their foster-parents and write their real parents to explain what had happened.' All of which meant Victoria hadn't got to bed until half-eleven and had then been awakened at three by an air raid siren which turned out to be a false alarm.

'I worry about how many hours you work. All the time you spend visiting evacuees in their foster homes and writing letters to their parents is a job in and of itself, let alone everything you do preparing lessons, teaching and general cheering up.' Louis folded his hands on the lap of his ragged garden trousers. 'That's why I'm especially sorry we missed our date in Cromer. I'll make it up to you, I promise.'

'That's this war for you.' Victoria stared at her own hands. She had to trust Louis. Miss Hetty did – but had Louis told her the whole truth? He hadn't told his great-aunts everything about his broken engagement.

'No, I mean it. You tell me where you'd like to go and when, and subject to where His Majesty's Navy might send me, I'll make it happen.' He patted her wrist and Victoria unclenched her fists. 'Supper, dancing, the cinema. I should warn you that now things have hotted up, I won't be here as often. I'm needed elsewhere. We can still write, though, and I hope you know how much each moment we spend together means to me?'

'They're important to me as well.' In these snatched moments, whether working in the garden, cycling along a leafy

202

lane or picnicking, Victoria's feelings for Louis grew but at the same time, so did her fears. 'I don't need suppers or dances or the cinema, although all of them are nice, but I need to know...' There was one thing Louis could be honest about. She took a deep breath and stared at him, unflinching. 'Was Miss Bertram, now Mrs Wallace, the girl you were once engaged to?'

His light laugh held a new and bitter note. 'Yes, Evelyn Bertram is the girl who threw me over as soon as a better prospect came along. I didn't tell you, because it's in the past. The same reason I presume you didn't tell me much about your former fiancé?'

'Roy isn't on our doorstep, is he?'

'True.' Louis hesitated and a muscle twitched in his jaw. 'Village gossip being what it is, I suppose you were bound to hear something about Evelyn. She was always headstrong, but I... foolishly as it turned out, thought she returned my feelings, which were sincere at the time.'

'Do you still see her... in London or here?' Victoria's voice hitched as she remembered what Miss Grainger had said.

'I've seen her several times in London but always in a group with others.' Louis let out a heavy sigh. 'Never here, but as far as I know, she's not often home. Hazelbury's dull for a woman of her sort. While I admire and respect Major and Mrs Bertram, Evelyn means nothing to me now and never will again. I was virtually a boy when we became engaged and in the intervening years... I suppose I became a man. You have no need to concern yourself about my feelings for Mrs Wallace.'

A weight she hadn't been aware of lifted from Victoria's chest. 'Mrs Wallace is very beautiful. I saw her at Whittleton Hall when I was there with the school, and she was visiting her parents.'

'Now you're fishing for compliments.' Louis glanced around and then took Victoria's hand. 'Come here. I'll show you how much you mean to me.' He tugged her around the back of the arbour where they were hidden from the house.

His lips met Victoria's in a kiss that began light and sweet, and deepened until neither of them wanted to break apart. She forgot about Mrs Wallace, Miss Hopson's visit, Miss Grainger's disapproval and those fears and suspicions about this clandestine work that Walter Clarke's comments had resurrected and added to.

All that mattered was Louis and what the two of them had in this scarce moment, here, now and, she let herself admit it… what she wanted forever.

Chapter Thirty-Two

On Monday at mid-morning, Victoria answered Miss Hopson's knock and stood aside to let the headmistress enter the village hall ahead of her. Behind her back, she crossed her fingers for luck. After Louis had left before supper on Saturday, and except for Sunday church, Victoria had spent most of the intervening hours in the library at Hazelbury Manor working on her lesson plans. She was as ready as she'd ever be but even all the preparation hadn't quelled her nerves.

Instead, from the moment Beatrice had arrived with Miss Hopson late on Sunday evening having met her and a small group of new evacuees in Norwich, Victoria had been on edge, fearful of putting a foot wrong in front of the imposing, silver-haired headmistress.

'Good morning, children.' Miss Hopson greeted the infants' classes who sat in long rows on either side of their tables in almost unnatural silence. 'I was with some of your brothers and sisters at the village school and now I'm happy to join you here.'

Beatrice had organised Miss Hopson's visit so she'd welcome the older children at the village school first and then come to the hall to see the infants. After that, she'd go back and forth between the schoolrooms to join as many classes as she could before tomorrow, the last day of her visit, gathering all the pupils together in the parish church for a school assembly.

At a nod from Victoria, Diana presented the headmistress with a bouquet of wildflowers in an empty jam-jar, followed by Albert who gave her his best drawing of Norfolk red poppies.

'How kind, thank you.' Miss Hopson's nod was gracious and then Victoria guided her to the most comfortable chair which she'd placed at the front of the hall beneath a framed photograph of the king. 'Don't mind me. Go on as you would ordinarily.' Miss Hopson sat, placed the flowers, drawing and her handbag at her side and pushed her spectacles further up her nose.

Victoria swallowed and smiled at her pupils. She was the one in charge of these classes and they looked to her for everything, not only during lesson time but their wellbeing out of school as well. Miss Hopson had been evacuated and would understand what Victoria and these little ones were coping with.

'The youngest children are doing art and the others are reading aloud. Ralph? Please begin where Joan left off.'

'Yes, Miss.' Seemingly awed by Miss Hopson's presence, Ralph found his place and began to read, following the simple text with one stubby finger.

As lessons followed one after the other, Victoria's breathing eased. Writing, arithmetic, a break for lunch, singing and then Miss Hopson returned for the final lesson of the day, nature study – which now, in summer, Victoria took with the children outdoors.

'I hope you don't mind but I've set them a scavenger hunt "I-spy" activity.' As Victoria put on her summer straw hat and checked her book bag to make sure she had the needed materials, she turned to the headmistress. In her navy skirt suit, white blouse, stockings and lace-up brown shoes Miss Hopson looked as crisp and well-turned out as she had that morning. 'It helps the children appreciate the natural world.'

'A splendid idea.' Miss Hopson adjusted her hat pin. 'As I said to Miss Wentworth and Miss Potter, we are all doing the best with what we have. Where better than places such as Hazelbury to forge a lifelong love of the English countryside? I grew up in rural Sussex and attended a village school myself.' Miss Hopson's penetrating pale-blue eyes softened. 'I still hold country people and places dear and close to my heart.'

Victoria and Nell had gone to bed soon after Miss Hopson arrived. As such, their only conversation with the headmistress had been a brief greeting the night before and then over breakfast with Beatrice and the Misses Grainger. Since nothing personal had been discussed, this was the first time Victoria had glimpsed Miss Hopson as an individual rather than her headmistress.

'Shall I take the boys and leave the girls with you?' As they left the hall, Miss Hopson put on the gloves tucked in her jacket pocket.

'The boys?' Victoria darted a sideways glance at Ralph, Albert and several others who she privately referred to as her more 'boisterous' pupils. 'Are you certain? They can be rather lively.'

'I trust you don't doubt my capabilities, Miss McKaye?'

'Of course not. I… the boys it is, then.' Victoria separated the group and distributed worksheets. Owing to the paper shortage, she'd prepared one for each class and reminded them to share. 'Miss Byrne, I'm leaving the smallest girls in your care and I'll take the older ones and new London arrivals.'

'Yes, Miss McKaye,' Ivy said as she gathered her charges.

For a moment, Victoria watched Miss Hopson with the boys as they fell into step behind the headmistress and the group moved towards the lane. 'Diana, Sheila and Margaret, please partner with Phyllis, Vera and Ruby.' The latter, three new girls who'd arrived from London with Miss Hopson, were still frightened and uncertain.

'Right,' Victoria clapped her hands. 'Work in your pairs to find something in nature that you can see, hear, touch, smell and taste and then draw a picture of it on your group sheet.' She distributed pencils. 'Remember, don't eat or even have a quick taste of what you find in case it's poisonous.'

'Miss?' Pale, spindly-limbed Ruby tugged on Victoria's skirt. 'I needs to go to the toilet.' Ruby came from one of the poorest homes in the new and larger area served by Park Road School.

While Miss Hopson had hinted at Ruby's family's struggles, which had begun long before the war with the economic depression of the nineteen-thirties, it was one thing for Victoria to hear about it and another to see Ruby beside other healthy, rosy-faced children.

'The lavatory. Yes, I'll take you. We'll all walk in that direction. In pairs, remember, Joan?' She shepherded them around the outside of the hall.

'I see the sun.'

'I see Mrs Meldrum in her motor.'

'She's not in nature. Neither's her motor.'

Voices rang out, followed by laughter as the girls moved towards the lavatory and then the garden allotments and field behind.

'In you go. I'll wait for you out here, shall I?' Victoria opened the lavatory door for Ruby and stood outside where she could also keep watch over her other pupils and Ivy.

'Ta, Miss.' Ruby scuttled inside and closed the door behind her.

'I see a red-and-black ladybird on a daisy plant.' Diana's voice rose above the chatter.

'The grass tickles my legs. That's something I feel.' Joan laughed.

'All done, Ruby? Go and wash your hands.' As the lavatory door opened again, Victoria pointed towards the hall's kitchen.

'Miss McKaye?' Diana appeared at Victoria's side with the other girls behind her. 'See what we found in one of the allotment gardens?' She held out a cone-shaped paper bag. 'It's aniseed balls like Miss Mills sells in the village shop. Phyllis and Vera wanted to eat them but I said we mustn't because you told us not to. They also don't belong to us. It would be stealing.'

'You did right bringing them to me.' Victoria took the bag and considered the shiny, round, reddish-brown boiled sweets. In both appearance and their strong liquorice scent, they were identical to the confectionery she'd seen countless times in the shop beside the post office. 'Where exactly did you find them?'

'Beneath a potato plant at the end of one of the rows in Mrs Mann's allotment,' Sheila said. 'I know it's her garden because I've seen her working in it after school.'

'I thought Mrs Mann only had a garden at her home.' Victoria poked in the bag where her fingers caught a second layer of paper.

'She did,' Diana said, 'but when Mrs Green sprained her back and couldn't work in her allotment, Mrs Mann offered to help. I overheard the ladies talking when Mrs Russell had the W.I. meeting at the vicarage.'

'I see.' Victoria refolded the top of the bag and held it tight. 'You're quite right that these sweets don't belong to you. Mrs Mann or someone else must have dropped them so I'll look after them for now. Here's Ruby coming back. Finish your worksheet and then we'll sit in the shade of the hall and hear what everyone has found. Is that Miss Hopson and the boys already?' Victoria cocked one ear in the direction of the lane. 'Quick as you can, girls.'

Diverted as she'd hoped, they ran to rejoin the others.

Victoria stood at the edge of the allotments and tucked the cone with the sweets in her book bag. Once hidden, she made as if to rummage inside the bag but instead dug further around the sweets.

The second layer of paper was thinner, like onion skin. She dumped out the aniseed balls and squinted. Then, her eyes widened. Centred around Hazelbury's parish church marked by a cross, the confectionery concealed what appeared to be a hand-drawn map of England's North Sea coast.

'Miss McKaye?' At Albert's voice, Victoria shoved the map to the bottom of her bag and schooled her features.

'Yes?'

'You'll never guess what Miss Hopson showed us. She knows lots about fossils and…'

'Speak one at a time, boys,' Miss Hopson interjected while giving them an indulgent smile.

'How exciting.' Victoria nodded and smiled at her pupils. Yet she hugged her book bag closer and a cold chill crept along her spine. The aniseed balls and map had been left in Mrs Mann's allotment by someone for someone.

After the fall of France and with Germany controlling French sea ports, Britain's situation was desperate. Night after night, RAF planes battled German aircraft in the skies overhead and all the armed forces were determined to protect the country from invasion. Had this map been drawn by someone working to thwart Britain and her allies?

Along with fear, pride surged inside Victoria. She might only be a civilian teacher but she'd do her part to try to defeat the Nazis in whatever way she could.

Chapter Thirty-Three

'I am proud of all of you, pupils *and* teachers.' Outside Hazelbury's parish church after the Park Road School assembly, Miss Hopson shook Victoria's hand. 'Well done. It's not been easy, I know.'

'Thank you.' Victoria acknowledged her headmistress's praise with a restrained smile.

She'd been perpetually on edge for several days. Miss Hopson's assessment of her teaching and pupils' progress and behaviour had been difficult enough, but since yesterday afternoon she'd been hyper-aware of that map and sweets, now transferred to her handbag and which she hadn't let out of her sight.

'You have nothing to fear when the school inspector visits.' Miss Hopson gave a decisive nod as she thanked Nell and then Beatrice. 'If his report notes any fault, no matter how minor, I shall deal with him. These are extraordinary times and we all, even school inspectors, must recognise when corners have to be cut, including adapting the curriculum to best meet our children's needs.'

As Miss Hopson turned aside to say something privately to Nell, Beatrice and Victoria exchanged relieved glances.

'Please do thank the Misses Grainger again for their hospitality.' The headmistress once more included all three teachers in her remarks. 'My visit here has been regularly splendid. Rather like visiting my maternal grandparents at their home before the last war. Such larks I had with my cousins in a house much like

Hazelbury Manor.' She turned to the vicar. 'If you're ready, we can be on our way.'

Mr Russell nodded. 'Your case is already in my car waiting by the gate.'

As Miss Hopson had decreed, they'd dismissed the children early after the assembly. Since the vicar, rather than Beatrice, was taking Miss Hopson back to Norwich, the three teachers had some rare free time.

'Move along, Ralph,' Beatrice chided the boy. 'No dawdling. You'll see Albert again tomorrow. And you, Albert, I expect Mrs Russell will have chores waiting at the vicarage. Diana and Wilf must be partway home by now.'

Victoria put a hand to her mouth to repress a smile.

'What?' Beatrice turned back to her. 'We can't let standards slip because Miss Hopson is leaving.' She waved as the vicar's car carrying their headmistress went by.

'You do sound fierce, but we both know that Mrs Russell treats Albert as if he were one of her own boys,' Victoria said. 'Chances are Albert and Ralph will reunite at the vicarage and enjoy their playtime.'

'True.' Beatrice laughed with Victoria. 'However, I don't want them to think they're getting away with anything. Miss Potter?' She called to the younger woman who still stood somewhat apart. 'All right?'

Nell re-joined them and her face glowed. 'Miss Hopson was so kind and encouraging. She said I'm already a good teacher, and that I have the makings of a first-rate one. Then she said I shouldn't be afraid of smiling in the classroom.' One of Nell's shy, sweet smiles flowered across her face. 'Fancy her saying something like that to me. She also said I should keep asking you both for advice when I need it and learn from your experience but that I should trust myself.'

'Miss Hopson is right.' Beatrice's voice was gruff as the three of them followed the last of their pupils out of the churchyard and then walked towards the village green and high street.

'Beatrice and I have been telling you much the same for several months now.' Three WAAFs on bicycles passed them, and as Victoria moved closer to the hedgerow she gripped her handbag tight.

The previous evening, she'd gone to the outside lavatory, the only place she could count on being alone, and by torchlight had examined the map more closely. It showed military bases throughout North Norfolk as well as the North Sea coastline between Cromer and Sheringham, with a faint line connecting Hazelbury, Whittleton and Upper Yarrow Farm. And in one corner there was a date and time, Saturday evening a week hence. Although the aniseed balls still looked innocuous, Victoria couldn't shake the sense that they'd been left with the map for a reason.

Nell beamed. 'Miss Hopson thinks I can be a real career girl.'

'If that's what you want, why not?' While Victoria liked teaching, she hadn't thought of being a true career girl until after her broken engagement. Then, she'd felt forced into the role of independent working woman but, while she enjoyed her independence, a big part of her still hadn't let go of the dream of having a husband and family of her own. Did Louis think about her like she thought about him? If so—

'Get down.' Nell shouted and grabbed Victoria's arm as aeroplanes thundered low overhead.

'Ouch.' Victoria tumbled backwards into a blackberry bush.

'Girls?' Beatrice still stood in the road. 'They're ours. See?' She waved at one of the pilots and pointed to the RAF roundels.

'Oh.' Nell's voice was chagrined.

Victoria took Beatrice's outstretched hand as the other woman helped her to her feet. 'I didn't ladder my stockings, thank goodness.' Even though clothing wasn't yet rationed, some thought it soon would be.

'Sorry.' Nell brushed leaves and twigs off the grey herringbone skirt and jacket she'd made from an old suit Miss Addie had given her that had belonged to the Misses Grainger's father.

'It's fine.' Victoria gave Nell's arm a reassuring squeeze. 'Better safe than sorry – and these days you can't be too careful.' Of the three of them, Nell was the most fearful and easily startled. Had she always been that way or had something happened to make her so? Victoria suspected the latter but, respecting her friend's privacy, had never pried.

'How will you use this unexpected hour of freedom?' As if sensing a change of subject was necessary, Beatrice landed on a topic that gave Victoria the opening she needed.

'I want to telephone Louis.' They entered the village high street proper and Victoria gestured towards the red phone box.

'Of course you do.' Beatrice's tone was dry. 'Aren't daily letters enough?'

Victoria's face warmed, and she straightened her hat.

'Sometimes she needs to hear his voice. I expect that's the reason, isn't it?' Nell, always the peacemaker, looked between them.

'It is. I miss him.' Which was the truth – but not the primary reason for this call.

Beatrice sighed. 'We'll wait for you on the green. If we don't return home together, Miss Hetty and Miss Addie will wonder where you are. I hope you know what you're doing, Victoria. The Grainger family is…' Beatrice stopped as if she'd already said too much.

'I know.' But did Victoria really know what she was doing? No, not with Louis and certainly not with whatever was going on in Hazelbury and a potential German spy network in their midst, but she was far too involved to back out now.

Luckily, the telephone box was free and as Victoria put coins into the slots and dialled, her heartbeat sped up.

'Grainger, here.' Louis answered, his voice clipped and with none of its usual warmth.

'It's Victoria, I…' She hesitated. She'd expected to get Miss Skene and now she'd reached Louis himself, she didn't know what to say. 'I have news.' That's what she'd said in her note, although he likely wouldn't have received it yet.

'Yes?' He barked out the word.

'It's urgent.' Was Louis in a meeting with other officers? Was that why he sounded so unlike himself? 'I found… well, it was my pupils, really. Some aniseed sweets and a piece of paper with what looks to be important local military information.'

As the weeks and then months had gone by, she'd become more guarded until now, neither in letters nor telephone calls, did she say exactly what she meant. Along with Louis's veiled warnings about intercepted post and overheard telephone calls, she read the papers. Even the most ordinary-appearing people could be involved in enemy espionage.

'I see. Sweets, you say?' There was a slight hitch in Louis's voice, discernible only because Victoria knew him well.

'Yes.'

'Right.' He cleared his throat. 'Thank you for keeping us informed. I'll do what I can. In the meantime, sit tight.' He rang off.

Victoria held the handset several seconds longer before replacing it in the cradle. She'd reached Louis at work. She couldn't expect the same warmth and affection as in his letters or when they were together in person. Yet, even given those circumstances, something about his manner was off and he hadn't mentioned coming to Hazelbury any time soon, either.

She tucked her coin purse back in her handbag and left the telephone box, nodding at the man, a farmworker, judging by his clothes and the mud caked to his boots, who'd waited at a respectful distance for her to finish her call.

What should she do now? Post the map to Louis and wait for him to respond? Although he'd told her to 'sit tight', given that date on the map and the line joining Hazelbury, Upper Yarrow Farm, Whittleton and the Cromer coast, action might be needed sooner. She couldn't go to the authorities on what was, admittedly, flimsy evidence and a vague sense of things not being 'right'. Besides, if she did, she'd have to tell them she was working with Louis – and he'd asked her to trust him. If he found out she'd doubted him, he'd hate her.

Yet Britain was fighting for its very existence. Despite what Louis had said, she couldn't stand by and do nothing. Since there wasn't anyone she could ask, she had to make her own plan without him.

Chapter Thirty-Four

'Here's to our summer holiday.' In the late July twilight, Victoria sat on the bench outside the scullery at Hazelbury Manor and raised the blacking brush she'd used to polish her school shoes.

Almost a week later, she was still no closer to knowing what to do with that map or formulating a workable plan, and except for a postcard and letter, both of which had been sent before she'd rung him, she'd had no further word from Louis. What if he wasn't really a naval officer and that telephone number wasn't for an office in Whitehall? Could he have got the uniform from somewhere? No, that was ridiculous. The country was at war. It wasn't a fancy-dress party.

'Such as our holiday is,' Beatrice said. From a cushioned wicker chair she'd brought out from what had once been an orangery but had fallen into disrepair, Beatrice set the heel on the sock she was knitting. 'Despite lesson preparation and what are sure to be ongoing issues with our evacuees and their families, I'll be glad to have a fortnight's break from the classroom.'

'As will our pupils, I expect.' Nell sat on a wooden kitchen chair and held a bowl filled with fresh-picked raspberries. 'What do you think, girls? Shall I make a crumble? I can replace the sugar with honey. Between all of us, we've enough butter.'

'Yes, please.' Victoria set aside her clean shoes and started on Beatrice's. 'We're lucky here in the country with so many fresh fruits and vegetables.' Nightbirds circled high above them, and a light wind brought welcome coolness after the heat of the day. 'In her last letter, my mother said she and my sisters are growing their own Victory gardens. Mother tended one for our family in the First World War too.'

'My dad's got his allotment,' Nell said. 'I miss going down there with him of a Sunday afternoon. I also miss my mum and brothers and sisters. They're all working now. Even Gladys, she's the youngest, got herself a job at Woolworth's. With so many of the lads being called up, Mum's got a place there as well. She's in ladies' hosiery like she was before she married, and Glad's in the canteen.' Nell patted Lady who was sprawled by her side. 'Mum wrote that it's a rush with shopping, fixing tea and keeping the house, but everyone's pitching in. My brothers grumbled, but Dad said this war means everyone has to do things they didn't expect. If it's only dusting, mopping and helping with the washing-up, the boys should count themselves lucky.' Her laugh turned into a sigh. 'I've never even met our Fred's fiancée.'

'Why don't you visit your family during our holiday?' Victoria said, exchanging a covert glance with Beatrice. Nell rarely spoke of her London life, and along with that being possibly the most she'd ever said about it at one time, she'd also never before shared anything so personal.

'You certainly don't have to stay here,' Beatrice added. 'While it's not precisely a holiday, my four days with my mother near Henley will be a change of scene.' She grimaced before turning away to count stitches.

'Oh, I couldn't go to London.' Nell shook her head. 'You know what the government says about essential journeys and leaving the railways and trains free for troops.'

Her expression was so earnest that Victoria almost believed her. 'But you haven't seen your family in almost a year. Surely—'

'No.' Nell's mouth set in a firm line. 'Besides, it's better here, isn't it? In almost every letter, Mum says she's glad one of her children is where it's safe.'

'If anywhere *can* be called safe.' Beatrice gestured with a knitting needle as the now daily aircraft rumbled in the distance.

Victoria's heart squeezed. She'd be safe in Canada, but even though she missed her family, she'd never regretted coming to – or staying in – England. If she hadn't, she wouldn't have made this new life for herself or met Louis. Since there was no formal understanding between them, and to forestall questions, she'd continued to refer to him as a friend in her letters home. However, it was also a way of keeping herself safe. If her family didn't know Louis was important to her, she wouldn't have to face their pity if the worst happened.

Poor Victoria. She's been dreadfully unlucky, hasn't she? At her age, it's almost too late unless she sets her sights on a widower. Mr Wahoski wouldn't be choosy and he does have money. He's not British but at least he's a Protestant thanks to his mother. Such a pity when you think of the matches Victoria could have made if Roy hadn't kept her dangling. Mark my words, I always thought she'd be a bluestocking in the end. It's not good for girls to be so clever. Thank goodness her sisters married well.

Victoria shuddered inwardly at the memory of a conversation she'd overhead between two of her great-aunts at a family birthday party. It was then she'd known for certain she had to change her life, and she'd applied for the boarding school post the next day. Mr Wahoski indeed. He was almost sixty, had nine children, all of whom she'd taught, and with his thinning white hair, a fondness for waistcoats, his pocket watch and his nervous, hurried air, he'd always reminded her of the White Rabbit in *Alice in Wonderland*.

'Victoria?' Beatrice's voice jolted her back to the present. 'Miss Addie asked you a question, and surely you're finished with my shoes? You've been rubbing that spot as if it were Aladdin's lamp.'

'What? Oh, sorry.' Victoria lifted her head. While she'd been absorbed in the past, Miss Hetty and Miss Addie had returned from what they called their 'evening promenade' around the garden. Now, both carrying their knitting, they occupied a wrought-iron bench that no one else, not even Louis, dared sit on. 'What did you say, Miss Addie?' She set the shoes and cleaning materials aside and folded her hands on her apron.

'My sister and I had a note from Louis this afternoon. I wondered if you'd heard from him, dear?' The last rays of sunlight gleamed on Miss Addie's white hair that tonight curled in loose strands around her face. With her soft blue eyes, faded pink-and-blue floral-print dress and sweet smile, she radiated warmth and kindness.

'Not recently, no.' Victoria glanced between Miss Addie and Miss Hetty and, not for the first time, wondered how two such different women could be sisters. Miss Grainger's steel-grey hair was pulled back in a tight bun, her severe grey dress with its white collar wouldn't have been out of place on a New England Puritan and her piercing blue eyes usually held more censure than approval.

'I expect you'll hear soon. The darling boy hardly has time to write. His note to us was only a scrawl.' Miss Addie's hands fluttered like a bird's wings. 'Louis is being sent away from London. Of course, he couldn't tell us where and now we are only to write to him care of one of those service Post Office Box addresses. Somewhere on the south coast, isn't it, Hetty?'

'Yes, but he could, of course, be anywhere.' Miss Grainger's voice was stiff. 'I suppose we – and he – were fortunate he stayed in Whitehall as long as he did. Major and Mrs Bertram's sons were scattered to the four winds months ago thanks to the vagaries of military postings. Their daughter, though, is in London. Louis mentioned he'd seen Evelyn at a party.' Her sideways glance at Victoria was laden with unspoken meaning.

Louis had said Evelyn Bertram, now Mrs Wallace, meant nothing to him, and Victoria believed him. It wasn't jealousy that made the hair on the back of her neck prickle. Rather, it was the sense that Miss Grainger knew more about Louis and his activities than Victoria did.

'I shall send Louis a parcel straight away. I hate to imagine him lacking home comforts. What do you think?' Miss Addie's bright gaze darted around their circle.

While Miss Addie chatted with Beatrice and Nell about socks, magazines and the practicality of making a mock marzipan topping and sending Louis's favourite cake by post, Victoria studied Miss Hetty, who focused on her knitting as if the entire Royal Navy depended on it.

Victoria wouldn't wait for an opportunity. She had no other choice than to speak with Miss Hetty privately and tell her about the map and sweets. It was time to set her personal feelings and any doubts aside. Louis's wellbeing – and maybe even Britain's future – might rest on it.

–

'Even if your suspicions about Walter Clarke are correct, what do you suggest we do?' An hour later Victoria was seated in a drawing room chair, with the lamplight flickering and high-lighting Miss Hetty's sharp cheekbones.

Victoria leaned forwards. 'Both of us need to go to Upper Yarrow Farm tomorrow evening. Going together will look less suspicious than I would alone, especially since it's the school holiday and I can't say I'm bringing work for Jimmy. We could go under the pretext of it being an urgent W.I. matter.'

'On a Saturday night and wandering around up there in the blackout?' Miss Hetty gave a disbelieving, yet remarkably ladylike, snort. Lying at her feet, Lady huffed in an echo of her mistress. 'What would be so urgent we couldn't wait until morning?'

'We wouldn't be that late and we could motor part of the way.' Except for a narrow slit, all car headlamps had to be covered as part of the government's blackout regulations. While Victoria didn't fancy driving in the countryside after dark, she needed to do something rather than sit here worrying. 'Louis wouldn't have taken either of us into his confidence if he hadn't thought we could be trusted. You don't want to let him down, do you?'

'Of course not.' Miss Hetty's tone was curt. 'But you're very sure of yourself, aren't you? In my day, young women weren't so bold. Conventions mattered.'

'Maybe if you'd defied convention and been more, as you call it, "bold", you'd have played at Wimbledon. Beatrice said you were good enough.' Victoria held her breath. She had nothing to lose by being direct and perhaps everything to gain.

A heavy silence hung between them, broken only by the rhythmic tick of the clock on the fireplace mantelpiece.

'You care for my great-nephew, don't you?' Miss Hetty's eyebrows raised almost to her hairline.

'Yes, I do.' Victoria didn't let her gaze waver. 'None of us know what the future might bring but I...' She took a deep breath. 'I want to help Louis. I *need* to.'

Because she loved him with every part of her heart and soul. Awareness slid through her as comforting, right and constant as a cup of hot cocoa on a cold winter's day at home. It was so simple yet profound and she wanted to tell Louis, tell everyone, shout it from the rooftops, even. Warmth shot through her and her entire body trembled.

'All right, then.' Miss Hetty nodded. 'However, we'll leave earlier and go by bicycle. We'll be less obvious that way.'

'But—'

Miss Hetty cut Victoria off. 'I'm not so old I can't manage a bicycle. How do you think Addie and I get around when you girls are at school?'

Victoria hadn't thought about it at all – and maybe that was the problem. All she'd seen was that Miss Hetty and Miss Addie were elderly. Not that they both had lived lives Victoria had never considered and were in many ways still living them. 'I'm sorry.'

'Perhaps we've both misjudged each other. You don't only care for Louis. You care for this country.'

'I do.' Victoria said it almost like a vow.

'Then look.' Miss Grainger traced the line on the map with a gnarled finger. 'If you're right that whoever is involved is planning something for tomorrow, it likely has to do with high tide. If Walter Clarke or whoever it is plans to go to from Hazelbury to the coast, they'll have to account for travel time.'

'I hadn't considered the tide.'

'Why would you?' Miss Hetty took a piece of writing paper and pencil from a drawer in the table beside her chair and made several notes. 'It's not as if you grew up near the sea, is it?'

'No.' Victoria bit back a smile.

'See here.' Miss Hetty passed Victoria the piece of paper. 'I reckon we need to be at Upper Yarrow Farm by half-seven at the latest.'

Victoria nodded as she checked the notes and calculations. 'I'd thought of telling the police constable but I'm afraid it would sound absurd.' What did Victoria truly have to go on? The map was the most damning piece of evidence, but even it wasn't conclusive. 'Besides, if Louis had wanted me to go to the police I expect he'd have said so.'

'He would have – and Constable Smith is… well.' A small smile hovered around Miss Hetty's mouth. 'Not the most perceptive or imaginative of men, shall we say. Very much by the book.' Yes, that was a definite twinkle in her eyes. 'I also expect the police have more than enough to occupy them at present without following up on wild-goose chases. If we are to believe what we read and hear, there are German spies and fifth columnists lurking behind every bush, leaving their marks on everything from fences to coded messages sent through the post.'

'Do you believe those stories?' Victoria had read about and heard the same lurid accounts which, more often than not, turned out to be false.

Miss Hetty let out a breath. 'I have lived a long life, so there are few things that surprise me anymore, even that there are those who choose to betray their country. As for what I do or do not believe? Certainly, some of the stories are far-fetched, but with a German invasion expected at any moment it's natural that the British public is apt to see or imagine evidence of foreign espionage with minimal or even no provocation.'

'Is that what you think I'm doing?' Victoria clasped her hands tight together to hide their shaking. 'Or Louis?'

'Louis certainly not. He's a Grainger.' Miss Hetty's voice was decisive. 'As for you? I know nothing of your family.' She studied Victoria for several moments. 'But I believe you have a loyal heart. Beatrice speaks highly of you and, unlike many young women today with their brazen red lipstick and chasing after any man in uniform, you seem sensible and not prone to silliness or flights of fancy.'

'Thank you.' Albeit a back-handed one, Miss Hetty had given Victoria a compliment – which she had to consider as progress. 'Until tomorrow evening?'

'Until then.' Miss Hetty stood to indicate their interview was at an end.

Although Victoria found herself wanting to curtsey, she took a step back and waited to follow Miss Hetty from the drawing room.

'Oh, and Victoria?' Miss Grainger turned before she opened the drawing room door.

'Yes?' Victoria tensed.

'While I never agreed with Mr Chamberlain's policy of appeasing the Germans, you may remember what Shakespeare said in "The Tempest".'

Victoria had read the play at school but, having always taught younger children, she hadn't had any occasion to revisit it.

'Yes, we've a copy upstairs in the library. Shakespeare was referring to "misery" but war also "acquaints a man with strange bedfellows". Wise, don't you think? Come along, Lady. Deal with the lamps and check the blackout before you turn in, won't you?'

As the door closed behind Miss Hetty and the dog, Victoria stood in the shadowy room and then snapped her half-open mouth closed. Miss Hetty was doing what she thought was her duty, nothing more.

Chapter Thirty-Five

Never had a day gone by more slowly. Although Victoria tried to keep herself busy with mending, writing letters home and reading *Clothes-Pegs*, a romance by Susan Scarlett she'd borrowed from the village library, she'd kept checking the time, sure it must be later than it actually was.

As for *Clothes-Pegs*? The fictional heroine, an ordinary girl who caught the attention of a well-born lord, had also drawn the ire of an honourable lady. Despite such things working out in a romance, the chances of them doing so in real life were slim. She'd tossed the book aside and taken up an Agatha Christie whodunnit instead.

In what had once been Hazelbury Manor's carriage shed, which housed the rarely driven motor-car, she double-checked the chain on what was now 'her' bicycle and pulled on the cardigan she'd left in the basket. If Walter Clarke wasn't doing anything wrong, he had nothing to worry about. But if he was? Then Victoria would try to foil his plans.

Seeming as unconcerned as if they were making an ordinary jaunt to the village, Miss Hetty came into the shed dressed in a light-grey A-line skirt suit, with her hair covered in a surprisingly chic floral-patterned scarf. She also carried a small black handbag which she placed in Beatrice's bicycle basket. 'Ready?'

'Yes.' Victoria jabbed at her hat pin to fix her straw boater more firmly. In her white blouse, blue cotton skirt and hand-knit cardigan, she felt decidedly underdressed and at a disadvantage. However, she couldn't think about her clothes at present. They were suitable for what for all intents and purposes would be an ordinary summer evening bicycle ride.

She sat on the bicycle's seat and pedalled out of the shed leaving Miss Hetty to follow. Beatrice, Nell and Miss Addie had all accepted their excuse of going to see Alma Clarke about a W.I. matter, and since Marjorie was on holiday and they'd already planned an early supper, the questions Victoria expected hadn't been forthcoming.

As they rode along the lane between the hedgerows, the summer air perfumed with lavender and wild roses, swifts darted above them, their small, slender bodies and long, curved wings grey-smudges in the dark-blue sky. In open spaces, vibrant red poppies bloomed, interspersed with fields of more muted brown and gold grain.

For a brief moment, caught up in the beauty of the countryside, Victoria could almost forget the war. Then, an aeroplane from Whittleton broke the quiet and roared overhead, the first in a squadron which soon turned sharply towards the coast.

How many of them would return to base after their mission? Victoria's stomach lurched as the fleet of aircraft disappeared into the misty blue, and her clammy hands slipped on her bicycle handles.

'Don't.' Keeping pace at Victoria's side, Miss Hetty's scarf billowed like a sail behind her.

'Don't what?'

'Let yourself think or worry over what might happen to them.' Miss Hetty sat stiff in the saddle but her voice was softer than usual. 'My fiancé died in the Boer War and then Louis's father, Rupert, my elder brother's son, in the last war. Rupert's parents died when he was a baby so Addie and I indulged him, I suppose. When Rupert was killed, he was an airman and served in the Royal Flying Corps, I… we'd let ourselves love him too much. Since then, and although we did our best to bring Louis up, unlike Addie I've found it's best to not let myself care.'

'I'm sorry.' How could you love anyone *too* much?

'Also unlike my sister, I don't let myself think about the past.'

'I see.' As they cycled through the village and then into the lane that led by the vicarage and towards Upper Yarrow Farm, Victoria turned what Miss Hetty had said over in her mind.

From the sounds of it, grief had made the woman close herself off from others until it became part of who she was. Prickly, distrustful and standoffish had been Victoria's first impression of her, and even after living at Hazelbury Manor for so many months now, she couldn't say she'd got to know Miss Hetty any better to change that initial opinion. If she hadn't taken steps to change her life, would she eventually have become like Miss Grainger? Victoria didn't want to think so, but Roy's betrayal had left her hurt, angry and, as time had gone on, bitter. Before moving to England, she'd been well on her way to hating the world and everything in it.

She waved as they passed the vicarage garden where Albert and Wilf were playing with the Russells' labrador. Being evacuated had changed those boys' lives for the better but what would that mean when they eventually returned to their family in London? They wouldn't be the same boys who'd left home in September 1939, and neither would their family. When Victoria thought about it, she and her family in Canada wouldn't be the same either. How would she fit there with them again? And did she even want to?

It was an uncomfortable thought, but not one she had to consider at present. Maybe Miss Hetty was right. It was better to live in the moment and not ruminate on either the past or future.

'We're almost there.' Miss Hetty broke what had become an awkward silence and gestured to the farm gate ahead of them at the top of a low rise.

'Yes.' Victoria swallowed and tried to work moisture into her dry mouth. 'If Mrs Clarke asks why it's so pressing to talk about the autumn programme, I thought of saying it's because my mother's W.I. branch may be interested in partnering with us and have members exchange letters, read and discuss the same book and similar. To start something like that, we'd need to begin planning now.'

'Have your mother or her W.I. branch made any such suggestion?' Miss Grainger glanced at Victoria as they dismounted to walk their bicycles the rest of the way up the hill.

'Not exactly… well, no. However, I'm sure it would be something they'd find appealing.' A rabbit darted across the lane in front of them, and Victoria suppressed a startled gasp. She was nervy, was all, but she couldn't let herself show it.

Miss Hetty shook her head. 'If Mrs Clarke, as the committee member responsible for organising meetings and activities, requests your help to coordinate such a scheme, are you willing to contribute?'

'Of course.' The farm gate was shut, so Victoria opened it for them to wheel their bicycles through and then closed it behind them again. One of the many ways the previous months had changed her was in her attitude to the W.I. Now the women who belonged to it were her friends, and she wanted to help and support them, secure in knowing they'd do the same for her.

'Good.' Miss Hetty retied the ends of her scarf which the wind had tugged loose. 'It doesn't look as if anyone is at home.' She motioned to the deserted farmyard and house where the curtains were drawn, then propped her bicycle against a fence and rapped on the farmhouse's front door.

Still holding her own bicycle, Victoria quaked in her shoes. What if they'd come to Upper Yarrow Farm only to be forced to turn around and go home again with nothing to show for their efforts?

'Hang on.' She put a finger to her lips and cocked her head towards the barn. 'Quick, around the back.' She grabbed Miss Hetty's bicycle and ran with it and her own machine towards a small apple orchard behind the house. She'd hardly noticed it the day she'd looked in at the kitchen window but, fronted by a small storage shed, it offered an ideal vantage point with a view across the property, as well a place to conceal themselves. 'Here.'

'What on earth?' Miss Hetty joined her behind the shed. 'We weren't doing anything wrong knocking on the front door. I agreed to that but not skulking about and—'

Victoria clapped one hand over Miss Grainger's mouth. While the farm had at first appeared to be deserted, it wasn't.

With their heads close together and apparently deep in conversation, Walter Clarke and Mr Knight came up the track from the barn followed by Joe, the man who drove the Cromer baker's van. She drew in a shallow breath. There were also two women with them.

Evelyn Bertram as once was, now Mrs Wallace, and Mrs Mann, Hazelbury's schoolteacher.

Belatedly, Victoria took her hand away from Miss Hetty's mouth and they stared at each other wide-eyed and for once united.

The question now wasn't *if* something was going on but *what*?

Chapter Thirty-Six

Victoria stood as still and silent as a statue beside Miss Hetty as Walter Clarke and the others approached the shed – and their hiding place.

Her thoughts whirled. If they were discovered, she could try to brazen it out – but even if Walter Clarke believed her, Mr Knight, Mrs Wallace and Mrs Mann were undoubtedly less likely to be fooled. What on earth was the village teacher doing here? Victoria had never considered that the map being found in her allotment was anything more than coincidental.

Victoria would have had a better chance of having them accept her story if she'd stayed near the front door. But, lurking behind the shed, she'd appear guilty before she said a word.

A chain rattled and then a creaking noise suggested the shed door was opening. Victoria glanced at Miss Hetty who shrugged and raised her eyebrows.

'I kept them all in here like you told me.' Walter's voice reached them, followed by a sound of boxes or crates being dragged across a stone floor.

'Good man.' That was Mr Knight. 'Look smart there, Joe. You and Walter need to leave with the van before it gets any later. And before anyone sees you moving this lot into it in the barn. We don't want Frank nosing around.'

'I already told my brother that if he knows what's good for him, he'll stay out of my business,' Walter grunted.

'Where did those guns come from? You said I'd be part of a peaceful, Christian organisation. That's the only reason I sent on your letters. I never wanted to kill anyone. And blowing up a ship is wrong.' Mrs Mann's voice quavered.

'Don't be such a fool.'

Although Victoria had never spoken to Evelyn Bertram Wallace, her clear, upper-class voice was unmistakable.

'You were there when Mosley spoke, the same as I was. We all were. Now he's in prison, you said you wanted to help him. That's what we're doing, along with ending the war. As I recall, you've always been in favour of appeasing the Germans since your parents—'

A man's muffled curse stopped whatever else Evelyn had intended to say. 'You got any bandages? I cut myself on that there knife.'

The speaker, who had a broad Norfolk accent, was presumably Joe.

'Use this rag. You'll be dripping blood across my farmyard and then we'll be in a fine fix,' Walter said.

'But I…' Joe moaned.

'Oh, be quiet, both of you.' Evelyn's voice held exasperation. 'Here, I have a scarf in my bag. Wrap it around your hand for now and we'll go to the house. Goodness knows where that rag has been. Joe could get blood poisoning and how would he explain that to any of the local doctors or even the bakery owner? That cut is bad enough when in a few hours Joe is expected to be at work baking bread. If you hadn't sent Mrs Clarke and your sons away, they might have helped. Surely you trust your family?'

'My Alma asks too many questions.' Now it was Walter who sounded exasperated. 'As for the boys, all they're good for is farm work. I'd like to be shot of the lot of them.'

Victoria exchanged a horrified glance with Miss Hetty as the voices faded and then the front door of the house slammed shut.

'We must go for the police constable.' Miss Hetty grabbed her bicycle handles. 'What we heard is treason. It's un-British.'

Victoria gestured around their hiding place. 'How can we get back to Hazelbury without going through the farmyard?'

'Plenty of ways. I know the footpaths and farm tracks around here better than almost anyone.' Miss Hetty rearranged her scarf so it almost covered her face. 'I am not the first Grainger to do my bit for king and country. In the English Civil War, another Henrietta Grainger...' She stopped and sat astride her bicycle. 'Coming?'

Victoria shook her head. 'I'll stay here.' While they'd heard treasonous talk, they hadn't actually seen anything. 'While they're in the house, I'll look inside the shed and then go to the barn. It sounds as if they intend to leave from there.'

Joe. Van. Mr Clarke's cousin from near Cromer was called Joe. And he drove a baker's van. As a commercial baker, he was important to the war effort and exempt from military service. The pieces slotted together like the Meccano model Albert and Diana had brought to school last week.

'Besides, if they find one of us then the other can still...' She stopped and put a hand to her face. There were different kinds of fear. While not as instantaneous as that day in the field with the German planes overhead, the present fear was no less potent nor the risk of death any less.

Miss Hetty nodded and then, for the briefest of moments, touched Victoria's hand. 'I'll be as quick as I can.' Then she wheeled her bicycle into the orchard and disappeared.

As Victoria hesitated, making sure she wouldn't be detected, the shadows of dusk deepened and the sky turned from indigo-blue to mauve and the first stars twinkled overhead. If she couldn't be fearless, she could try to be courageous. After looking towards the house once more, she crept around the shed and ducked inside through the half-open door.

There was still enough light to see shelves that would ordinarily have held tools for the garden or farm were stacked high with boxes. An open box of leaflets, several metal plates, more aniseed sweets and magnets were scattered across a table. She'd borrowed a similar horseshoe-shaped magnet from the local ironmonger's to give her pupils a simple introduction to pull force.

Victoria grabbed a leaflet from the top of the pile and folded it into her skirt pocket. Where were the guns Mrs Mann had mentioned? In the barn – or had they taken them into the house?

After another cursory look around, Victoria scuttled out of the shed, grabbed her bicycle and made for the path to the barn. She wheeled the machine and crouched low until she reached a turn that put her out of view of the house and then broke into a run.

Once safely behind the barn, she propped the bike against a wall and stood on tip-toe to peer through a cobweb-hung slit window. Along with the window's small size, dusk and the last glare from the setting sun made it impossible to see anything clearly. She couldn't go in via the main barn door, but with any luck she'd find that side door Louis had mentioned. Victoria crept along the pebble-dashed wall, all the while alert for any sounds that could mean Walter Clarke and the others were returning.

Her hand closed on a round metal handle to what indeed proved to be a door. As she opened it and slipped inside, her mouth dropped open. Louis had said the barn was empty. Now, it held the baker's van she'd seen that day at Cromer railway station.

As she walked around the vehicle and investigated the rear, where bread and buns would usually be stored, her breath caught. Instead of baked goods, it was filled with crates, along with several pairs of wire cutters, more aniseed balls – although these had holes drilled in them – and more magnets and steel plates.

As if for easy reference, another hand-drawn map of local airfields and pencilled notes about Royal Navy ships and their positions off the coast sat on the front passenger seat, and in the footwell, an open, small metal box of what looked like ammunition. A black uniform shirt hung on a hook by the door she'd entered through, and a picture of Hitler, which appeared to have been torn from a newspaper, was pinned to one wall.

Oswald Mosley. Blackshirts. The British Union of Fascists. Victoria had seen photos in the press of that same shirt being worn by violent political protesters, Nazi sympathisers and anti-Semites closely allied with Hitler who'd marched through London streets before the war. With Mosley's arrest and imprisonment, the British government had declared the movement he led 'unlawful' and banned it. But from what she'd read in the papers, there were other groups like it – so what if…

Voices echoed from outside, and, seizing the map, Victoria darted to the open side door, slipped through it and eased it closed as softly as she could. Facing this way, towards the fields, she put a hand to her mouth.

There was indeed an airstrip back here, flat and, by the looks of it, freshly ploughed.

'Put them boxes in with the others. We're late.' Walter's voice was all of a sudden so loud it could have been on the other side of the barn wall. 'It's all because of you – so move along, you fool.'

'You need me and me van, don't you?' Joe mocked his cousin.

'Get in, then, and look sharpish,' Walter said. 'Them explosive things don't look half bad, do they? Let's hope they work and that fellow is waiting for us where he's supposed to be… Hang on, that door were latched before. Did you…?'

The door Victoria stood beside was flung open and she shrieked.

'What the devil are you doing here?' Walter grabbed Victoria by one arm and held her in a vice-like grip.

Chapter Thirty-Seven

Victoria flinched as Walter's fingers dug into her shoulder through her cardigan and blouse. *Think. Stay calm.* 'I came to see Mrs Clarke about W.I. business. I knocked on the front door but nobody answered so then I... ouch.' He twisted one arm behind her back and the map fell to the ground. She wouldn't mention Miss Hetty. She might have already reached the village and found Constable Smith, who could be on his way even now.

'You thought you'd have a good look round, did you?' Walter's mouth curled and he tightened his hold on her.

'No, I...' She pressed her lips together so she wouldn't cry out in pain. 'I was riding back to the village and my bicycle made a... squeaking noise so I stopped to check it.'

Walter picked up the map and then dragged her fully into the barn, kicking the door shut behind them. 'What's this then, eh?' He waved the map in front of her.

Victoria blinked when he flicked on a torch and aimed its light in her eyes. 'I found it when I was looking for grease. For my bicycle chain. I also thought I might have a puncture so I...'

Walter whacked her head against the barn wall, and Victoria saw stars.

'Now, now, take it easy.' Joe pulled Walter away from her. 'He always did have a temper on him. Sorry, Miss.' Joe touched his flat cap with a hand wrapped in a makeshift white bandage stained with dark-red blood.

'If you know what's good for you, you'll keep your mouth shut.'

While Walter berated Joe, Victoria rubbed her head and risked a look around. No Mrs Mann, no Mr Knight or Mrs Wallace either. 'I'm sorry for disturbing you. I'll be on my way.' As she made a move towards the door, Walter grabbed her again.

'Not so fast, Miss McKaye. Now you're here and had a nosey round, you're coming with us.' He tugged her to the van and shoved her into the back between the boxes. 'I warned you, didn't I? Said I didn't want you getting into no trouble but you didn't listen.' He found a piece of twine and bound her hands behind her back.

'This is a mistake. I swear, I wasn't…' She twisted and glanced wildly around.

'Not another word or I'll shove a rag in your mouth and that'll keep you from talking, won't it? All your fine words and book learning won't help you any now.' Walter slammed the van's rear door, clicked off the torch and leaned into the front passenger seat across from Joe. 'Drive out alongside the field. I'll close the main door after you. Wait for me.'

The van's engine sputtered, turned over and the vehicle began to move.

'There.' Walter was back and even as he slid into the passenger seat and closed the door, the van rattled along a rough track.

Victoria wiggled this way and that, trying to ease one hand free from the twine binding them together, while also scooting closer forwards to try to hear anything the two men might say.

'If that Mann woman turns herself in we're all done for.' Walter's voice rumbled in the growing darkness. 'As for that posh bird and her fancy man, you can bet they'll deny they ever knew us. Their sort merely has time for the likes of us when we can be useful.'

'I only said I'd drive you to the coast. I don't know nothing about the rest. And what about Miss McKaye?' Joe's voice resembled the whine of her youngest pupils when they were tired.

'Don't worry about her.' Walter glanced over his shoulder towards her, and Victoria tried to make herself smaller. 'Lots of places for folk to disappear.'

'All you said was, if I didn't like Mr Churchill I should join you. I don't want somethin' bad happening to Miss McKaye or anyone and between Mrs Wallace talking about cutting telegraph wires and what that fellow said about attaching timed explosives to ships—'

'Be quiet, you idiot.' Walter swore. 'It's more than not liking Churchill and his cronies – but you'll see. When the Germans land – and mark my words, they soon will – we'll have our country back and things will be better. Mr Hitler knows what he's talking about. All of them Jews running the banks means folk like us don't have a fair chance.'

As the van turned a corner, Victoria slipped to one side and, as she did, her right hand came free of the clumsily tied twine. She rubbed her wrists to work feeling back into them.

'But what about Mr and Mrs Edelman and their kiddies in Whittleton? They're Jewish and came here as refugees and don't have any more than us. Likely less.'

The van lurched back to the right, and Victoria curled into a ball and rolled with the movement.

'That's another thing, there's too many of them so-called refugees taking over our country. They should go back to where they came from and let their own look out for them.' Walter made a sharp sound. 'What are you doing slowing down? Keep driving. What the hell...?'

Brakes squealed and Victoria scrambled towards the rear door, wrenched it open and jumped out, crashing into the woods that bordered the road.

Men's voices shouted, a shot rang out and she ducked behind a tree trunk and crouched low to the ground, covering her head. Where was she? They couldn't have travelled far from Upper Yarrow Farm, but in the growing darkness, and thanks to that bang on the head, she was disoriented.

'What's going on here?'

A new voice spoke, and she peeped around the tree.

'I told you to stay out of this, Frank.' Holding a revolver or pistol, Victoria couldn't be sure which, Walter faced his brother in the middle of the narrow lane.

'It's too late.' Outlined by the gleam of the moon, Frank shook his head. 'I know what you've been up to in the barn and I don't want no part of it. And what's with that airstrip? How'd you think you could hide it?'

'Get on home and mind your own affairs, then.' Walter waved the gun. 'You got no business being out here with the tractor anyway. What do you think you're playing at, cutting us off?'

'Mam and Dad would be ashamed of you.' Frank raised his arms as if giving himself up to an enemy. 'And what about our Florrie? She worshipped the ground you walked on. Remember her? Come over here with me, Joe. You don't want no truck with Walter's new friends, do you?'

'If you do, I'll shoot both of you.' Walter's voice rose.

Victoria risked another cautious look around the tree. The two brothers still faced each other, and Joe sat as if frozen in the van's driver's seat.

'Don't you bring our Florrie into this. She'd still be here if it weren't for that foreigner calling himself a doctor. He weren't fit to tend a sick cow and that's the truth.' As he bent his head, Walter's hand, which held the gun, went to his side nearest Victoria.

'Dr Cohen did his best and you know it. If not for him, we'd have lost Mam too. He was also as British as you and me. He were born in Manchester and even went to Cambridge.' Frank moved closer to Walter. 'Come on home with me, both of you and we won't say anything more about—'

The sound of an aircraft reverberated in the distance, not the steady drone of an RAF plane but the uneven one Victoria had learned to distinguish as the Luftwaffe.

When Walter took a step back to look up, Victoria sprinted from the cover of the trees and pushed him as hard as she could from behind.

Startled, Walter dropped the gun and before he could scramble and retrieve it, she grabbed for the handle and clasped it tight.

'I'll… you…' As Walter lunged for her, Frank tackled him and the two of them pummelled each other in the dirt.

The aircraft noise grew louder and, still holding the gun, Victoria dived back into the woods, crashing through undergrowth in search of a place to hide.

Her ears rang, tree branches swayed and when she looked up, the aeroplane's wings were almost directly above her head.

Then, almost as suddenly as it had appeared, the German plane roared upwards again, but now with the familiar steady drone of an RAF fighter aircraft in pursuit.

She collapsed against a tree trunk and pressed a hand to her heaving chest.

The gun. It could go off. *Always check the safety mechanism.* Long ago, her uncle and father had returned from a day of duck hunting and, since she'd been curious, they'd showed her how to use a gun safely. She stared at this one, found and secured the safety and then, her hands shaking, dropped the weapon by her side.

Shouts and grunts still reverberated from the lane as she once again tried to get her bearings. If they hadn't gone far from Upper Yarrow Farm, they hadn't gone far from Hazelbury either. The village must be further along this road, one of the many that criss-crossed the North Norfolk countryside.

Miss Hetty. If she'd made it to the village, the police constable should have arrived by now – except he'd follow the main road unless… She listened, scarcely daring to breathe, as a car engine grew louder.

Vehicle doors slammed and new voices, urgent ones, rose above the cacophony.

'Miss McKaye? Where is she? What have you done to her?'

At Louis's voice, Victoria went limp and when she tried to call, her voice came out in a weak croak.

'Victoria?' Footsteps crashed through the bracken and then Louis's arms were around her. 'You're safe.' He buried his face in her hair and then kissed her. 'You've been so brave, so terribly brave. If you only knew what… you could have… oh, my darling.'

Victoria sagged against him as his words washed over her.

'I've found her and she's safe,' he shouted.

'Miss Hetty… is she all right? Did she find Constable Smith?'

'She not only found him, she's here with him. He's making arrests as we speak.' Louis touched Victoria's face and hair as if to reassure himself that she was real and alive. 'I'd have searched every inch of the county, all of England and beyond to find you. I love you, Victoria, with all that I am, now and forever. I should have told you before but I thought we had time. I waited and it was almost too late. I can't hope that you love me in return but—'

'I do, I do love you.' As she gazed into his eyes, the last bit of doubt was swept away.

Explanations, how Louis had found her and talking about everything and everyone else, even Miss Hetty and Constable Smith, could wait.

Victoria wanted to savour this one perfect moment, enveloped in Louis's arms and in the certainty of his love – before she, and they, had to face real life again.

Chapter Thirty-Eight

'I'm all right, honestly.' The next morning, Victoria sat propped up in her own bed at Hazelbury Manor, the breakfast tray Nell had prepared balanced on her knees. Sunlight and a soft breeze came through the open bedroom window along with the murmured voices of Miss Pilch and another land girl in the garden below.

'That may be, but the doctor said you're to mostly stop in bed today, what's left of it. It's after midday.' From where she sat on the edge of her own bed, Nell's worried face studied Victoria. 'He also told us to keep checking on you and be on the lookout for any new or unusual symptoms. If your headache worsens or your vision gets blurry and such.'

'Yes – and while *we* follow the doctor's orders we're also to make sure *you* abide by them.' In a chair she'd moved from their sitting room, Beatrice nodded. 'If you feel up to it, he said you can come downstairs and sit in the garden with one of us later, but that's all. Constable Smith wants to speak with you, but Miss Hetty said he had to wait. She was quite fierce.'

Victoria flopped back on the pillows and put a hand to her head. Although her whole body hurt, the bumps and bruises would heal. Despite the instructions of the doctor, who'd come from Whittleton to check her over, she was anxious to be out and about. To see Louis most of all. *He loved her and she loved him.* Her face heated at the memory of his words and his kisses.

'Where's Louis? He said... I... have to get out of bed and dress. I need to speak with him.'

'Louis had to return to London early this morning.' Beatrice plumped Victoria's pillows and gave her a sympathetic smile. 'He left a note for you, though. Smuggled it to Nell in the kitchen while I kept Miss Hetty and Miss Addie occupied in the dining room. After last night, neither of them wanted to let Louis out of their sight.'

Nell took a small envelope from the table by Victoria's bed. 'Here you are.'

Victoria took the precious letter and tucked it beneath the top pillow. She'd read it later when she was alone. Of course Louis needed to return to his work, but she still hadn't pieced together why he'd been here at all.

'More tea?' Nell gestured to Victoria's empty cup and the teapot covered in a knitted cosy. 'You haven't finished your toast.'

'I'm not hungry.' Instead, and despite the joy of knowing Louis felt about her as she did him, as other memories of the previous night returned, unease curled in her tummy.

The brief journey back to the village with Louis driving Joe's baker's van, and Victoria and Miss Hetty squeezed together in the front passenger seat. Walter Clarke hurling insults as he, Frank and Joe were arrested and bundled into Constable Smith's police vehicle. At the police house, Miss Hetty stopping Constable Smith from asking them any but the most basic questions. Victoria asking Louis questions. Had he answered? She couldn't remember.

Louis had taken the gun, Victoria recollected that much. She'd given it to him and tried to tell him about the map and aniseed balls. The leaflet. She'd put it in her skirt pocket. The police would want to see it. And what about Mrs Wallace, Mr Knight and Mrs Mann? Had the police caught them as well?

'My skirt, the one I wore yesterday. Where is it?' One problem at a time. She glanced around the room.

'I put it with your other clothes to be laundered,' Beatrice said. 'It will need mending. There's a rent in it on one side that's a good four inches. I'm not certain it *can* be mended, but Nell says she'll do her best. Since she's as good as a professional seamstress—'

'Yes, but I need my skirt now.' Victoria made to get out of bed. 'I left something important in the pocket.'

Nell gave her a gentle push back. 'Nothing is so important it can't wait.'

'Might it be this pamphlet?' Beatrice took the crumpled paper out of her own pocket and smoothed it atop Victoria's eiderdown.

'Yes.' Victoria leaned forwards to look at it. Last night, she'd only glanced at what was in those boxes in the shed but now she took in the full horror of what she was reading. 'It's... it's treason and antisemitic and... and...' Un-British, that's what Miss Hetty had said, although she'd only been referring to what they'd heard – and this pamphlet was far worse. 'Who could write such things about Hitler? That he... his way... will be good for Britain and the British people?'

'A person who believes it and then convinces others to follow them, I expect. Fascists like Oswald Mosley and his ilk have no qualms about betraying their country and putting all of us under Hitler and Germany's control.' Disgust curled Beatrice's mouth. 'The village is, of course, in an uproar and talking of nothing else. The police arriving from Norwich and Cromer would have set tongues wagging even before news of the arrests got out. Mrs Meldrum called in on her way to church to see how you were, but also undoubtedly to see what she could find out. I sent her on her way, but not before accepting the dish of strawberry jam she brought with her for you.'

'Beatrice stayed home,' Nell said, 'but after church I heard that the police are all over Upper Yarrow Farm. Lower Yarrow, Mr Frank Clarke's farm as well – although the police have released him.'

'As they should.' The throbbing in Victoria's head worsened, likely from when Walter had bashed it against the barn wall. 'Frank tried to stop his brother.'

243

'And got himself a broken nose and several cracked ribs for his trouble, I also heard.' Nell shook her head. 'It's a bad business all round. Wilf and Albert brought your bicycle back earlier. They said it's not part of what Constable Smith calls 'evidence', but word is the police are even interviewing Mrs Mann. As if she'd have anything to do with anything. When I think about what could have happened… You should have come straight back to Hazelbury with Miss Hetty.'

Victoria couldn't tell Beatrice and Nell that she'd only stayed at the farm because of Louis, or even why Mrs Mann was being questioned. 'One of us needed to stay to find out what was going on. At the time Miss Hetty left we'd only heard some careless talk.' Victoria fiddled with the edge of the quilted eiderdown.

'There's a time to be brave and do your bit, and there's another time to be sensible and scarper.' Nell took away the breakfast tray. 'You're a teacher, not someone trying to catch Nazi sympathisers. Nobody would've blamed you for haring off to the village at the first sign of trouble. Wouldn't it have been something to see Miss Hetty on Beatrice's bicycle? Bob was coming out of the pub as she flew by and said he hardly recognised her without a hat and her hair all down.'

'One of the farmers found her scarf in his field,' Beatrice said. 'Perhaps after the holiday we should set a combined maths and PE lesson to retrieve and count scattered hair pins.' With a soft laugh, Beatrice stood. 'But now we must leave you to rest.' She indicated a small silver bell at Victoria's bedside. 'If you need anything, ring. I'll draw the curtains, shall I?'

Victoria nodded and slumped on her pillows as Beatrice and Nell left her alone and the bedroom was plunged into shadows again. Stuck up here, she was useless. Worse than useless. She thumped the top pillow and drew out Louis's letter.

Her head felt like it was stuffed with cotton wool, and even sliding a finger under the flap to open the envelope was an effort. She found her torch, turned it on and tugged out the single sheet of paper filled with his now familiar handwriting.

My dearest Victoria.

As the bedroom and soft light from the torch spun around her, she blinked and lay flat to continue reading.

> *I can't say much, but know that last night you and Aunt Hetty foiled a Nazi plot that could have cost Britain and her allies hundreds of lives, including those of innocent civilians. But in doing so, you risked your own life, darling, and I don't know whether to be proud or cross. For now, I'll settle for proud but I also regret more than I can say having put you in such danger.*
>
> *When I asked you to keep watch on certain people and report back, that was all, nothing more. When I got to the farm and found your bicycle, I must have died a thousand deaths imagining where Walter Clarke might have taken you. What a man like him and his friends might have done to you. When I came upon the Clarke brothers and their cousin, I'd have killed all three of them with my bare hands if not for Constable Smith and Aunt Hetty arriving at almost the same moment. Promise you'll never give me such a fright again?*

She could easily promise that, because from now on she'd stick with teaching and everyday war work like other women.

> *As soon as you're well enough, Constable Smith and someone from Special Branch will interview you. I know you'll answer their questions honestly but remember that as far as anyone knows, you and Aunt Hetty were only at the farm on W.I. business.*
>
> *I'll write again as soon as I can. I'm also hoping for a twenty-four hour leave pass in a fortnight's time.*
>
> *For now while we are parted, I send you all my love.*
> *Louis*

After switching off the torch and setting it aside, Victoria tucked the note back into its envelope and under her pillow, battling the need for sleep with a similarly pressing need to make sense of Louis's note. Did he mean she wasn't to mention he'd asked her to help him? He hadn't asked her to go to Upper Yarrow Farm yesterday evening, so that was the truth. However, all along she'd reported back to him about Walter Clarke. And what was Mrs Wallace's role? Beatrice and Nell hadn't mentioned *her*, or Mr Knight, either.

Before sleep claimed her, Victoria couldn't shake the unease that lurked at the edges of her mind. Until now, she'd assumed Louis had arrived with Constable Smith and Miss Hetty but hadn't been able to work out how and where he'd met them. However, in his letter he said he'd gone to the farm and found her bicycle.

What had he been doing before he reached the farm and with whom? Even if he truly was a Royal Navy officer, that didn't mean he couldn't also be spying for the Germans. Someone in his position, privy to the kind of military intelligence that Louis must be, would be the ideal recruit. And what was Miss Skene's role? Was she really his secretary or were the two of them working together in some other way?

Along with the pounding and dizziness in her head, Victoria now felt sick as all her previous suspicions roared back, even stronger. For weeks, months now, she'd gone back and forth, talking herself into distrusting Louis and then convincing herself she was wrong. But what if she was right and now she'd fallen in love with him too?

Tomorrow. She'd think about it all tomorrow.

Chapter Thirty-Nine

'Are you comfortable, Miss McKaye?' Two days later, in a box-like room at the village police station where mid-afternoon sun cast ribbon-stripes across the floor and pale-green walls, Constable Smith fussed around Victoria.

She shifted on the straight-backed wooden chair where she sat across a table facing Constable Smith and Mr Bowie, the detective inspector from Special Branch in London.

'Here, a cushion, perhaps?' Constable Smith bounced to his feet, found a crochet-covered green one, and tucked it behind Victoria's back. He'd already made her a cup of tea she didn't want and insisted she take one of his wife's rock cakes, which she had no interest in eating.

'We'll begin, shall we?' Mr Bowie, who looked to be somewhere in his early fifties, was portly and bald, and had protruding blue eyes topped by bushy, sandy brows that reminded Victoria of spring caterpillars at home.

Constable Smith, younger but also balding, and deferential to a superior officer who carried the prestige of both the capital and Special Branch, sat down again. 'Now don't be frightened, Miss McKaye. It's not as if we're going to lock you up. You're a witness, not a suspect.'

Mr Bowie silenced him with a frown and rapped a pencil on the scarred wooden tabletop.

Victoria wasn't frightened, not exactly. Instead, although the doctor had given his approval for this interview, her head was still too much like cotton wool. She also had a curious feeling of somehow being outside herself, almost as if she were an onlooker rather than an active participant in this meeting.

Mr Bowie opened a black-covered notebook and held his pencil poised. 'If you would be so good as to leave us alone, Constable?'

'Yes, of course.' Constable Smith gave Victoria an encouraging smile before scurrying from the interview room like a mouse trying to escape a cat. 'Now, would you please start from the beginning, Miss McKaye? Tell me why you and Miss Grainger went to Upper Yarrow Farm.'

As Victoria recounted going to see Mrs Clarke about a W.I. matter and, not finding her at home, hearing voices and deciding to investigate, she kept her voice steady.

'Then Miss Grainger went for Constable Smith, correct?' Mr Bowie wrote notes as Victoria spoke.

'Yes. You see, from what we overheard, we thought they could be working for the Germans against the British government.' Victoria swallowed and took a sip of the now lukewarm tea. 'Perhaps members of a Fascist organisation.' She passed the leaflet she'd taken from the shed across the table to him.

'And that "they" you are referring to is Mr Walter Clarke and his cousin, Joseph Taylor?' Mr Bowie glanced at the leaflet and set it aside.

'Yes, but I only ever heard him called "Joe".' As Mr Bowie studied her, Victoria got a creepy-crawly feeling in the pit of her stomach. 'At first, there were several others there as well. Mrs Mann, the village schoolmistress, Major Bertram's daughter, Mrs Wallace, and a Mr Knight. I'd seen Mr Knight at Mr Clarke's farm before when I was giving his son, Jimmy, extra tuition in reading. Mr Clarke said Mr Knight was from the government. Something to do with identifying more land to grow crops.'

'Mrs Mann?' Mr Bowie's expression didn't change but Victoria sensed that, like Mr Clarke, she was already known to the authorities.

'Yes, she and Mrs Wallace and Mr Knight went up to the farmhouse but didn't return to the barn.'

'Then you were discovered, physically assaulted and forced into Mr Taylor's bakery van?'

As Victoria recounted the horror of that evening, she clenched her hands together. 'It sounded like they were driving to the coast, possibly to meet someone else with a plan of attaching timed explosives to blow up ships. Cutting telegraph wires was also mentioned and they had a map of the Norfolk coast, military bases and ship positions. With all the talk of a German invasion and spies, I assumed...' She faltered. Her work for Louis was secret. She couldn't explain why she'd really gone to the farm.

'Quite right.' Mr Bowie nodded. 'Keeping your eyes and ears open as anyone would do in these dangerous and distressing times.' He paused. 'What I don't understand is why Mr Grainger was involved as well. Constable Smith said he was already there when he and Miss Grainger arrived.'

'I don't know. I'd hidden in the woods and then... well, I told you about the gun and the rest.' Cold sweat trickled down Victoria's neck beneath her hair. 'I heard his voice, that's all.'

'Who *is* Mr Grainger to you?' Mr Bowie fixed Victoria with a hard stare.

'Mr, rather Lieutenant Commander Grainger, Louis, is Miss Grainger's great-nephew from my billet. He's serving in the Royal Navy. I thought...'

'You thought what, Miss McKaye?' Mr Bowie's gaze held hers.

'That he might have been working with you, the security services?' Her voice caught.

'Why would you think that?'

'Well, I got the sense he might be doing intelligence work. By putting two and two together.' She stared at her hands. Louis had told her he worked in naval intelligence. Was that supposed to be a secret? Had she said too much? Unless Victoria had been right to doubt Louis all along, why would Mr Bowie suspect him?

'I see.' Mr Bowie snapped his notebook shut, and Victoria's head jerked up. 'You do realise, Miss McKaye, that at the present time you can trust no one?'

'Yes, but you're with Special Branch. You showed me your badge.'

'I didn't mean myself and Constable Smith, of course.' He tutted as if she were a foolish child. 'Is Lieutenant Commander Grainger someone that you have… feelings of a more personal nature for?'

'Yes.' Victoria's face flamed. 'But it's not, he's not… I trust him.' Or had she been a fool and Louis, like Roy, wasn't worthy of her trust?

'You and Miss Grainger did indeed foil a Nazi plot, and although I can't tell you the specifics, the British government is grateful for your service. Those aniseed balls contained a device to detonate a timed explosive that would have destroyed one of His Majesty's ships and everyone and everything in its immediate vicinity.' His bushy eyebrows drew together. 'We are already questioning Mrs Mann. As for Mrs Wallace and Mr Knight, they were detained this morning when they arrived together at one of the London railway stations.'

Victoria pressed a hand to her mouth to suppress a gasp. 'But Major Bertram, he…'

'Major and Mrs Bertram were unaware of their daughter's regrettable associations.' He cleared his throat. 'Unfortunately, I can't say the same of many others of their class.' Mr Bowie took out a white handkerchief and wiped his forehead. 'Be mindful of whom you bestow your affections upon, Miss McKaye. Simply because Lieutenant Commander Grainger comes from a good family does not testify to his character or trustworthiness. As you have so recently seen, there are many British people who have not hesitated to betray their country to the enemy.'

'Yes.' Victoria spoke around a lump in her throat.

'There are men and women like Mr Clarke all across the country, but they are the foot soldiers. They are being preyed on and led by others far more intelligent and well connected.' Mr Bowie tucked his handkerchief away. 'Your Grainger fellow may be innocent of any wrongdoing but likewise he may not. While I cannot divulge my reasons, I shall be speaking with him and his superiors as well. Keep that in mind, won't you, Miss McKaye, when you join in any talk in a shop or with your friends in the W.I.?'

'Of course.' Victoria's heart gave a dull thud. She wasn't a gossip – but Mr Bowie had no reason to believe her.

'You aren't the first woman to be deceived by a handsome, charming man pretending to be someone he's not and you won't be the last.' He stood. 'Likewise, nor would Miss Grainger be the first genteel and unworldly elderly lady to be duped by a trusted member of her family. I hope you understand me?'

'Yes, Mr Bowie.' Victoria's head pounded and when she got to her feet she tasted bile.

Could Louis be a double agent, and had Victoria unwittingly been helping the Germans? Had he lied about his work to her and Miss Grainger? She kept one hand on the edge of the table to steady herself. Had Mr Bowie kept Louis under surveillance too?

'All right, Miss McKaye?' Constable Smith reappeared and gave her his arm. 'I'm sure you did splendidly. Here, why don't you sit down again?' He led her back to the chair. 'If I may say so, you do look rather faint. I'll show Mr Bowie out, but I won't be a moment.'

'I'm fine.' She sank back into her seat. She'd never fainted in her life and wasn't about to do so now.

Still, amidst the dizziness and whirling in her head, one thought stood out in stark relief. She had to speak with Louis and, once and for all, find out what was truly going on.

Chapter Forty

In a teashop tucked away on a side street in Norwich city centre, Victoria stared out the window into misty afternoon rain and twirled a spoon around in her empty cup. It had been almost a week since her ordeal at the hands of Walter Clarke and now she waited for Louis who was late.

She checked her wristwatch again and resolved to give him another five minutes. This meeting had been arranged through Miss Skene, but the secretary, if that's who she really was, had promised Victoria he'd be here. Since the Misses Grainger and Beatrice were away for a few days, she'd only had to tell Nell, who hadn't questioned her story of catching the Norwich bus from Hazelbury crossroads to do some shopping in the city. And since Nell never wanted to go anywhere larger than Cromer, Victoria hadn't worried she'd ask to come along.

'Victoria, I'm sorry.' Louis stopped beside her table.

'I'd almost given up on you.' She forced a smile. He was in uniform and, as he bent to kiss her cheek, she smelled damp wool, cigarette smoke and a hint of crisp lemon soap.

'I was on a troop train and it was delayed. Come.' He took Victoria's coat from the back of her chair and she stood as he helped her into it.

'I need to pay for my tea and bun.'

'I've already taken care of it.' He nodded to a nearby waitress in a black dress and white apron. 'I thought we could walk in the cathedral grounds. It's a miserable, wet day but—'

'I understand.' They couldn't risk being seen here together or overheard. She picked up her umbrella, handbag and parcel containing a book and pair of gloves she'd bought at Jarrolds department store.

'Going round the shops, were you?' He gestured to her parcel. 'Here, let me carry it for you.'

'I can manage.' She clutched the parcel to her chest as he guided her out of the tearoom and outside onto the pavement.

'As you wish.' His tone was formal and, dropping her arm, he put up his umbrella to shelter them both. 'I hope you're feeling well again?'

'I am, thank you.' She navigated the wet pavement, avoiding puddles and wishing she'd worn her overshoes. 'The doctor said I can return to school when term begins the week after next.'

He'd also said she might have headaches for several more weeks from that thump on her head and if she did, she'd have to stop work and rest. Except, who would replace her? She couldn't burden Beatrice and Nell with even more work, and although everyone in the village knew the teacher's house beside the school was empty and rumours flew thick and fast, there'd been no news of Mrs Mann.

'That's good, then.' Louis took Victoria's arm again as they crossed a busy main road and then walked into the cathedral close.

'Yes, it is.' She paused as two young women on bicycles rode by giving Louis covert looks as they passed. 'Thank you for meeting me. I don't expect it was easy to get away.'

'It wasn't but I… I suppose you'd like an explanation.' He drew her away from the main path towards the green that spanned one side of the cathedral.

'I would.' There was a book about Norwich Cathedral, a city icon since medieval times, in the manor's library and Victoria had pored over it. Now she was too anxious and focused on Louis to admire the building's imposing spire and magnificent Romanesque architecture. 'I don't understand why, that night in the lane, you were with the Clarke brothers and their cousin. When I heard your voice I almost thought I'd imagined it.' The rain fell harder now and despite them sheltering under a tree, fat drops pattered Louis's umbrella.

'It's difficult.' Louis exhaled and his warm breath brushed Victoria's cheek. 'Did that detective inspector from Special Branch ask you about me?'

'He did but…' She looked up at him but his expression was unreadable. 'How did you know I'd be interviewed by a detective inspector or even someone from Special Branch?' He'd mentioned the latter in his note and until now she hadn't put the pieces together. 'And why did Mr Bowie tell me he'd be speaking with you and your superiors?'

'That's difficult as well, although let's just say that our intelligence and security services aren't as joined up as perhaps they ought to be.' He gave Victoria a smile likely meant to be reassuring but it didn't reach his eyes. 'Mr Bowie's eyebrows would make even the most hardened criminal confess.'

'But I'm not a criminal, am I?' She was making a hash of things, but Louis was the one who'd dragged her into this situation in the first place. If not for him, she'd be the conventional teacher everyone else thought she was, either in her classroom or having picnics and nature rambles. Not traipsing round the countryside after Nazi sympathisers. 'I'm worried, is all. About you and…' She gulped. 'I could have been killed. You didn't see as much of Walter Clarke and the others as I did, including your friend Mrs Wallace.'

'Mrs Wallace is no friend of mine.' Louis's face was grim and as immovable as the cathedral's stone face. 'I told you before that she means nothing to me and hasn't for a long time.'

'I know, but Miss Hetty said…' Victoria's face heated. Was she more upset about Mrs Wallace betraying Britain or her past connection to Louis? Now the two things were intertwined, as was the possibility that Louis and Mrs Wallace had been working together all along, and Victoria had been played for a fool.

'Aunt Hetty was meddling, was she?' Louis turned and cupped Victoria's chin in one hand. 'I thought you trusted me.'

'I did, I wanted to believe you but now I…' She gulped. As she stared into his blue eyes, he blinked and then took his hand away from her face.

'I know you could have been killed and when I found your bicycle I was desperate to reach you. I had a hunch which direction Walter was headed in and fortunately I was right. If you'd been badly hurt or worse, I'd never have forgiven myself. Walter Clarke is… well, I know what he's capable of. While he didn't have anything to do with the hall roof falling in, it *was* him behind the lavatory that day. He was waiting for a delivery and further instructions which all the roof commotion foiled.'

Victoria trembled and clutched the book parcel like a shield. 'If that's true, then why can't you tell me what's going on? You must realise I'm thinking all sorts. If Walter and the others were helping the Germans, maybe you are too.' There, she'd said it, put her worst fear out into the open. Although part of her wished she could take it back, any relationship, even friendship, had to be founded on honesty. 'And what about Miss Skene? Did you fool her as well?'

'I *had* hoped you thought better of me.' His voice was curt.

Her stomach lurched at the bleakness in his expression. 'I want to, truly, but the country could be invaded by the Germans at any moment – and *that's* not village gossip.' Mr Bowie's comment about her joining in talk in a shop and at the W.I. pricked at her. 'We all have to be on our guard.'

'We do.' He stared into the distance where wisps of fog hovered over the River Wensum. 'If you're worried about Walter Clarke, don't be. Along with his cousin Joe he'll likely be imprisoned for a good long time.'

'And the others?'

Louis shrugged. 'It's not for me to say. Evelyn Wallace has friends in high places so she may escape prosecution entirely. As for Mr Knight, and Mrs Mann? They're both German nationals. Evelyn met Mr Knight on a trip to Berlin before the war.' He hesitated. 'She had a husband, and he still has a wife – but apparently that was just a minor inconvenience.'

Victoria put a hand to her mouth to cover what her mother would call an unladylike gasp. Although she'd heard that such liaisons happened, she'd never imagined someone like the Bertrams' daughter engaging in one. 'What about the school? Mrs Mann shouldn't be teaching British children.'

'Even though she's been teaching them for over thirty years and has lived in Britain since she was a young child herself?' Louis shook rain off the umbrella. 'I gather that Mrs Mann thought she'd joined some kind of Christian pacifist group. Her parents were German, and – certainly in places like London and Manchester – that isn't unusual. There are good Germans, you know, and some of them are as appalled by what's going on under Hitler as the rest of us.'

'I'm sure they are, but…' Victoria's thoughts spun. She'd been raised to believe there was right and wrong and nothing in between. At home, church and school, and until her broken engagement, she'd followed the path that had been set out for her without questioning it. Despite what she'd considered her 'escape' to England, as the child of British parents, and unlike refugees, she'd been sheltered. 'Does anyone in Hazel-bury know about Mrs Mann?'

'Not yet – but it will soon come out. In any case, village gossip being what it is, I doubt she'd be welcomed back with open arms, especially because it's also likely to surface that her late husband was Italian. As she did, he came to England when he was very young. The family name "Mann" was "Mancini" before they anglicised it.'

'She once mentioned a son.' Victoria's heart pounded.

'He was killed in the First World War. Only a boy. He ran away from home and lied about his age to enlist.' Louis still stared at the rain and fog. 'As a bereaved mother, she wanted to work for peace.'

A lump rose in Victoria's throat. It was a mess, all of it, and between Mr Bowie and Louis she didn't know who or what to believe.

Or trust. She'd trusted Roy and he was the reason she'd ended up here, although unlike Louis's possible betrayal, his had been a personal failing, not a matter of political allegiance. There was also Miss Hetty to consider. She'd warned Victoria away from Louis. Even if Louis *could* be trusted, knowing his great-aunt's reservations, would he go against his family's wishes to marry Victoria?

'I love you, Victoria, and that hasn't changed. It won't ever change. Can't that be enough?' Louis's voice and face pleaded with her.

She loved him too, but she also couldn't promise herself to any man who wasn't truthful. If she gave Louis her whole heart, he could break it as Roy had. Even worse, Louis could also lead her to betray the Allies. Britain and Canada, both her countries and her family, her heritage and everything she held dear.

'I'm sorry, but love isn't enough, not for me.' Without trust, love was meaningless. She choked back a sob and fumbled in her handbag for a handkerchief.

'I'm sorry as well.' Louis's voice caught. 'I thought you… we… Although I can't tell you everything about myself, the feelings I hold in my heart for you are true, honest and honourable.'

The silence stretched between them. 'I'm sorry,' Victoria said again. In books and films, love was happy and wonderful. It wasn't supposed to rip you apart and trample on the scattered pieces.

Louis stood even straighter. 'In wartime, one would be particularly foolish to accept as truth that which cannot be proven. Here.' He held out his arm. 'I shall see you safely back to the bus stop.'

Mutely, Victoria took his outstretched arm. There was nothing else left to say. She'd made her choice, one that would save her from more heartache and, like the gentleman he was, Louis had accepted it.

She'd also done her duty, which king, country and her family would expect. What Miss Hetty would expect. In the lonely days, weeks and months ahead, Victoria would have to remind herself of all those things, even if they seemed cold comfort now.

Chapter Forty-One

'Did you hear about Mrs Mann? I can hardly believe it.' Several days later, Mrs Meldrum came out of the village shop and stopped Victoria on her way in. 'It goes to show that you can't trust anyone nowadays, can you?' The cherries on Mrs Meldrum's summer hat bobbed in time to her words.

'I did hear the news about Mrs Mann, yes.' Victoria glanced around, but apart from several young men in RAF uniform clustered outside the newsagent's, the high street was deserted. 'If you'll excuse me, I—'

'And Walter Clarke as well.' Mrs Meldrum tutted. 'I saw poor Alma Clarke in the post office. It's a wonder she can show her face in the village.'

'Why would you say that?' After mostly sleepless nights ruminating over how she'd left things with Louis, Victoria was in no mood to be tactful. 'If anything, we women should be rallying round to support Mrs Clarke.'

Mrs Meldrum's mouth dropped open and she crossed her arms over her ample bosom. 'Well, I should think that after what Walter did to you—'

'Walter, not his wife, remember?' Not caring if she was impolite, Victoria held Mrs Meldrum's gaze until the other woman looked down. 'As for Mrs Mann, from everything I've heard, she made a mistake, an error in judgement, if you will.'

A costly one, however, because if the rumours were true, the schoolmistress would soon be sent to an internment camp for enemy aliens. Although Canada and Britain were allies, would Victoria be sent away somewhere too if Louis were found to be an enemy agent and the authorities discovered she'd helped him? She gripped her handbag and shopping basket tighter.

'And what about Mrs Wallace? I haven't heard anyone say Major and Mrs Bertram shouldn't show their faces.'

'That's different.' Mrs Meldrum's voice trailed away and red patches bloomed on her cheeks. 'The Bertrams must be devastated. The major's mother has a weak heart, you know.'

'I didn't know, but Mrs Clarke and Mrs Mann must be devastated as well.' Victoria stepped around Mrs Meldrum.

'Miss McKaye, I... You're right, of course.' Mrs Meldrum touched Victoria's gloved hand. 'I don't know what this world is coming to.'

What was left of Victoria's wounded heart squeezed into a tight and painful knot. 'I must get back to the manor so—'

'Yes, no... please wait.' Under her hat, Mrs Meldrum's face was now the colour of a ripe plum, and beneath a navy dress with a white collar her chest heaved. 'We *should* rally round Mrs Clarke and maybe even Mrs Mann. The two of us fell out years ago, something trivial, the flowers for a W.I. event, but then that pageant of yours brought us back together. Still, while I didn't put my finger on it before, Mrs Mann's secretiveness always bothered me. Now, of course, we know what she was hiding. An actual German right here in our midst and married to an Italian as well. While we shouldn't speak ill of the dead, I always thought her husband odd. So demonstrative, not British at all.'

As Mrs Meldrum rattled on, Victoria stopped herself from interrupting. Although Mrs Mann and her husband had come to England as small children and had lived here far longer than in Germany or Italy, to someone like Mrs Meldrum they'd always be foreign. Despite her British ancestry, did Miss Hetty also see Victoria as 'not British at all'?

Victoria thought she belonged here, but she didn't – and maybe never would. She couldn't change who she was and nor did she want to, even for Louis. Despite a fresh niggle of doubt that perhaps she'd misjudged him, it was too late to make amends. He'd seen her onto the bus and then, after touching his cap, he'd disappeared around the corner of the crowded street. And Victoria had sat stiff in her bus seat all the way back to Hazelbury, trying not to cry.

However, even if she couldn't help herself, she could help someone else. 'Mrs Mann must want some of her things from home. Photographs, clothing and such. I could put together a parcel. Someone must have a key to her house.' While it would be uncomfortable going through the teacher's possessions, perhaps Mrs Russell would help. Unlike Mrs Meldrum, the vicar's wife was discreet.

Mrs Meldrum made a harumphing sound. 'Next door will have a key, I expect, but otherwise there's likely to be one under the outdoor mat by the scullery window. You shouldn't be settings your sights on her house, mind.' Mrs Meldrum shook her head. 'Mark my words, it'll either be evacuees or the army moving in.'

'I haven't been "setting my sights" on Mrs Mann's house or anywhere else. I'm perfectly happy at Hazelbury Manor, as are Miss Wentworth and Miss Potter.' How happy would Victoria be at the manor without Louis's regular visits? But even if he did come to see his great-aunts, that would be awkward. She'd have to pretend there had never been anything between them. Or what if he brought a girl home, a fiancée even? Oh, it didn't bear thinking about. 'I'm sorry, what did you say?' She returned her attention to Mrs Meldrum.

'I'll call a special meeting of the W.I. to discuss how we can support Alma Clarke. I suppose she's the one in the greatest need, left with that farm. The older lads were off to join up as soon as Walter was arrested.' Mrs Meldrum frowned. 'As for Mrs Bertram, I'll invite her to the meeting as well. Perhaps she might even host it at Whittleton Hall. The major's in London seeing what can be done about Mrs Wallace. In that case, even though honesty is usually the best course, I think we should simply carry on as if nothing has happened. Don't you agree, Miss McKaye?'

'What? Oh, yes, of course.' Victoria nodded.

People should be honest with each other – but what if they couldn't? Mrs Mann had to keep the secret of her German parents and Italian husband. Otherwise, some in the village would likely have turned against her. What Victoria had seen as her initial unfriendliness might have stemmed from fear. While she'd never know for certain, perhaps she'd been too quick to judge the village schoolmistress.

After saying goodbye to Mrs Meldrum and assuring her she'd speak to Beatrice and Nell about the special W.I. meeting, Victoria went into the shop, ducking her head to avoid a low beam. She pulled Nell's list and their ration books from her handbag and, ignoring the chatter around her, joined the queue for the attention of the assistant serving behind the counter.

While right now she wanted to run as far away from Hazelbury as possible, she couldn't. She had to stay and do her duty.

–

'I hardly feel I've had a holiday. Still, needs must, especially with the three of us now having to teach the village children as well.' At the wooden table they'd moved over beside a sunny window in Hazelbury Manor's library, Beatrice gave Victoria and Nell new notebooks, pencils and fountain pens. 'They're from the school supplies I brought back from London with me.'

Victoria opened the hard-backed notebook and inhaled its crisp, fresh scent. Due to their shortened holiday, the autumn term was starting much earlier this year. Despite not having a true break, perhaps returning to the classroom would be a distraction from Louis and everything else that had happened in the past fortnight.

Nell gestured to the plate with the oat biscuits she'd made earlier. 'With Miss Hetty and Miss Addie having had to stay longer in Ely, Marjorie's happy to let me use the kitchen as much as I want. Although I'm sorry that the Misses Graingers' cousin is ill, I'm making the most of being able to cook and bake as and when I please. Any news from Miss Hopson?'

'Not much beyond what she wrote in her last letter.' Beatrice added a dash of milk to her cup and then poured tea into it from the pot that Nell had also prepared. 'As you might expect, the mood in London is – well, for want of a better word, on edge. Oh, everyone is calm, almost resigned, but underneath, there's an indescribable anxiety.'

'What about visits from the London County Council Care Committee organiser and school inspector?' Victoria poured her own tea and took a biscuit. Despite being in the countryside, they were far from forgotten when it came to inspections, and someone official always seemed to be popping up, whether to do with education, billets or a health authority.

'Both in the middle of September, apparently, although that could change depending on what happens.' Beatrice bit her lip.

'You don't think the Germans will bomb London, do you?' Behind her teacup, Nell's face went white and her eyes were wide and frightened.

'Why wouldn't they? It's better to be prepared than stick your head in the sand and pretend such things will never happen.'

'Beatrice.' Victoria shook her head. 'Some of us are more sensitive. Nell, I'm sure your family will be fine. They don't live near a military base or factory do they?'

'Not nearby no, but still…' Nell dropped her head into her hands.

'Here, put more sugar in your tea. I don't need it.' Beatrice's voice was gruff as she found a clean spoon and dropped a generous amount into Nell's teacup. 'Now, we need to plan for our first day back and how we'll cover Mrs Mann's absence.'

'By mixing the London pupils with the villagers, I expect. It's the only way, at least for my infants,' Victoria said. 'Thank goodness we have Ivy to help. Otherwise, I could hardly manage. Even so, it will be a squash in the village hall.' Victoria suppressed a sigh and began taking notes as Beatrice went through curriculum updates, government education legislation and other never-ending planning matters.

'I wish we could have a decent blackboard in the hall.' As Beatrice drew the meeting to a close, Victoria raised her familiar complaint.

'As I'm sure you're aware, there's a war on and there are other priorities, Miss McKaye,' Nell said.

Beatrice laughed. 'I did raise it with the authorities, but I'm afraid they didn't see my point.'

'Despite the war and all the alarms round here, those authorities still expected us to set and mark examination papers, didn't they?' Nell nibbled on a biscuit with a gloomy expression. 'Yesterday when Ivy and I took the bus to Cromer, we actually glimpsed a dog-fight. It was miles away but still, seeing those aeroplanes battling overhead, we couldn't rightly enjoy our day out for thinking of the poor lads.'

Louis was in the navy, not the air force, but no matter where he was and what he was doing, Victoria wanted him to be safe. 'How did you find your mother, Beatrice?' Since Beatrice had only arrived back in Hazelbury late the night before, they hadn't had a chance to catch up. It was as good a subject as any to divert tender-hearted Nell's thoughts away from the war.

'Much the same.' Beatrice closed her notebook and refilled her teacup. 'She's still living her life as if the world hasn't changed since the summer of 1914 and expects everyone to wait on her hand and foot. Did you have other days out, Nell? How is that dress you're making coming along?'

Victoria wasn't the only one adept at changing the subject. As Nell chatted about her sewing and a church outing, Victoria knew she wouldn't be able to avoid telling Beatrice and Nell about Louis – but how?

'Don't you think Victoria looks peaky?' Nell's question drew Victoria out of her thoughts. 'If you need to stay at home for a few more days, Beatrice and I will cover for you.'

'Of course we can,' Beatrice said. 'And Nell's right. You don't look or seem yourself.'

'I want to go back to school. The doctor said I could.' Staying at the manor with only Marjorie for company would be even worse, as Victoria would have more time to brood.

'Then what's wrong? Something certainly is.' Beatrice took off her spectacles and rubbed her purple-shadowed eyes.

Did Beatrice look more tired than usual? She worked harder than any of them, as in addition to classroom teaching she had more administrative responsibilities, but surely she'd had a few days' rest on her holiday.

'Beatrice is right,' Nell said. 'You'd finally started looking better after the business with Mr Clarke, but that day in Norwich seemed to set you back. If you can't tell us, who can you tell?'

'Nobody.' Emotion clogged Victoria's throat. 'It's Louis. He… we… I broke things off with him.'

'But why?' Nell wrapped her arms around Victoria and made soothing noises.

'I can't…' Victoria gulped back a sob. Although not as unemotional as Beatrice, she'd never been prone to tears, but now she couldn't seem to stop crying. 'It's for the best.'

'Is that what Louis wanted?' Beatrice's voice held an unexpected softness.

'No, but he accepted it.' Victoria found her handkerchief. 'It's the war, and his work, and Miss Hetty doesn't approve.'

'None of which should matter if you truly love each other,' Nell said.

'But unfortunately the way of the world is that they do.' Beatrice gathered up books and papers. 'Under those circumstances, the best place for you, Victoria, is at school. However, please be assured that no matter the situation, Nell and I will do whatever we can to support you, including with Miss Hetty should the occasion arise.' She stood. 'It's our last Saturday afternoon of holiday freedom. I'd thought of going for a walk in the woods. Would the two of you care to join me? Nothing like exercise and time in nature to lift the spirits. Later, we could do a new jigsaw I got in London and listen to a wireless programme.'

'Yes.' Victoria sniffed and put away her handkerchief.

'If you'd like, I'll retrim your summer hat before school on Monday. I still have some pretty ribbon from those remnants Miss Addie gave me.' Nell gave Victoria's hand a last squeeze. 'There's a rich blue that will suit you.'

'Thank you, both of you.' Victoria glanced at Nell, then Beatrice. Even without Louis – and with a war on – Victoria had friendship and many other things to be thankful for. So, as Beatrice would say, she'd 'buck up' and rather than mourning what she'd lost, once again she'd make the best of what she had.

Chapter Forty-Two

'Ladies, ladies.' On a mid-week evening in the large drawing room at Whittleton Hall, Mrs Meldrum rang the small brass bell Mrs Bertram had provided for the special W.I. meeting. 'If I may have your attention for one more moment, please.'

'She likes the sound of her own voice, doesn't she?' Nell leaned into Victoria and muttered while retrieving her ball of navy-blue wool. 'When I met her on my way in, she told me that although she was sure the new term was going "swimmingly", she'd drop by the school tomorrow for a little chat.'

Victoria suppressed a smile. After only two days of the new term, she'd already experienced several of Mrs Meldrum's 'little chats'.

'Now.' Mrs Meldrum's voice rose above the babble. 'You understand, not a word to Mrs Clarke of this meeting. Above all, we must be discreet in giving this aid so as not to cause any discomfort or embarrassment.'

Alma Clarke was likely already embarrassed enough, given Walter had been sentenced by a London court to several years in prison for 'collaborating with the enemy'. However, to her credit, Mrs Meldrum was trying to be tactful.

'Now to the matter of employing land girls at Upper Yarrow Farm.' As Victoria concentrated on turning the heel in the sock she was knitting, Mrs Meldrum's words washed over her.

After the first furore, talk in the village about Walter Clarke, Mrs Mann and Evelyn Wallace had died down. Leading by example, Mrs Bertram had kept a dignified silence and even opened her home to tonight's meeting. Still, suspicion and betrayal simmered beneath the surface, and even the youngest children in Victoria's class talked about "wrong 'uns" and fretted that Germans would soon be marching down the streets of Hazelbury.

'Finally. I'm gasping for a cup of tea.' Nell folded up her knitting as Mrs Meldrum drew the meeting to a close. 'Mrs Clarke will be grateful for our help. Jimmy came back to school yesterday, and the poor boy cowered like a beaten dog. The other children were good as gold, though, better than their elders in some cases. They know Jimmy had naught to do with what his dad was up to.'

'School will likely be an escape for him.' As it was for Victoria. 'I'm going up to the farm on Saturday morning to continue tutoring Jimmy.' That would be after she had posted the parcel to Mrs Mann which, along with packing up the contents of the small, neat house beside the school, Victoria and the vicar's wife had worked on together.

'I'll come with you.' Nell stood and stretched. 'I expect Mrs Clarke could use some help in the house. She might even talk to me. It's not good to keep everything bottled up.' There was a sadness in Nell's voice that belied her youth and suggested she'd experienced more than her share of life's troubles.

'If you ever want to talk about anything, my sisters say I'm a good listener.' Victoria glanced at her colleague. Nell wore a navy dress Miss Addie had given her, and which she had altered by embroidering red accents at the collar and cuffs and adding buttons salvaged from a jacket destined for rags. She looked a perfect fashion plate.

'Oh, don't bother about me.' Nell's smile was too bright. 'I'll go and see if I can lend a hand pouring tea, shall I?' Without waiting for Victoria to respond, she darted away to where Ivy and Mrs Russell stood behind a table with cups and saucers laid out.

'All right, Miss McKaye?' Several minutes later, Mrs Bertram appeared at Victoria's elbow where she stood apart from the other women near one of the long windows which overlooked a garden.

'Yes, thank you.' Victoria gazed towards the massive globes of pink, white and blue hydrangeas that bordered the neat rows of a potato field.

'Good, good.' Dark shadows bracketed Mrs Bertram's eyes, and even her stylish nipped-in-at-the-waist, two-piece grey peplum dress with white piping couldn't conceal that she had lost weight. 'I expect you're wondering why we didn't dig up the hydrangeas as well to free up even more land to grow food.'

'No, not at all.' In truth, Victoria was musing over what would happen if people genuinely said what they meant. She wasn't 'all right', and she doubted Nell, Mrs Bertram or many of the other women here were either. Yet they all had to keep up a pretence of social niceties because even if there hadn't been a war on, that was how life worked.

'Hydrangeas were my late mother's favourite flower. It sounds silly, I suppose, but I needed a bit of cheer and a reminder of home, and dear Sidney indulged me. You must miss your family and Canada.'

'I do.' Her mother loved hydrangeas too, and grew them by the porch at home. However, as the weeks and months of war continued, Victoria had tried to resign herself to the fact that she likely wouldn't see her mother and the rest of the family again for years. By then, they would almost be strangers to each other but she had only herself to blame. The familiar guilt curled its icy tentacles around her. 'How is your mother-in-law?' Grasping for a neutral subject, she landed on Major Bertram's mother who hadn't come downstairs for tonight's meeting.

Mrs Bertram shrugged and, for an instant, her brittle social mask slipped. 'Well enough, but she decided she'd be happier living with Sidney's sister in Suffolk. Barring any bombing scares, I'm taking her down at the weekend. Being so near to Whittleton air base, she finds the aeroplanes buzzing about overhead here... disturbing.'

'I see.' There were plenty of RAF bases in Suffolk too, but whatever the real reason for the elder Mrs Bertram's departure, it was no concern of Victoria's.

'No, I'm sure you don't "see" and there's no need to be so polite, not with me.' Mrs Bertram's face flushed. 'Out of everyone, you're the only one likely to understand. I'm not like the others here and nor are you, not really.'

Victoria swallowed and tried to school her features. 'You mean because, like you, I didn't grow up in England?'

'Yes.' Mrs Bertram fingered one of the cream-velvet curtain pulls and studied the fields and trees gilded in gold by the setting sun. 'Sidney told me what you did and what happened that night when you saw Evelyn at Walter Clarke's farm.'

Victoria glanced around, but all the other women were clustered on the opposite side of the vast drawing room near the tea urn. 'I didn't intend to—'

Mrs Bertram waved away her protest. 'Evelyn is a grown woman, but she's always, unfortunately, been flighty and easily led, especially by men like Mr Knight. Unlike her, you, my dear, were brave and patriotic. Oh yes,' she continued in response to Victoria's stunned expression, 'Evelyn is my daughter, but I'm not blind to her faults. Thanks to Sidney's efforts she's avoided prison and been let off with a warning, but we've agreed it will be better for her to stay at the house in London and engage in some useful war work. My mother-in-law holds a different view. So far, *her* only contribution to wartime life has been to suggest we have dinner in the middle of the day to give Cook less to do. Hence the Suffolk plan.' Mrs Bertram's smile was wry as she raised her eyebrows.

'I... I...' Victoria stammered.

'Even those you love most can disappoint you.' The other woman's brown eyes were troubled. 'War brings out the best in some and the worst in others. Did you know that Mr Knight's real surname is Ritter? As a boy, he had a British tutor. That's why he speaks such good English. I suppose he thought he was being clever, since translated into English, the German "Ritter" means "Knight". Evelyn's behaviour has been disgraceful and repugnant. I'm sure many would expect us to disown her.'

'But you can't.' Victoria wasn't a mother but, in the past eleven months, since having to become an almost de facto mother to her pupils, she had some understanding of the maternal tie. 'You want to help her, give her another chance.'

'Indeed.' Mrs Bertram sighed. 'With the boys away serving in the Forces, and remembering the carnage of the last war, I understand too well the fragility of life. If Evelyn had not acknowledged her mistakes and accepted the consequences it would be a different matter, but if there's any chance she can put this painful interlude behind her, I'm bound to offer my support.' Mrs Bertram scrutinised Victoria. 'I understand Louis Grainger may be caught up in certain things as well.'

'He... I really couldn't say.' Victoria pressed her lips together and her face warmed.

'Quite so.' Still Mrs Bertram studied her. 'However, remember that even if it may not seem so at present, life does go on. While one's vantage point at my age is much different than yours at thirty, I've known Louis since he was born. From then until now I've never had a reason to suspect him of any wrong-doing. Right.' She brushed her hands together as if dispensing of unpleasant topics. 'The bushes in the lane behind the church are simply full of blackberries and they should be ripe in a few weeks. I shall organise a party to pick them and make jam. What do you say?'

'I've never made jam but yes, of course.' Victoria blinked. Why had Mrs Bertram mentioned Louis?

'Then I'll teach you jam-making while I still have use of the Hall kitchen. Nothing is fixed yet, but it's likely this house will soon be requisitioned for military use. If Sidney and I move into one of the estate cottages, we'll have no need for a cook or any of the other remaining house servants. It will be like our flat in London after we married. Hardly room to turn round – but we were so happy.' Her eyes glistened and she patted Victoria's arm. 'Now, let's see about a cup of tea and a piece of undoubtedly dry carrot cake which we shall savour as if it were the finest French pastry.'

As Victoria walked alongside Mrs Bertram to rejoin the rest of the W.I. ladies, she reflected on what the other woman had said.

Before the war, Victoria had been privileged and protected, but that life was gone forever. She had to make a new one and in doing so, she was bound to make mistakes. Had she made one about Louis?

Chapter Forty-Three

'Well done, Albert. That's ten different wildflowers, three birds, a rabbit and the post office cat you and your group spotted on our nature walk.' On Friday afternoon at the end of the first week back at school, Victoria sat in the shade of the village hall with the now combined village and evacuees infants' classes grouped in a big circle around her. 'Diana? Would you go next, please?'

'Yes, Miss McKaye.' The girl had grown at least an inch since last September and, along with Albert and Ralph, was the oldest child in the infants' classes. There was no room for the three of them in the schoolhouse, though, so Victoria had agreed to keep them here for now and set different lessons. 'We saw a thrush, a sparrow, three pigeons and a black-backed gull.'

'You never did. A black-backed gull's a sea-bird.' Leonard, one of the village boys, shook his head and shouted. 'I knows 'cause me dad showed me one.'

'We did see it so it must have flown inland,' Diana said. 'There's a picture right here in Miss McKaye's book. I know what I saw.'

'Children.' Victoria made a calming gesture.

'Miss?' Peter nudged Victoria's sleeve. 'Mrs Meldrum's here. In front of the hall in her car.'

'Oh, again?' Victoria almost added 'bother'. What did the woman want now? Surely between the W.I., WVS, church and various other worthy endeavours, Mrs Meldrum should be too busy to take more than a general interest in the school. But this week she'd dropped by once a day and sometimes twice. 'Miss

Byrne, it's almost time for dismissal. Could you please take the children inside and oversee them washing their hands while I speak with Mrs Meldrum?'

'Yes, Miss McKaye.' Ivy grinned and began organising the children into groups.

When she gave thanks for her blessings, Victoria counted Ivy ten-fold. Without the girl's cheerful help, she'd never have managed the London evacuees and Hazelbury children nearly as well – if at all.

'Mrs Meldrum.' She greeted the woman who'd now left her car and stood in the sun at the front of the hall. 'What can I do for you?'

'Oh, it's the most dreadful thing.' Mrs Meldrum's face was grey, the colour of putty. 'The vicar has had a telegram.' She pressed a handkerchief to her mouth. 'The Russells' eldest son, Gilbert, has been shot down and killed. His entire crew but one, dead, and the one who survived is in hospital badly burned. I thought you'd want to know so the children… could you possibly take Albert and Diana back to the manor with you and give them their tea?'

'Certainly. I'm so sorry.' Victoria's vision blurred.

Gilbert had attended church with the vicar and Mrs Russell on Victoria's first Sunday here, the day war was declared. A tall, brown-haired lad of twenty-three with laughing hazel eyes and an easy smile. On his last leave at home, only a few weeks ago, he'd begun teaching Albert how to play cricket, holding the boy's small hands on the bat with his larger ones as Wilf tossed the ball towards them.

'Is there anything else I can do?' She stole a furtive glance over one shoulder but the hall's outer front door was closed, and Ivy had taken the children in through the back way.

'Not at present, no.' Mrs Meldrum's lower lip wobbled. 'The vicar said he'd tell the children about poor Gilbert himself. It was his duty, he said.'

So the good man had saved Victoria from having to tell them. Her heart skipped a beat. 'Do the Misses Grainger know?'

Mrs Meldrum nodded. 'I went there first. I was at the vicarage speaking to the vicar about hymns for Sunday when a boy came with the telegram. Took the news ever so calmly, Mr Russell did. Mrs Russell too. It was her who asked me to go to the manor so the Misses Grainger didn't hear the news unexpectedly and have an even greater shock. Miss Grainger is one of Gilbert's godparents, you know. His second name, Rupert, is after the Graingers' nephew, Mr Louis's father, who died a few months before Gilbert was born. The vicar is distantly related to the Misses Grainger through his mother's family.'

'I didn't know.' Victoria brushed at her face, all of a sudden aware she was hatless with someone who was invariably critical and to whom standards mattered. 'I'm sorry. It was so warm in the hall I brought the children outdoors and forgot to put my hat on.'

'As if a hat is of any importance now. Gilbert is… was…' Mrs Meldrum sniffed. 'He was in my Sunday-school class and had the kindest heart. I can only hope he didn't suffer. He's in a better place, of course, but such a young man. He'd become engaged only last week, the vicar said. They planned to announce it at church on Gilbert's next leave when his young lady could be here. She's from Cornwall. He met her there on a training course. Now she'll be burying rather than marrying him. It's not for me to question God's will but…' Mrs Meldrum buried her face in her handkerchief again. 'You must get back to the children, and I'll go on to the schoolhouse to speak to Miss Wentworth. She and Miss Potter will need to bring young Wilf home with them. Mrs Russell said to tell the children the vicar would collect them in his car around seven.'

'Of course.' Victoria reached out to touch Mrs Meldrum's gloved hand. 'I am sorry, truly, for everyone. You, the vicar and Mrs Russell and their family.' And Gilbert's fiancée, that unknown young woman whose life and hopes had also been wrecked. All the other families, sweethearts and friends of the men who'd been in that aeroplane, their grief rippling out like a pebble tossed into the still waters of a pond.

Tea at Hazelbury Manor would be a special treat for the children, only to be followed by news that would upend their world, Albert's especially. Gilbert had been a good influence on him, showing the boy through both his words and deeds the kind of young man he could aspire to become.

Mrs Meldrum's hand clasped Victoria's for several seconds before she took it away. 'While Gilbert is the first of our men to be taken in this war, I fear he won't be the last. As you well know, my own boys are in it too… and so many others.' Her voice hitched and then she straightened. 'None of us in Hazelbury will let the side down, you can be sure of it. The sacrifices our brave young lads are making will not be in vain.'

It was an admirable sentiment, and as Mrs Meldrum made her way back to her motor, her bearing as upright as any gallant soldier, Victoria tried to share both her conviction and patriotism.

Except, all she could think of was Louis and that one day he might be one of those injured, killed or missing in action. And – unlike Gilbert Russell's fiancée – Victoria had given up any right to be by Louis's side in life *or* death.

–

'If I may have a word, Miss McKaye?' After Victoria had finished helping Beatrice and Nell give Wilf, Albert and Diana their tea, Miss Hetty cornered her by the dining-room door, almost as if she'd been waiting there.

'Of course, but the children, we're taking them out to the garden so they won't disturb you any further.' Victoria glanced back into the dining room where, under Beatrice's direction, Albert and Wilf were stacking plates and Diana was collecting up the silver napkin rings. 'I was only popping upstairs for a cardigan. It's got chilly.' She rubbed her bare arms beneath her short-sleeved lilac blouse.

'I'm sure that, along with my sister, Miss Wentworth and Miss Potter will be able to manage. Addie has always been fond of children.' Miss Hetty's gaze flicked towards Miss Addie, who was descending the stairs carrying a ball, several books and a skipping rope and cricket bat.

'There's also the washing-up. I don't want to leave it to Nell and—'

'I asked Marjorie to stay late today. *She* will do the washing-up. After all, it's rightfully part of her duties, even if she does it the next morning. Miss Potter is far too obliging and Marjorie takes advantage.' Miss Hetty gestured to the drawing room across the hall.

'All right.' With no more excuses, Victoria turned to follow her.

Behind her sister's back, Miss Addie gave Victoria an encouraging smile as if to say nothing could be as bad as Victoria might imagine. However, except for that night at Upper Yarrow Farm when they'd both, briefly, been united, most of Victoria's interactions with Miss Hetty had been if not downright unpleasant, decidedly awkward.

'Yes, Miss Hetty?' Victoria remained standing as the other woman closed the drawing room door behind them. If only she'd insisted on retrieving her cardigan first. Since it only got the early-morning sun, even in summer this room was cold. But now, with the furniture – apart from one sofa, the piano and several chairs – covered in dustsheets for what Miss Addie called 'the duration', it had an almost ghostly feel of disuse and genteel decay.

Miss Hetty stood near the window where greenish light filtered in through a tall hedge that lined this side of the property. 'Louis used to write to my sister and me several times a week. Now, we've heard from him once in the past fortnight.' Miss Hetty crossed her arms over her bony chest. 'Even then it was only a rushed scrawl on the back of a picture postcard.'

'Oh?' Victoria gripped the back of a chair.

'Don't hover over there. I can hardly see you. Come.' Miss Hetty made an impatient gesture. 'Sit.' She dragged another chair nearer the window before Victoria could offer to help her. 'I remember what this room was like in my girlhood. All lit up for parties with candles in the wall sconces, musicians playing in the hall, women in exquisite gowns and the men in white tie. Look at it now.'

'There's a war on.' Even as Victoria repeated the trite phrase, she knew it was a mistake.

Miss Hetty's upper lip curled and she rested one hand on a window frame. 'Please, you are many things but one of them is intelligent. You're not a parrot or one of the village girls such as Marjorie.'

'No, Miss Hetty.' As the older woman sat in the chair opposite Victoria, she appeared almost frail. 'May I get you anything? Your shawl, perhaps?' Miss Hetty's face was as white as her filmy lace collar, and her lips were the same bluish-purple as her dress.

'I do not need a shawl or anything else except to understand what has gone wrong between you and my great-nephew. Louis won't tell me and...' Her voice faltered. 'I'd never want him to be unhappy.'

'Mr... Lieutenant Commander Grainger is undoubtedly busy with war work but... he... I... you didn't approve of any attachment between us.' If Louis hadn't told Miss Hetty the truth, Victoria wouldn't either. It was none of the old dragon's business.

'Fair enough.' Miss Hetty's mouth worked before she squared her shoulders. 'Gilbert Russell's death has... I suppose it has reminded me of my fiancé and Louis's father as well. Such terrible losses of young and promising lives. You'd expect men would learn, but somehow they don't.'

Victoria clasped her hands in her lap.

'I expected better of *you*, though.' Miss Hetty's gaze drilled into Victoria. 'As you may recall, before that mad caper to Mr Clarke's farm I said we might have misjudged each other but now... If you truly cared for Louis, you wouldn't doubt him or be so easily dissuaded in your affections.'

If Louis truly loved her, then he'd be honest and not shut Victoria out of his life. 'It's not that straightforward.' Her heart gave an agonising thud.

'Do you love my great-nephew?' Although Miss Hetty's expression was grim, there was a new and fleeting softness in the depths of her eyes.

'Yes.' The word came out of Victoria's mouth before she could stop herself. 'But it doesn't matter any longer.' Her face burned. She loved Louis like she'd never loved Roy – and like she'd never love anyone again – but it was too late. She had her job and her friends and they were enough. They had to be.

'I see.' Miss Hetty stood. 'Well, you're in a fine fix, aren't you?' She clicked her tongue against her teeth. 'I hold Louis responsible as well. He's proud, like his father, and in weaker moments inclined to be a romantic like his mother and Addie. Put the two together and while it may be a recipe for great love, it can also result in considerable heartache.'

'Please don't say anything to him. Whatever was between us is over, and I'm sure that Louis has forgotten all about me.'

'If he has, then he isn't a Grainger. We don't show our feelings, but we also don't bestow them lightly.'

'I thought you wanted Louis to reunite with Mrs Wallace, Major and Mrs Bertram's daughter. She's everything I'm not.' Victoria gulped.

'Yes, she's a traitor and you most certainly are not. Along with everything else, consorting with a German and a married man as she did is beyond the pale.' In the dim light, Miss Grainger's jet beads gleamed against the front of her dress. 'I'm going to read in the library. I can't hear myself think with those children and their racket. Tell Marjorie to bring my supper on a tray and to fix that frayed piece of carpeting on the landing before she leaves. I almost tripped on it earlier. It was so much easier when staff lived in.'

Except in the grandest families and even at Whittleton Hall, the days of staff living in were long gone. If village gossip was correct, the Misses Grainger wouldn't have Marjorie for much longer, either. In a few months, as soon as she was old enough, Marjorie would be off to join the women's branch of one of the services. She was young and lively, and if not for needing to help her mum with younger children at home, she'd have left to work in one of the Norwich factories long before now.

'If you wish, I can nail down the carpet for you. I'm handy with a hammer.' Victoria held out her arm. 'Before I speak to Marjorie about your supper, let me walk with you upstairs. You don't want to risk tripping again.'

'Thank you.' Miss Hetty gave Victoria a grudging smile. 'None of us were the same after the last war, and I suppose this one will change us more. However, there are certain things that don't change. Love and loyalty, trust and respect. Those are the values that endure and you'd do well to remember them.'

'Yes, Miss Hetty.'

But even if his great-aunt was right about Louis's feelings, it was up to Victoria to see and talk to him to try to make things right. She couldn't say what she meant in a letter, not with the censor, and after what she'd said and done she couldn't call his office from the village telephone box, either.

Now Louis was the one who had good reason not to trust her.

Chapter Forty-Four

On Sunday evening, Victoria put the exercise books she'd finished marking back into her school satchel and rubbed a hand against her forehead. She'd had a dull headache all weekend, and two early nights and staying home from church this morning hadn't helped mitigate it any.

'All done?' Across from her at one of the tables in the manor's library, Nell finished her own marking and closed the last book. 'Those compositions were frightful and the maths problems even worse. Between our juniors going backwards and forwards to London to be with their parents, and now the village children mixed in with the Londoners, I don't see how we can maintain any educational standards at all.'

'We can't – but that doesn't mean we aren't expected to.' Victoria held back a weary sigh. 'I haven't heard Beatrice come back, so she must still be at Mrs Meldrum's for the church young people's meeting.'

'How the vicar and Mrs Russell could be at church this morning as if nothing had happened I'll never know. Beatrice said he had to set an example but surely… Oh, that blackout curtain is askew again.' Nell got up and went over to one of the tall windows. 'We don't want the warden round telling us he can see light. Along with the fine, we'll be hearing the manor has to set an example, like the vicarage. The old ladies have gone to bed early, thank goodness. If Miss Hetty were here, she'd be telling me off for certain.'

'I expect they'd both understand that curtain is—' Victoria stopped as a pounding sounded on the downstairs front door.

'What on earth? It can't be the warden already.' Nell tugged at the blackout with a frightened expression.

'Surely not.' Victoria took the lamp from the middle of the table. 'Get that cricket bat Miss Addie brought out for Albert. It's still by the scullery door.' After her experience with Walter Clarke, Victoria wasn't taking any possibly foolish chances.

Holding the lamp in one hand and her torch in the other, Victoria went down the main staircase. As the pounding continued, Miss Hetty's bedroom door opened and then Miss Addie's, and they stood in the hall in their nightcaps with Lady wagging her tail between them.

'I'm sure it's nothing, but stay where you are for now.'

'Not much of a watchdog, is Lady?' Nell – who must have taken the servants' stairs and sprinted from one side of the manor to the other – muttered as she re-joined Victoria in the front hall with the cricket bat.

'With planes overhead at all hours that poor dog doesn't know when to bark or not. Here.' Victoria handed Nell the lamp in exchange for the bat. 'Who is it?' she called through the front door.

'Two of the kiddies are missing and we're forming a search party.' Bob the publican's voice rang out from the other side.

'Two kiddies?' Victoria flung open the door, thankful she was still dressed in her skirt, blouse and sturdy shoes. 'Which ones?'

'Albert and Diana. Two of them evacuees from the vicarage.' Bob's usually florid face was pale.

'Put out that light.'

'Now, Herb. Give us a minute,' Bob began again.

'Get the light out now.'

Victoria and Nell joined Bob outside and closed the door behind them. 'The warden's right, and I didn't think. I'll come with you.' As Nell made to follow her, Victoria shook her head. 'Stay here with the Misses Grainger and put the kettle on. The children can't have gone far. It's only beginning to get dark.'

Although it was a warm night, Victoria shrugged into the cardigan she'd had around her shoulders and joined Bob to hurry back towards the village, their shaded torches, covered with tissue, illuminating the grasses waving eerily from both sides of the lane. 'Tell me exactly what happened. Who discovered the children were missing?'

'Mrs Russell. She said Diana and Albert were playing in the garden, and she only went inside the vicarage for a minute to answer the telephone, but when she came back out again they were gone. The fellows that were in the pub are checking the pond. I left my missus to close up and knocked on doors as I went.' Bob shook his head. 'I mind the time a little lad, only two he were, wandered off from one of the farms in winter. He froze to death before anyone found him.'

'It's not winter and Diana and Albert are older, so more sensible.' Victoria hoped they were. 'What about Wilf, Albert's elder brother?'

'He were reading in his bedroom. The lad's right cut up as you'd expect but he insisted on going to the pond with the men.'

As they approached the village crossroads, a vehicle came towards them and drew to a stop.

'Victoria?' From the front passenger seat, Louis peered around Constable Smith through a half-open window.

'It's Diana and Albert.' Her legs trembled and she took a step nearer the car. 'They're lost and we have to find them. We're forming a search party.'

'I'll help.' Louis was out of the motor before Victoria finished speaking. 'We'll find them, I promise.' He held her gaze for a brief moment and then turned back to Bob and Constable Smith.

Adrenaline surged through Victoria. It didn't matter why Louis was here or her discomfort at facing him again, especially so unexpectedly.

Nothing mattered except Diana and Albert. Two children who weren't only her pupils, but whom she loved with the same fierce protectiveness as if they were her own flesh and blood.

–

An hour later it had gone full dark, and from where Victoria stood outside the village hall, grey clouds and misty fog obscured the shadowy sliver of moon.

'Bob and you lot, go back to the woods. The rest of us will head towards the stream and outlying farms.' Constable Smith had taken charge of the search party, but despite combing the village, pond and nearby outbuildings, Diana and Albert were still nowhere to be found. 'Anyone know where Mr Grainger got to?'

'Last I saw, he were with the vicar and them going up towards the Clarke farms. Wilf says Albert's mighty fond of Frank's dog, Captain.' Herb, the ARP warden, had joined the searchers and slung a coiled rope over one shoulder.

Victoria sank onto a wooden bench and buried her face in her hands. There was no reason for the children to go to Upper or Lower Yarrow Farm in the evening, but presumably the men had to consider every possibility.

'Don't lose hope.' Beatrice patted Victoria's shoulder. After Bob had raised the alarm, the church young people's meeting had broken up and Beatrice had joined Victoria in the search. 'Are you sure you won't return to the manor? As Constable Smith said, the two of us can't do anything more.'

Victoria shook her head. 'I need to stay. The village hall is the designated meeting point so when the searchers find Diana and Albert, I have to be here. They'll be tired, cold and frightened, and wanting their mums.' She choked back a sob. 'I'm a poor substitute for their mothers but they'll need me.'

If the children were found. No, she couldn't let herself think such a thing.

'I understand.' Beatrice's usually guarded face was soft with compassion. 'Between us, Nell and I will manage your infants' class tomorrow, but go inside the hall and drink some tea.' She set the flask Mrs Meldrum had provided on the bench at Victoria's side. 'You'll catch a chill out here.'

Victoria stood and faced Beatrice, senior teacher but also her friend. 'Diana and Albert can't have vanished into thin air.'

'No, so there has to be somewhere or something we haven't thought of.' Beatrice's brows wrinkled. 'I'll go back to the vicarage and speak to Wilf. Perhaps he'll have another idea. The poor fellow will likely be glad to see me, and although Mrs Russell is being a brick, she really shouldn't be left with only Ivy right now.'

'Before I go indoors, I'll check around the hall and allotments again.' Victoria had to do something except drink tea and sit and wait, or she'd go mad.

After Beatrice went in the opposite direction to the vicarage, Victoria, with new resolve, put the flask of tea inside the hall, then gripped her torch and pointed it towards the allotments. Since Albert and Diana enjoyed working in the school garden, it was one of the first places the men had searched earlier.

Apart from the dim light cast by the torch, owing to the clouds and fog, the usually familiar world outside her classroom was shrouded in shadows. Although the Germans had begun to send over more bombers at night, surely tonight they'd struggle to find their way, just as she was doing. Still, she listened for the sound of any approaching aircraft, ready to find shelter or dive to the ground if needed.

Picking her way through the darkness, Victoria rounded the rear corner of the hall and squat lavatory building, inching forwards to avoid wrenching her ankle in a hole or tripping over an edge of one of the raised beds.

At the entrance to the allotments, a profusion of bean vines covered a trellis and beyond, tomatoes tied to supporting stakes stood tall and proud. From the school plot several rows back, and behind a potato patch, the corn Victoria had planted with the children grew thick and high almost as it did in her mother's garden in Canada.

A lump formed in Victoria's throat, and she had to force herself to keep going, around Mrs Meldrum's carrots and then Mrs Mann's allotment, now being cared for by the postmistress. When, if ever, would the other teacher return to Hazelbury? That was something else Victoria couldn't let herself think about.

A low hum of voices echoed from the corn, and Victoria stopped, a chill prickling along her spine.

'We all, young and old, have to do our duty for king and country.'

'But what if it's too hard?' Diana's high treble answered Louis.

'When it's hard and others doubt you, that's when staying steadfast and doing your duty is even more important,' Louis said.

Frozen in place, Victoria put a hand to her chest as shame rolled over her. She'd doubted Louis. And she'd been wrong. So very, very wrong.

'We thought we were doing our duty and a kitten would help Mrs Russell feel better after Mr Gilbert's aeroplane was shot down. We didn't mean to get lost, Sir.' Albert's voice was unusually meek.

'Or fall asleep,' Diana added. 'Except it got dark and in the fog and blackout we didn't know which way to go home. Is everyone cross?' A small sob erupted.

'No, not cross but terribly worried. Here, put your arms around my neck and I'll carry you. There's a handkerchief in my breast pocket. Keep hold of my jacket, Albert. There's a good boy.'

'I want me mum.'

At Albert's hoarse cry, Victoria made her frozen limbs work and darted forwards.

'I'm here, darlings. You're safe.' She crashed through the corn stalks to where Louis huddled with the children. 'We'll have you home soon.'

'Miss McKaye.' Diana cried harder. 'We followed a kitten and got lost. We were afraid the Germans would get us so when we couldn't find our way back we hid in the corn and then Mr Grainger found us when Albert sneezed and…' Whatever else she said was drowned out by more sobs and then, as Victoria crouched on her knees, Albert and Diana were in her arms.

'Oh, Louis. Thank you for finding them.' Over the children's heads, Victoria's gaze connected with his.

'I promised – and I never break my promises.' His voice was gruff.

'I know, and I was mistaken. Please won't you believe me? I'm sorry. I was foolish and misjudged you and I… Forgive me?' She stuttered to a stop when Albert raised his tearstained face and looked between them.

'If you want to kiss Miss McKaye, Sir, I won't tell nobody.'

'You won't tell *anybody*,' Victoria said and then gave a choked laugh. 'What are you saying, Albert? I'm sure Mr Grainger doesn't want to kiss me. Come, take my hand. If Mr Grainger carries Diana, we'll have you back at the vicarage in—'

'Would one of you let Mr Grainger get a word in?' Louis's eyes twinkled as he took Diana from Victoria's embrace.

'I… oh… sorry.' Victoria's face burned.

'Mr Grainger can speak for himself, and you, Miss McKaye already said you were sorry.' Louis lifted Diana so her curly head rested on one of his broad shoulders.

'I need you to know I mean it.' Victoria held Albert's hand tight as they made their way out of the garden.

'I do know.' Louis's smile told Victoria she had all the forgiveness she could ever need, and more. 'I made a case to my commanding officer for a twelve-hour leave pass

287

so I could come here and see you. Speak with you, and tell you…'

He stopped and Victoria's heartbeat sped up.

'Tell Miss McKaye what?' Diana asked from the safety of her perch, distress and fear seemingly forgotten.

'I have a great deal to tell Miss McKaye – but in private.' Once again, Louis's gaze locked with Victoria's, and the promise and longing in his face sent heat flashing through her.

'If you and Miss McKaye get married, may I be a bridesmaid?'

'Diana!' Victoria let out a horrified gasp and jerked her attention away from Louis.

'In lessons last week you said we should ask for what we want. I want to be a bridesmaid.'

'I meant that Sheila should ask for a new pencil rather than taking Margaret's.' Thank goodness it was dark because Victoria must be all shades of red.

Louis's warm laugh rolled out. 'You two listen to your teacher, and when it comes to choosing bridesmaids we will certainly keep you in mind, Diana.'

'Told you Mr Grainger was sweet on Miss McKaye.' Albert nodded up at Diana. 'I don't tell no lies.'

Victoria put a hand to her mouth. She'd forgo correcting Albert's grammar and everything else right now. Louis had said 'when' not 'if' they chose bridesmaids, which must mean he still loved her.

Like she loved him. With that love, and although they only had a few hours left in his leave, they'd work everything else out.

A piercing miaow sounded from somewhere near Louis's chest.

'What on earth?' Victoria looked around.

'It's the kitten, Miss McKaye. When we found it, I put it in the pocket of my dress and…' Diana's eyes filled with tears again. 'I didn't hurt it, did I?'

'No, it's fine.' Louis extracted what at first glance appeared to be a scrap of tortoiseshell fur and held it in his palm. 'Everything will be all right now, darling, you'll see.'

Although he spoke to Diana or maybe even the kitten, Victoria sensed his words were also meant for her.

Chapter Forty-Five

Victoria glanced at the longcase clock that stood in one corner of the front hall at Hazelbury Manor. Its hands pointed to just before midnight. The search party had been called off, Diana and Albert had been delivered to the vicarage, and then – following tea and biscuits with Beatrice, Nell and the Misses Grainger – she and Louis were finally alone. 'You need to get some sleep before you have to leave again.'

'Sleep can wait.' He took both her hands in his. 'I love you still, and I'll love you always. When Aunt Hetty wrote to me, I let myself hope that you… well, I had to try again.'

'I love you too and I've been such a fool. I… no wait.' When Louis would have drawn her into his arms, Victoria stopped him. 'I need to tell you the truth, every part of it.'

'All right.' He drew her over to one of the hall chairs and, once she was sitting, sat beside her keeping hold of one of her hands.

'I know you can't tell me about your work and it's fine. It has to be secret but I… I was using your work and that need for wartime secrecy as an excuse. After Roy, I was afraid to truly trust anyone, even you. I thought I had to protect myself from being betrayed again.'

'That makes sense, but if you remember Evelyn betrayed me as well. Then, that business with Walter Clarke had her fingerprints all over it. She was disloyal and treacherous yet again, but to her country, not only me.' Louis rubbed his free hand through his hair. 'She also attempted to get me to disclose military and other classified information at parties and such.'

'How vile.' Victoria squeezed his hand tight and moved closer.

'By that point, we already had Evelyn and the others under surveillance but still… That day in Norwich when you implied you couldn't trust me, I was hurt and angry. But I also understood and then I cursed my job and this godforsaken war.'

'They don't matter.' Emotion clogged Victoria's throat.

'They do, and I can only tell you that I'm continuing to work undercover for British intelligence. On my honour, though, I'm not a double agent.' He gave her a half-smile. 'Nor is Miss Skene, a very efficient and patriotic grey-haired martinet who keeps me in order as if I were the son she never had. However, I'll be sent on another assignment soon, maybe even to France. That's why it's not fair of me to ask you to wait for me.'

'I want to wait for you, no matter how long it might be.' The backs of Victoria's eyes burned. 'Don't you see? When Gilbert Russell was killed, all I could think of was that if something happened to you, I'd never be able to tell you how wrong I'd been. I wouldn't even be able to grieve for you properly. But loving you as I do means I have to open my heart to trust in love and any hurt that might come with it.'

'I'd never hurt you but if something were to happen to me—'

'I'd still have known your love. Our love, forever, no matter how long I live.' Tears rolled unheeded down Victoria's cheeks. 'That would be everything to me.'

'To me as well with you.' Louis cleared his throat and clasped both her hands again, the light from the lamp Victoria had lit earlier flickering across his beloved face. 'Here, now… it's not how I planned to ask you. I should have written to your father first but we have so little time and I don't want to leave you without knowing… Will you marry me, Victoria? My love?'

'I will, Louis. I will marry you.'

He reached into his jacket pocket and brought out a small, worn blue-velvet box. 'Then I hope you will wear this ring for me and as a symbol and promise for our future. It's a Grainger

291

family ring and was my mother's and grandmother's before her.' He opened the box and took out a large, marquise-cut sapphire, surrounded by diamonds and more sapphires, and slipped it onto the fourth finger of Victoria's left hand.

'I'd be honoured to wear it.' Victoria's eyes widened as the stones sparkled in the light. 'It fits.'

'Then it must be even more meant to be.' Louis drew Victoria gently to her feet and wrapped his arms around her.

'But what about Miss Hetty?' Victoria didn't want to marry Louis without his family's blessing.

'Who do you think gave me this ring to give to you? It's been in Aunt Hetty's jewellery box all these years waiting for you. It wasn't right for anyone before but now it is.' Louis's breath warmed Victoria's cheek. 'When I got Aunt Hetty's letter, that's when I requested leave.'

'I asked her not to say anything to you.' Victoria rested her head on Louis's chest, the steady thump of his heart reassuring against her ear.

'Aren't you glad she did? It happens rarely but even Aunt Hetty will on occasion admit she was wrong.'

'How did she send you a letter? We only spoke on Friday afternoon and she went upstairs to the library and then had her supper on a tray and went to bed.' After, in her usual brusque manner, she'd rebuked Victoria for the racket she'd made hammering the piece of stair carpet into place.

'She gave Albert double the amount of his weekly pocket money to hold his tongue and smuggle out her letter in time to catch the last post.' Louis touched Victoria's cheek. 'I hope you don't have any more questions because I've wanted to kiss you since seeing you in the lane.'

'No more questions.' She smiled up at him.

And then Victoria's lips met Louis's in a kiss both passionate and sweet. A kiss which held the promise of their future and a bond that nothing, not even what the war might bring, could ever break.

'Chin up,' Beatrice said. The following morning as the rising sun cast a rosy glow across the lawn, Beatrice and Nell linked arms with Victoria on the front steps of Hazelbury Manor.

Victoria straightened, although she still stared at the lane where a car from RAF Whittleton carrying Louis had disappeared moments before. 'You didn't have to get up with me but thank you. More than ever, I have to be brave.'

'We all do.' Beatrice's voice was crisp but now Victoria knew it wasn't because she didn't care. Rather, it was one of the ways the other teacher hid her feelings as if, for reasons Victoria was still unaware, she feared any display of emotion.

'Let me see your ring again.' Nell raised Victoria's hand. 'My word, that centre sapphire and those other, smaller stones all look even bigger in daylight.'

After Victoria had said good night to Louis, Beatrice and Nell had been in her bedroom, waiting up for her to celebrate or console as might be called for. Then the three of them had talked into the night, and Victoria had only managed an hour or so of sleep before getting up again as Louis had to be at Whittleton by six.

'It is a very fine ring indeed,' Beatrice said. 'To my mind, inherited family jewellery is far more significant than—'

Aircraft engines rumbled overhead, Nell gave a frightened squeak and Victoria ducked and reached for the door handle.

'They're RAF, girls.' Beatrice's smile was amused. 'Really, by now I'd have thought you'd be able to tell the difference between their planes and ours.'

'Sorry.' Nell bobbed her head in her instinctive gesture of respect, almost deference. 'If you two want to go back to bed, I'll bring up a tray with tea.'

'Of course not.' Inside the manor and with the door closed again, Beatrice took Victoria's and Nell's arms once more. 'We'll all make tea, as you and I, Nell, will go to school in a few hours and teach the children who turn up to the best of our abilities.'

'As will I,' Victoria said. 'No, I need to be there.' She waved away Beatrice's protest. 'For the children, Ivy and you both as well. You're my friends and we're in this war together. A bit of missed sleep is no reason for me to shirk my duty. I need to be up and about and useful. Teaching is war work too.'

'That's the spirit.' Beatrice gave an approving nod.

And today, and each day that followed, Victoria would hold to that spirit for herself and now Louis and their future together.

Acknowledgements

I'd like to thank my UK literary agent, Kiran Kataria, of Keane Kataria Literary Agency, for her staunch support, encouragement and advocacy. I'm also grateful to Kiran for her superb editorial skills which help me continue to grow my writing craft.

Much appreciation as well to my Canelo editor, Emily Bedford, for her enthusiasm for my 'teacher evacuees', helpful feedback, and reassurance as I launch my historical fiction career as Rose Warner. Thank you, too, to the Canelo team for their work at all stages of the publication process to bring this book to readers.

I'm grateful to research room staff at London's Imperial War Museum (IWM) for assistance in-person and online when accessing the IWM's collections, including accounts by real WW2 evacuated British teachers, and other wartime records. Additional thanks to staff at the Home Front Museum in Llandudno, North Wales, and RAF Oulton Museum at the National Trust's Blickling Estate in Norfolk. Material held by all these museums helped me create my story world and blend historical fact with fiction.

Thank you to my family, friends and, especially, dear author friend Susanna Bavin (who also writes as Maisie Thomas and Polly Heron) for being there for me in writing and life. Susanna regularly boosts me with wartime 'Blitz Spirit' and, when beneath the metaphorical rubble, there's no one better with whom to share virtual tea and cake.

Finally, I'm grateful to the readers, reviewers and bloggers who support my books and help make my author career possible.

If you're discovering me for the first time writing historical women's/saga fiction as Rose Warner, welcome.

And if you've followed my contemporary romance career as 'Jen Gilroy', I hope you enjoy these new 'Rose Warner' historical stories.

Author's Note

Whilst the village of Hazelbury, Whittleton Hall, Whittleton village, and the RAF base are fictional, they're inspired by real places in the British county of Norfolk – especially the North Norfolk coast and nearby area.

Long before I became a published author, I spent many wonderful family holidays in Norfolk and fell in love with the county's beautiful countryside and North Sea coast. On these holidays, I discovered Norfolk's Second World War history, much of it, including remnants of military pillboxes and other coastal fortifications, still visible on the landscape today.

Like all historical novelists, in *The Teacher Evacuees* I've blended certain historical facts – for example, the Luftwaffe's bombing of Cromer in July 1940, and rise of British fascism in the1930s – with that which is fictional. In the early years of WWII, when British people feared a German invasion was imminent, many seemingly ordinary, patriotic British citizens worked on behalf of Hitler's Germany. Those British traitors inspired part of Victoria's story in *The Teacher Evacuees*.

I've always read widely about UK wartime life and, as a child, was engrossed in Noel Streatfeild's *When the Siren Wailed*, and *Carrie's War* by Nina Bawden. However, although a range of fiction and academic research has focused on child evacuees, the teachers who accompanied them to the British countryside, sometimes for the duration of the war, are often overlooked.

Reading letters by some of these teachers, and listening to audio interviews with others, via archival materials held by London's Imperial War Museum was sobering, poignant and, at times amusing. I hope I've done justice to those, many of them women, who gave up their own lives, often for years, to care for their pupils in a strange place, in wartime, both inside and beyond the classroom.

Like my fictional teachers, the real teacher evacuees were on occasion forgotten when it came to accommodation and some did temporarily stay in barns and village halls. Other anecdotes – Victoria cycling to an ARP post to secure replacement gas masks for pupils who lost theirs in a pond, and the elder Mrs Bertram's only concession to wartime life being that the family's cook make dinner in the middle of the day – come from real accounts.

Neepawa, Manitoba, Canada – where Victoria is from – is also a real town near where my much-loved late dad, a naval officer like the fictional Louis, grew up. The lake where Victoria's family has their summer cabin is Clear Lake in Riding Mountain National Park, another place of happy family memories.

The Teacher Evacuees blends my Canadian and British lives and, in that sense, was a particular joy to write. And, although I was first published in contemporary romance as Jen Gilroy and continue to write in that genre under that name, I originally started my journey to publication writing historical fiction. Releasing *The Teacher Evacuees* as Rose Warner realises a long-held dream of writing fiction rooted in women's history – focusing on ordinary women's lives and loves, and their friendships, families and communities – but also their often extraordinary and unrecognised courage.